FROM THE ASHES

A Psychic Visions Novel
Book #16

Dale Mayer

FROM THE ASHES
Beverly Dale Mayer
Valley Publishing Ltd.

Copyright © 2019

ISBN-13: 978-1-773362-84-7
Print Edition

Books in This Series:

About This Book

This is the 16th Psychic Visions Novel from USA Today Bestselling author Dale Mayer.

Born and raised in a cult with a fanatical father who believed she was destined for greater things, Phoenix endured a childhood of pain and torment. Not only was her father preparing her for the future he saw, he hated that she was stronger, better than he was.

When she's finally rescued, her life slowly improves, but still her past hinders her future. Her father has gifted her with one special note, written on a material she has yet to destroy. In order to get rid of it forever, she travels to Iceland to her father's hometown to visit a fissure of lava that opens every summer. Surely the material will burn in the lava? And she can then be rid of her father and the special note forever …

Detective Rowan Einar hates when the damn fissure opens as it always signifies the suicide season—a despicable time of year where people travel to his small corner of the world to end their lives. When a waif shows up with huge eyes and scars, both external and internal, he wants to ensure she won't be the next suicide in town. But, when he hears her story, he wonders what is going on …

Then the deaths begin, … and he witnesses the visions and energies that he's always been able to see have now merged with Phoenix's energies, making the two of them stronger and more powerful. What they see though is even more terrifying …

Sign up to be notified of all Dale's releases here!

https://geni.us/DaleNews

CHAPTER 1

P HOENIX RISING STEPPED off the tour bus and was
engulfed by the sights and sounds of the small Icelandic
town they would spend the next few days. An odd ashy
aroma filled her nostrils, even as a fresh breeze lifted her long
blond strands of hair.

She'd spent her whole childhood being told about this
place. Then spent the rest of her life researching, studying,
trying to figure out exactly what her connection was to this
place and to the Eternal Fire that burned here.

Or rather the Eternal Fire that always burned beneath
the ground but rose to the surface once every year. It had
resurfaced weeks ago.

Finally she was here.

Her father had prophesized how she would die by the
Eternal Fire—and then be reborn.

Her delusional mom had believed him and, after way
too many sessions of drugs, had named her daughter Phoenix
Rising, as supposedly the epic answer to this burning in hell
and subsequent resurrection.

Phoenix had no clue what the truth of the matter was.

Then again, not many children from cults escaped, and,
if they did, they needed a lifetime to deal with the BS they'd
been spoon-fed. Rescued at eleven, she was old enough to
understand what had happened and how her rescue from

that nightmare had been a gift.

Her father, the cult leader, who had impregnated almost all of his followers, had decreed Phoenix was special. Very special. But she'd had no idea what that meant or why she needed to be *special*.

The rational part of her mind understood her father would say that just to make himself more special because he was *her* father. He'd filled her head with stories of this fire that burned here, but he'd never answered any of her questions.

Instead, he'd patted her on the head and said, *You'll learn, child. You'll learn.* But, when the cult had been raided by the cops, she only learned that her father had been a pedophile and a psychopath.

And, with his blood in her veins and his words still in her mind and his torture ever evident on her body, that meant she was damaged.

But, even as broken as she had started out in this life, she'd gone to a wonderful foster couple, both professors, who'd quickly filled in the gaps of her education with intensive tutoring. Now she had her own degree and had been an associate professor in mythology at the same Seattle University she'd attended, until recently but had volunteered to take a layoff from her struggling university.

Now she had severance money in the bank and was foot-loose and fancy free.

Only for her, *true freedom* meant finding answers. She reached up to touch the scar on the side of her face. Just another reminder of some of the things her father had done to help her remember who she was and what she was here for. In his uncontradicted opinion, she was the Chosen One, and as such was required to endure the pain of training to achieve that status.

The scars on her body ached as they always did with the memories of the torture she'd endured on a regular basis.

Her mother had cried with her afterward but had never stepped in to stop the abuse.

Phoenix had screamed and wailed, asking the others to stop him, telling whoever would listen how she didn't want to be this special child. The other children had laughed, had taunted her more. But they'd also been afraid of her—maybe a tiny bit jealous too of the Chosen One moniker.

"We aren't special, like you are," they would say and, instead of helping her, had often beaten her more.

Her lessons about humanity had been learned at the hands of a madman and his all-too-willing disciples.

When she had finally become an adult, she had a very twisted view of man *and* religion, how distorted beliefs could distort people and how so many of them had taken their beliefs in a very wrong direction, like her father had.

He had died in a shoot-out with the cops, choosing to die a *martyr*—as he had put it—than to go to jail and to suffer at the hands of others.

His disciples had chosen to die with him too—taking the poison they had ready and waiting for the one day when it was needed.

Her mother had tried to drag Phoenix into the closet to die with her. "Come. We must go. We must follow Father," her mother had insisted harshly.

But Phoenix had fought back. "No. I don't want to follow him anywhere."

Slap.

Phoenix had taken several hard blows from her mother's very capable hand before her mother gave up to dash into the closet alone. Phoenix hadn't even tried to follow.

When the cops had surrounded her, she had pointed at the closet where her mother was. When they opened the door, they found her mother dying on the floor. And that was the last Phoenix had seen of her family. That vision sat at the edge of her consciousness, never giving her a chance to move past it.

Now, so many years later—eighteen years to be exact—she had decided to finally put this all to rest.

"Phoenix?"

She shook off her tortured memories to see the whole tour bus had emptied, tourists already storming through the gift shop and heading toward the hotel.

The driver stood beside her.

"Are you doing okay, Phoenix?" he asked in his jovial tone, but his fatherly gaze studied her with concern.

She smiled and nodded. "I am. Just a little tired, so thought I'd wait for the crowd to disperse first." A fib as she'd been lost in her thoughts.

"Understandable," he said. "This afternoon you are on your own. After we get you into your hotel, you can rest. Tomorrow morning we'll head out to the Burning Fires." He paused and studied her. "Excited?"

"Very," she said. "I've come a long way to see it."

"People come from all over the world," he replied and shrugged. "I don't understand the attraction myself. It's just a fire."

"But a fire that has burned for a long time," she said gently. "With very specific start and stop times. an eternal schedule that surpasses our understanding."

"But still just a fire. It's burning because of an opening in the ground with an endless amount of lava fuel for it. I understand a lot of people believe in the mythology of the place. And, of course, the few missing people cases we have around here help to fuel that fire's legend. But it's just gossip. None of it makes much sense to me."

At his words, she stumbled, righted herself and then asked, "What do you mean, *missing people*?"

"Ah," he said. "It's nothing. Just a few missing tourists every year. But it's to be expected. Hundreds of thousands of people come here. Some with good intentions and some not. And some come deliberately to commit suicide," he said, his gaze sharp as he studied her. "We have a weird season here—*Suicide Season*. For anyone choosing the fires as a way to die, the lava leaves nothing to see afterward. A way to disappear completely. It's not a bad method if someone is dead set on dying. Just hell on those left behind."

"Suicide?" she exclaimed and shook her head at his nod. "I'd never even considered something like that." She looked at the quaint town around them. "Such an awful concept against such a picturesque background."

"Oh, the town is definitely picturesque," he replied. "But the townsfolk play into that. They need the tourist dollars so they give it their all. As much as they love the tourists, they hate them too."

"I can understand that," she said. "They need what we have to offer, but they don't really want us in their space. I'd probably feel the same."

As the only surviving cult member, she was left to the foster care system. It hadn't been a kind system to her, but she could sleep in a warm bed, eat real food and not deal with her father. A few years later she'd landed at one foster home and had stayed. She had gone to school for the first time. Although she knew her numbers, reading and writing, she had been so far behind that she'd had to focus hard to catch up.

By the time she hit grade ten, she was there and well past. Her final foster parents had tutored her steadily. Both of them were professors and put high stock in education.

Patrick had tutored her incessantly on all things mathematical, whereas the woman, Merry, had tutored her on all things scientific. And then Phoenix got into mythology, making them both stand back and look at her in surprise.

She had done it more because of all the training she'd received in the first years of her life. She had also taken a lot of forensic courses on serial killers and psychopaths and the damaged mind, in an effort to understand how her birth family could have been so bent on destroying her childhood.

Nobody understood what she had been through, except maybe the cops, who sat listening as she answered their questions. She had watched the looks of shock and horror, then the pity.

Her father's teachings were always in the back of her mind. She was afraid some code word existed that somebody would say, and she would then turn into this mass killer or something.

Maybe that fear had kept her on the straight and narrow. She had never been into drugs or sex or boys. She never cheated at school. She was always too wary that maybe this learning opportunity would be taken away from her, and somebody would lock her back up again.

It was funny. With another eighteen years had gone by in this whole new world, she wondered if maybe it had been a myth—a dream—or rather a nightmare.

In the back of her mind, she worried there were eleven-year cycles, starting with the first eleven years in the cult.

The second eleven years in foster homes and college, before finally having her own place. She'd made it about two-thirds of the way through the next set of eleven years. Which so far had been about independence and loosening the shackles of her history. Who knew what the rest of this set would bring?

"You're off in your own world again," he said with a kind smile. "Come on. Let's get you to the hotel. You look tired." His eyes once again went to the scar alongside her face. She let him look. Everyone did. Her foster parents had wanted her to get plastic surgery to cover it up. Phoenix wouldn't hear of it. It was a reminder of who she really was—inside and out.

A monster.

Just like her father.

CHAPTER 2

PHOENIX HEADED INTO her hotel. Three buses were in town, adding an easy couple hundred people to the small town. She winced at the numbers in line at the registration desk but stood obediently at the end. She knew the receptionists would get through this process as fast as they could, and being difficult and or having a tantrum wouldn't help.

Her mind caught on the simple wood furnishings as she studied her surroundings. Outside, she could see a cop having an argument with somebody. Whether the suspect was drunk or just being argumentative was hard to determine. But the cop looked more exasperated than anything. Finally he shut the door to the police cruiser with the man now inside and hit the hood so it could drive away with its passenger. Then, as if sensing she was watching, he turned toward the hotel, seemingly staring right at her.

Instinctively she ducked back, even though she was inside and shouldn't have been visible from where he stood. But something was so compelling about that gaze. She waited, her breath caught in her throat, as he strode through the front doors of the hotel in the loose-limbed stride of a man in control. He was a man in charge. He was a man who knew what power was all about, and she could feel the waves of energy coming off him. She didn't know how people created that aura, but her father had had the same over-whelming "I'm in charge" presence.

Her father had said she was a sensitive and could under-stand energy like he did. Then he had said a lot of things. Supposedly he'd been looking for that one special child to rise up and to lead the group with him. As far as she knew, she was the only one in the group of children he'd shown any interest in—lucky her.

She definitely was sensitive to others—sensitive to her surroundings, sensitive to danger. She had this supervigilant instinct to run. She called it her scaredy-cat genes. Because anytime there was a confrontation or something was about to get ugly, she knew somehow and tried to get away before things got bad. Of course, in her mind, she was still escaping her father.

Now she was avoiding the policeman. She deliberately turned her back on the front door and waited in line. She refused to look back, but her skin crawled as that presence walked toward her.

Her breath caught in her chest as she stepped forward once again. She was next in line. The cop stepped up beside her and called out, "Hey, Reethra. How's it going?"

The receptionist on the left side of the long counter smiled up at him and said, "Just like every other day."

He chuckled, and then, in a deliberate move, he turned and looked at Phoenix.

Phoenix refused to look at him. She kept staring at the three receptionists, waiting for her turn.

"What brought you here?" the cop asked in a nonchalant tone with a slight thread of steel running through his voice.

She turned to look up at him and replied, "Just looking at the touristy things to do here. I came off the bus."

"I talked to John. He said everybody was up here registering."

She nodded. "I am part of his group," she replied with a shrug.

Just then the male receptionist called out, "I can help the next person, please."

Pulling her small suitcase, she walked away from the cop and headed toward the man at the counter. She gave him her name and told him which bus she was on. It was a process they must deal with all the time. He nodded and went through her paperwork, looking at her passport and checking her identification.

"You're supposed to be in a double room," he said. "I have one more person booked into that room with you, but they haven't checked in yet."

She didn't say anything, just waited. Every stop was a double-booking per room. That was how they managed to get the prices so low. So far every time she got the room to herself. Perfect. She'd wondered if she'd been putting out a special "stay away" energy or if it was coincidence. Regardless, it had been working in her favor on this trip.

He handed her a key and gave her directions to her room. She gave him a soft smile and said, "Thank you."

He nodded but still didn't bother looking up. He called out, "Next."

She unhooked the handle on her suitcase and rolled it toward the elevator. Her room was on the second floor. High enough to be out of danger in case somebody tried breaking in through a window but not so high she couldn't escape out a window if needed. She shook off that thought.

Of all the things her father had drilled into her brain, the most prevalent was that they were *always* in danger. They *always* had to be on the lookout for the police. *Always* had to take safety measures, even to the point of being ridiculous. And she had continued the habit all throughout her ensuing years.

One foster family had thought Phoenix was nuts and had asked for another foster child because Phoenix's idiosyncrasies used to set off their nerves, making them aware of all the dangers around them. They said they didn't want a child constantly on the lookout about being attacked.

She wasn't looking to be attacked, but, as her father would say, it was looking out to not be persecuted.

In the elevator she pushed the button, and, as the door closed in front of her, she saw the cop watching her from the lobby. She didn't say anything, just stared right back. She had learned a long time ago not to withdraw if she couldn't do it without being seen. It was better to stand your ground and to wait for whatever it was to blow over.

ROWAN EINAR STUDIED the elevator as it closed. He turned toward the receptionist who'd registered the woman he had been speaking to. "Paul, what can you tell me about her?" he asked.

Paul looked up in surprise and shrugged. "Honestly the day's been bus after bus. I have the registration with a copy of her passport. If you want to take a look at it, Chief, go for it."

Everybody called him *Chief*, even though their chief of police was in a coma. Rowan hadn't been promoted, and neither had anybody else. He was still a constable, as the top job hadn't been given to him yet. But he didn't make any comment over his presumed title, just snatched up the paper and read it. Seeing her name, his eyebrows shot up. "Did you see her name?"

Paul looked up, his eyes already distracted. "Yeah, right?"

Phoenix Rising. Rowan looked at the copy of her passport and realized it really was her name. He shook his head and said, "Can you get me a copy of these, please?"

Surprised, but willing, Paul walked to the office behind the counter and photocopied both documents. He brought them back over and said, "Is there a problem with her? She didn't look like much."

Rowan's lips kicked up. "Maybe not," he said. "But sometimes you got to watch out for those. They're a little more dangerous than the others."

Paul didn't appear to care. He barely nodded and went back to his computer. "It's been a hell of a day. I should have left over thirty minutes ago. I'm heading out now, if I can slip away." He glanced at Rowan and asked, "Unless you need anything else?"

Rowan looked up. "What room did you give her?"

"Room 232," Paul replied.

Rowan's frown deepened. "Didn't the last person in that room commit suicide?"

Paul shrugged. "I have to fill the rooms. You know that."

Rowan did know that. He turned and walked out of the hotel, stopping just outside the front door and took a deep breath. Only he thought these suicides were something other than normal. He had tried to talk to the chief about it before he was hospitalized, but the chief had told him to shut down that line of inquiry. The last thing the town needed was any bad publicity.

Rowan took several long, slow, deep breaths, inhaling

the sweet scent of the warm air. Even though they were still a good distance from the fires, the heat always seemed to settle on top of the town.

And, right now, it seemed as if everything was heating up. He didn't know what it was about her, but something was off. Something … ancient? He couldn't quite put his finger on it. But if she'd come here to commit suicide, that was the last thing he would allow.

They had a lot of missing persons' reports from their town and surrounding areas as travelers checked in with friends and family one last time, then nothing. A lot of suicide notes were left behind with no bodies to go with them. The Burning Fires was a perfect way to dispose of the bodies. The town had a perimeter set up around the Burning Fires so nobody should get close enough to commit suicide, but somehow these determined people found their way in regardless.

Rowan had often wondered if somebody in town wasn't facilitating the suicides, maybe making money off them by helping them complete the act. Which would be a sad situation, but, with human nature being what it was, he had to acknowledge it was at least a possibility. Just sucked if it was.

He ran his fingers through his hair, shifted his shoulders slightly and headed back to his vehicle. He would stop at the hospital and check on the chief. Something was odd, off, about his condition.

Rowan saw energy in Technicolor all around the chief— floating greens, yellows, blues and reds. Always red. Something about this town turned tempers into a hard, red, angry, mobsterlike energy. Rowan had only seen the phenomenon a couple times, and that it was happening again bothered him.

Always involved a death at the end of it. Something ugly was brewing, and just dealing with it made it uglier. This was a tourist town. People came here to have fun.

HE RUBBED HIS host's hands together, staring around the town center with its cobblestone streets and old-fashioned lights. He loved this place. He came and went freely, disguised as a local and yet, at the same time, not. He appeared human to get the job done ... Entities by right weren't defined by their previous incarnations as to what sex they were. He identified as male in his head but could be either depending on his host at the time. He had one main one but sometimes needed to hop out to give that one a break. A holiday so to speak. He smirked at his own joke. At least he was highly gifted. His ties here could never be disputed, but he loved leaving here just as much. After all, he was reincarnated each time to feed the gods, the Elders. Every time he came back to the Burning Fires of Iceland in his newly-reincarnated body, it was with a rush of power. That surge of need. Although with each new life he didn't fully understand his powers or his purpose until he hit about age ten or eleven. Then that thirst-quenching desire for what was to come clarified, which he could not deny.

Today he was already looking for his next offering to the gods, having already provided them with more than seventy so far for this lifetime. The Elders demanded *live and conscious* offerings, which made his job a bit more challenging.

Plus he needed to find the right one, the best one for a sacrifice to the Elders, so to speak. He'd been communicating with this god of the Icelandic Burning Fires for centuries and knew nobody could understand that, and that was okay by him. As long as people didn't try to stop him, then he could do what he needed to do. And, if they did try, ... well then, he had more sacrifices for the Elders—or more victims for himself.

His powers had grown with each reincarnation, so he knew to cloak himself from the readers and the seers, from those other gifted humans, so they couldn't detect what he really was. So, when he did get found out, each time had been because he had wanted too many, too much, too soon, without proper planning. Something to keep in mind each time ...

This was a perfect little town for his needs. The fact that he traveled all over the world to many sacred sites and repeated this process over and over should have gotten old by now, but it hadn't. His own blood bubbled at the thought of this sacrifice. The ones from here were special. Something was special about these eternal fires. Something about *this* fire and the fact it left no trace. It was the perfect killing machine.

These people intent on suicide were perfect offerings. They were people with no lives, no land, no space, no wish to go on. Some of them left notes at his suggestion, and others just simply disappeared without a final word. He couldn't do too many from each location, which was why he traveled constantly. But he was here in Iceland now, and three new buses had arrived. Surely he could find somebody to fit his purpose among one of the new arrivals.

The buses would be here for a day or two, and then they'd be gone. But he knew that, as soon as they left, more would come. He wanted something special this time. A pregnant woman maybe? Maybe a single father with a little child to help make the sacrifice all that much sweeter. The twins last time had been supremely wonderful. He smacked his lips together at the memory.

Under his breath he whispered, "I promise you that I'll find the perfect victim. She'll be absolutely perfect." He always rotated from men to women to men again if he could. But he wondered if he needed to up his game. Things could get boring if he didn't. He wasn't sure the Elders themselves cared as long as he kept them with a steady supply, but, considering he'd been doing this forever, it was important he find pride in his work.

He was a Supplier, which was not exactly a job description to raise joy and delight, but it was definitely a job he loved and had been doing all his many lives, doing it in previous lifetimes too. He kept coming back, doing the same thing over and over again.

People didn't understand reincarnation. They didn't understand faith and duty that transcended time or physical reality. That was their fault. The Supplier had been born blessed with purpose, and he knew it right from a young child on. As soon as he could, he'd shaken loose of the family ties and had dived back into his purpose. In this lifetime he expected to perform even more sacrifices for his Elders than ever before.

He had tried hard the last lifetime but hadn't quite succeeded. He had offered one hundred sacrifices to his Elders, but still they hadn't been happy. Instead they'd made sure he was caught and killed. This time he knew he had to up his game and do a lot more. He was only at seventy-two so far.

It wasn't enough.

As long as the Supplier kept on the move, nobody would know. Nobody would ever know. He realized that would be a problem, which it was with every lifetime, but this time even more so with the extent of travel he could do now. He always made sure he kept a steady supply of income flowing in so he could travel. And, of course, every lifetime he shifted bodies, sexes, professions. *Whatever worked* was his motto. His awakening to his real purpose in life was always harsh. A refusal first to understand—to believe—followed by zealous commitment to his higher calling, no matter who thought he was nuts. They didn't understand. Who could? Except him.

Depending when he got the call for a sacrifice, he ran the feeding of the Elders in rotations. Occasionally one of the Elders got hungrier and needed more. It was his duty; it was his honor, and he was here once again to make sure this god, this Icelandic Burning Fires god, got exactly what he needed.

As that familiar hand was placed atop his head and gave him a gentle squeeze, the Supplier felt a shiver run down his back. He dropped to his knees and whispered, "I obey your command."

He was on the sidewalk at a bench digging through his pockets. As if looking for something lost. And he was, but what was lost was a soul that needed to go home. A soul that needed to reconnect with his god. And his job as Supplier was to make sure that happened.

CHAPTER 3

P HOENIX HEADED OUT as soon as she had dumped her bag onto one of the two beds. She caught sight of the cop as he got back into his vehicle and left. With him out of the way, she put her hands in her pockets and strolled from the hotel. She perused the town, wondering at the weird buzz she felt. Something unusual was going on here. Maybe caused by the lava fires? The Burning Fires stopped at fall and restarted in spring all on its own. With a sudden awareness, she realized no ash fell. No ash floated in the air or fell from the sky. This close to the fire, she expected a layer of ash to be everywhere. Was eternal volcanic fire the same thing as a volcanic eruption? She thought so but couldn't be too sure.

It was hard for her to even know why she was here except for the damn Burning Fires recital from her father. She didn't even want to call him her father. A DNA test to prove otherwise would be reassuring, but was that even possible to do now? She knew the police had his DNA because he'd done a lot of other things wrong besides abusing his other cult family members.

She wandered from store to restaurant to café, picked up a coffee to take on her walk outside. She stopped at the edge of an alley and stared down it while she sipped on her coffee. That she was here after all these years filled her with a heady excitement, and yet brought a deep-seated worry to the surface. What if she didn't find what she was looking for? What if no answers were to be found?

She took deep breaths and reveled in the feeling of being here. The alley ahead of her was dark, and yet didn't have an eerie feeling she would have gotten from where she lived in Seattle. A lot of predators were in Seattle. Were there any here? In reality, predators existed everywhere, yet this was but a small town that bustled innocently around her. At least it seemed innocent—on the surface.

She was puzzled by suicide season. Surely there were easier, cheaper ways of committing suicide. Not understanding the mind-set, she continued walking down the alley, checking out the small side streets that came and went. The streets were lovely—cobblestone and unique.

She took out her phone and took several pictures. She didn't know what she would do with any of them. What did any tourist do with this stuff? At least she had avoided buying the T-shirts that read I Was in *blah blah*.

She smiled at that because she had picked up a couple small baubles along her travels, and she would likely pick up something from here as well. Her tour group didn't leave until the day after tomorrow, so she had a little time to explore. Part of the appeal of taking the bus tour was she didn't have to do any of the driving or navigating where to go or where to stay. The disadvantage had been that she was on a bus, full of people.

Not being a big fan of crowds was why she was off exploring the less-traveled corners of the town. She came out on the other side of the alley to see a much smaller area of town, nowhere near as well-lit, nowhere near as nicely decorated as the main center. This area was likely more for the locals. Not such a tourist trap as the rest of the city and, with a little luck, might offer something a little more unique. She wandered up and down a few streets, happy to see some of the stores were still open. She stepped into a tea shop, but it appeared to be more of an apothecary store. She found it fascinating and spent twenty minutes browsing the shelves before buying a lemon balm and leaving.

Tucking her purchase into her pocket, she went to a couple other stores and heard her stomach grumbling. Meals were provided with the tour, but she'd missed a bunch of them, as she didn't always want to eat at the same time as the other travelers. She knew the hotel was supposed to give them a meal, but she had a two-hour window in order to get it. So she kept on walking. She finally came to the far end of the street and took a left, intent on returning to the main center of town.

As she rounded a corner, she heard a cry off to the side. She stopped and spun around. "Hello? Is someone there?"

She stared at a large grove of trees, sure she had heard a woman's voice. She crossed the street on an overpass that looked down into a creek that was likely a raging river at some points during the year. Trees grew down the gully on either side, and the gully itself was at least thirty, if not fifty feet down.

She frowned, wondering where the cry had come from. At either end of the overpass were wooded sections too. She hesitated, then turned her back on the noise and kept walking toward town. When the cry came a second time, she stopped and turned around. Only she saw absolutely nothing.

"It must be a bird," she wondered out loud.

Resolutely she turned again and kept walking. She

wasn't sure what she heard, but an almost electric atmosphere surrounded her. Then again, it could be her sensitive instincts kicking in. Maybe a bird of prey had picked up something for dinner, something that hadn't wanted to be dinner.

Shaking off her nervousness, she rushed faster toward the main part of town. It turned out to be farther than she had expected. More streets coming in and off than she had left. She chastised herself for forgetting to pick up a map of the township.

One of the first lessons when traveling was to always make sure you knew where you were, or else you got lost. She wasn't good at navigating without her phone, and the cell reception since she'd arrived had been terrible. So, with a sense of relief, she saw one of the big buses parked up ahead. Her shoulders sagged, and she continued forward, relieved to see she was on the main street again.

She stopped at one of the benches and plunked down, controlling her breathing. She hadn't realized just how those odd cries and finding herself so far from her hotel had agitated her. When an old woman sat down beside her and smiled, a half toothy smile, Phoenix smiled back. "I'm not from around here," Phoenix asked. "Any idea where I can get a map?"

"Staying at a hotel?" the woman asked.

When Phoenix nodded, the woman stated, "They should have them."

"I meant to pick up one before I left," Phoenix confessed. "Do you live here?"

The old woman nodded. "I was born here," she said. "I've traveled plenty, but I'm still happy to come home. It's a hard place to leave permanently."

"Why is that?" Phoenix asked.

"It's hard to walk away from everything you know." She looked at Phoenix. "Don't you feel that way about your family?"

"I don't have any family anymore," Phoenix replied in an abrupt tone. She stood and gave a small nod of goodbye and rushed away. She should be used to the questions by now. She'd gone through school having to answer all kinds of them, and every time it had gotten easier, but, for some reason, this woman's reasons for staying seemed foolish to her, but Phoenix couldn't really determine what that would feel like because she did not have anyone to stay for.

As she continued walking, she looked behind to see the woman staring after her. Something was creepy in the look on her face. Feeling chills running down her back, Phoenix hunched her shoulders and hurried away, hating that she saw evil everywhere she looked.

That was because of her father, still showing up everywhere in her life. Every time she'd seen him, she'd cringe and would try to hide, and he'd always catch her and pull her forward for punishment. He never called it punishment though. He always said it was time for her to learn something new. He called it *teaching*. But she'd be tortured in front of everyone because she was the Golden One. And because of her status, the others used to love to see her suffer.

Family didn't have the same meaning to her as it did to others.

She rubbed her temple, feeling the scar on the side of her face ache as she remembered the old traumas. When would this end? When would she leave it all behind? Her breath was still rough in her throat, her chest still sore from the fear of those memories.

She shook her head and headed straight for the hotel. Inside, she noticed the crowd had dispersed, and a lot of noise was now coming from the dining room. She raced up to her room to change, realizing the other person sharing her hotel room hadn't checked in, and maybe she'd get lucky again. The bus had been full, so there was no reason for somebody to not take that other bed in her hotel room. Only it hadn't happened yet. Likely her stay-away energy. She headed out again with her hair brushed, feeling refreshed.

She stood at the open door of the dining room and waited to be noticed. Soon a waitress approached, and she was seated at a table for two. Maybe it was her energy, maybe it was something else, but, no matter where she went, she was placed off to the side alone—never with a group or even another individual traveling on the same bus. She'd long gotten used to it, but it made her wonder if she was putting out energy that said she didn't want anything to do with anyone or if people were picking up on that on their own.

And she didn't understand her impulse to always be alone. She didn't want to be alone, but neither did she want to be left with inane conversation from people who asked questions she had no intention of answering. She sat, staring out the window, her back to the door, a menu in her hand. A shadow fell beside her, and a man pulled out the chair across from her and sat down.

She looked up only to rear back in surprise. It was the cop. She gave him a quick frown. "What's the matter?" she asked.

He looked at her, surprise lighting the deep gaze in his eyes. "Now why would you look at me and ask what's the matter?"

"You're a cop," she said bluntly. "You sit down without

asking and just stare at me."

"I'm staring at you now," he confirmed. "But I wasn't when I sat down, and I did sit down abruptly because I figured you'd probably get up and run away."

Again she could feel herself withdrawing, looking for a way to run. Because of that she jutted out her chin and glared at him.

"And now you're looking to run again but then got mad," he said. "Interesting."

She let out her breath slowly. "How do you know I was running away?"

"Because I can see it in every line of your frame. You're tense. You're worried. You're afraid. Possibly afraid something will come up in this conversation you might not want to answer."

At his observation, her eyebrows rose slowly. "Did you read my aura or something?"

He inclined his head, but all he said was, "Or something."

Frustrated, she stared back at him. "I don't understand what you want. Have I done something wrong?"

"Not that I can see," he said cheerfully, shifting closer to the log wall. "Yet."

"So why are you here then?"

"Because I heard through the grapevine how you appeared nervous and unsteady earlier this evening."

"Grapevine?"

"We're a tight-knit community," he affirmed. "Somebody spoke to you on a bench, and she was worried about you. So much so that she called me as soon as you took off."

"She doesn't need to be," Phoenix replied, surprise raising her eyebrows as she understood this was a compassionate visit. "She made a comment about family that hit a nerve. I had gone down an alleyway that ended up taking me to some other streets, and I got a bit turned around. I ended up on an overpass, coming back into the main part of town."

At that, his mouth dropped open. "You found Fellow Alley?"

"I have no idea what I found," she said bluntly. "But, by the time I made it back to the center of town, I was a bit frazzled and more than happy to just sit there for a moment. Then this woman sat down beside me, so you must see I was already geared to be upset. If you see her again, please give her my apologies. I am fine."

"I'll pass the message on." He leaned forward, his hands clenched in front of him. "Did you see anything down the alley?"

"Some stores that were open. An apothecary masquerading as a tea shop," she said with a half a smile. "A couple shops with nothing I wanted to pick up for myself. Everything was dark and ghoulish. Plus a couple empty stores. It was the cries in the woods that got to me. I presume some bird of prey is around here that makes a cry like a woman's voice."

"Where was it?" he asked, his voice low and urgent, his eyes narrow and glinting. "Where did you hear it?"

Surprised and a little daunted by the tone in his voice, she replied, "At the bridge," she said. "I mean, I was standing there, looking down, when I heard it in the trees again."

"Did you go looking?"

She shook her head. "Not when I was walking across the overpass. I heard it again, and I thought maybe it was a bird. It was so very clear though."

"Why would you think it was a bird?"

"Because it was exactly the same pitch and length," she said. "Nothing differed between the two cries, so I figured it must mean something about it was normal. Like the call of a bird."

His expression eased back some. He nodded. "That's good to hear," he said. "We always have to watch out when we have so many transient people through the place."

"Does *transient* equal *tourists*?" she asked.

"In some ways, yes," he replied. "There's also the worry we are some sort of a suicide destination," he said, and this time his tone wasn't light at all. "And that's the last thing we want to become."

"Suicide season." Her face fell at his nod. "The bus driver mentioned something about that," she said slowly. "Honestly that sounds terrible."

"Exactly. But that overpass you were standing on? We've had four people jump off it."

She gasped. "Really?"

He nodded. "Absolutely no way to survive that fall. Two were locals, and two were tourists. The locals were several years ago, and, once the events were on the internet, it seemed like that became the next favorite spot."

"I thought they were all committing suicide at the Burning Fires," she said in surprise.

"We still lose several there a year," he admitted. "We've extended the security on the place. There's rope and all kinds of measures to keep people back from the edge, but it never seems to stop people from trying."

"The barrier would stop those looking for attention or those easily persuaded off their path but not the serious ones."

He smiled at that. "We don't get too many just getting

attention," he said. "This is a permanent answer."

"I'm sorry," she said. "That's terrible."

"Indeed," he said. "So make sure you don't become one of the victims, okay?"

She sat back with a slump and stared at him. "Is that what you think I am? Somebody who came here to commit suicide?"

He watched her for a long moment. That was exactly what he thought. The woman she'd been speaking with on the bench had likely found their conversation upsetting. Phoenix had been distressed before the woman had asked her a question, and obviously the combination had been enough for the older woman to worry about the young tourist's mental health.

"I didn't come here to commit suicide," she said, her voice hardening and low. "I get that woman might have been worried, but that's not what this trip is about."

"Good," he said. "Then I've nothing to worry about, right?"

"Not in any way," she said in a neutral tone.

"So, why are you here?"

She was starting to get angry with his interruption of her dinner and with his interrogation. Not to mention no one had come to take her order. "Do you give every tourist the third degree?"

"The ones who pique my interest and make me question what they're all about, yes, I do," he replied with a nod.

"I came to see the Burning Fires," she said. "Don't worry. I'll be on the bus and out of here in another day and a half."

He smiled and stood. "Good to know," he said. "Enjoy your stay." He turned away from her and walked off.

She still had yet to see a waitress or a waiter, and she was cold. As she turned, she heard her name called out. It was the cop standing at the door, with two other people huddling at his side. He motioned with his hand for her to join him. Frowning, but not having much choice, she got up and walked toward him. "Now what?" she asked with a hiss. "I'm just having dinner. I'm starving."

"We got word a girl is missing in the woods. Tell me more about what you heard and where."

ROWAN STARED AT her, seeing the fear and the horror of his words reflected in her face. But his phone had just rung, and his fellow cops were here to talk to him. Irene Hansen was missing. She had gone out for a walk, even after being told many times not to, and hadn't returned home. She was still depressed, and her mental state was not something Rowan wanted to consider, given the conversation he'd just had with Phoenix. He watched the young woman in front of him. She appeared to be distressed, but was that over a young woman missing or at potentially missing her dinner?

She shook her head. "I told you what I heard."

He opened the front door and said, "Come with me. I want you to show me exactly where you heard the noise."

She frowned. "I told you. It was at the bridge overpass."

"Get in the car." He motioned to his cruiser out front.

Frowning and obviously hesitant, she walked out of the hotel and got in the cruiser.

He got in on the driver's side, sent a message to dispatch about what he was doing, then headed down the street, out of town.

She didn't say a word. They arrived at the overpass and

pulled off to the side. "Show me where."

"We need to get out and walk," she said, sending him a hurried glance.

She hopped out a little too eagerly for his liking, as if she didn't trust him. But then she didn't appear to trust anyone or anything around her. She was skittish, not exactly shy but reserved. And she did have a massive thick wall all around her. He didn't know what it was about, but a part of him wanted to rip it apart. You couldn't live like that. It wasn't living. It was being a prisoner, walled up inside, and he didn't want that for her. He didn't want that for anybody.

Again his ability to read energy allowed him to see some of what was going on, but it didn't give him the whys.

She walked ahead of him, her steps clipped and fast.

He kept up easily enough. Compared to his six-foot frame, she was tiny. At a guess he'd have to say she was around five seven and slim, to the point of being scrawny. She moved with a litheness that spoke of a healthy body; it was her mental state that worried him. The scar on her face was another issue altogether. He knew no way in hell he could ask her about that and get a reasonable answer. Besides, he had no reason for asking, outside of curiosity.

As they crossed over the overpass, she stopped, looked around and pointed to the alleyway that came up close to it and said. "I came out from there, and I was somewhere around the middle of the road when I heard the first cry."

"How many cries did you hear?"

"Just two," she said. She pointed. "First was here."

"Okay, and the second one?"

She walked out to where he stood in the middle of the overpass. "This is about where I heard the second cry. I looked down over the side, but I couldn't see anybody."

He nodded, his gaze on the woods all around. "She lives not too far from here and is known for walking these woods."

"Sounds like *she's* the one you need to be giving a warning too. For all you know, she's the suicidal one."

"It's possible," he said with a frown. "She lost her infant son four months ago and hasn't recovered."

Phoenix's face scrunched up with sorrow. "I'm sorry to hear that," she said in a hushed tone. "That's tough."

"It is," he said. "Very sad for her. And her husband."

They continued to walk back to the cruiser. As they neared it, she stiffened. "There it is again."

He looked at her in surprise and asked, "There's what?"

She glanced at him and frowned. "The woman screaming," she said urgently. She looked back at the woods and headed across the overpass. "It came from over here. Didn't you hear it?"

He followed her footsteps and muttered, "No, I didn't hear anything."

At that, she froze, turned to look at him and said, "How could you not? It was a woman. A woman screaming for help."

She ran over to the other side and dashed around the edge.

He ran behind her, calling out, "Stop. It's dangerous. There're no barriers."

She froze, looked at him and then continued to walk ahead. "I heard her," she said. "We have to go in this direction." And she kept going, following something; somehow her own mind directed her to some place.

He searched the area around them, looking for the energy that would tell him what was going on. And there was energy all right. It was colorful and cloudy and swirling around them. But a stronger energy was around her. He followed her carefully. "Do you hear it again?"

"No." Her tone was waspish.

"Look. I'm not being difficult," he said, hurrying behind her. "But I didn't hear the scream."

He watched her shoulders hunch tight and knew in her mind she really had. And he was good with that. "Take me to wherever you heard it," he said suddenly.

"Even though you don't believe me?" she snapped.

"I'm trusting that you believe what you heard."

And, with that, her feet took flight, and she ran ahead. But she didn't know the area, and the cliff edge was right at her left.

"Hey, not so fast," he cried out. "You're likely to go over the edge."

"No," she said. "The woman is up here." She ran faster.

It was all he could do to keep up. He didn't know who this woman was, but she either raced toward something important or ran away from something important. He hoped to hell it wasn't her running away from him …

Suddenly she came to a stop and held up her hand to stop him. Coming around her, he could see a woman stretched out, lying sideways on the top of the cliff. *Irene.*

Phoenix reached out a hand and whispered, "Grab my hand. I'm here to help you."

The woman raised her hand; it was broken and bleeding. She whispered, "Nobody can help. Nobody can help."

"Yes," Phoenix whispered. "I can."

Out of nowhere, a heavy gust of wind picked up the woman and threw her into the middle of the gorge. As she fell, she screamed all the way to the ground, leaving both of them in shocked silence.

The echo of her cries boomed through his head even as his brain screamed out, "What the hell just happened?"

"THE LOOK ON her face," the Supplier whispered to himself. He started to laugh but kept his laughter silent, just ripples in the shadows. He absolutely loved to scare the crap out of people. They thought they were so safe and secure in this mundane world of theirs. But they weren't. *He* had control.

He could feel that hand on the top of his head, digging in deeper. He shrugged and said out loud, "Allow me a moment to indulge. I know I'm not supposed to be playing with the humans but the temptation …"

There was never any answer, just an increased pressure in his head. He winced as he was forced to his knees. He took several deep breaths and gave a gentle nod. "Of course I will fix this."

CHAPTER 4

PHOENIX STOOD THERE, a silent scream still pouring from her mouth, as she stared where the poor woman had been flung across the cliff. Phoenix took several steps back, her hands reaching out for the tree for safety, for stability, in a world suddenly gone awry. She glanced at the cop, and his face reflected her own shock.

He took two steps forward, completely the opposite reaction she had had, and stared down at the cavern. He turned to look back at Phoenix, a question in his eyes.

She nodded. "I just saw what you saw," she said, her voice harsh and raspy. "That woman was picked up and tossed into the air, to drop down, screaming all the way." She took a shuddering breath. "I don't know what the hell's going on in your town, but this is sick."

He walked to her, reaching out to grab her arm. She flinched as soon as his hand closed around her skin. "I don't know what just happened," he said. "I don't understand any of this."

"Neither do I," she mumbled. "I just got here today. I heard a woman screaming. You insisted I show you where, and we just watched some unseen force pick her up and throw her to the bottom of that ravine." She shook her head, loose tendrils of long auburn hair flying loose from the braid down her back. "Dear God, did you see her? Did you see her fly out there?" She tried hard to control her voice, but it rose into a shriek regardless. She grabbed his shirt and shook him. "She's dead. She has to be dead."

He turned to look over the cliff again, a strangled exclamation escaping his lips.

Her gaze shifted to where he looked. And cried out.

There was the woman, once again on top of the cliff. … Just as she'd—they'd—first seen her …

They froze. And then he broke contact and ran to the poor woman.

Phoenix followed. All she wanted to do was get away from that edge and wasn't at all surprised when Rowan snatched the woman up and ran back several hundred feet. She applauded his actions, racing at his heels until he finally slowed and lowered the woman to the ground, checking for a pulse.

"Is she alive?" Phoenix asked.

He nodded. "She is. But I don't know what that just was."

"I don't know either," her voice replied softer. She stared over at the cliff's edge. "I'm starting to wonder how we could both have seen the same thing."

"It wasn't a mirage," he said. "It wasn't something we made up in our minds."

"Are you sure?" she asked. "Because I really want it to be."

His look was understanding but hard. "We can't forget what just happened," he said abruptly. "This woman was thrown off the cliff and somehow returned."

Phoenix rubbed her temples. "There has to be another explanation."

"Sure, and I'd love to hear it," he said harshly. "Because,

if that ever happens again, … what if she isn't returned to safety?"

Phoenix sank back on her heels and stared down at the young woman, still shocked at what she'd just witnessed. She couldn't get her mind wrapped around it. She tried to see the woman's energy, but, whether because of what just happened or because Phoenix was off-balance, she wasn't seeing it. "Will she remember any of this?"

"I have no idea," Rowan replied. "We need to get her some help." He looked at her. "And don't say a word."

Her mouth dropped open. "And just what would I possibly say?" She motioned toward the cliff's edge. "Anything I say will make me sound like a crazy person."

"I know," he said. "We came upon her like this. That's the end of the story. Okay?"

Phoenix nodded slowly because he was right. That was exactly what they needed to say. And he already had his phone out, calling for help.

She stroked the woman's waxy cheeks. "Please wake up," she whispered. "Please." The woman's cheeks were cold. "It's almost like she's hypothermic," Phoenix said. "But the evening is warm."

"She's definitely suffering from something," he said. "I don't know if that had something to do with what we just saw or not, but it's impossible to discount it."

"Ghostly or spiritual encounters often have that reaction, don't they?"

His initial response was to study her intently. "What do you know about such things?"

"Nothing," she said with a shake of her head. "Nothing like this."

"Interesting," he said. "Because I've heard the same

thing."

"And what do you know about such things?" she asked, flipping his words around at him.

He smiled and said, "Nothing."

She glared at him and then looked back down at the woman, picking up her hand and gently stroking the back of her wrist. "I want her to wake up," she said. "I want her to wake up and tell us she's okay."

"Do you really believe she is?"

"I've seen a hell of a lot of nastiness in my life," Phoenix whispered, her voice very soft, almost faint. "But I've never seen anything like that. I want it to be a mirage. I want it to all just go away and be erased from my mind, so I never saw it …" She shook her head. "But I can't."

He nodded. "Neither of us can." He gently patted the woman's cheeks. "Irene, wake up. Please, wake up."

First came a moan, and the woman's chest shuddered, then she took a great big breath, and her eyes opened. She looked over at the cop in confusion and then in dawning horror. "What just happened?"

"I'm not sure," he replied, keeping his tone neutral. "What do you think happened?"

"I was being held down by some weird pressure all around me," she said. "It was like somebody was squeezing the life out of me. And I kept hearing the word *sacrifice*. I fought, but it wasn't doing any good. I could scream sometimes, but I couldn't handle it." Her voice broke off, and the tremors started.

"And then?" he prompted, taking off his jacket to drape it over her.

"I swear to God, I was thrown off the cliff, and I fell," Irene whispered, horror reflected in her eyes, "screaming all the way down the valley to the bottom. She shuddered and closed her eyes again, tears leaking out. "Dear God, that nightmare was so real."

"You're here. You're alive, and you're safe," Rowan said, his voice strong and reassuring.

Phoenix wanted to step in and say, like hell, but there wasn't any point. The woman's words confirmed exactly what they had both seen. Phoenix placed her hand on the woman's belly. "How are you feeling now?" she asked, infusing some warmth into the chilled woman.

Irene turned her head slowly to look up at her. "I feel better," she said. "Of course I'm not caught in that nightmare, so anything is better than that."

Phoenix nodded. "That sounds like it was a pretty rough trip."

The woman gave a gargled laugh. "Absolutely." She looked up and said, "Everything seems so much brighter. So much stronger."

"*Brighter? Stronger?* In what way?" Rowan asked, his tone deepening suspiciously.

She smiled at him. "I can't really explain. … I must be still caught up in a dream state. Everything looks odd."

"In what way is it odd?" Phoenix asked, bending slightly so she could look into the woman's eyes.

"Like I said, everything is brighter. Like, your face," she said. "An unworldly glow is around your head." She looked over at the cop. "You too, Rowan."

Rowan, Phoenix thought. *So that's his name.*

"Can you see anything else?" he asked, leaning back slightly.

"Everything seems gentler," she said. "If it wasn't for the nightmare, I'd be feeling really good. Like waking up from a good dream."

"Maybe that's what you needed then," Phoenix said slowly. "What if that nightmare was enough to kick you out of whatever fog you were in? I understand you've been dealing with a lot of grief and loss lately." She'd brought it up deliberately—not sure what reaction she'd get from Irene.

Rowan wasn't happy with her. He shot her a hard look and gave a small shake. But the damage was already done.

Irene looked up at her and smiled. "That's the thing," she said. "It's like I'm at peace with it now. As if whatever crazy nightmare that tumbled me off that cliff, when I came back up again, I could leave it all behind."

Phoenix settled back slowly and looked at her. "That would be lovely if that was the case." Just then they heard sirens in the distance. Phoenix looked down at the woman and asked, "Can you move? Are you okay? Do you have any injuries?"

Irene stretched her hands up, rotated her shoulders, then her head. "I know it sounds foolish. I know I was crying out, screaming in pain earlier, but I feel much better now." She slowly sat up. "Now I feel foolish that you called the ambulance."

"You were unconscious," Rowan said. "No way I wouldn't have you checked over."

She smiled and gently patted his cheek. "You're a good man."

"So is Pelchi," he said. "He has been really worried about you."

She sighed and gave an oddly beautiful smile. "I know. It should be better now," she said, and, against their protests, she stood and stretched. "I do feel so much better. I don't know why. I don't know what that was all about, but I feel really good now."

The ambulance stopped, she turned and waved at them as the men raced toward her.

"Hey, John. Hey, Crem. I'm fine. Really."

The men looked at her, surprised, and turned to Rowan.

He shrugged and said, "She was unconscious."

The two paramedics stood with their hands on their hips. "Let us take you in and get you checked over," John said.

Crem reached out his hand. "Come on, Irene. You've had a tough couple months."

She smiled and said, "I have, haven't I? But that's all over with." She gave everybody a beautiful smile and then turned to face the cliff.

Phoenix got a horrible feeling.

Irene bolted as fast as she could away from them and did a swan dive off the cliff.

Phoenix screamed.

Rowan ran past her, reaching for Irene before she went over, barely stopping himself from falling off the cliff after her.

Phoenix sat on the ground, arms wrapped tight around her knees, shuddering, hating what she knew happened. She buried her face in her knees and rocked back and forth. She could hear sobbing—great big gulping sobs from somewhere around her.

Finally hands—big, thick, warm and comforting—wrapped around her, and she was tugged into a man's embrace.

She raised her head and realized it was her sobbing, tears pouring hot and fiercely down her cheeks. She stared up at Rowan.

He placed a finger against her lips, as if to tell her to not speak, pulling her tight against him and together, the two were silent as they tried to process the horror of what they had just seen.

ROWAN LOOKED OVER at the paramedics, keeping the still-shuddering Phoenix tucked against his chest. The shocked look on all their faces, the distress. One of the EMTs walked to the edge and then turned to look at his buddy and shook his head. "I can't even see her."

Rowan had to admit he was staring at the same location on the top of the cliff, wondering if by chance she would return again after the same crazed fall she'd had the first time. But he knew in his heart it wouldn't happen. Whatever Irene had gone through, she had made a decision to run for freedom. Whatever freedom death offered.

The woman in his arms let out great big devastating sobs as she clung to him. And he couldn't help thinking of all she'd been through since she'd arrived in town. He held her close, watching as their energies blended and fused. He shook his head at that too. How was that even possible? It was too fast. He didn't even know this woman, but either they shared a bonding experience over what they had just both witnessed or something about their individual energies was pulling them together into one connected river as it flowed around the two of them.

He closed his eyes, dropped his chin on top of her head and held her, realizing that a ball of energy was wrapping up and around them, sealing them off from the rest of the world. Bits and pieces of her past flowed through him, revealing images he could only hope had been from a long time ago, and he hoped to God it was her past lives. He didn't always get information as easily as this, and these were some he'd wished he'd never seen.

There was so much torture, such fiery flames that he could feel his arms clenching, as if to protect her, and yet knowing that all this was history. He didn't know why he was seeing it all. He didn't know what he was supposed to do with the information, but, as he slowly looked up, he saw the two paramedics calling out to him. He lifted a hand and waved them off.

They nodded and walked away. He could see them back over by the ambulance, calling in for search and rescue. He couldn't even imagine telling Irene's husband what they had just seen. And yet, somebody had to. And that somebody would be him.

Seemed liked suicide season had begun early.

43

CHAPTER 5

P HOENIX SHIFTED IN his arms, tilting her head back, her eyes hot, her body anguished. "Please tell me that didn't just happen," she said in a broken whisper.

"I'm so sorry," he said, "but it did."

She shuddered, wrapping her arms tighter around his chest. "She looked so happy. It was like she was this otherworldly being," she whispered. "As if she thought she could fly."

Privately he agreed. "I don't know what that experience was," he said, "but we have to be careful about what we say."

She gave a heavy sigh. "That's all right. I've had a lifetime of being careful of what I say." Tears still ran down her cheeks. "But I have to admit to being more than a little terrified of closing my eyes tonight. Because this will play over and over again."

"No, you need to sleep," he said. "Your body is now in a state of shock, and, when it wears off, you are likely to collapse from exhaustion."

"Does something like this ever wear off?" she asked, thinking about how absolutely insane what she had just seen was. What *they* had seen. And thank God he'd been here too. No one would believe her if she tried to tell them what just happened.

"But we only saw the beginning part," Rowan added.

"The paramedics saw the rest. They're witnesses that she just took off and flew over the edge. Committing suicide."

"As if her second chance at life changed something inside her," she theorized.

"But remember. Nobody else but you and I saw that first fall," he said. "And you need to *not* bring it up. I don't want to make it an order, but it's pretty damn hard not to. Stay quiet."

She nodded, hating the need for secrecy, but understanding. Some women were good with that, and some had to talk things out over and over again, and then there were the gossips, who embellished everything they heard and saw, until the end result was something completely unrecognizable from the original story.

"I need to move around," Phoenix said quietly. "I'm stiff, sore."

He stepped back slightly, letting his arms drop to his side. But she swayed unsteadily. He shifted position and tucked her up tight against him.

"I should have taken her farther away from the edge," he muttered. "I hate the guilt of knowing I could have, should have done more."

"I don't think it would have mattered," she whispered. "I don't think we could have stopped it. Or maybe I just want to believe that. Maybe I just want to be absolved of my own guilt."

His gaze was hooded. The light in his eyes shadowed as he looked around.

"I suppose they will mount a rescue now?" she murmured, not sure what to do at this point.

"A retrieval," he corrected. "They'll retrieve the body."

"Because, of course, no chance she is alive." And then

she gave a broken sigh. "Or is there?"

"I'd love to see her reappear," he said, his voice heavy. "At this point, for such a thing to happen, we'd have a bigger problem."

"You mean, a resurgence of the talk about the Burning Fires here?" she murmured. "The craziness that happens here? The weird supernatural events? … The evil?"

He squeezed her shoulders and said, "That's enough of that talk. We work hard to calm those rumors."

"I can tell you that you won't quell this one," she said. "It's one thing if it was just you and me and what we saw at the beginning. But the paramedics. What will they say?"

"They'll say, she stood up, appeared to be fine and then took off running to do a swan dive off the cliff. They'll assume she was in an altered state from having fallen or taken something or having tried to commit suicide, not having the strength, and, when she woke up, finding the strength, she took off."

"Had she tried before?"

He nodded slowly. "Twice."

"Ouch," she said. She shook her head. "At least maybe now she's at peace."

He slowly turned her in the direction of the paramedics and asked, "Do you need to be checked over?"

She gave a strangled laugh. "They can't see into my crazed mind now," she said. "Or see my heart that aches for a young woman's life cut so short. Or the spiritual side of my life, standing here and staring at whatever good or evil stood on that cliff with us today."

"You realize it could have been a premonition," he said, suddenly stopping in his tracks and looking down at her.

She frowned. "The fact that she flew off the first time?

That was a premonition of her committing suicide?" She shook her head, seeing the wheels turning around in his mind. "Can premonitions be shared?"

"I don't know," he said. "I've never seen one before."

"Well, I can't say I'm thrilled about seeing this one either. But it is an explanation." She smiled up at him. "And that's what the mind needs, isn't it? An explanation. Some way to understand. To fit this into our record of experience and move forward. Maybe a premonition is a good way to look at that. Of course she didn't exactly fly peacefully the first time, did she?"

"No, and, maybe for that reason alone, its better this way. Maybe we are happier to know that, when she did fly over that edge, she was in an altered state, and she was happy with her decision."

"How wrong is that?" she asked.

"I understand she just lost her child, but she had a husband who loved her. She had a life ahead of her. And what we can't do is judge," Rowan said softly as they slowly walked toward the paramedics. "Because, even though to us, she had all those things, we don't know the truth because we never looked that closely into her life."

"Will you now?" she asked.

He stopped to consider her question and nodded. "I pretty much have to."

ROWAN WALKED BACK into his office, his head full of all he'd seen. Questions streamed through his mind. He didn't understand so much; he wasn't sure he could ever understand enough because there just weren't answers to be had.

Above all else he still couldn't let go of what had happened to Irene. And the fact that he was here with Phoenix, a woman he was attracted to, and yet even he could see the danger of being associated with her—that too made no sense. That their energy melted together had stunned him. He did see auras. Not all the time. Not with everyone. And that was something else that just blew him away.

Why wasn't it all the time? Why wasn't it like math, when two plus two always made four? When it came to psychic energy, there was always this level of *sometime, some* days, with nothing ever *certain*. That bothered him.

He could also see Phoenix kept her energy extremely tight against her body, as if afraid to let anybody in. But not only did she keep it tight against her body but it was hard, tense, almost like a shield.

He needed to research her background, and he wanted to talk to his grandmother to see if she had picked up anything about Phoenix, but he figured that would lead him down a path he didn't want to go. His grandmother had more than her fair share of Gypsy blood. She'd come and gone throughout his life. She'd spent most of the last few years in town, except for short trips to visit the rest of her Gypsy family wandering all over the globe. He liked her independence, but some of her messages were dark.

And she often saw what he didn't want her to see. She'd see his attraction to Phoenix. Sometimes his grandmother seemed to slip into trances, and what came out of her mouth then was stuff that even he didn't want to question. He had tapes of some of her messages somewhere. He'd often considered destroying them but couldn't bring himself to do it.

After the chief had tried to commit suicide, Rowan had wondered if something was wrong with the entire town. Was something psychic going on here? Irene's death seemed to confirm it. Rowan sat down in this big chair with a heavy *thump.*

When he brought up his emails, he groaned because, of course, there were dozens and dozens of them. While he sorted through the list, one of the office staff walked in with a sheaf of paperwork in her hands. He shook his head, his palm up in a stop signal.

"You know, until he's back up and running, if he's ever back up and running," she said quietly, "somebody has to handle the paperwork."

"I get it," he said. "I will temporarily step up to the plate to do what's necessary. But that doesn't mean it's my job."

"Doesn't mean it isn't either," she said cheerfully.

With that, he went through the pages and initialed the ones that needed initialing and signed the ones that needed signing. He handed the stack back to her. "I'll take an hour so. If you can hold calls for me, I'd appreciate it."

"Will do." She stopped at the doorway and said, "I'm really sorry about Irene."

He nodded. "So am I," he said. "So am I."

She went out and closed the door behind her.

Immediately he delved into Phoenix's history. But in order to get into the files he wanted, he needed access. He sent off several requests for information on Phoenix Rising. After researching several databases, he ended up contacting law enforcement in New Mexico, drilling down to police officers who had handled the surrounding area to the north of Albuquerque. He mulled over a reason for his request, then finally typed in, "Possible connection to the death of a local here." And left it at that.

He was surprised when he got an answer almost immediately, and a file was attached. Except it was just a summary.

He opened it and gasped. His breath caught at the back of his throat at the sight of the photos of a young girl taken on the day she was rescued. The damage to her face, her body. The scars were incredible.

With that heavy introduction he sat back and read through the summary. Her father had run a cult on private property twenty minutes from the closest town. On the day the cult had been raided, he'd shot at the cops, and his body had ended up riddled with bullets. At the bottom of the page was a notation saying *suicide by cop*. And Rowan understood that. Because, at the end of the day, not all cult leaders were capable of killing themselves. They usually shot everybody else around them or had everybody else die and then couldn't do the last deed themselves.

Also, according to the report, the police found multiple women and children deceased in the building. The fire had burnt a large portion of the building but not all of it. Further autopsies showed they'd died from poison. It was suspected the father had started the fire, and the only surviving member was eleven-year-old Phoenix.

He shook his head. "In black and white," he muttered to himself. "This is beyond devastating." He just couldn't imagine what she'd lived through or how.

What a shock her condition would have been to the doctors at the time too.

At the bottom of the summary was a file number to request more information.

He followed up, asking for the full file. Rowan closed the email, saving it to a personal folder and sat back. So far everything matched with what little Phoenix had said and so much more. All this did was bring up more and more questions. Just like Phoenix herself.

CHAPTER 6

B ACK AT THE hotel Phoenix found she'd missed the dinner hours and was now in her room alone. So far nobody had shown up to claim the other bed, and she was damn grateful.

Her body and emotions were exhausted, and yet her mind wouldn't shut down. Her stomach was empty and wouldn't stop growling. Everything was complete opposites. She wanted to relax, but every muscle was tight, tense. Before she left for her room, Rowan had asked for her cell phone and room numbers, although she had a suspicion Rowan already had them.

She had said, "Can't you just get all this from the hotel?"

They were walking through the front lobby at the time. "I already have," he said. "I'm just confirming."

She'd been too tired to care what that meant. As they'd passed the dining room, she had whispered, "And I missed dinner too. I don't know if I can make it till morning."

"I'll take care of it," he said at her room door, which he unlocked, swiping the card down through the lock, opening it for her. He glanced at her. "You sleep here alone?"

"Apparently. It's supposed to be two to a room but ..." she replied. "Every other night on this tour has been the same."

While he watched, she threw herself on the bed and buried her face in the pillow. "Will you be okay?"

She rolled over and glared up at him. "Hell, no, I won't be okay."

He winced. "Okay, I deserved that. I'll go down and get a couple cups of tea and find something to eat. Why don't you get up and wash your face? Do anything you can to make yourself feel better, and I'll be back, okay?"

She'd nodded. Now she was back on the bed, looking around the small room, wondering why she was in Iceland.

Of course she knew. Her gaze went to her travel bag and the weird letter her father had shown her so long ago.

Her father had powers and abilities she'd thought were normal. Only later had she realized it wasn't normal to light a flame on the end of a finger. As a child, she'd been terrorized because she had been the one on the receiving end of that fire. But it also seemed normal. Only she'd never seen anyone else do anything so strange and otherworldly. She'd never seen anything else quite like it until today. That black hole of ugly memories she wanted to avoid.

It had never occurred to her that other people could be in a position of power, like her father, as he'd pounded it into her that she was special. Now she knew others were out there too who were special. She sat cross-legged with her laptop—a small cheap one for traveling.

She keyed in the internet password for the hotel. Very quickly she had it up and working and searched terms like *suicide season* and *premonitions*. By the time a knock came on her door, she was well into the research. And feeling a little better. She hopped off the bed, walked across the room and opened the door.

Rowan had a trolley in front of him and one of the staff members with him.

She looked at the stranger and smiled gratefully. "Thank you."

He nodded, and such compassion and understanding was on his face that she realized Rowan must have said something to him. With the door closed after the employee's exit, she looked down at the trolley. "What did you get?"

"Leftovers," he said with a small laugh. "But the leftovers Patro makes are pretty fine indeed."

"And who is Patro?" she asked, lifting the lids to see large plates of what looked like roast beef, gravy, mashed potatoes and veggies. Her stomach growled again. She motioned at a small table by the window. "Let's sit over there."

He pushed the trolley so it was right beside the table and then, from underneath, pulled out plates and cutlery.

"I'm surprised they gave you this," she said.

"Once they realized what had happened, they were all too willing to make our evening a little easier."

She nodded. "Meaning, I wouldn't have anything bad to say about the town or the hotel after I leave?"

"You can't blame them," he said, putting a plate in front of her. "Their livelihood is dependent on tourists."

"Keeping the suicide season quiet has got to be difficult."

"It is," he said. "The internet picks up on things like that and runs with it like crazy. Embellishing the truth and making it out to be something it's not, driving more people to commit suicide," he ended grimly.

"I've been doing research since you left." She rubbed her eyes. They were dry and scratchy and still hot from all the tears. She blinked to ease them, noticing, as she opened them, a pot of tea. She smiled. "In a way this is much nicer than in a dining room. Plus I don't have to eat alone."

"Are you always alone when you eat?"

She tilted her head to the side as she thought about that. "Since the bus tour, yes, but I'm not sure why."

"It's an even number of people on the bus," he said. "I asked, so I'm not sure why you're alone in this room either."

"I'm not sure either, unless there's an odd number of women, so I'm the odd one out," she said. "Or why, every time I go into the dining room, I'm given a table alone. Maybe they expect I'll have a partner join me, but I never do. I've often wondered what others know that I don't."

"Interesting," he said. He picked up his knife and fork and motioned at her plate. "Eat while it's hot."

She didn't argue, and, with the first bite, she was lost. "I'm so hungry," she said. She chewed several more bites and then smiled. "Patro is truly talented if this is his cooking."

"He is indeed," Rowan agreed. "He's lived here all his life, except for the years he went to France and Italy for special training. But he came back and took over his father's position at the restaurant."

"Did his father want to be taken over?"

At that Rowan looked down at the plate and didn't answer.

She slowly lowered her hands. "Don't tell me that suicide season hit?"

He winced at the term. "Yes, that's exactly what happened."

"I'm sorry for Patro," she said. "Does anybody know why or what the extenuating circumstances were?"

"In his father's case, he had just found out he had stage four cancer," Rowan replied. "He had no intention of following the recommended course of treatment, according to the hospital."

"Ouch," she said. "I understand his thinking."

"Except for what it does to the families left behind," he said, his voice harsh.

"Right," she said, admitting that point. Something in his voice said either he'd known Patro's father and had been really close, or he'd known somebody else who had done the same thing. "It must be tough policing a part of the world where people come to kill themselves."

"Not only that," he said, "one of our own police force just tried the same thing. And I'm sure you'll hear about it from the gossip, if you talk to anybody locally tomorrow. The suicide chatter will be loud again after today. Our police chief tried to commit suicide almost six weeks ago."

"*Tried?*" She pounced on that word. "Is he still alive?"

"Yes," he said. "He's been in a coma ever since. In the meantime, I've been doing his job."

"Oh," she said. "Any worries you'll end up the same way?"

He lifted his head and studied her features. "Meaning?"

"Meaning, maybe policing a place where so many people choose to kill themselves would have a negative effect on you. As if maybe you will eventually choose that as the answer for your own future."

He looked at her in surprise. "I hadn't considered that as a reason behind why my boss made that choice, but," he said, "I suppose it's possible. He was the police chief here for over forty years."

"That's a long time," she said in surprise. "Didn't he have to retire?"

"Because he was in such good health, he stayed well past the point he should have retired. But he was now heading into forced retirement, and I think that's what precipitated his actions."

"When would he have retired?"

"Two weeks after he attempted to take his life," Rowan replied. "So this helped him to avoid those last couple weeks where everybody would say goodbye, when that's the last thing he wanted to do."

She nodded. "I can understand that too. If this was my entire life, and I was being forced to leave it, I'm not sure I would want to continue afterward either, particularly if I didn't have family and other things I wanted to do." She glanced at him. "What about his family?"

"His wife died of cancer years ago."

"Oh," she said. "And if he didn't commit suicide back then …"

"He didn't," Rowan replied. "Obviously. As far as I know, he didn't make any attempts either. I think he just was ready to go this time. He wanted to join his wife."

"Was he talking about her a lot?"

"He was. Not that he was planning on joining her, just that she was always on his mind. He did tell me how he thought he'd seen his wife, and that's when he realized he was starting to lose it."

She slowly lowered her knife and fork and placed it on the empty plate, her thoughts shrouded by his words. "And what if he really did see her?" She picked up her water glass and took a sip. "After what we saw today, maybe he did see her and realized the only way he could join her was to die."

"I've thought of that," he said. "It's been on my mind since watching Irene. I keep going through all the other suicides I know about personally in the last few years, wondering if something like that didn't also happen to them."

"Were they all the same?"

He shook his head. "No. The police chief ate a bullet. He just didn't do a complete job of it."

She winced at that. "But that makes sense too. He was on the job. And I guess he wanted to go out the same way he lived his life."

"Maybe." He cleared away their empty plates, put them back on the trolley. "Patro also sent up dessert."

She smiled up at him. "I'm not sure I could eat anything else," she said. "I am feeling much better with a full belly though."

"Exactly," he said. "That's why it was important you get a hot meal." He poured her a cup of tea and then brought over the third silver tray. When he lifted the lid, there were two plates. Each with a large slab of a multilayered chocolate cake and some fluffy filling in between.

"Wow," she said. "That looks gorgeous."

"I hope you're not allergic to anything," he stated. "A bit late to be asking now though, isn't it?"

"Much too late," she said, reaching for a plate. "And, no, I'm not allergic to anything that I know of."

"What do you do for a living?"

"I was recently laid off from my position due to budget cuts," she replied. "I was an associate professor at a college. I used to teach mythology and several art classes."

"Oh, I don't see you as a teacher," he said in surprise.

She lifted her gaze. "What do you see me as?"

He thought about it and frowned. "I'm not really sure."

"I didn't do a lot of teaching," she said. "I was there for four years, hoping to get into a full-time position, but the college suffered because of multiple sexual harassment lawsuits, bringing the enrollment numbers down, plus the legal fees from the lawsuits impacted their bottom line. They were forced to do layoffs. Six of us were offered a payout, so I took mine."

"And came here?"

"Yes," she said. "I was putting some other issues of my own life to rest." At that, she gave him a half smile. "I thought maybe, if I could see one of the places I'd heard about, I could walk away from my past and start fresh."

"Interesting," he said. "Because walking away from the past is often what people do by committing suicide. They can't handle their life, so they walk away from it permanently."

"I didn't come here to commit suicide," she said, her voice firm. She could feel the intensity of his gaze, and she smiled up at him. "I get that, after what we saw today, you're worried about me. I presume that's why you brought dinner and why you're sitting here, babysitting me. But I promise I'm not planning on committing suicide."

"Good," he said. "Because that's not a memory I would want to live with."

"That would be tough, wouldn't it? I'm already struggling with Irene's swan dive as it is. And I never met the woman until today. The thing that really gets me is the joy and the peace that settled on her face as she made some decision and then took off on us. But what if we could have grabbed her faster?" She stared at her teacup. "That's what'll haunt me—the what-ifs."

"And that'll be my nightmare," he said heavily. "I mean, I was close. I was so close. And then it was like she had wings on her feet and just flew."

"I was afraid you would go over the edge too," Phoenix said. "You were following her so closely. I was afraid you wouldn't stop."

"That's something I didn't tell you," he said. "It's almost as if this unseen wall stopped me. I'm not sure I could have gone over."

Her eyes rounded. "Wow. Okay, that takes this into the realm of something else yet again."

"Something else?" he said with a laugh. "What else could there possibly be?"

"Fate? Angels? Decisions from above? Your time? Not your time? Things like that." She shook her head. "I've already questioned those concepts. It's one of the reasons I'm here. I keep thinking of the Burning Fires. If I could just find a way to close it, maybe it would not bother me anymore."

"*To close it?*" he said. "You realize this thing is massive, right? And it's burning on gases from deep in the center of the Earth. That it shuts down every fall and restarts every spring, like clockwork, all on its own."

"I didn't mean to close off the fire," she said. "I just want to find closure in my world."

"That fire? Or the fire of your childhood?" he asked almost delicately.

She looked up at him and frowned. "What do you know about that?"

Silence.

ROWAN DIDN'T KNOW what to say. That he'd looked into her history? That would seem incredibly intrusive. Particularly when his reasons for doing so were a little thin as well. "When I was holding you in my arms after Irene went over the edge, I saw all these images, … visions, insights. I don't know what else to call them," he said with a shrug. "Just these pictures and I don't know if it was from your childhood or from a past life."

At that, she stiffened.

He nodded. "I know that probably sounds horribly invasive. But I didn't try to see them. I didn't *want* to see them."

"What did you see?" she asked in a crisp tone. "Not that I believe in past lives."

"I haven't had too much to do with them myself either," he said. "But I will admit that I do see a lot of different energies and auras."

"Auras like what Irene saw around you and me? I wondered if that's what she saw. She commented on the lights around our heads."

"I don't know what Irene saw," he said. "If you think about it, it could have been anything."

"Right. So, what did you see?" she asked, her voice challenging. "About me."

"Fire and being burned," he said softly. He watched her withdraw and nodded. "Over and over again. As if you were being tortured."

Her eyelids slowly closed. She opened them to stare at the table.

An almost invisible wall went up between them. Only it wasn't invisible because he could see it. "I'm sorry," he said. "I am not trying to intrude."

"Maybe you're not trying to," she said, "but intruding you are." She picked up the tea, took a sip, and when she replaced the cup on its saucer, she took a bite of the chocolate cake. Chewing quietly, she sighed, settling back happily. "It's wonderful cake. You should try it."

He realized, as far as she was concerned, the conversation

was over. He let her change it, knowing it was obviously something horrifically painful. "It is good, isn't it? You can come in during the daytime and have tea and a treat here. It's quite reasonable."

"Good to know," she said. "We're here tomorrow and then leaving the day after."

"Where do you go from here?"

"I don't really care," she said. "My destination was here. I didn't really think about what came afterward."

More alarm bells went off. "That brings me back to my suicide worry," he said. "That's what people often say when they don't make plans after coming here." And that was one of the biggest warning bells he'd learned to take note of.

"I still have an apartment at home," she said. "I still have bank accounts open. It's not like I sold everything or gave everything away."

"Do you have family?" Again his research came to mind. She'd been the only one to survive, but that didn't mean other family members weren't still alive at other locations.

She stared up at him before finally answering. "So, so many. But to my knowledge none are still alive."

"Wow, that's sad." In fact, something was wrong about her tone.

"It happened a long time ago," she said dismissively. "It's possible an extended family is out there, but I never bothered to look."

"Oh," he said. "Maybe you should make that your mission. Find the other family members."

"Why?" she asked. "The memories I have of my family aren't good. And I highly doubt I want anything to do with any of them as adults either." She returned her fork to the plate and said, "I think I'll brush my teeth and go to bed now. Thank you for bringing the food."

It was an obvious dismissal. "I'll take all this back out again."

"That's a good idea." She got up and walked into the bathroom, where she closed the door and locked it.

Talk about hiding something, but even hiding behind that door wouldn't hide everything. She needed to be watched. He didn't know if suicide was on her mind, but she definitely didn't want him to know about something.

The last thing he wanted was for this woman with the too-big eyes, scrawny body and scars that ran soul deep to commit suicide. She was young and had a whole life ahead of her. That her job was over and that she had traveled this far to see something of a curiosity worried him. This location attracted people heading toward a final end. He couldn't bear to see his town be *her* final end.

CHAPTER 7

WAKING THE NEXT morning was a slow, painful process. Every time Phoenix closed her eyes, she saw Irene making the swan dive off the cliff. But it was always intermingled with her reappearing at the top of the cliff. Phoenix didn't know what was going on, but shock and fear had rattled her system. Every time she'd come up with an answer, something would refute it as being stupid and illogical. Phoenix ended up taking melatonin to try to sleep. Thankfully she kept a little bottle with her while traveling so had it available.

She got up, took a hot shower to wake up, then tidied up her clothes and bag so she was ready to check out. A habit she had gotten into since the police had collected her that fateful night so long ago. Her bag was on top of her made bed, waiting to leave, even though she had another day and night at the hotel. It was early yet but she picked up her purse, determined to not lose out on breakfast this morning.

As she walked out of the room, she pocketed her key card and headed downstairs. The reception area was quiet. Somebody worked at the front desk, but she walked past them to the dining room, since she couldn't see an area set up for breakfast.

A young woman walked over to her and smiled. "Breakfast is served in the morning room," she said. She led

Phoenix to the correct area.

"That makes sense," she said. "Sorry."

"Not an issue," the woman said. "Let's find you a nice seat by the window."

Oddly enough, once again she sat at a table for two, and once again she was alone.

The woman called over the waitress, and, within minutes, Phoenix had hot tea and a menu. She turned to look outside at the scenery.

She was distracted by the beautiful and quaint village around her. Something called to her. The wildness of the mountains, … the quaint little cottages, … the cobblestone streets. She shifted in her chair, so she sat sideways with a better view. A few people were out walking, and a vehicle or two passed by but not much else. A blanket of serenity covered the place. Or had something lurking beneath …

In the distance she could see the red halo of the burning fire, and it finally hit her. After all this time she was finally going there today. The tour group had to meet at nine in front of the hotel, and she wanted to make sure she didn't miss out.

She pulled her attention back to her cup of tea as she perused the menu. When the waitress came by, she ordered the breakfast special, surprised at her appetite after eating so well and so late last night. The woman looked a little surprised but smiled and nodded.

She returned a few minutes later with some French bread that appeared to have been fresh out of the oven. Phoenix sliced a piece and buttered it, then topped it with a dollop of jam. She didn't want to fill up on bread because she wouldn't have room for her breakfast.

Something pulled her attention to the door. She looked

up to see Rowan standing there, talking with the waitress. He caught sight of Phoenix, smiled at the waitress, tipped his head and headed in Phoenix's direction. Phoenix wasn't surprised. Somehow she had been expecting to see him. He sat down in the chair opposite her.

She said with a half smile, "We have to stop meeting like this."

He chuckled. "Glad to see you have a sense of humor this morning."

"It's better than all the thoughts I slept with," she admitted.

"You're not the only one," he said. "I had a pretty rough night too."

"I imagine we will both feel that way for a while," she murmured.

Just then her breakfast arrived. He looked at it in surprise. "Wow, that looks great. And a healthy appetite, I see." He turned to the waitress. "May I have exactly what she's got, please?"

The waitress laughed and disappeared.

Phoenix's plate had pancakes, hash brown potatoes, eggs and sausages. She shook her head and smiled. "I wasn't expecting this much." She pointed at the French bread. "That is delicious."

"Good," he said and picked up the knife, cutting himself off several slabs. "I seem to have an abnormally strong appetite this morning."

"I wondered about it as well. I'm starving," she confessed. "Maybe we just need to carb up."

"Or we need the protein to keep us going," he said with a shrug. "Either way, we're better off to eat if we're hungry."

As she dug in, a comfortable silence followed. She finished chewing her bite, then lowered her head and asked softly, "Do you think our appetite has anything to do with the energy from last night?"

He swallowed his bite of bread, looked around and said, "I hadn't considered that."

"Maybe we should," she said. "I don't know why one would have such a healthy appetite after an experience like that, but it just seems to be something else that's abnormal. We ate a big dinner too."

The waitress arrived with Rowan's plate. He smiled, thanked her and dug into his breakfast with obvious enjoyment. "I'll dissect the answer after we eat. How's that?" he said with a smile, then stuffed in a bite of pancake.

The waitress asked if they wanted more tea or French bread. They shook their heads no.

They both dug into their breakfasts with gusto, until they finally sat back, full. "I don't think I could normally eat that amount of food in two days," she said. "So I'm putting that down to another supernatural effect of yesterday."

"Another one?"

"It's not like we need more, do we?" she said with a grimace.

"No," he said. "What we need is a way forward and to put that to rest."

"I leave in an hour," she said. "The tour bus is heading out at nine."

"Because of yesterday's events," he said, "I've doubled up security around the Burning Fires, and I'll be on-site myself today."

"You think something'll happen?" she asked curiously. She leaned forward and, in a low voice, asked, "Are you expecting somebody else to commit suicide?"

He glanced around the room as more and more of the bus people had moved in and were eating breakfast around them, but nobody seemed to pay any attention to them. Usually, if people saw an officer of the law, they would be looking over more often. It was almost as if Phoenix and Rowan were invisible.

"I don't know," he said, his voice equally low. "But I don't want to take that chance."

"Okay," she said. "The bus isn't terribly full. You can probably get on with us."

"No, I want my own wheels," he said. "I'll be connected to my own equipment and communications."

"Ah, that makes sense." She had no idea why she had offered him a spot on the bus. She couldn't even legally do that. More disturbed by her friendliness, she tried to pull back. "I'll head up to my room and pack up the rest of my things, then wait in the lobby until it's time to leave."

He nodded.

As she stood from the table, she looked out the window and said, "It really is pretty out there."

He stood beside her, and they walked to the lobby. "It'll be a nice day," he said. "You should enjoy it."

"I hope so," she said. "I need something to replace the memories of yesterday."

"I hear you," he said.

"See you up there." She turned away, walked a few steps toward the elevator and stopped. Her heart slammed into her chest. She spun to Rowan.

He looked at her and mouthed, "What?"

In a low murmur, she said, "Look at the doorway."

He turned and looked in that direction. She heard him suck in his breath and look back at her with wide open eyes, mouth dropped open.

"It's Irene, isn't it?" she asked in a hoarse whisper.

He nodded. "It so is."

ROWAN LEFT HER in the lobby and ran out, slamming his way through the double doors, rushing past people and darting around the crowd. His gaze searched for what he was sure was Irene's ghost.

It had to be a ghost. Four of them had seen her dive off the cliff. No way she could be alive. Yet she'd come back once before.

As far as he knew, the search and rescue retrieval mission was due to start later this morning. They'd had trouble getting enough skilled men with ropes for this job, as this would be a part-helicopter, part-repelling mission. He wasn't sure how any of it would go and was thankful it wasn't his job. They had specialists for that.

But no doubt he had seen Irene in the doorway, looking at both of them. This time she wasn't wearing that same lively look she had had before.

Instead it looked like an accusation was on her face, as if she blamed them. He already blamed himself enough. What he didn't know was whether he was tuning into Phoenix's psychosis or if seeing Irene now was because they had seen the original vision together? Were they still seeing bits and pieces of the same energy? None of it made any sense, but, if he could find a way to talk to this vision, maybe he could help her cross over.

Only he saw no sign of her now.

He had searched to the left and then the right. He wandered around, hands on his hips, swearing under his breath.

"Any sign of her?"

He turned to see Phoenix standing beside him, arms wrapped around her chest, as if cold.

But he knew the chill was deep inside. He shook his head. "No."

"She's really dead, isn't she?"

He knew what she was asking. "Yes," he said. "She's really dead."

"Have you retrieved her body yet?"

He shook his head and turned to listen to noises coming from the left. Realizing it was just a group of kids, he turned to Phoenix. "The retrieval process will start later this morning."

Her shoulders hunched, as if she'd taken a physical blow.

He reached out a hand and gripped hers. "We couldn't have done anything."

A sigh worked up her chest, rattling every bone.

He swore he could hear it as it coursed through her body before releasing from her chest.

"I know that, in theory," she said. "But, in reality, my mind won't accept it."

"I know."

She gave a brisk nod. "I was doing much better, until I saw her standing in the lobby."

"The question is, why was she there at all? And does she want something from us? If so, what?"

"No clue. Maybe because we didn't save her? Did anybody else see her?" She looked around, her hand gesturing to the crowd. "And how is it possible they couldn't have?"

"We're back to that shared premonition again," he said, pinching the bridge of his nose. "I'm sure there's an explanation. I just don't know what it is."

"It could be all kinds of things, but I'm not sure what you are talking about."

"When two people see the same vision," he said, "like we saw earlier here and on the cliff, it's like her energy is attracted to both of us."

"What about the paramedics?"

"They were there when she committed suicide, not for the shared premonition," he said, his voice low. "Both were distraught enough at her final moments. Neither of them showed up for work today."

"I wouldn't have shown up either," she stated bluntly. "I'd like nothing better than to be at home in my bed."

He turned and studied her. "Yet here you are, ready to get on a bus and go to the Burning Fires."

She gave him a ghost of a smile. "It's what I came for," she said. "I have a letter I wanted to burn in the Burning Fires, but that probably is not allowed, is it?"

"You can't get close enough," he said. "It's not safe."

"Is there any place where it could be dropped in?" she asked. "By someone who is allowed to get close enough?"

He shook his head. "No, and there shouldn't be. Because it would mean somebody had to risk their life in order to get close enough to throw it in."

She frowned as she thought. "I haven't seen it, so I don't really know. I guess I was thinking I could use a long tong or something to drop it over the edge."

He smiled at her. "People come with all kinds of preconceived ideas, but we've had to tighten security because of the reasons I explained already."

She nodded and glanced at her watch. "I need to leave. They'll start boarding in a few minutes."

"I'll walk you down," he said.

"Nobody else noticed, did they?" she asked. "I expected screams, or people crying, saying something."

"I highly suspect it was only us," he said.

"Weird to be bonded in such a way," she murmured.

"Very." He slid her a sideways look. "Just don't let it freak you out too much."

"I said I'm fine. And again, I am not here to do anything crazy."

"I remember what you said, but I'm here day in and day out as people say things and do the opposite."

They approached the line of people getting on the bus. Rowan stood to the side and waited.

She glanced back at him and smiled as she walked up the steps. She sat in a window seat.

He waved, turned and walked away. He'd meant it. No way in hell he would miss her trip to the Burning Fires. He didn't know what the heck was going on, but it was linked to her. And to him.

Now he had to figure out why.

CHAPTER 8

PHOENIX SAT ON the bus, patiently waiting for it to leave. As she'd found with every stop, stragglers always delayed their departure by at least five minutes. It was often the same couple. Sure enough, it was them again. Probably in another argument.

She didn't understand it. She often wondered about combative relationships. Did these people have any joy? Why stay together if all they did was fight? Or worse, how could they enjoy or derive any benefit from all the conflict? And, from the looks of them, they were in their early sixties and had been doing this for a long time. Maybe they got comfort living with the certainty of this same routine. They certainly argued loud and long to make sure they couldn't be ignored. Maybe they did it for attention?

After the bus driver called for a head count, he finally closed the bus door, sat down, put the bus in gear and backed up. One of the buses was ahead of them, and another was still parked, gathering the last of its group. They had only a half-hour drive to get where they were going, but, on a bus, it would probably take ten minutes longer.

When they arrived at the massive parking lot, their bus stopped, and everybody filed out. The heat from the Burning Fires could reach them even here. Why had she never considered that? She should have. She listened to the spiel as she got the history on the hows and the whys and the whens.

And the fact that science couldn't explain the consistent start and stop of this burning fire.

Several other such Burning Fires were found in other places around the world too. This was one of the smaller, lesser-known sites, and the only one she cared about. This town? It was her heritage. It was where her father was born.

It was where she had to return to.

They walked up to the lookout, feeling the noise and the heat increase with every step as they got closer. She sighed with disappointment. The entire area had been truly commercialized. Not only were the tourists kept back enough to stay safe, but also because of the extreme heat. Again, why had she never considered that? How foolish to think she could just let go of her letter and drop it—and everything attached—into the fire. She could throw it into one of the many tourist garbage cans readily available, but she wouldn't get anywhere closer to the lava than where she now stood.

Heartache ate at her. She'd hoped and planned this for years. And to come so close and to not complete her mission was a crushing blow.

She stared at the fire, mesmerized by the flames that continued to burn bright. Something was both devastatingly horrifying and exhilarating about seeing something contained, and yet so powerful within that space.

She listened as the bus driver droned on. She thought about what Rowan had said about suicides and wondered how one could even do that. They were set back so far. With the heat pouring out from the fire, how could anybody knowingly and willingly throw themselves into the flames? It didn't seem likely. She began to wonder if he was teasing her, yet he had been too serious and too worried about her intentions to not take his words literally.

As she walked farther along the path, she came to an area much less traveled and found it was hotter. She also spied steps going down, probably for maintenance. A gate stopped people from traveling in that direction. But, if somebody was seriously interested in committing suicide, they wouldn't let a gate like that stop them.

She frowned, wondering if she should follow the same path. If Rowan caught sight of her down here, he'd think she was about to take her own life. And yet, nothing inside her said she was supposed to do that; yet the letter on the strange paper in her hand burned hot.

She so badly wanted to release it in the fire. But how could she make that happen?

Frustration ate at her. She had been dreaming about this single act for years. Dreaming of walking away and being free. Free of the influence of her father and all the nastiness she had endured. She stroked the scar along the side of her face. One of so many. Yet the most visible one. The one that pained her the most because it was always there, something that other people looked at, glanced away and then, almost as if they couldn't help themselves, glanced back at again.

She glanced at the gate and the sign she presumed read Do Not Enter, although she couldn't read the local language. A voice called out from behind her.

"Phoenix? What are you doing?"

She looked up to see Rowan.

She gave him a crooked smile. "I was just thinking to myself that, if you saw me, you'd think I was about to commit suicide. I'm not," she said. "But the fact that people were doing that here made me wonder how they could breach the fire with this protective barrier."

"Which is, of course, why we have it," he said. "A lot of space exists where people can get away from the tourist area and head to the trees and come up on the other side of the fire. More often than not, they are not even close to the tourist trap here."

She motioned at the steps. "Which is why I was thinking that might be important."

He looked down at the fire. "It's one of the servicing areas," he said. "We do have to deal with the gases sometimes. Plus the concrete here has to be maintained."

She nodded and smiled. "That's what I figured. I was thinking anybody down there would likely have better access for taking their own life."

"I sincerely hope I don't have to find out," he said, his tone quite abrupt. "Please come back up here."

Hearing the tone in his voice, she nodded and headed toward him. She could see him relaxing more as she got closer.

"I'm really not suicidal," she said in a low voice. "It is just very important to me that I get this letter into the fire."

He looked at the paper she had clenched in her fist. "Why?" he asked bluntly.

She hesitated and shrugged. "It would be nice if you would just accept the fact that it's important for me."

"Does it have to do with the scar on your face?"

She flinched. "Definitely," she replied, her voice turning more defiant. "I've been through more than most people could even dream of. I tried to write some of it in this letter, but that didn't work well. And I really, really, really wanted to let it all go into the fires, as that represents my childhood to me."

He didn't appear to be reassured.

She slipped her arm through his. "I promise. I'm not in *that* mental state."

He nodded and looked again at the letter in her hand. "Why can't you just light a match to it?"

"Because *he* always told me about the Burning Fires," she murmured. "I figured, with that refrain always working through my mind, I needed to come to the actual Burning Fires and toss this in."

"He? Your father?" Rowan asked, his tone dry. "But you can't do it from here."

Her father? Had she told him about her father? Her family? Her suspicions arose. Then, after what they'd been through with Irene, if Phoenix could get information on Rowan, wouldn't she have tried? And her name would flag a mess of files. Determined to not let it bother her, she looked at him. "Is there another way to do it?"

He frowned. "Do you have to do it yourself?"

She bit her bottom lip. "No, but I think I have to see it go in."

"I might be able to help," he said. "It would mean calling in a favor."

"Understood," she said. "I really did think I could just stand here and throw it in." She gave him a wry smile. "I know that's naive. The heat hit us way back at the parking lot. I can't imagine getting any closer."

"If you tied it to a rock, you might be able to throw it in," he said, eyeing the distance.

"Only if it's with a trebuchet," she said with a laugh.

"Or a slingshot," he said, cocking his head at her.

"Oh," she said, staring at him. "That seems highly possible."

"You'd only get one chance."

"True," she said. "I'd have to practice for a bit." She glanced around. "How late does this stay open?"

"We didn't used to close it, but now, unfortunately, it gets shut down at sunset."

"But you could come in, couldn't you?"

He frowned.

She looked up at him hopefully. "It's why I came. I know it doesn't seem like much to you, but, with what I've gone through, I've always thought I needed to do this very thing." To her own mind and ears it sounded foolish.

Why the heck would anybody care, when he was right. She should just light a match to it. How did she explain all the horrors she'd been through and the pounding recitals about the Burning Fires? Or that the paper didn't burn …

"Maybe if I understood a little more."

She glanced around at a lot of people, literally hundreds. She clutched his arm tighter chest again.

"Does it have anything to do with what happened to Irene?" he asked finally.

Startled, she stared at him. "I don't even know what to say about Irene," she whispered. "I've never seen anything like that before."

"So, what you're doing here isn't psychic stuff?"

She wanted to say no but wasn't sure. "My father believed he had powers," she said. "I don't know if he did or not."

From Rowan's quick frown, she decided that wouldn't be enough of an answer. She wished she knew how much he already knew about her. She looked around once more to make sure they were out of earshot of anyone, and then, in a lowered voice, she said, "I'm the child of a cult." She searched his face to see if he had any inkling of what that meant. From the look in his eyes, he already knew.

"Tell me."

She nodded, and, with her suspicions confirmed, she said, "My father was a cult leader, and my mother was one of his many followers. He had abilities that seemed to keep everybody fixated on him and only him. The way the women swooned and gushed over him was awful. But what was even worse was the way he treated me."

"You? Or everyone?"

"Me, and only me."

"Why is that?" he asked, his eyebrows pulling together, and a heavy frown crossing his features. He leaned against one of the retaining walls. "Why were you so special?"

"If only I had the answer to that million-dollar question," she said with a bitter laugh, "I might understand."

"Is that why your name ..."

She nodded. "He felt I would rise from the ashes," she said, unable to keep the bitterness from her tone. "He felt he had to prepare me for the fires to come."

At the term *fires*, Rowan sucked in his breath.

"So you can see why I have an affinity for the Burning Fires," she said.

"Maybe," he said. "But I don't want you getting any closer and testing that theory."

"I'm not planning on it," she replied adamantly. "I spent my life being tortured by him and his fire."

His gaze darted to the scarring on her face.

"That's nothing," she said, her voice hoarse. "He usually managed to stop himself from scarring me where everybody could notice."

Rowan's gaze widened, and then his face hardened as he

understood. "Why did nobody stop him?"

"Not only did nobody stop him but they all joined in."

He stiffened. "Your mother?"

"She was proud because I was the Chosen One," she said, her tone bitter. "The thing is, my father was the one and only all-powerful leader in that clan. He seemed to think I would have his abilities, and, therefore, I would be a threat to him at the same time."

"What did he think would happen?"

She shrugged. "The thing about cult leaders is they're greasy salesmen," she said. "Their stories change from day to day to suit the situation. All I ever really understood was that I was special, and I had to be prepared for my future. The other kids hated me because they were supposed to treat me like I was something special. They also loved that I was tortured on a regular basis and did a lot of chanting and laughing at me because of it. Let's just say, I had an incredibly dysfunctional childhood."

"That's not a childhood at all," he said, his voice hard. "How long did it go on for?"

"Until the property was raided by the cops when I was eleven. My mother tried to kill me and herself at the same time. I managed to get free, and she took her own life."

"I did check into your history a little," he offered, "but it was missing quite a few details."

"Good. Who wants to relive those?" she snapped. "I hope it said he'd been shot during the raid. I wanted to see his body. I insisted on it. I know the cops thought something was wrong with me because of it, but I had been tortured for so long. He was the stuff of my nightmares. I needed to know he was dead and gone and couldn't come back and hurt me anymore."

"I think even the cops would have understood that," he said.

"At the time they didn't realize how badly abused I had been," she said. "Only after I was taken to the hospital, and some of my more recent wounds were treated, did they understand how extensive it had been."

"Do you really think throwing this letter into the fire will give you closure?"

She could tell he was working hard to keep the doubt and the disbelief out of his voice. But he didn't understand everything she'd been through.

"He kept talking about me rising from the Burning Fires. I believe this one here is the one he referred to."

"Why the hell would you even want to come here?" he asked. "That is absolutely insane."

"Not as insane as what I went through," she said calmly. "When you spend eleven years being programmed by an insane father, it's hard to toss that programming away. You understand it doesn't make sense, but, at the same time, you can't *not* listen."

He nodded. "But you're an adult now. You should know the insanity of who he was is why he tortured you."

"He kept saying I was special," she said with a sad smile. "So special he used to burn me all the time."

"He tortured you with fire?" he asked, standing up straighter. "Burn marks are horrific to heal."

She stood back from him. "You think I don't know that?" She turned her gaze to look at the fire burning in the distance. "Now I understand how foolish what I wanted to do is, but I can't let go of the idea regardless."

He looked once more at the crumpled letter. "How long have you been carrying that around with you?"

"He gave it to me," she said. "A long time ago. It's all I have left of him and of my mother."

"Your mother obviously wasn't much of a mother," he said. "No mother lets their child be tortured."

"Oh, she tortured me too," she said. "And she did it with great joy."

Rowan shook his head sadly, the pain obvious in his eyes.

"All I can ever remember was that vacant blissful smile on her face when he told her to do something. Whether that was getting on her knees and servicing his sexual wants, cooking dinner, doing laundry for all the other women. She didn't seem to have any sense of reality anymore."

"Drug use?"

"Lots and freely," Phoenix replied with a nod. "But alcohol was considered a poison so wasn't allowed. Like I said, it was a very twisted lifestyle."

"And yet, you seem moderately sane."

"Moderately," she said cheerfully. "Foster homes were pretty rough for a while. I finally ended up in a good one, and my foster parents were both professors. When they realized how lacking my education was, they stepped up and helped."

"Didn't you go to school growing up?" he asked in surprise.

"Homeschooled, of course," she said. "Which meant I knew how to cook. I knew how to clean, and I knew how to service our father."

His body stiffened at that.

She slid him a sideways glance. "Don't ask."

"The fact that you're a normal-sounding human being is amazing," he said. "That was why you said you had family of a sort?"

"Yes," she whispered. "A lot of other kids were in that cult. I don't know how many of the mothers survived, but the children, if they are alive, were all his."

"Your file said no one else survived, just you. How many women?"

"In my mind, dozens," she replied, "But it was seven, maybe eight. And I wonder if the cops are correct? It was such a crazy time. I was told no one else survived, but I'm not sure I believed them."

"Did all the women have children?"

"All of them. Most of them had five or six apiece."

"And your mother?"

She shook her head. "Just me. Something went wrong during my birth, and I think she couldn't have any more." Phoenix frowned at that. "Or he did something to her. I don't know."

"Sounds like she didn't have an easy life either. And maybe drugs were the escape she used in order to survive."

IF ROWAN HAD ever heard anything this disgusting, this immoral and this horrifying, he couldn't remember it. Just thinking of what she'd gone through blew him away. It was one thing to read some of this in the file in black-and-white format, but to hear her retell it in such a dispassionate voice? … And yet here she was, standing in front of him as normal as anyone else. But was she really?

Scars like that had to go deep. They would last a life-time. No way she could possibly be this normal, this well-adjusted.

"How far behind in your education were you?" he asked.

"Almost an entire lifetime," she replied quietly. "The first couple foster homes had tutors for me and special classes, but it wasn't enough. I had a voracious need to learn, a voracious hunger to get out of the history of my life. I honestly don't know what happened to the other kids, and I can't say I care. I know that makes me mean, selfish, but I remember how they all hurt me. How they all jeered and made my life hell. Maybe they had no choice. Maybe they were forced to do so. I don't know, and I'm doing my best to put that all behind me."

"Are you still in touch with these foster parents?"

She gave a brief nod. "Yes, to a certain extent. They got me through school to the point where I went to university, got an education and landed a job as an associate professor. They were very proud of that. Without them I'd be a basket case. They were stable, sound, practical people. Whenever my nightmares or memories would overwhelm me, and I'd go into panic mode, their sensibilities brought me back. They would tell me how I could do nothing but walk away, and then I needed to write it all down. I needed to get it out of my head. I saw a shrink for years. That helped. As much as people make a mockery of the profession, I needed to tell someone about the horrors I'd been through."

"And the counselors handled that okay?"

"No," she said. "One left the profession after me. Another had to seek a professional to talk about everything I'd been through, for their own sake. But over time I managed to find a new normal."

"And this is the last thing you need to do?"

She looked down at the letter clenched in her fist.

He watched as she stared at it with loathing. "Or is it the fact that it's the last thing you have of your father and you want to throw that into the pit?"

Finally after a pensive pause, she said, "It's a lot of things, I think. It's the only thing I have of my father's, except for my DNA, and that's something I can't get rid of. It's also a message he left me. A message that's been emblazoned on my brain, and I don't know why I feel like I have to throw it in here, but I do."

"What's the message?" he asked. She may not want to tell him, but it was important. He just didn't know why.

Her lips twitched. "I'm really not making this up, you know? Neither is this some big horror movie that'll go bump in the night. I just want to throw this into the lava."

"I might know where there's a stream of lava you can throw it in," he said. "But I guess I'm not willing to do that until I know what it is you're expecting from this."

"Expecting?" She looked at him in surprise. "I just want to let it all go," she said. "I want to know his wishes for me won't be fulfilled and that he was wrong."

"Wrong in what way?"

"He felt I could walk through fire," she said. "I was named to rise from the ashes and to become someone special."

"But you have already lived out that legacy," he said.

She shook her head. "How is that possible?"

"Look at the purgatory you were raised in," he said. "Look at the horrors of what you've already survived. You lived through that. You rose from the ashes of that cult life to become someone completely different."

He could see from the shock in her eyes that she had never once considered that. She sagged against the retaining stonewall and looked at him. "I don't think that's what he meant."

"Doesn't matter what he meant," Rowan said. "What matters is what you do with the information. It's obvious it's good for you to be here, if for no other reason than to understand he isn't here. He wouldn't have had the strength to exist in a place like this. I don't understand his fascination with fire," he said. "Do you?"

"He could make fire," she said simply. "It didn't burn him like it burned me."

"What do you mean, *he could make fire?*"

She shrugged. "At least, to the child in my mind, he made fire. Whether it was a magic trick or not, I don't know," she said for clarification. "But he didn't have to use a match or a stick to burn me. He would just use the flames coming off his fingers."

Rowan made a strangled exclamation. How unbelievable was that story?

"I know you don't believe me," she said. "I get that. But I'm not sure how else to explain the memories."

"So then why would he burn you? And why didn't it burn him?"

"It did burn him, *if* the flames touched him anywhere else on his body but his fingers," she said. "And he figured that I was the same."

"Could you make fire come out of your fingers?"

She hesitated.

He leaned forward and repeated, "Can you?"

She glanced away and shook her head.

He stared at her. "I don't believe you."

"Doesn't matter if you believe me or not," she said, turning to face him. "It's the truth." But her voice lacked conviction.

"Even if you could do that, why would he want to kill

you?"

"Oh, he didn't want to kill me," she said in surprise. "He was training me."

"For what purpose?" he asked. "That's nonsensical. It's not as if you'll be a fireman and walk into a burning building and rescue people—not without a fire-retardant suit."

"I don't think he thought it through," she said, her lips tilting. "Remember that insane part? That whole premise that he was the cult leader and could make up whatever he believed or wanted his disciples to believe? He kept telling me that I was supposed to walk through fire, and I would be the Phoenix that rose from the ashes."

"And so, your real name is Phoenix?"

"Even worse it's Phoenix Rising," she said with a laugh. "My first name and last name."

"He thought he knew who you were, already from your birth?"

"I did ask my mother that a couple times, and she said I was special right from the beginning."

"What about the other kids?"

She gave a headshake. "As far as I know, none of the others were"—she paused—"special."

"Were they tortured or hurt in any way?"

"Oh, no," she said. "They were considered normal. Sure, they did chores and were homeschooled, but they were never tortured like I was."

"Did they understand why you were being tortured?"

"They understood I was being prepared for something nobody could understand yet, but it was super important," she said.

"That sounds just vague enough to be believable." But he certainly didn't understand it. "What's your father's name?"

"I don't know."

He waited and she groaned. "Why? You want to listen to all that lovely garbage on the internet about him? His name was 'the Ancient One,'" she said with a snort. "And, yes, that's what he was called."

"What name was he born with?"

"That's more mundane," she said with a smile. "He was John Hopkins."

"Like Johns Hopkins University?"

"Yes, but no relation. *John* has got to be the most popular name in the US. Or the second-most popular. And *Hopkins* is not far off."

"So, in other words, it will be hard to find information about him?"

"Oh, I doubt it," she said. "The news was pretty full of details at the time. Everybody had ideas of how he managed to stay under the radar for so long."

"What did he do for money?"

"No clue," she said. "I was only eleven when he died. Remember?"

Rowan had forgotten that. He settled back. "Sounds like your foster parents were a godsend."

"They were. I think one of the biggest benefits was the fact they were so pragmatic. They knew my history, but they weren't full of visions and dreams and prophetic statements. They didn't pretend to be God or my boss or my leader or my whatever you want to call it. They made it clear who they were, what they were, what they expected of me and what I could expect from them. Those rules were never broken, and I appreciated it. It gave me an understanding of what life should be and what life could be. And I flourished within those boundaries, within those restrictions."

"What about boyfriends?" he asked. "I can't imagine that was easy."

"The boyfriend part definitely not. Even just having friends was something I struggled with a lot."

"Because you didn't trust them?"

"As far as I was concerned, they would betray me, like all the siblings did."

"But these were friends, not siblings?"

"True," she said. "But we didn't have any friends outside of the cult family, so they were one and the same for me."

"Did you have any boyfriends growing up?"

"Not until I was quite a bit past the normal dating age," she said. "I could only handle so many new experiences at once. I was all about learning in school. I wanted freedom, and, to me, education and money would give me freedom. I didn't want anybody to have any power over me ever again." She smiled, looked around and said, "I don't have a clue why I am standing here telling you all this."

"Because you want something from me," he said. "And I have the power to make that happen." He could feel her gaze on his face. But he was busy staring down at the fistful of crumpled paper. "I still want to see what's in there."

She turned her palm up, uncrumpled the paper and spread it against the stone wall. "There," she said, holding it for him.

He frowned when she refused to hand the letter to him, so he read it out loud. "*Dear child, Remember you were destined to die and to be reborn. We are one with the Burning Fires. Only if we have prepared you well and truly will you rise again as the Phoenix you are bound to become ... and save us all. I made you. I will guide you. Remember it. Remember it*

*well. Don't cross me because I will travel from this plane to
yours, and I will make you pay. Or you will triumph as the
Phoenix you are, and we all will achieve immortality."*

Rowan let out a long whistle. "Wow, that's a hell of a
letter."

"That's the epitome of my life with him," she said quietly.

"Are you sure you don't want to keep this?"

She gave a broken laugh. "Would anybody want to keep
something like this?"

He shook his head. "Maybe not but I think you should
keep a copy."

"I have one, and the cops have a copy too."

"What happened to all the other mothers?"

"They all committed suicide," she replied solemnly. "For
all I know, all the kids died too. I really don't know."

He nodded, but, in the back of his mind, he knew he
had to confirm that. He didn't really have a reason to help
this woman, but they were already bonded and connected in
a way he didn't understand. "We'll find a way. Just don't do
anything without me, please."

"Why's that?" she asked, crumpling the letter back up.
The paper almost instinctively shriveled into a ball as she'd
done it so many times. She was surprised it had lasted all this
time, but something was weird about the paper's texture—
almost a plasticity.

"Because I don't want you getting into trouble over this.
Enough weird things are going on, and you have this odd
energy about you. So let's not have a combustion where
things go really bad."

"You'll help me then?"

He thought about it for a long moment, then nodded.

"I'll help you throw that letter somewhere into lava—"

"It has to be in the Burning Fires lava," she insisted.

"That's fine," he said. "As long as it can be a runoff or run into the lava. I can't get it into the actual gates."

She liked that answer.

"I'll try. I don't know for sure yet. I do have a couple things I could check out, but …" His voice trailed off.

Phoenix let her shoulders sag slightly. She looked at the spot where they stood and, as if realizing she couldn't do it on her own, said, "Fine, but please, you must understand how important this is to me. I get that it doesn't matter to anybody else, but, to me, it's huge."

"Understood," he said. "Leave it with me. I don't have an answer right now. I'll have to check into it."

"You've got the rest of today," she said. "We're leaving first thing in the morning."

"No pressure, right?"

They laughed together and returned to the crowd.

THE SUPPLIER SAT outside at a table, drinking a coffee, watching the world go by, waiting for the last bus to come in. Finally he heard its heavy engine shifting gears as it slowed and came in to park alongside the other two.

He had been waiting to see which one would hold his best opportunity. So far, the first bus had been an incessant array of loudmouthed overweight people, who seemed to only glorify in themselves.

They didn't understand the wider world at large. They definitely weren't sacrificial material. The Supplier must have someone good enough to give to the Elders. Someone clean. Someone healthy. Someone full of spirit and life. The Elders deserved the best.

Sure, some he could easily throw into the pits of the Burning Fires, but they didn't deserve the honor. They weren't all goodness. They weren't clean. They were nothing.

The first bus had been full of disgusting specimens. So, when the second bus had arrived, the Supplier had been full of hope. Surely, out of the three buses, there had to be somebody. The tourist attraction of this town had swelled massively. But, when the tourists left, so did most of those people. And that left him with only the locals. It was one thing to play with the locals like he had, but he had to choose the right ones.

Irene had been his choice. His treat. She deserved death whether she understood it or not. He knew the rest of the town was still in shock over her suicide, and they probably would never learn any differently. He could never forget why he was here and what he was here to do.

All he could do was make it fun and make his days less of a hardship. But he had to find his next sacrifice first.

The second bus yielded little potential. Again filled with more older people, some fighting, some just so tired and exhausted that they dropped immediately. Others eating as they got on and eating as they got off. Unclean bodies. Some so diseased he couldn't believe they were still walking. The Supplier could see the disease in their souls and in their physical forms.

He could not anger the Elders by tossing in somebody already with one foot at death's door. The Elders needed the pure energy of the young. They could take the old if they had to, but it took so many more to do the job. And these were already nasty pieces of humanity. He would never insult his Elders with such offerings.

It was getting harder and harder to find acceptable sacrifices, and his time was running out. If he couldn't find somebody soon, he'd have to settle for a local again. Or somebody who had moved in temporarily. Lots of people came to the region to work for the summer and then left. Some people were so rotten, they could not be allowed to exist, and that was where the Supplier stepped in. He wished he had a well where he could toss in the despicable ones at will. Like a sorting process. Cleaning up the garbage.

The longer he waited to find his perfect sacrifice, the worse it made him feel, and, in order to appease that anger and frustration within himself, he had to find victims for his own stress relief. Yet too many victims were dangerous. He couldn't get greedy, as it could get him caught.

The last bus finally parked, and the double doors opened. The Supplier had also visited the Burning Fires today, a chance to inhale the essence of the Elders, even as the Supplier searched for their next sacrifice. The buses had all been there today. And many more people. Too many people. The Supplier had been forced to leave early and had been sitting here ever since, watching the buses return and the visitors disembark.

One bus at a time.

From where he sat, he watched the passengers of the third bus as they stumbled out. The first out was a couple, arguing. They were almost having a physical altercation. He watched in amazement, wondering how people could go through life like that.

He should toss them into his despicable well, just to dispose of their pain and suffering and how they inflicted that onto others. People should pay the Supplier to take care of those two. But, of course, they wouldn't. Humanity had a problem cutting short a life.

In this case it wasn't much of a life. Sometimes he chose to end their suffering, and sometimes he chose people who deserved it. They were either nasty or vile. Sometimes the line between the two blurred, but the Supplier didn't give a damn. His job wasn't the easiest and, if it gave him an outlet for fun and games, then fine.

He used to justify every person's life he took; now he didn't bother. Why? Nobody ever knew who he was and what he did. After all these years he'd never been questioned about the deaths. That just blew him away.

On the one hand, he was very good at what he did, and he had a few extra tricks that helped preserve his secret. So whatever. All he had to do was keep doing what he was doing, and the Elders would take care of him. Or, if they didn't take care of him, he'd know it was time for him to be replaced, to be reincarnated. That time would come; he just didn't know when.

The issue right now was that the Elders needed another sacrifice, and, so far, nothing appropriate was in sight. Another couple exited the bus, so bent over they needed help to get down the steps. And a middle-aged couple, much younger, waited politely behind.

The Supplier looked at them with interest. Then he searched into their souls and snorted. Both were using fake IDs. They were married to different people but here to have a holiday together. The lies and fabrications people lived with astounded the Supplier.

Nobody was honest anymore. Another young woman exited. She then turned and snapped something at the person behind her, who shook his head. When she turned around again, he realized she wasn't as young as she first appeared.

In fact, she was a good twenty to twenty-five years older. He sighed and settled back, watching as everyone exited the bus.

The bus driver got down and then turned to look back inside the bus. How was it possible yet another bus was full of rejected potentials?

And then he saw her.

She had shoulder-length brown hair and moved slowly, as if her body wasn't as young. He glanced into her soul and froze. She was physically young, but her soul was old, and she had scars everywhere. He frowned. A strange light surrounded her.

He watched as she walked slowly to the hotel, not looking left, not looking right, but intent on the building in front of her. Yet she didn't race; she just moved confidently to her destination. Fascinating in a way. And maybe he'd found his offering to the Elders.

"May I get you something else?"

Startled, he looked up at the young waitress, standing beside him with a coffeepot in hand. He looked down at his empty cup and shook his head. "No, thank you. I'll be fine."

"Okay," she said but hesitated. "Are you feeling okay?"

He froze, then surged his energy up around his host's body so the waitress felt more secure in his presence. The energy was draining from him faster every day. He'd hoped Irene would have helped him more but he'd need another victim to feed his own needs soon. Irene had been fun, being inside her body when she jumped—exhilarating—but feeling her silent scream as she understood her fate … intoxicating. Keeping her spirit on a leash, even now … well that just kept him from being bored. Of course it only worked that way with the weak-willed ones. Others fought to the bitter end.

Still, his games came at a price. Energy. If he wasn't careful, he'd give away his presence. And that would never do. He was here with his host's permission but secrecy was the price they both had to pay to keep his work moving forward. He smiled up at the waitress. "I'm a little tired today. Thanks for caring …"

She smiled in relief. "Would you like to pay for your coffee here or inside?"

He looked down and realized she was worried he'd bail on his bill. She was another young arrival just here for the summer. Otherwise she'd have recognized who she was serving. Still better she didn't know him … or his host. He stood, pulled money from his pocket and handed it to her. It was way too much, and that was fine. Money didn't matter to him. He took note of her features, confirming her youth as she had to be in her twenties, and he nodded and walked away.

She stood staring after him as he left.

He crossed over to a park bench, where he was out of sight from the restaurant and sat down.

Just then a cop car pulled up and parked beside the bus. Out stepped Rowan, who lifted a hand at the sight of him, then turned and walked into the same coffee shop.

The Supplier walked unhurriedly away, deliberately not looking back. When he got to the alleyway, he slid against the wall to rest for a moment and then peered around the corner. And found Rowan strolling in his direction. His heart froze, and he didn't understand what was going on, but he felt fear. Absolutely unending fear as adrenaline shot through his system.

The cop was almost at the entrance of the alley when a woman called out to him. Rowan hesitated, looking into the shadows where the Supplier leaned against the wall, then frowned at the woman running to him.

"What's the matter?"

He heard Rowan speak but couldn't hear the woman's response. The Supplier took this opportunity anyway. While the cop wasn't looking, the Supplier disappeared. As he got to the end of the alleyway and turned to look back, he knew he was out of sight. The cop stood with hands on his hips, glaring in the Supplier's direction, and he knew this wasn't over.

In truth, it had just begun.

CHAPTER 9

P HOENIX WALKED BACK into the hotel, exhausted, both mentally and physically. But, on an emotional level, something had spiked an energy surge within her. Standing before the Burning Fires, it seemed. Just further confirming her destiny to be here. She couldn't tell whether she trusted the cop or not, and that bothered her. She had good reasons for not trusting people. Yet not so much in recent years. But then everything she and Rowan had been through so far, where Rowan had been involved, had been steadfast and solid. She had no reason not to trust him.

She knew his name and that he was a cop, but that was it.

Lunch had been a picnic at the site, and it was now three-thirty. She had the rest of the afternoon and evening free, and tomorrow they would leave at nine a.m. Sharp. She had so little time left …

Phoenix decided she needed tea first and a chance to just sit and destress a bit. Seated once again at the same small table at the window in the hotel café, she waited for her tea to arrive. Once again a shadow loomed behind her as Rowan approached and sat across from her.

She looked over at him. "Well?"

One eyebrow lifted. "You don't give a guy much time."

"I don't have much time," she said curtly. "I leave tomorrow morning, in case you've forgotten."

"I know," he said. "I've spoken to the local geologist. He thinks your need is foolish and dangerous, but, as long as I'm willing to support you in this, he will take us where you can get the closest. He figures, with the addition of a rock, we could potentially throw it in the fire."

Hope surged within her. "That would be terrific. I know nobody else understands. But then nobody else understands what I went through either."

He nodded. "I didn't give him any details, so, as far as he is concerned, this is a frivolous quest." Rowan lowered his voice when he asked, "No one seems to have noticed anything odd going on. Have you seen Irene again?"

Phoenix gave a quick shake of her head. "No, but then I don't want to. I'm wondering if I can block this. Maybe if I keep telling whatever is out there that I don't want anything to do with this, they'll stay away."

"I doubt it," he said. "But, if it works, I'll try that too."

"And yet, I think you're more accustomed to this type of thing than I am."

He gave a humorous snort. "Anybody who was raised by a father who could create fire at the end of his fingers ..."

"I was tortured by that fire," she corrected. "I was just sitting here, wondering how much of his behavior was to train me for what was to come and how much was to expunge his anger because he was afraid of me."

Rowan leaned forward. "Why would he be afraid of you?"

She took several deep calming breaths, and just then the waitress arrived with the pot of tea and a cup. She smiled up at her and said, "Thank you."

The waitress looked at Rowan. "Do you want a cup for

tea too?"

He nodded. "That would be great. Thanks, Melissa."

The woman walked away, and Phoenix turned her attention to the tea steeping in front of her.

He wouldn't let it go. "What were you going to say?"

Her lips quirked. "I wouldn't say anything if I could."

"We're well past that," he said harshly. "You want my help. I want to know the details."

She picked up a spoon, lifted the lid off the teapot and gently stirred the contents. She wasn't terribly fussy about her tea, but it gave her something to do. "He felt he was geared for greatness," she said slowly. "You've got to understand. This is all coming from an eleven-year-old mind. And what I learned about him afterward."

"I'll take what the eleven-year-old has to say," he said smoothly. "So spill."

"He said, for every good person, there's always a greater evil. Somebody who tries to bring him down. And he said somebody is always poised to replace whoever is at the top. Evil is always pulling him down because he wants to take his spot. But he knew so much more than evil did and laughed at his attempts."

"He thought you were the evil replacement?" Then Rowan gave a shake of his head. "Did anybody seriously listen to this guy?"

"The other women and children did. I'm not sure about anybody else."

"Right. I wanted to get back to the office and do some research on that group."

"Why?" she asked. "It was a long time ago."

"Not long enough apparently," he said. He looked at her, motioning at the tea. "Don't you want to pour that?"

She picked up the pot and gently poured herself a cup. "It wasn't that long ago," she admitted. "At least in my head. Everybody else involved, I suspect, are all dead."

"And yet, you think some kids are still alive?"

"I don't know if they are or not," she said. "I don't remember much about that day, and I never saw or made contact with them after that."

"You don't want to find out, do you?"

"No," she replied. "I really don't."

"Why? Because you think they'll still treat you the same way?"

"Maybe," she said. "You aren't treated like that without getting a huge sense of insecurity about future behavior."

"Were you terrified of them?"

She gave him a flat stare. "Let's just say, some of the torture didn't stop because my father stopped."

He froze, stared at her and said, "What do you mean?"

Now she wished she hadn't brought it up. "You heard me." And she clammed up.

He waited for several moments. Then finally said, "You think he saw you as competition? That you would replace him?"

"I think he thought I would be bigger and better than him. He couldn't stand that I might have more abilities than he had."

Rowan sat back, his fingers running a staccato pattern on the tabletop—his nails going *click, click, click*. She didn't say a word, just waited. "And why would he think that?"

She lifted her gaze to him. "I have no idea," she said, lying through her teeth.

His gaze narrowed, but she stared back with the same

look she'd given him earlier. Daring him almost to question her further.

The waitress returned with a cup and pot of tea for him. She smiled at the two of them. "Are you sure you don't want a bite to eat? We have lovely cinnamon buns, just out of the oven."

Rowan nodded. "We'll have two."

When the waitress left again, Phoenix asked, "How do you know I wanted one?"

"Because you're hungry," he replied with a smirk.

She stared out the window beside him and then admitted, "I wasn't even thinking about it, but you're right. I wanted one."

"See? I do know," he said smugly.

"You know some things," she corrected. "When are we going?"

He checked his watch. "When the geologist is off work. At six."

"Good," she said. "It will be great to get it done."

He motioned at her hands. "Do you still have the letter?"

"I've had this letter since I was a child," she said coolly. "Obviously I still have it."

"What were the stains on it?"

She froze and then settled back. "Blood."

"Yours or his?" he asked, his tone hard.

"I imagine both," she said.

"When these other children tortured you, well past the time he stopped, were other adults around?"

"Depended on which child was involved," she said. "Alice used to come in and poke my fresh wounds when I was sleeping. Jessica poured vinegar on an open burn any chance she could. And then there was Elisha. I would finally get to sleep, and she'd start banging things by my ear, waking me up again, so I could never rest. And they did it all with their mothers' permission. You really don't understand gang mentality until you live it."

"I'm so sorry," he said.

She stared out at the bright green lush world. "I am too. It's one of the reasons I need to throw this letter in that fire."

"That's the part I don't get," he said, his tone turning thoughtful. "How has that letter got anything to do with that horrible childhood?"

She shrugged irritably. "All I can tell you is, it's something I feel I must do."

He settled back and nodded. "Good enough then. Six it is."

The waitress arrived with two large plates, displaying the massive cinnamon buns.

For the first time in a long time, Phoenix smiled. "These are gorgeous," she said. "Amazing."

Melissa chuckled. "I did pick out the two biggest ones for you guys."

"I appreciate it. Thank you," Phoenix said.

She had no clue why she was getting special treatment and was afraid to hear the answer. But Rowan didn't appear to have any problem with it. He picked up his fork and pulled open the cinnamon bun, hot steam escaping. She did the same. The icing on top still hadn't hardened. "I gather because I'm with you that I get special treatment," she said.

"No clue," he said cheerfully. "Normally I don't get this kind of treatment."

She took several bites, thoroughly enjoying it. Her gaze once again drifted outside. "It's really beautiful here."

"It is," he said. "I've been here most of my life."

"You never wanted to live anywhere else?"

"Not now. I spent almost a decade in Kentucky but finally couldn't resist the urge to come home. I too have a few issues that made it easier to spend my life here."

"And so those issues weren't ones you wanted to run away from?"

He smiled and shook his head. "My grandmother is a psychic. She has a lot of Gypsy in her. Has traveled extensively and often knows things ahead of time."

Phoenix's mouth parted slightly, and she put down her fork, staring at him. "Is she still alive?"

He slowly raised his head to look at her. "She is. Do you want to meet her? I've told her about you."

"Really? Do I want to? I'm not sure," she admitted, even more unsure to think he'd told his family about her. "But need to? Yes."

At that wording, he stared at her in surprise.

She shrugged. "I know. I know. It doesn't make any sense, but I have to honor those instincts."

"As soon as we're done with this, we can go see her. She lives in town here. Just a few blocks away." He pulled out his phone. "Let me see what she's up to."

He sent a text, which surprised her. "You don't call her?"

He shook his head. "She's not a big one for calls. She has a hearing aid and finds it difficult to hear on a phone."

His phone buzzed a moment later. He smiled. "She said I'm supposed to bring you." His smile fell away. "And she added, … *Leave Irene behind.*" His gaze flew up to Phoenix.

She looked around but saw no sign of Irene. As she

glanced back outside, her breath sucked in, and she pointed.

He turned and swore.

"I WONDER WHY we're seeing Irene?" Rowan muttered under his breath. "I suspect we'll find out from my grand-mother."

"Then we need to see her as soon as we can," she said. "Preferably before I go to the Burning Fires."

"Good point." He sent a text to his grandma, telling her that they'd be there in half an hour. He got an immediate response.

The sooner, the better.

He winced at that. "Although I don't know how we're supposed to ditch a ghost," he said. He watched as Irene stared at them. This time the look on her face was more vacant than anything. "What does she want from us?"

Phoenix shrugged and asked, "Did you have a chance to do any research on her?"

"I did," he said. It was the last thing he wanted to talk about. He deliberately took one of the last bites of his cinnamon bun, so he could chew while he thought about the answer. But, from the look in Phoenix's eyes, she understood what he'd done. He sighed and replied, "Her life wasn't as simple as I had thought."

"Did she kill her child?"

He stared at her. "Why would you think that?"

She frowned. "Just answer the question."

"It's a possibility, yes. That's what we're afraid of," he said cautiously. "It's quite likely."

"So chances are, her extreme depression wasn't the loss

as much as the guilt."

"Possibly."

"I wonder if she was picked."

He stared at her blankly. "How do you go from suicide to murder? I don't think I like the direction you're going."

"Maybe not," she said, her voice harsh. "But, *if* somebody is doing this, they might potentially be looking for victims. How does one determine who deserves to live and who deserves to die?" She leaned forward. "How else do we explain what we saw first?"

"You think because somebody might have assumed that's what she did, she deserved to have this done to her?" He motioned to the outside window, where, by now, Irene was gone. He couldn't help but be amazed and grateful that he wasn't seeing her spirit again. "But we had a shared premonition."

"Maybe. I don't know," she said. "I've seen a lot of things in my young life that made no sense. I've always known there was more to understand. I just didn't know how to learn more."

"I can't imagine what you've gone through to get here," he said. "I'm familiar with this stuff because of my grandmother."

"Your parents didn't have the abilities?"

He shook his head. "No, it seemed to have skipped a generation." He swore in his head because he hadn't intended on letting her know. But, of course, she didn't miss that either.

"Meaning, you *do* have abilities?" she asked slowly. "Like what?"

"Well, like, seeing Irene for one," he replied. He motioned at her empty plate. "Are you ready? Maybe we should go now."

"You mean now, while we're alone?"

He looked out the window and nodded. "Exactly."

*

THE SUPPLIER WATCHED as the two walked out of the hotel. He could see their energy already blending and blurring together. That wasn't good. It would be that much harder to separate her from him the longer it went on.

He wasn't sure what abilities Rowan had. But it was obvious he had a protective energy around her, which was interesting, especially considering, up until now, there had been no threat against her. So why the protection?

Auras told the Supplier so much about a person—but not everything. He wanted to see so much more, and sometimes he could, but sometimes it was past his ability.

Rowan and the woman headed down the steps to the main street, crossed and continued walking. The Supplier followed at a slower pace. He wondered where the pair was going and why in such a hurry. As they walked, they turned and looked around, as if sensing a predator.

His interest piqued, he followed along, figuring out what they were up to. When they disappeared into a familiar alleyway abruptly, he picked up his pace until he got there and could see down the same lane. They were gone. He frowned. Now this was so much more interesting. Something about the hunt, the chase, added to his joy.

The fact that he might have found his sacrifice made it all that more interesting. But so much darkness existed in her soul. He wasn't sure if she was good enough for what he needed, to serve as a proper sacrifice to appease the Elders, especially the god of the Iceland Burning Fires. The Supplier needed to find out more about why she was here at Burning Fires. He ducked into a doorway—a shortcut only he knew. There had to be some advantages to having this job.

CHAPTER 10

P HOENIX WALKED AT Rowan's side, loving the trip away from the tourist center and was surprised when they came to a small narrow stairwell hidden in the wall of an alleyway. She looked at him and said, "Your grandmother climbs this every day?"

He chuckled. "You haven't met my grandmother yet." He led the way up the stairs and, at the top, was a double door. He opened it and exposed two more doors, as if two apartments were on this level. He opened the door on the right and called out, "Grandma, we're here."

"Hurry up and close the door behind you," came the hard voice.

He motioned Phoenix inside. "Just keep an open mind."

Surprised, she nodded and followed him through a hallway to a much larger open area. To the left was a kitchen, where sunshine streamed in. Phoenix smiled as they walked into a ray of particularly vibrant sunshine and stood with her face up into the sun. When she heard no voices, she opened her eyes and looked at the two people staring at her.

One small spry woman—who couldn't have been five feet tall and maybe eighty-five pounds—stood before them. Her gaze was intent, as if running an X-ray machine through Phoenix's soul to see what she could find. Yet she was oddly familiar. Then Phoenix realized this was the woman she'd met on the bench the first day. That was how Rowan had known about Phoenix. His grandmother had called him, worried about Phoenix's mental stability. And he'd likely kept her abreast of everything since.

"Grandma, this is Phoenix. Phoenix, this is my grandmother. Her name is Manru."

Phoenix smiled. "Good afternoon. My name is Phoenix. Nice to meet you again."

Manru nodded and said, "Yes, that is indeed your name. Interesting. You have already risen from the ashes," she announced. "Why are you here to do it again?"

Startled, Phoenix didn't know what to say. "I'm not sure I have risen," she said hesitantly. "I feel like I need to do this."

"It's dangerous," the woman announced. "Just coming here was dangerous."

"Here to your apartment?" Phoenix asked, slowly looking for clarification. "Or coming to the Burning Fires?"

"Coming to the Burning Fires," Manru said. "You've been ignoring the danger all your life. You wanted nothing to do with that part of your world. But that danger stalks you, always. And still you refute your destiny."

Phoenix could feel the shivers running up and down her spine. She glanced at Rowan, who frowned at his grandmother. She didn't know if his grandmother was deliberately scaring Phoenix or if Manru really had some weird insight into Phoenix's life. A weird buzz surrounded the old woman too, and she had an inner strength, if the fire in her gaze was anything to go by. Yet her energy had a roughness to it Phoenix didn't understand. It might have just been age … Or stress … Even disease … Whatever it was, Manru was unnerving, even with her small stature.

"I want you afraid," his grandmother snapped. "Have you so little disregard for your own life that you would ignore those things?"

"What things?" Phoenix asked, her voice stronger than she expected it to be. "As far as I know, I've only tried to rise from that horribleness of my childhood."

"No. You felt that energy stalking you here," she said. "You felt those eyes watching you here."

Phoenix winced. "Maybe," she said. "But surely that's my imagination."

"Ha! For you to say that is even more ridiculous."

Rowan held out his hands. "We saw her again at the tea shop, just after you said to leave her behind."

"Well, she's not here in this room, so I thank you for that," Manru said as she shoved her hands into the pockets of a bulky sweater. "She's a very disturbed soul. She was before her death, and now she is even after her death."

"Guilt will do that," Phoenix said quietly.

His grandmother nodded. "Yes, it will. She was ready to commit suicide. Had tried several times. The death of her child was part of that."

"Seriously?" Rowan asked. "It was to be a murder-suicide, and she chickened out?"

His grandmother nodded. "Exactly. But what you don't realize is, her husband was supposed to be part of it too."

Rowan shook his head. "No way Pelchi would have taken part in that. He said he loved that child."

"But the child was damaged," his grandmother said. "Not my words. His."

Phoenix gasped. "Damaged? How?"

"Born with a chromosome imbalance. Neither parent could deal with it. Irene felt, if she could return him to God, they could try again. When she realized there was no going back, and this was her life, she decided on a murder-suicide. Her husband's energy is confused, as if he was tempted to try too."

"Or was he also unhappy with his life? Was he intending to murder his child and wife and make it look like it was just her?" Phoenix asked carefully.

Manru started to cackle. "Oh my, I do like that," she said. "Very sharp. You understand the underbelly of society, don't you?"

"I've had more than my fair share of practical experience with them, yes," Phoenix admitted. "People who do one thing and say another. People who like to hurt for the sake of hearing and seeing other people suffer, if only for the joy of knowing it's not themselves suffering. People who show one face to the world and another to their inner circle."

Manru stopped laughing abruptly and stared shrewdly at Phoenix. "Your childhood was worse than I had thought. I didn't look too deep. It's not a gift to see the pain and suffering others have endured," she said. "I usually cut it off as soon as I realize it's there."

"Then I hope you cut it off early," Phoenix said coolly. "No joy was in my childhood."

"And no joy will be in your future if you go to the Burning Fires. You can't go back."

Phoenix shook her head. "I came all this way because I need to throw something into that fire," she said adamantly. "Rowan is helping me to do that this afternoon. It's important. I know nobody understands, but it's important."

"It's important all right," her grandmother said. "Important that you don't go."

"What difference does it make?" Rowan asked. "I'm confused here. I get that you see a lot of the history in her life. And I understand some things are more upsetting, and you're deliberately avoiding looking at it. Hell, I don't even want to see it all. But I don't understand how any of that applies to her throwing this letter into the fire."

"Because sometimes people with abilities can infuse an object with their energy. To move it."

"Sure. Telekinesis," he said. "The ability to move items. Not what we are dealing with here."

"So move it." She turned to face Phoenix, her voice challenging. "Show him how you can move it. That you can throw it away."

AN UNCOMFORTABLE SILENCE filled the small room. "What do you want from her? From me?" Rowan asked. "I had a reason for bringing her here. But it seems like you wanted to see her anyway."

"You can't go to the fires," she spat out in a hard voice. She turned her gaze on Phoenix. "Show him."

"I'm not a circus monkey," Phoenix said, her voice harsh. "I don't know what you're talking about with the letter."

"Let me see it," his grandmother demanded.

Phoenix hesitated.

"What will you do if you see it?" Rowan asked cautiously. "It's very important to her. She needs to do this."

"She needs to tell us why."

"Because I've tried to destroy it before," Phoenix burst out. "And I couldn't."

"What makes you think the Burning Fires will destroy it?" his grandmother demanded. "That you would bring something like that here …"

Phoenix stared at her in confusion. "What does it have to do with being here? It came from here. I'm just returning it. I know this thing is tainted. I know it retains pieces of his energy. It was his. I need to destroy it."

"Why here?"

"Because he always talked about the Burning Fires and his life here." Phoenix looked at Rowan, hoping he would understand. "I figured it had to be the one place where I could destroy it. Bring it back to where it came from, so I could get rid of this nightmare. Forever."

"Child," Manru said, her voice soft. "You have to destroy it from inside your own mind. Getting rid of that physical letter won't do it."

"It must," Phoenix said, her eyes feverishly bright. "Don't you understand? I've tried to get rid of this thing time and time again. And it always ends up back in my wallet."

At that, Rowan stiffened. "What?"

Her shoulders hunched, and she seemed to shrink within herself. "Never mind," she said wearily. "I'll solve this on my own." And she turned to walk back down the hallway.

Rowan grabbed her. "Stop," he said. "It's not that simple."

"I know," she said.

That tone of defeat in her voice got to him. He tugged her backward. She came willingly, and he forced her into his arms, where he could hold her. He stared at his grandmother over the top of Phoenix's head and raised an eyebrow.

She glared at him.

He shook his head ever-so-slightly and then said, "She needs help."

"She's brought danger here," his grandmother snapped.

"Then help her, so she can leave."

Phoenix snorted as she turned to face his grandmother. "Right. That's a good reason for helping me," she said. "So I can leave and never come back."

Such bitterness and a sense of abandonment were in her tone that made Rowan ashamed of his grandmother and himself. "Look. We don't mean it that way. But obviously we don't want anything to bring danger to the people around here."

"Do you think I brought whatever it was that happened to Irene?" she challenged him, stepping farther away.

He watched her spine stiffen but not with outrage. It was more like being beaten down time and time again and to find out the only way she could survive was to be the strongest she could be against whatever foes. He hated to see he was now a foe in her eyes. "No, of course not." He turned to his grandmother. "What danger?"

She shrugged. "I can't see the details. All I can tell you is that she is dangerous."

"Which is a whole different story than bringing danger to the town," he snapped. "Enough games. She's terrified. She's had one of the shittiest lives anybody could possibly have. If we can do anything to help her move on and to make some better life for herself, I would like to do it."

"Why?" his grandmother challenged. She turned that laser gaze on him, searching his eyes, his face and deep into his soul.

He stood there and let her. "You've seen into the heart of me many, many times," he said softly. "Why are you so against me helping her?"

His grandmother seemed to collapse in on herself. And

she cried softly. "You must protect yourself. She could kill you too."

"How?" he snapped. "Enough of these vague threats and turbulent fears. I need facts. I need something concrete I can go on."

"You know better than that," she said, her voice fatiguing, her face aging in front of him.

"Maybe," he said. "But it's not that bad. And you need to help us."

"No," she said. "There's nothing anybody can do to help you." She waved at the front door. "Go," she said. "Just leave for now. Let me think."

"No time for thinking," he said sadly. "And you never did tell us about Irene."

She stiffened and turned to look at him. "Something's wrong with Irene. Something's wrong with her spirit."

"We know that," Phoenix said. "She's haunting us. She's always there with us, as if we could have stopped her, and we didn't, and so we're to blame."

"Are you to blame?" his grandmother blurted out. "Is that how you feel?"

Phoenix hesitated. "I don't want to feel guilty," she said, "but she was there. She was in our arms, and then she was up. Walking, talking and running away from us and flinging herself off the cliff."

"But that's not all of it, is it?"

Phoenix stared at Rowan and shrugged.

"No," he said and proceeded to explain the rest of it. About her going over the edge while they watched and then coming back.

"That is the evil surrounding her and you at the moment," his grandmother said quietly. "Why Irene was chosen, I don't know, but you have also been chosen." Her gaze eyed Phoenix. "Not only must you be careful but anybody around you must be careful too."

"Is that the danger?" Phoenix asked softly. "Is that the danger you feel I'm bringing? Do you think this entity who has targeted me, like he did Irene, will take Rowan as well?"

His grandmother nodded. "That's part of it," she said. "But I see something else. Something much darker, and it's coming from you. Not from whoever it is who hurt Irene, who even now captured her soul as a pet. I have less fear of that person than I do of you. Because you're much stronger. You might not know, might not even understand, but you're much stronger than that evil. And that makes you even more dangerous because you have no clue what you can do, and, therefore, you have zero control when this blows up. Everybody around you will go up in flames." She turned away from Phoenix. "Lock the door on your way out." And she disappeared into a small room off the kitchen.

Rowan motioned at Phoenix to follow him. "Let's go."

He led her out of the apartment and down the stairs. Inside he was more disturbed than he had ever been in his life.

THINKING ABOUT THE young woman he'd seen, the Supplier returned to the hotel. He had to find out who she was and why she was here. He walked over to the reception desk and said his friend had been on the bus, and he'd meant to meet her in town. She was leaving tomorrow, but he wasn't even sure if her bus was back from the Burning Fires yet. The receptionist smiled and confirmed the buses had all come in. So it would probably be hard to find somebody.

Better to call right away and set up a meeting.

"Wouldn't that be nice?" he said with a small laugh. "But I don't think her phone will work over here. She is American."

"We get a lot of Americans. Sometimes they have cell phone plans that work worldwide, but most of the time it's a problem."

"Right. I should have asked her for her room number first."

"The room numbers aren't assigned until they get here," the receptionist replied cheerfully. "Maybe just sit in the lobby and wait for her."

"She just left," he said. "I tried to catch up with her but lost her in the crowd."

"Oh, you're talking about Phoenix," the receptionist said. "Such a fascinating name too."

"Right. I was thinking of the bird rising from the ashes when I heard her name," he said. Inside he was jumping for joy at the perfect name.

"Especially with her surname too," the woman said in a low voice. "*Phoenix Rising.* Like, wow."

"Can you imagine going through school with that name?" he said with a laugh.

The woman smiled and said, "I bet it would have been rough when she was younger but perfect when she was a teenager. And, of course, Rowan is a very interesting name too."

"They appeared to have hit it off quite well," he said. "We've been friends a long time. So, if she's found some-body, I'm delighted for her."

The receptionist looked relieved, as if afraid the Supplier was here for a relationship with her and hadn't expected she'd have hit it off with another man. The Supplier just smiled. "Not to worry," he said. "She's a beautiful woman."

"Except for the scars," the woman behind the front desk said. "I wish I knew what that was all about. And the fact that she was there with poor Irene ..."

He gave her a smile. "Thank you. I'll keep an eye out for her." In fact, he planned to do a lot more than that.

He sat down with his laptop in the lobby, punched in the hotel's Wi-Fi and searched her name. It was incredibly unique, so the information flowed. As soon as he realized where she'd come from and what her history was, sheer joy speared through him.

"Wow," he murmured. "She'd be perfect. The Elders would be happy with her." He smiled, closed his laptop and hurriedly walked outside. He headed in the direction of the woods on the other side of the overpass. He often came here because it was such a calm center, with the town on one side and the wilds on the other.

Lots of houses, farms and small cottages dotted the landscape, but he saw mostly woods, and that was what he needed. He stood in the middle of a clearing he'd taken for his own the other day and called out, "She's perfect. She even has the perfect name and the perfect history. She is exactly what you need. You won't need anyone else for a long time."

He waited for an answer, but there wasn't one. Disappointed, he frowned. "I will come back. But know I'm on the right trail. She is literally the best thing you could have, ever. I just have to make sure it works out."

A voice in his head spoke. *Irene.* "I know. I know," he said. "I think I can make it work."

He could feel the nervousness and fear sliding through

him again. Something he had to watch out for. He shouldn't have touched Irene. But he'd needed that for his own soul. She'd been perfect for him. He had heard the rumors about her and her baby. It hadn't taken long to befriend her husband, to hear his side of the story and to realize he was conflicted about staying with his young wife.

That she'd killed her son, then made it look like an accident? ... After that discovery, it had been an easy decision. The Supplier could only take those lives he could justify. She'd fit his need perfectly.

CHAPTER 11

"OH, MY GOD," Phoenix whispered as she stood outside Manru's home, taking several deep breaths. "How was any of this possible? I came here to throw a letter into a fire." She shook her head, watching the flames in the distance. "That's all I ever wanted."

"You need to explain what ways you've tried to destroy that letter."

She pulled her hand out of her pocket, along with the letter. She held it out for him to see; then she tried to rip it up. But it wouldn't rip. She pressed it to the corner of her mouth and tried to bite off a piece, but she couldn't tear it. "I've stuck it in the oven to burn it to a crisp. I've tried to light it on fire with matches, but the fire goes out. I've taken scissors to it, and it won't cut. You don't understand. It was one of my father's pieces that he hung on to all the time. He said it was special and had been in his family since forever, and it has my name written on it. The writing has long since worn off." She held it up for him to see. "But it used to say Phoenix. And that's when he used to get violent, hitting me, slapping me, eventually burning me, because he could find no other way to assuage the pain within him."

"What kind of pain?"

"I think the pain of realizing he wouldn't be *the Chosen One*. He would be replaced. And at a young age. He never believed he was long for this world. He couldn't handle it. And yet I was *special*. He used to say it—half the time in a mocking tone and half the time in a way to make you know he hated you. And, when that happened, I knew it would get bad. It was always terrible, but, when he got into that mood, it was beyond terrible. He used to get everybody else to help. He would get them to torture me at the same time, and they just wouldn't stop."

"I'm surprised they didn't kill you," he said quietly.

"Twice," she said. "Twice they went that far, and twice I came back from the brink."

"And I bet you didn't want to," he said, eyeing her carefully.

She smiled up at him. "The trouble is," she said, "I wondered if it was me who wanted to come back or me who wanted to die. Each time, it's like I heard a voice that told me that I couldn't. It wasn't time. It seemed like an angel's voice. Someone out there watching over me. At least I wanted to believe that. Except, if I didn't die, I was doomed to lie there and suffer so much pain. It used to make my father so angry. He beat me to the point where I lost consciousness for days," she said. "They thought I had died. They didn't give me food or water. They were just waiting for it to happen. But, instead of getting weaker, I got stronger. After that, he realized he couldn't kill me. That I wouldn't die, no matter what he did. So he upped the torture to make me suffer as much as he could on a day-to-day basis."

"He died too young," Rowan said, his voice harsh. "He died too easy."

She gave him a sad smile. "Well, I'd agree with you. He took several bullets to the chest, and it was such a relief to know he couldn't get up again. I worried he could. I worried that, like me, he would get up and walk again, but he never did."

"That you know of," he said cautiously.

She stared at him, her eyes getting wider. "Okay, that's not a thought I want to think about," she said slowly.

"Maybe not," he said. "But you have to admit, it's something you must consider."

"Maybe, but I don't want to. Isn't it time to meet your friend?"

"What if that letter can't be destroyed in the Burning Fires? Then what?"

"I don't know what then. As long as it separates from me, I'll be okay to let the Burning Fires be the new caretakers of this letter."

"May I hold it?" he asked.

She smiled. "Yes, but you won't like it."

Surprised, he reached out a hand, and she placed the letter in it. Instantly he cried out, and she nodded. "It's like an electrical shock to anybody else."

He stared at his hand, then the letter and said, "That's not paper. It's like plastic. And the shock you get when touching the letter? This is more energy crap, isn't it?"

"I don't know about *crap*," she said, "but it's definitely freaky energy, yes. I don't know anybody with an ability to help us deal with this. And that's one of my biggest concerns."

"Right," he said. "I don't know anybody either."

"What about your grandmother?" Phoenix asked. "Would she know anybody?"

"I don't know," he said. "So few people can do this kind of work."

"Well," she said, "I guess it doesn't matter then. I'll face whatever my future is. And hope I live through it."

He shook his head. "I really don't like the sound of that."

"No," she said. "Maybe not, but it doesn't change the fact that something, somehow, will change if I can get this letter out of my life."

"It seems so wrong," he said.

"I know, and yet it doesn't give me any answers. And that's something I can't live with. I have to find out how to get this letter out of my life and hopefully, with that, will come the end of my father for me."

"You mean, the end of your father or the end of your father's torment?"

She smiled. "Interesting dilemma, isn't it? To think that's all I have as a choice."

"And not necessarily a good one," he acknowledged. "Just the thought of it is enough to give me the heebie-jeebies."

"How do you think I feel? Especially now that you have mentioned how maybe he isn't dead."

"How close to death were you?" he asked. "When they thought you were dead."

"You can listen to the rumors of those who were there at the time. According to them, I was *dead* dead. Of course for me, who was living, I didn't feel dead, but I knew something was very wrong. I was not conscious for a long time, and, when I did wake up, the looks on their faces were terrible. I don't think they realized that, although he said I was one of the special ones, that it meant I would survive what they had done to me."

IT WAS ALL so far-fetched for Rowan. But he understood that—from her tone, her words and her face—that she believed it. It wasn't that he *didn't* believe it, but he didn't *want* to believe it. It was so far from his concept of reality. Nothing inside him could understand what these people had done to her. He did understand that, as far as she was concerned, something was wrong with her and why. That her body had survived everything they'd done to her, so he could only imagine how they viewed her afterward. Their treatment would be even harsher. She'd be a target for their fear and their hatred. And then she'd survive, so they'd ramp up their efforts all over again. How had she survived? How could anyone have survived?

This letter was something else. He wanted it to be protected. To go into a special archive somewhere. But where? He'd ask his grandmother if she was in any way amiable to helping, but she wasn't. In truth she'd not been the warmest of grandmothers at any time. She'd been reclusive and irritable as far back as he could remember. His grandfather hadn't been around much either. *Off traveling the world,* she'd said anytime Rowan had asked. For all he knew, his grandfather had passed away a decade ago. And, if he had, his grandmother wasn't telling.

Then Rowan remembered an article he'd read a few years back. Some psychic in the US had come up against something bizarre. Many had mocked him. His response had been to laugh and to say that, when reality hit you on a personal level, it didn't matter what other people said because you knew how completely twisted some things in life really were.

Rowan had to admit, right now, reality had hit on a personal level. Could he contact that man and get his advice?

Would he help them, or would he just tell Rowan to go away? "I have to go back to the office for a few minutes. If you want to come with me, you can wait in the lobby until it's time to go. It'll only be a few minutes."

She looked at him in surprise. His suggestion had come out of the blue. She smiled and nodded. "Okay, let's do that. I'd prefer that to meeting up later."

He nodded and started walking. "The station isn't here. We take the overpass to the other side of town."

She winced and said, "Fine. Let's just get this done."

He led the way to the car, helped her in. As they turned the corner, heading to the overpass, she sucked in her breath.

"Don't look," he said. "Irene is standing guard at that cliff now."

"Dear God," she whispered. "Is that for eternity now?"

"We don't know," he said. "But, with any luck, we can find a way to help her. If we figure out how this happened, and stop it, she could be released from this prison."

"I'm not sure about that," she said. "According to your grandmother, it's somebody else, somebody evil, doing this."

"Maybe. But that doesn't mean he gets to have the final say."

"What do you think about it being my father?" she asked. "Do you really believe it could be him?"

"I wasn't there to see how bad your torture was," he said. "I want to see now how close to death you were decades ago. As a child, your memories will be very different than as an adult. I'm hoping to contact somebody who might help."

"There are people who could help?" she asked.

"Maybe," he said. "I can't guarantee it."

She laughed. "Of course not. Like your grandmother, they probably have more to say and none of it helpful."

"She sees a lot," he said. "If she sees danger around you and because of you, then I believe her. The trick is to make sure we keep you safe."

"Like we kept Irene safe?" she asked.

He winced. "That's not fair. If I'd had a chance to do that all over again, obviously we would do some things differently."

"Sorry," she whispered. "You're right."

"No, it is fair. I've been racked with guilt over it myself. But I don't know what I'm supposed to do about it now." They drove over the overpass, and he could still see Irene in the rearview mirror, staring after him. He felt fingers sweep down his soul. "I hate that she's always around, watching us."

"Can your grandmother find a way to get Irene home?"

"I don't know. She has never been terribly powerful in that department. She's much more about premonitions and precognition. Now my granddad, if he were around, might be of more help, but he went traveling, and we haven't heard from him in a long time."

"Is he still alive?"

"My grandmother says so and gets angry anytime I push it. They are both of Gypsy ancestry and hate to be caged or questioned," he said with a lopsided grin. "And, if he's gone, not much I can do about it now."

"Which isn't terribly helpful, considering how vague she was. Specifics would be helpful at this point."

"It would," he agreed. "But, given this work, there never seems to be any of those."

CHAPTER 12

ROWAN TOOK HER back to the office. "If you could stay here, I promise I won't be long. I'll try to get in touch with this person. If I can't, I'll try later." He gave her a distant smile and headed across the large room.

As he walked away from her, she understood he had things to do, and she felt bad for adding to his workload, but she needed to do this.

That she could give so little by way of explanation made it that much harder for anyone to believe her.

But it was all true.

She sat in the reception room and stayed as calm and as out of the way as possible. He'd gone to a private office and had closed the door. She wanted to be in that room with him. She didn't want to lose sight of him at all. In her mind, although irrational, she couldn't help worrying he'd take off and not keep his word. Yet she knew he was honest, honorable. Still, she'd thrown him a curve ball.

As she watched the busy station go about its day, she could see the energy inside the station was clean and fresh. She wondered at that. She'd never seen a place so lacking in drama and trauma and pain and fear. All emotions she'd have expected to see here.

All emotions she was very good at seeing. Then she'd had a lifetime of observing the world around her—both before her rescue and afterward. She'd had so much to learn. So much to figure out in the real world and all it did was show her how incredibly dysfunctional her childhood had been.

A woman walked toward her. "May I get you something to drink?"

"Oh, water if you don't mind."

"No, of course not. Do you want a coffee as well?"

Phoenix shook her head. "No, thank you though. We'll be leaving soon enough. I'd be afraid I wouldn't get time to enjoy it."

The receptionist looked at Rowan's closed door and then back at her, a smile splitting her face. "When he shuts the door, it's usually serious."

Phoenix chuckled. "That's okay. He's helping me out."

The woman nodded and disappeared, only to reappear a few moments later with a bottle of cold water. "Here you go."

Phoenix accepted it gratefully. "Thank you very much."

She relaxed as the receptionist returned to her seat behind the counter, leaving Phoenix alone with her thoughts. She'd never had premonitions before. To have had a shared one with Rowan went beyond anything she'd experienced. Then the visit with Manru had been just as upsetting but in a completely different way.

That woman had been freaky.

Her messages—in fact, everything she'd said—had been disturbing. And it was obvious she hadn't liked anything about Phoenix. She should be used to that, but it still hurt. More so in this case because she really liked Rowan. She had no business having any feelings for him, but they were there nonetheless.

She was only here for another day, then her visit to Iceland was over. She'd go her own way, and he'd go his. With any luck neither of them would have to see anything like Irene's strange death again. She wondered at this person Rowan was contacting.

Something was there in her mind's eye, … some tiny thread that confirmed people were out there who could help her and Rowan, only she didn't know how to contact them.

When she'd been a child, desperate and calling out for help mentally, she had heard a response sometimes. She just hadn't known in her pain and torment who or what it was. After she'd been rescued, she'd never tried to call out for help again, so she had no clue if that was even possible. Or was it all part of her very traumatized memories?

She took another sip of her bottle, then, seeing a washroom, went to use the facilities. She took a moment to wash her face and to refasten her hair back. Feeling refreshed, she headed to the same spot and sat down again. She didn't want to clock-watch. But it was hard to sit here and wait.

How much longer would he be?

SAYING HE WOULD contact this person was a lot easier than making it happen. All of Rowan's information and research kept turning up the same person but no contact number. When Rowan found an article about this Stefan Kronos working with the Seattle Police Department, he looked up the Seattle PD and the person named in the article. With that down, he called him. He realized he'd forgotten to check the time. But a quick internet search said it was close to ten a.m. for Stefan's time zone.

"He's not in right now," the receptionist said.

"I'm looking to get into contact with Stefan Kronos," Rowan said, identifying himself from the police force in Iceland.

A moment of silence came on the other end, before she said, "Just a moment." Rowan was put on hold. A few long moments later a male voice came on and asked, "What's this regarding?"

"A very strange set of events," he said. "I was thinking maybe this Stefan person would have some insight."

"Give me your information, and I'll contact Stefan. If he's interested, he'll contact you."

That was the best Rowan could hope for. "Please let him know this is urgent."

The other man said, a weariness in his tone, "It's always urgent."

Rowan hung up. He looked at pictures of Stefan online and read up on his life's work. Rowan didn't know how to contact Stefan other than leaving that message. Unless he was incredibly strong and could hear messages on the ethers? That was how his grandmother would have described her form of communication. With that in mind, Rowan leaned back in his chair, closed his eyes and thought, *Stefan, I really could use your advice.*

His phone rang. He picked up the department's landline but then realized it was his cell phone. He didn't recognize the number on the other end. "Hello?"

"Stefan here," a voice said briskly on the other end. "Don't bother asking how."

Rowan's jaw dropped. "Okay," he said, when he finally could. "Then considering what you've just pulled off, I'm really hoping you can help."

"Then start," he said. "Tell me everything."

Rowan told him about Phoenix's arrival, her life in the US. Her childhood. Irene, the first scenario. Where they both saw her flung off the cliff and then returned, only to have her wake up and commit suicide and now being haunted by her ghost. The fact that Phoenix had this letter that wouldn't burn. She had come to his small town, looking to put it in Burning Fires. Rowan took a deep breath and added, "And we live on a lot of seismic activity, so it's not totally unexpected, but it's the timing ..."

"What else?" Stefan asked.

Frowning, Rowan racked his brain and then added his grandmother's words. "And I think that's it."

"What about your own intuition, feelings, premonitions?"

"I do see some energy," Rowan said. "But I'm not saying I'm proficient. Something has been odd around the place for the last couple years. It is coming into suicide season, which is a terrible name, but it's an apt description. Something about this location attracts tourists to come and commit suicide. I think that's the only reason for my heightened awareness, as I'm trying not to lose anybody."

"But you already have. Correct?"

"If you mean Irene? Yes. Irene may have had something to do with her child's death four months ago."

"What was that bit about *sacrifice versus victims?*"

"I don't really know," he said, frowning. "Did I say that?"

A moment of silence followed before Stefan said thoughtfully, "Maybe not. But that's what I'm getting. Something about a sacrifice versus victims. There is an energy there that I half recognize but it's changed. It's connected to this ..." his voice trailed off as if he was off in deep thought.

"Irene might have been a sacrifice?" Rowan asked in confusion. "I'm not sure what you mean about this energy."

"I'm not sure either. And no. I think Irene is a victim," Stefan said, confusing the issue further.

"Are you saying somebody is behind this?"

"Somebody's always behind it," he said. "The trouble is, we don't know if it's somebody in this plane or somebody who has already crossed over to a different existence."

At that, Rowan could feel his heart wrenching and his stomach sinking. "Are we talking a ghost?"

"What would you say Irene's status is?"

"I haven't a clue. Every time I see her, it's like she's transparent, except for the look on her face, which is clearly accusatory. And honestly I blame me too. When I saw her body reappear at the top of the cliff, I snatched her up. I carried her away from the cliff's edge. I knew that edge was seriously dangerous, ... but what I didn't expect was that she would wake up, stand with this blissful look on her face, talk almost normally and run so fast we couldn't catch her before she did a swan dive over the cliff. The recovery team said she was found facedown against the rocks below, her body with multiple broken bones and just absolutely no chance she could have survived."

"No, she probably wasn't intended to survive," Stefan said thoughtfully. "Has something like that ever happened before?"

"Not that I know of," Rowan said. "I've worked here for eight years, and every year the suicides get a little worse."

Again came a long silence. "There's something you're not telling me," Stefan said.

Rowan shook his head. "If it is, it's because I'm either

not thinking of it, or, to me, it doesn't appear important."

"Who was the last person to try to commit suicide before Irene?" Stefan asked.

Rowan sucked in his breath and whispered, "My boss. The police chief."

"Was he somebody you would have thought would have committed suicide?"

"Absolutely not," Rowan replied.

"How did he try?"

"He ate a bullet," Rowan replied bluntly.

"Usually that's pretty guaranteed, isn't it?"

"Unfortunately not. Too often the angle isn't right. It should be up and back, and I guess, in his case, it was slightly to the side and back, so went out the upper cheekbone."

"Interesting," Stefan said. "How did he feel about suicide season?"

"He hated it. He had extremely strong feelings about anybody who would come to our town to commit suicide. He felt it was a person's duty to keep that to themselves and to do it at home."

"And where did he commit suicide?"

"In his office, at his desk," Rowan replied. "I think I'm the only one who ever questioned it might not have been a suicide attempt."

"Any reason why?"

"The energy," he said simply. "It was red for anger, for frustration."

"Which would fit a suicide, wouldn't it?"

"Maybe," Rowan said. "But I was also looking for a cause. I was looking for sadness or grief or something that would say he had no other option. He is in good standing in the community. His finances are decent. He owns his own home. His wife did pass away about eight years ago, but he never showed that he was so traumatized that he felt the need to join her."

"Okay. We'll put him aside for the moment. Who else?"

"This year? No one. The season generally ends around October. We had two in October and four in September last year alone. More earlier on."

"That is definitely intriguing," Stefan said. "How many in a season normally?"

"There is no *normally*," Rowan said, rubbing his temples and easing back into his chair. He looked around the chief's office, where he currently sat. It didn't feel like his job though. "Every year it's different. Every year it's worse."

"How are these people dying?"

"Well, unfortunately a lava fire opens every spring and closes every fall. It's the favorite suicide method here. Maybe something is in the gases? When the fissure is open, all of a sudden we have a bunch of people committing suicide. I'm searching for answers, and there just aren't any."

"There is always an answer," Stefan replied. "But it doesn't mean you'll find it easily. What is it you want from me?" he asked.

"I'd like to know how to stop it."

"*Hmm*," Stefan said. "This Phoenix person is the one I find very interesting. And her unique letter. She's familiar to me, but I'm not sure how or why ..." He cleared his throat. "And she went there to throw it into the fire."

"Maybe. She said her father, this cult leader, used to burn her with fire. That this fire came from his fingers. She also said he was in a love-hate relationship with her because he hated that she would be stronger and bigger and better than him, and yet, as his child, he was also proud. It was his job to teach her and to train her, so she could withstand all this fire because she was supposed to rise from the ashes."

Stefan sucked in his breath. "Now I remember her," he murmured softly. "I'm glad you called. She's been a puzzle. One of those niggling things I can't forget."

"I'm sorry? What was that?" Rowan asked in confusion.

"A memory from a long time ago. And a reminder of everything coming back around again," Stefan said. "Have you seen any signs of abuse on Phoenix's body?"

"No, not personally," Rowan replied slowly. "She does have a pretty bad scar along her face, but I haven't seen her without her clothes on."

"*Hmm.*"

"Do you think she made this all up?" Everything inside him refuted that. He didn't want her to be a liar or a fraud. But, at the same time, he didn't want her story to be real either because that was just too horrifying.

"It's hard to say, isn't it? I'll have to look into this. I understand that time is of the essence ..."

"More than you realize. I'm afraid she's more interested in committing suicide than just getting rid of that letter."

"She figures the Burning Fires will be the answer to burn this letter with her father's energy on it?"

"Yes," Rowan said. "It appears to be on some very anti-inflammable paper, and I don't understand what that would be. It's very thin. Looks like paper but almost with a weave to it. Yet it seems plastic. Makes no sense, I know."

"Lots of unique materials are out these days. It's possible it wouldn't burn in a fire. What does it say on it?"

"Something about Phoenix's destiny."

"Definitely enough to give any child nightmares," Stefan said.

"The other thing is," Rowan said, "she has no idea if any of her family, and I use the term loosely, are still alive. Because it occurred to me that maybe somebody else was making her life difficult. Maybe they were behind all this. Telling her that she needed to come here, but, at the same time she's putting the letter into this fire, she's not planning to jump, but this voice in the back of her head, belonging to somebody else, will tell her to jump."

"Autosuggestion?" Stefan thought about that for a long moment and finally said, "Too many variables are here."

Rowan waited at the pause in the conversation.

"Iceland, huh?"

"I know it's a long trip, and, by the time you would even make the journey, we could have ten dead people already."

Stefan chuckled. "If I were to come over, I wouldn't be coming on a traditional flight. But it would help a lot if we had somebody there to investigate over there. I'm dealing with a lot here that is keeping my energy split and very needed here."

"Wouldn't that be nice," Rowan said, a note of humor in his tone. "Do you have psychic investigators?"

"It's not that *I* have any," Stefan said, "but several are out there, yes."

"It would be good if one could be here now," Rowan said. "I'm feeling like the blind leading the blind."

"Try to keep Phoenix safe," Stefan said. "Anybody who's been through what she has, and we are assuming her story is true, deserves a chance at a decent life."

"I hear you. All the research I found about her father says he was definitely a bastard. A cult leader who abused and tortured his children. Her name itself isn't mentioned, but then she was a young child, so I'm not sure where the ban on names happens over there."

"She shouldn't have been named," he said, "but I wonder how many cult children survived."

"The article said none. I haven't told her that."

"And honestly that could have been done to protect her," Stefan said. "By the same token, if it was to protect her, was it to protect anyone else?"

"Her mother also tried to kill her, and Phoenix ended up getting away, but her mother took her own life."

"So Phoenix is already preprogrammed for suicide," Stefan said. "And you're sure she had nothing to do with Irene's death?"

Rowan stiffened. "It never occurred to me that she might have, but I don't see how. She's the one who told me about the woman crying in the woods. She's also the one I took to pinpoint the location where the woman was in trouble," he replied. "Phoenix did see what I saw in the sense that she saw Irene's ghost at the restaurant and in the lobby of the hotel later too. I don't think Phoenix is involved."

"Anybody who has seen Irene after her death to the extent Phoenix has is definitely involved. Sounds like she brought things to a head."

"What does that mean?" Rowan demanded.

"It means, she's likely the catalyst. The reason this is happening. I wish I could see what that letter looks like." There was a strange silence to the phone followed by an odd buzzing sound. When Stefan spoke again, there was an odd tone to his voice. "It feels like I'm being blocked. Or that this person has a massive wall I can't get around."

"I have a picture of it," Rowan said trying to be helpful. He'd met enough people he couldn't read to understand Stefan's frustration. "The material has the strangest feel. She called it paper, and it crumpled and stayed crumpled, but then it could straighten out."

"She got it from her father?"

"Yes. He said it was a very special letter, had been in his family for generations, had come from here in Iceland."

"Okay," Stefan said. "If you can send a photo, that would be great. I'll see if I can find any of my hunters in your area."

At the term *hunters*, Rowan backed up. "What do you mean?"

"A few gifted people who investigate these types of incidents globally," he said. "They wouldn't like it if I didn't tell them this was happening."

"A lot of tourists are here now," Rowan said. "We're not fond of the influx, but, at the same time, the storekeepers can use the money."

"Of course they can," Stefan said. "Things like this always bring people and, with people, come problems." And with that he hung up.

Rowan sat in the chair for a long time, wondering if he'd done the right thing. When he looked up, he saw the receptionist walking toward him, holding something in her hand. She knocked then opened the door.

"What's that?" he asked.

"I need signatures," she said simply. "Order forms for people working, consents for meals for prisoners." She gave him a hard smile. "It's your job now."

He snagged the paperwork, gave it a quick perusal and then started signing. "The chief is still alive," he said.

"Alive is one thing, but obviously he's not capable of returning to full duties," she said. "In other words, it is up to you."

CHAPTER 13

P HOENIX WAITED. WHEN she watched Rowan stride
from his office, she knew something was wrong. "I'm
over here," she called with a slight wave.

He changed direction and came toward her. He sat
down in the empty chair beside her and said, "I got hold of
him."

"That's good, isn't it?" She brightened at the thought of
an expert involved.

"Maybe," he said. "He'll see if he can get somebody to
come over and give us a hand."

Her eyebrows rose. "Seriously? That's great but ... *time*.
I'm leaving in the morning." She glanced at the clock. "Is it
time to meet our six o'clock appointment? I don't want to
miss it."

"Yes, I told you that I'd take you there." He pulled out
his phone, dialed somebody and then had a conversation,
which she presumed from the subject was with the geologist's
staff. When Rowan said he was heading out to Haro's place,
she wasn't sure where that was.

He got off the phone and motioned for her to go before
him. She asked, "Where now?"

"To the geologist," he answered softly.

"Oh, good," she said, excitement overtaking her. "I hope
he doesn't mind."

"I've already cleared it with him," he said.

As he stepped out onto the street, she watched as his gaze searched the crowd around him. "You're really bothered by something. What's going on?"

"Not necessarily anything," he said. "Just being cautious."

"Can this guy you contacted come over?"

He shook his head. "No. He's in Seattle and needs to stay there right now. He might be able to do something on an energy level but maybe not. It did sound like he was involved in something that was demanding all his energy there."

"Oh," she said, disappointed. "That makes sense. Not to mention we can't expect someone to just drop what they are doing and come help us. For all we know he's involved in a bigger crisis there."

"Maybe." He got into the cruiser and slowly drove out of town. He was just over the overpass when dispatch called. "Hey. There's a problem over at the Hogarth place."

"What problem?"

The language changed to something she didn't recognize. When the conversation was done, he growled. "Theo Hogarth, one of Haro's neighbors, is missing."

"Oh, no," she cried out. "Is it likely serious?"

"He's an old man, and his son called it in. Says he's at the place, and it looks like a struggle occurred."

She sagged into her seat, hating the huge punch to her gut at Rowan being called away. Why now? "Look. If you can't take me there, I can find somebody else, I'm sure."

"Like hell," he said succinctly. "Just hold on. … We'll get you there."

"Maybe," she said. "But you're a busy person. I should

have thought of that."

"Doesn't matter," he said.

As they drove, she didn't want to bother him, but her mind was brimming with questions. She wondered if his mood was because of something this other person had said. Hesitantly she started a conversation. "Who was this person you contacted in Seattle?"

"Stefan Kronos."

She felt a jolt a surprise.

He looked over at her. "Do you know him?"

She stared out the window. "I'm not sure," she said. "I think he came with the police that day." She frowned. "Or maybe someone with a similar name. … Something about him and that energy …"

"What day are you talking about?"

"I think he came with the police that day of the raid on the cult," she said. "At least someone … did."

"Why would he have done that?"

She shrugged. "I don't know. Remember? I was eleven."

"Right," he said.

He took a series of turns, while she thought about what a coincidence it would be that Stefan was the same man Rowan was now speaking to many years later. She decided it had to be the wrong person. "No, I don't think it could have been him," she said.

"He didn't seem to know the name of your father."

"Not many did," she said. "My father would have loved to have been famous but for all the right reasons. I don't know that infamy was anything he wanted." Then she shrugged and said, "Don't mind me. I'm in an odd mood."

"I did try to find out about your case, but you're right. Not a lot of information is available."

"No," she said. "I've asked the cops too."

"So you connected with them?"

"At one point, when I was feeling very lost and alone," she said. "But the cops wouldn't tell me anything or *couldn't* tell me anything."

"Maybe one of those DNA ancestry kits might be an interesting route," Rowan suggested.

"I thought about it," she said. "But when you do it, and your name is out there, then they can connect you with all kinds of things. I didn't want to be that vulnerable." And then she winced. "Wow, listen to me. Still terrified of other kids."

"With good reason," he said shortly. He took a right just then onto a long dirt road. He passed several houses, then pulled into the driveway of the third one.

She hopped out and said, "Why are we here?" She wrapped her arms around her chest, feeling a sudden icy coldness.

"This is the call I was asked to check up on," he said. Just then a middle-aged man came out and spoke to Rowan in a language she didn't understand. "Wait in the car," Rowan said. "I shouldn't be long."

She nodded but didn't get back in the car. She was more than happy to walk around and stretch her legs. Besides, sitting here wasn't any good. It just made her tense. She waited until Rowan was inside the house, and then she slowly walked around the vehicle down to the main road and back up again. It wasn't a very long distance, but she couldn't help feeling eyes were watching her. Such an unnerving feeling.

But, if anybody had seen or had heard something un-pleasant had happened to the old man who lived here, then, of course, they were watching. Nobody wanted to get involved, but everybody wanted to know what was happening. When Rowan still didn't come out, she made another trip up and down the driveway.

By the time she made it back to the car, she was worried about the timing. They still had to meet this Haro person, and it was getting late. She wandered to the front door, wondering if she should knock, and then decided Rowan might get angry, and she should stay at the vehicle.

So once again, she traipsed her way back down to the car. There she leaned against the hood and waited. And waited. And waited. And finally she couldn't wait anymore. She walked around to the back of the house. As soon as she got inside the yard, she stopped and cried out in horror.

An old man lay on the ground, naked, spread-eagle, his hands staked to the ground. Candles circled him. And he had crosses cut into his skin. Rowan ran toward her. "Don't," he said. "I told you to stay in the vehicle."

"You also told me that you were looking for somebody, who the son hadn't seen."

"Well, we found him," he said. "It's very important you go back to the vehicle and wait. Do you hear me?"

She shot him a wounded look and said, "He shouldn't be alone like this."

"He's not alone anymore," Rowan said. "I'm here."

She bit her bottom lip and left, wrapping her arms tighter around her body. She retraced her steps to the car. She sat inside and could feel the tears coming down her cheeks. Something was familiar about that sight, but she didn't know what it was. She closed her eyes and waited.

ROWAN SWORE UNDER his breath as he watched her disappear around the side of the house. He turned to look at Sven Hogarth, who stood at the back door, a shocked look on his face as he studied his father. "Don't touch anything," Rowan said. "I'm bringing a team over."

Hogarth nodded. "Do we know for sure he's dead?"

It was obvious. The old man's eyes stared up at the sky above him. Enough blood had seeped into the ground that proved it had been a long, slow process to die. "How long ago did you see him?"

"Yesterday at dinnertime," the son replied, his voice jerky. "And he was perfectly fine. Normal. Happy. We don't get many murders in this town. And usually they're brought on by the tourists."

"I know," Rowan said. "But something weird has been going on these last couple days."

Hogarth nodded jerkily. "Yes," he said. "More fights, more arguments. Long-term friends and relationships splitting up. Two women I know lost their babies. I just don't know why this is happening." Hogarth cast one more long gaze at his father, turned back to Rowan and said, "I know what you'll probably say, but could I please cover him up?"

"No," he said. "I'm sorry, but that's not possible yet."

"I didn't think so, but I was hoping. It is just so demeaning to see him like this."

"I think it was meant to be empowering," Rowan said, studying the old man. "Almost like he was a sacrifice."

"That's a horrible thing to say," Hogarth said. "My father was a lot of things, but he certainly wasn't anybody's sacrifice."

"What do you mean?" Rowan asked, turning to look at

him.

"I loved him very much, but he wasn't necessarily a good man, but, no matter his sins, he didn't deserve this."

"What sins? I don't remember hearing anything in relation to your father." Rowan also realized he didn't know everybody in this town as well as he would have liked. "Your father only moved here about a year ago, didn't he?"

Hogarth nodded. "When he was released from jail," he said sadly. "I have very mixed memories about him. I'd like to think they were all good, but, of course, they aren't."

"What was he in jail for?"

Hogarth stared down at the man with a mixture of revulsion and love.

And then Rowan knew. "He was a pedophile, wasn't he?"

Hogarth looked at him in surprise. "How did you know?"

"It was a lucky guess," he said, his tone heavy. "But that's it, right?"

"Yes," he said. "Little boys and little girls. He wasn't particular. He liked to abuse anybody."

"I'm sorry," Rowan said. "But it looks like somebody found out and decided he hadn't paid his debt to society."

"A part of me agrees," Hogarth said. "What kind of a monster does that make me?" On that note, Sven turned and headed back into the house.

Rowan knew he had his hands full. And how the hell was he supposed to fulfill his promise to get Phoenix right now with the geologist? He'd already called in the forensics team. By the time he made his way out to the front and to his cruiser, they were here. He set up a guard to watch for the coroner on the way and to keep out the curious.

The coroner was the local doctor. He doubled up his duties. Like most of them had to in a small town like his. As soon as he arrived, Rowan spoke with him for a few moments and then said, "I have to leave. I'll be back as soon as I can."

The coroner nodded and said, "You've done your job. Let me do mine. You hunt for a killer." And he disappeared. Rowan got into his vehicle, turned it on and slowly backed out of the driveway. He didn't say anything to Phoenix for several moments. His mind was caught on what he'd seen and heard.

So many vehicles were arriving now that it was hard to get out of the driveway. Finally he was on the open road again, heading for the geologist's house. He looked over at her. "Are you okay?"

"No," she whispered. "He was sacrificed, wasn't he? What had he done wrong?"

"I think he was a victim," he corrected. "And, yes, he had done something wrong. He was released from jail a year ago. According to his son, he was a pedophile."

"Damn," she said in a hoarse whisper. "Do you have a vigilante running amok?"

"Anything's possible," he said. "But let's not make any assumptions. Let's see if we can at least solve your problem."

"That's two then," she said finally.

"Yes," he said. "Two that we know about." At her gasp, he realized she got his message.

"So you're thinking there might be more?"

"If there's been two, then I have to consider that possibility."

"Do you know everybody who's committed horrible crimes in town?"

"It's not something I ever aspired to know," he said. "I know those we've taken off the streets ourselves, but that's not many. We do have a lot of people who call here home but weren't born and raised here, some of them obviously with criminal records."

"Great," she said. "And I came here, why?"

"Well, that's what I've been asking you," he said with a grin. "And hopefully we can solve your problem fast, as I have to get back to work."

He drove up to the cabin where the geologist was. No lights were on though. Rowan checked his watch and said, "We're five minutes early. It's not quite six yet."

"He isn't here though. Do we just wait?"

"Yes, but not for long. I'm on a tight schedule as it is."

"Any chance this guy's exactly the same?" she asked. "As in dead. Potentially sacrificed?"

He gave her a startled look. "Why would you think that?"

"I don't know," she said. "But we came to one empty house, and look what we found."

"That doesn't mean the next one is a duplicate."

"No," she said, turning her hard gaze on him. "It doesn't mean it isn't, either."

CHAPTER 14

T HE DAY HAD a gray overcast sky. Phoenix couldn't forget the image of the old man spread-eagled on the ground. She couldn't place why it felt so familiar, but it ate away at the back of her mind. Sitting in the car at the geologist's dark house, waiting, made her think all kinds of horrible things. Finally she turned to Rowan and said, "Go check."

He looked at her and raised an eyebrow.

She shrugged. "*Please,* go check."

He sighed and opened the car door. "He's not late."

"Only a few moments more," she said.

He nodded and walked up to the front door. He knocked. She watched as he stood there, waiting, and, when nobody came to the door, he walked back down the steps and headed around the side of the house. And again she was in that horrible position of sitting and waiting.

They were too damn close to the other crime scene, and she knew the cops would be spreading out through all the neighboring properties. But what if another murder had been committed here? She didn't know how this was suicide season, yet they had found a murder.

Rowan came back to the car a few minutes later and shook his head. "Nobody's here," he said.

"Good," she said and relaxed. "I was afraid we'd end up

finding him in the backyard too."

The radio crackled with static and dispatch spoke. Rowan answered, and again it was the language Phoenix didn't understand. When he was finished, he turned to her. "The geologist left a message to say he's on his way home."

She smiled up at Rowan. "Perfect. We should just sit here and wait then?"

A few minutes later, a vehicle drove in, and a burly man in a big plaid jacket and heavy work boots hopped out. He walked toward the cruiser and smiled. Rowan hopped out, and they shook hands. The two men spoke. Phoenix wasn't sure if they would walk from here or drive, but she assumed drive.

Rowan poked his head in and said, "Come on. We'll go in his rig. It's got better 4x4 capabilities."

She nodded and hopped out. She was introduced to Haro, and they shook hands.

The grizzled-looking man in a safety vest eyed her. She gave him a bland smile and hoped he wouldn't ask too many questions. He motioned toward his vehicle, and she took the front seat and Rowan sat in the back.

Haro reversed out of the driveway, talking to them about the changes in the lava. "I know we often get one fissure on this place every few years around this time," he said. "But this one is quite a bit bigger than what we've seen in the past."

"Any idea why?" Rowan asked.

"No," he said. "Mother Nature likes to keep us guessing." He looked over at Phoenix. "Have you seen lava up close before?"

"No," she admitted. "I haven't."

"Interesting that you want to do this."

"I'm not sure it's a choice," she said, refusing to lie. "Sometimes you just feel compelled to do something, and it won't leave you alone."

He gave a bark of laughter. "Is that not the truth? Even when it's against our better judgment."

She didn't have an answer for that. They drove into rougher terrain, where the road was more like a faint line. She expected a chill to the air, but instead it got hotter, and that was how she knew they were heading for the area. The windows were closed, the air circulating. Haro eventually pulled off to the side of the road and said, "We have to walk from here."

Phoenix hopped out, closed the door behind her and took several deep breaths. A sulfuric acid smell gently floated toward her.

Haro said, "The easiest place is a lookout up here. With any luck we can tie your letter to a rock and throw it in."

She smiled up at him. "Thank you. I really appreciate this."

"As long as it's harmless, I don't mind," he said. He led the way, picking as close a path through the woods as he could.

She kept close, with Rowan bringing up the rear. She felt an odd sense of being watched again too. She kept looking around, but there was nothing to see. They arrived at the top of a plateau. Haro led them closer to the edge, then pointed downward.

They weren't up super high, but, like the pictures she had seen of other Burning Fires, this was similar in that a red molten lava flow had burned all around. Instead of a big round circle, it was more of a small bubbling stream, like pus coming up from the center of the Earth. Red angry pus with a partial crust. She watched, fascinated, as it poured into a small river channel. "How far will it go down?"

"Eventually it'll run to the water," he said. "But this isn't a very large amount. It's still bigger than we've had in the past. This is only about twenty to thirty feet across. Not too bad. If it doubles or triples, that's a different story."

"This is just releasing pressure from inside the Earth, right?"

"Yes. This is a fissure that's opened, instead of a volcano. So the gas escapes, followed by lava coming up from down below."

She nodded. "The smell is something, isn't it?"

"The smell is disgusting," he replied. "And that's one of the reasons why we have to keep people away. You can't be here for long." He looked at her pointedly. "You have something you need to do, please do it now." He took several steps back, out of the way.

Rowan stepped closer. "I don't know that you can throw a sheet of paper that far."

She studied the distance and shook her head. "No, I can't." She glanced around for anything on the ground she could use. "We should have brought some rocks with us."

"Didn't think of it," he said. He picked up several rocks and held them out. "One of these?"

She took out the letter and wrapped it around the bigger rock and then frowned. "How do we seal it? Do you have any glue or tape or rope or string?"

He shook his head but checked his pockets and pulled out gum. She looked at it and smiled. "It might work." He popped it in his mouth and chewed vigorously, as she checked her pockets and the ground to see if she could use anything else. But nothing suitable was here.

When he had chewed up the gum enough, making it soft, he used it to hold the letter wrapped around the rock, mashing it together good and tight. "It shouldn't come off." He held it out to her.

She walked up to the edge, took several deep breaths, and, with the rock in her hand, she whispered, "With this act, I'm releasing my father and all the horrible things that happened in my childhood. From here on out, I move forward, without carrying the baggage from that time of my life." She stretched her arm back, about to throw it, when a shot rang out. She yelped and dropped to the ground.

"Jesus, you've been shot." Rowan kneeled beside her.

She couldn't speak because of the burning pain in her shoulder.

He checked her over, then looked around, but the geologist was long gone. His vehicle was still there at the trees, but Rowan saw no sign of Haro. Rowan picked her up and ran as quickly as he could to the vehicle for shelter. With every step she cried out in pain.

HE SWORE SOFTLY. "I don't know who the hell fired that shot," Rowan roared, "but they certainly targeted you."

"Did anybody else get shot?" she asked through gritted teeth.

He looked around and shook his head. "I can't find the geologist." He also didn't know if Haro had done the shooting.

At the vehicle Rowan crouched down in front, where there was a little protection. There hadn't been another shot. ... Phoenix started to shake, and he could see blood welling from her shoulder. He pressed his hand to the wound and held her down. "When I take my hand away, you need to put pressure on it," he said.

Rowan pulled off his uniform shirt and yanked his T-shirt over his head. He folded it up, using it as a bandage, and pressed it on her wound, then called out, "Haro, are you there?"

No answer.

Rowan looked around and swore. "Where could he have gone?"

"Did he shoot me?" She gasped.

He stared down at her. "I don't know," he said. "No sign of him though."

"Why would he do such a thing?" she asked.

"We don't know that he did," Rowan reminded her. "Hold that thought. We can't be sure. He had no reason to either."

"Maybe not," she said, "but he was the only other person here."

"I know. Did you hear one or two shots?" He had only heard one, but something had been odd about it, so he couldn't be sure. An odd hissing rumble here distorted everything.

"I don't know," she cried out. "Oh, God, it hurts."

"I have to get you back to town," he said. "Let's get you into the truck, and then I'll get you to the hospital."

"We can't leave Haro here. What if he shoots someone else? What if he's been shot too?"

"What if he wants a second chance at you? He's made one attempt, but what if he wants to make sure you're dead?"

"Will he let us leave, or will he shoot at us again?" she whispered.

"I don't know. Let's figure that out afterward. Let's get

you inside his truck first." Rowan managed to get her in the passenger side and turned to look at her. "Keep your head down, just in case."

She nodded and shifted to lean sideways, groaning at the movement.

He turned and crouched, making his way around the front to get to the driver's side. No shots rang out. Nothing stopped him. He squeezed into the driver's side, turned on the engine and backed up. They needed to get a little farther away before he could see anything. But it wasn't easy to do. As he backed up, he thought he saw something off to the side. It made his heart freeze.

He glanced at Phoenix and said, "I have to check something."

She stared at him in horror. "Please don't. What if you get shot?"

"I won't be long."

She gave a broken laugh and nodded. "Go," she said, "but hurry."

He drove up as close as he could to the overlook above the stream and hopped out, slowly making his way to the edge, a little farther away from where they had been—but where Rowan had last seen Haro before the shooting. As Rowan stood here, he peered over the edge and saw what he had been afraid of—just one corner of Haro's brightly colored jacket at the top of the cliff partway below. The jacket was empty. No sign of Haro. But directly below him was the river of lava.

Rowan's heart sank as he considered the implication. But was it staged just to make a man, who possibly shot at them, appear to be dead, or had the shooter also taken out their driver?

He dropped to his knees and peered farther over the edge, and what he saw made his blood run cold. A partial body was down below. But only *partial.* The lava had consumed most of it, with the top of a head and one arm sticking out, as if reaching up when he had gone over the edge. But no doubt Haro was dead.

Swearing, Rowan pulled out his phone and took several photos because, by the time he got back with a team, he was pretty sure the lava would have consumed the rest of the body. Even as he watched, the rocks gave way, and the arm fell in the lava, obliterating any remains. Now Rowan really had no evidence. He went back to the vehicle, got in, turned on the engine and backed up. He drove back the way they'd come. He looked over to see Phoenix staring at him.

"What did you see?" she asked, her voice hoarse.

"Haro is dead," he replied softly.

"Was he shot?" she asked, twisting her head to look back. "Are you sure he's gone? Maybe you were mistaken. We need to go back and help him."

"No," he said. "He's dead. I can guarantee you that."

She stared at him. "How can you tell?"

"Because I saw the lava take his arm and head, and then that's all that was left of him. He was consumed by the lava."

She sagged against the seat. "Dear, Lord. Did we do this?"

He looked at her in surprise. "Why would you think that?"

"Because he wouldn't have come here without us asking him."

"Not true," he said. "You have to consider the fact this is his job. He comes here all the time."

She nodded. "Right. So this could have happened anytime."

He doubted it, but he didn't want to tell her that.

She took several deep breaths. "I'm not feeling very good," she said, suddenly woozy.

"Hold on. It's probably the adrenaline wearing off after the shock of being shot. We'll get you to the hospital in no time."

She turned to him and said, "Maybe. But I think it's too late."

He glanced over at her, his gaze sharp. "What do you mean, *too late*?"

"I don't think I'll make it."

"No, don't pass out on me," he ordered, pressing his foot down hard. The main road was up ahead. He turned onto it as fast as he dared to go, the truck skittering sideways as his tires caught on the pavement to surge forward, and again he hit the gas. "Do you hear me?" he demanded. "You hang on."

But there was no answer. He turned to look at her. She was unconscious.

CHAPTER 15

P HOENIX WAS CAUGHT up in a weird state of pain and
confusion. She knew Rowan was here and someone else
too. But she couldn't figure out who the other person was.
He was familiar, yet not.

A third person joined them. They were wrapping Phoenix in golden tinsel. She couldn't make any sense of it,
but ... something haunted her at the edge of her thoughts.

Then she realized these other two were her same fictional
childhood souls, helping her in her injured state. Had she
called out to them?

*You don't need to anymore. We know. We can feel your
need.*

That was a musical female voice. And then came a gentle
male voice. *We are Stefan and Maddy. We have helped you
many times in the past. Let us work. There is much to do.*

Thank you, she whispered in her mind feeling a connection in a way she'd never thought possible. Her mind didn't
recognize them but her soul did. *I thought you were my
imagination. Or maybe angels ...*

Maddy laughed, her voice a bright light, whispering
around her body. *No, we are humans just like you. Just
skilled ... like you.*

The truck pulled into a parking lot, waking her up. That
vision disintegrated around her. Her body jolted from the

sudden motion, and she cried out, opening her eyes to see Rowan staring at her in fear.

She gave him a pained smile and said, "Well, at least you know I'm alive."

"Sorry, I should have been gentler," he said. He turned off the engine and raced to her side. He opened the door and helped her upright. She took several deep breaths, stopping the greasy waves of pain from taking over and knocking her out again. She could tell, by the look on his face, he knew how bad it was. He eased her feet out of the vehicle to the ground and asked, "Can you walk?"

She nodded. "I can walk." She proceeded to take three steps and collapsed. He caught her before she hit the ground but jarred her shoulder again. She began shaking, her body overcome with agony. In the distance, she heard him slam the vehicle door closed, and she was then scooped up into his arms, and he ran.

She didn't know where she was. "Are we at the hospital?"

"Yes," he said. "We are. Finally."

She felt the air temperature change and a soft hum and realized that large doors were opening, letting them in.

"If it's like any other normal hospital, we will wait for hours," she muttered against his chest. She lay her head back, finding everything took way too much effort.

"Not likely here," he said. "Not unless there's been a car accident."

She was placed on a gurney and heard rapid-fire voices speaking over her as Rowan tried to explain what had happened. She could hear the exclamation from the others; then she was wheeled away to a curtained bay, where she was surrounded by men. Her shirt was snipped off, and medical equipment was dragged closer. She cried out, "Rowan. Where are you?"

"I'm here," he said. "Let the doctors look after you. Don't fight it."

She opened her eyes, but the bright lights above blinded her. She closed them again. "Get that guy, will you?" she whispered. And then he was gone under the commotion of sounds and noises and efficiency as people cut, snipped, poked, prodded, pricked, tested and moved her body as they needed to. She groaned many times until someone whispered, "Just breathe deep. The pain will go away soon."

She breathed in slow and deep, and finally the pain eased back.

She was taken for X-rays, and the rest of her was checked over. She remembered somebody telling her that she would need surgery, and then she was wheeled into an operating room.

She couldn't be afraid. She couldn't worry about how to pay for any of this; it was all happening so fast. The anesthesia mask came down over her face, and she was out within seconds.

The next time she woke up, she was in a bed with curtains around her. She lay here for a long moment, assessing what had happened and how bad the damage was. She shifted experimentally, and the pain wasn't too bad. She took several deep, calming breaths, and it eased back a little more.

She could feel the burn now that she was more awake. She shifted again in the bed to get comfortable, and just then one of the curtains moved back. A nurse stood at the end of her bed, frowning at her. Phoenix tried to smile in return.

The woman asked, "How bad is the pain?"

"Bad," Phoenix whispered. "And getting worse."

The nurse nodded and made an adjustment on her IV.

It helped immediately. Phoenix drifted into sleep again. Only this time her dreams weren't nice. They weren't peaceful. They were full of people getting shot. Men ran everywhere. Lava threatened to burn everything.

Maddy? Stefan? Are you there?

We're here …

When she came to the next time, her body was soaked with sweat, and hot tears rolled down her cheeks. Again she heard more voices. A calm murmur. A damp cloth was pressed to her forehead, and then she went under again, this time already sensing Maddy's and Stefan's presence …

As she woke up once more, she recognized her surroundings. Her body felt as if it had been through a war and had come out on the other side. She lay here for a long time, remembering everything that had happened. And the weird Maddy and Stefan dreams.

Not a dream, said a voice in her head. *Rowan has been speaking with us. We're people. Just like you and Rowan, but we're also healers. And we connected to you as a child, … so that connection was already there when you needed us again.*

Thank you, she whispered in her head. *I'm not sure what all you did, but my body isn't screaming in pain anymore …*

Don't worry about it. Just rest …

Just then the curtain opened, and Rowan stood there, his forehead creased with worry.

She gave him a half smile. "So, are you a natural worrier, or was I in a bad state?"

"You were in a bad state after surgery," he admitted. "It was too early to get a fever, so they're thinking maybe you reacted to some of the medication."

"Maybe," she said. "I don't know."

"Are you allergic to anything?"

She gave a broken laugh. "I don't know. I never had any medical care."

Silence. "You probably didn't when you were younger, but what about in foster care?"

"Only psychiatric care," she whispered. "I made sure to stay away from doctors at all times."

"Why?"

She shifted her gaze to look at Rowan in surprise. "Didn't I tell you? Although he never practiced professionally, my father was a doctor."

ROWAN FELT LIKE he'd been kicked in the gut. He sat on the edge of the bed beside her and whispered, "Your father, the cult leader, was a medical doctor?"

"Yes," she whispered. "I always put that down to why he knew how to maximize the pain and to minimize the actual physical damage."

"Well, the doctors here have a lot of questions," Rowan said. "I haven't had time to study the X-rays yet, but they are something."

She stared at him, her gaze going flat.

And he nodded. "Yes, that's the thing about X-rays. They don't lie, and I imagine they show a history of abuse. I thought it was just about the burns," he said with a tilt to his head as he studied her.

He couldn't even begin to explain his reaction when the doctors had taken him to the side and shown him her X-rays. The multiple broken bones. The damage done over and over again. It was enough to make him want to upchuck. Not only was she scarred externally but she was badly scarred internally as well. There were punctures to her ribs, as if a spike had been driven in. The doctors had asked him for an explanation.

He told them about her father. The leader of a cult, her father had abused her, beaten her and tortured her until she was eleven. Something in the emergency room team changed at that point. Their touches became gentler, as well as their voices. They had softened, as if understanding this woman had been through absolutely everything that somebody should never have to endure, and it was up to them to make sure she had minimal pain from then on.

Rowan appreciated it, but, at the same time, just seeing those X-rays had been so very real and so very difficult. He couldn't imagine anybody having done this to a child. Even worse, to one's own child.

How could she appear to be even halfway normal after what she'd been through? As he studied her cloudy, pain-filled eyes, he realized it was a miracle. A little warning came in the back of his head though. How normal could she be?

Rowan picked up her hand gently. Having seen the images on the X-ray, where the baby finger had been snapped, where new bone had formed, he could see, as he stared at the finger, that it was stiff and didn't quite bend properly. He rubbed the top of her hand softly and asked, "How are you feeling?"

She gave him the same flat stare she used all the time, and he realized she probably had become so accustomed to pain that anything like this was minor. "I'm fine," she said.

"And, even if you aren't, you'll be fine, won't you?"

She raised an eyebrow but stayed silent.

He nodded. "I understand," he said. "But you don't always have to be tough."

"I'm not that tough," she said in a whisper. "I wasn't tough back then either. I screamed and cried like a baby."

He winced at that and knew she caught sight of it.

"I'm sorry if you saw the X-rays," she said. "I can just imagine what they look like."

"Have you seen them?"

She gave a shake of her head. "No, I have no idea. I lived through all of it, so I'm not sure I want to."

"I'll take pictures of them," he said. "I think you should see them. No, not as a memory of what you went through but a memory of how far you've come. How strong you are to have survived all that."

"It was either survive or die," she whispered. "And I wouldn't give him the satisfaction of dying at his hands."

He grinned at that. "That's what I mean. I like that spunk, that refusal to give in to the evil people who did this to you. I'm sorry they're all dead because I'd love to punish them myself."

"I don't know that they are all dead," she said. "Remember the siblings? They may or may not be alive. They did all partake in the joy of beating me up or targeting me."

"I still don't understand that."

"Maybe not," she said, her gaze shifting to look behind him, and he realized she still wasn't sharing something.

He hadn't shared everything in his life either, and she'd had no choice but to have her secrets ripped open for all to see because of now being shot. The medical staff were still talking in the hallway about what they'd seen. They wanted to take different samples from her blood and her tissue. He'd okayed some of them but only if it would help her heal. Not for study, not for research and not out of curiosity.

"I guess when you're ready to tell me everything," he

said, "then we can sit down, have a cup of tea and talk some more."

"I'll be gone by then," she said.

"You're not going anywhere for a while," he said, his voice calm. "The bus left this morning."

Her gaze slammed back into his and widened in shock.

He nodded. "They couldn't stay because you're injured," he said. "You have to understand that." He didn't know if he had released her hand or if she had jerked it away. He settled in the visitor chair near her hospital bed.

"Damn," she whispered. She slowly closed her eyes. "It was supposed to be a simple return trip. It's something that would have helped me move on. Instead, look at me."

"The thing is," he said, "you are alive. And Haro is not."

She lifted her gaze and stared at him.

"Right?" he said with a sad smile. "It helps put some of this in perspective. All we found was his jacket, and I did see his arm and head as it went under in the lava."

"That's so sad," she whispered. "I never intended for him to get hurt. I never wanted *anybody* to get hurt."

"Maybe not," he said. "But the bottom line is, I didn't force him. He was quite happy to take us. I don't think he had any clue what he was getting into, but neither did we."

"Was he shot too?"

"I'm not sure," Rowan said. "Because we have no body, we have no way to find that out. What I do know is I only heard one shot. But that doesn't mean I didn't miss something."

"I know," she said, her head twisting to look out the window.

"I don't know what I heard," he admitted. "But I was so busy focusing on you …" He had a hard time with that, but he wasn't sure what else to think. "… that I don't know if he was pushed or if … he jumped."

She sucked in her breath.

"But I'm not going there right now. We have enough issues to deal with. The last thing we need is to worry about something we can no longer change."

"That's easy to say," she said, "but it's not so easy to release the guilt. *Again*."

"It's not your guilt. It's mine," he said in a harsh voice. "I asked him. I'm the one who asked him to take us."

"So, now we can't ask anybody else anymore," she said. "It's too dangerous."

"And yet, why is it dangerous? Did you consider that?"

She stopped and frowned, as if she hadn't considered the question. "Right. Why was he shooting at us? We don't even know it was a man, do we?"

"No," Rowan replied. He hadn't considered that element, but their attacker could have been a female. "So, what reason is there for somebody to have shot at you at the edge of the lava fields?"

"Somebody who didn't want me to put that letter in the lava," she said immediately.

"And who would that be?"

"Someone from the cult."

THAT WASN'T EXACTLY the way the Supplier had planned the session to go. He'd hoped to separate Rowan from the girl. Instead Rowan had glommed onto her. He was supposed to go help Haro.

Talk about people not doing what they were supposed to do. How infuriating.

Particularly as Haro was his victim, and Phoenix was supposed to be the offering to the Elders. She had to be alive going into the fires ... instead she escaped. The Supplier placed the blame for this mess firmly at Rowan's feet.

Imagine his surprise when he'd seen Rowan at Theo and Sven's house. The old man should have been taken out a long time ago. As the Supplier's own energy reserves had been dropping with the constant need to mask his own energy, that Sven had been a simple easy answer. The Supplier had no idea Sven was so close to his father though, whether geographically or emotionally. The Supplier had hoped to have much longer before the body was found. Hearing footsteps, he'd been forced into the woods, only to see Phoenix there, waiting. They were surrounded by men soon enough, and the Supplier had lost his chance. But he'd heard enough to understand Haro was taking her somewhere interesting.

His plans had been quickly made, and the Supplier had paid the price.

Still, he'd taken out Theo and Haro. The need for vengeance inside him settled. He'd be good for a bit now.

CHAPTER 16

T O CONSIDER THAT somebody from the cult was still alive and trying to stop her from putting that letter in the lava was enough to make her stomach revolt. She realized her thoughts must be evident on her face when Rowan hopped to his feet and leaned over. "Easy. Take it easy," he said.

She gasped several times, to get enough air into her lungs. "Oh, my God," she said on an exhale. "Just the thought of somebody still being alive ..."

"And yet, you always knew it was a possibility?"

"Children, yes. But it never sunk in that children grow up into adults. Although I saw my bullet-ridden father's body, that doesn't mean he was dead. I just have an image of a man on his back with five holes, covered in blood. The cops told me that he was dead, but were they correct? He was very wily. If he'd wanted to escape, I'm pretty sure he could have made that happen."

"I can contact the police in that area and see if we had a body and DNA tests of any kind or forensic material back then."

"Maybe," she said. Her fingers nervously pleated the sheet in front of her. "It does add a different element to my trip though."

"Why did you come here? Specifically?"

"The paper itself came from here, although I only have *his* word on that," Phoenix said. "It just seemed like everything was telling me that I needed to do this finally." She didn't know what else to add. It sounded lame to her too.

"We do try to keep the Burning Fires a secret," he said. "Along with suicide season. It would not be to our benefit to have any of it brought out in the open. Somehow the tourists find out anyway."

"Understood," she said. "I can't really explain how this came about from my perspective. All I can tell you is that, when the opportunity arose, I knew I had to come."

"Anybody else know you came?"

"Not really," she said. "I haven't had many friends to tell. If somebody from the cult is still alive, the only reason for them to be here now is if they knew I would be here. If they wanted to stop me from doing this, that would mean they would have some way of knowing who I was, how I lived, what I was doing and what my plans were."

"Do you have *any* close friends?"

"I have a few colleagues who are friends," she said cautiously. "But nobody I'm close with."

"Who did you tell about what you were doing here?"

"My foster parents," she said. "But just in brief. I didn't explain why. They don't know anything about Iceland being my father's homeland."

Rowan's body stiffened. "What?"

She looked up at him. "Yes, my father is from Iceland. I told you that."

"Wow. You never mentioned that last part," he said.

She watched as his hands fisted in front of her.

"I thought I did," she said. "A lot of details I didn't tell you. I'm not sure of my mother's nationality, but I think she was American. My father is the one who told me about this fire. He's the one who said the paper itself came from here, and the only way to destroy it was to return it."

"Then I need to do some research into your father's family," Rowan said. "Because that is a different avenue of inquiry. What if he has family here?"

"I never considered that," she said, frowning. "It never occurred to me that I had a family over here. He told me that he was an only child and that his parents were dead."

"But that doesn't mean somebody else hasn't been following him, or you, all these years."

"That's a little disturbing," she whispered.

"Any newspaper articles? Anything that would have put you back into the news?"

"I don't think so," she said. "I graduated and was hired by the same university I'd attended, but it's not as if I'm married or I'm involved in any litigation. I mean, police files exist regarding the raid on the cult obviously, but it's not something that's been resurrected."

"Has the case been closed?"

"As far as I know it has been," she said as honestly as she could. "But I don't know that they tell the whole story either. Do they ever?"

"For the moment," he said, "I want you to not worry about any of it. I want you to lie here and focus on getting well."

"As if. You just brought up a whole mess of other issues. That will stop me from sleeping, possibly for the rest of my life," she said. "Somebody tried to kill me. How am I supposed to think it's anybody other than a local?"

"It has nothing to do with being a local," he said. "It could have been anybody. We had three busloads of people in town just on the day you arrived. Remember?"

"Well, maybe you should start by finding out who else missed their spot on the buses," she said. "For all I know, the killer came with me. Did you check to see if anyone else missed the bus?"

"We checked the numbers yes. You were the only one that missed the next leg of the trip."

"Doesn't that figure. I'd only been planning this for a lifetime …"

"And maybe this is as far as you needed to come …" He spoke with a smile but his gaze was searching.

As soon as Rowan left, she lay back on her bed, wondering. She could remember the other cult kids, but she didn't know for sure there weren't more. She had younger siblings too. But she couldn't remember the names of them all. She remembered those who were the worst. The more she thought of it, she realized no sons were in her family. They had all been daughters. Yet she had tidbits of memories regarding boys.

Had it been that her father could only create daughters? Or had something happened to the boys? She didn't even want to contemplate that. Just as she thought she had no way to tell Rowan, he stepped back into the room and said, "I've arranged for the hotel to bring over your laptop, phone and personal belongings."

She smiled up at him. "And I just thought of something else. I don't know why I never thought of it before. But I think only girls were in my family."

He looked down at her and frowned. "What do you mean?"

"I have vague memories of boys but not toward the end. I can't be sure."

"Are you saying other girls were the ones who were mean and tormented you during the night too?"

She nodded. "Don't ever think we're the fairer sex," she said bluntly. "Everything I experienced proved to me that women were deadly vipers. But I don't know what happened to the boys. Maybe there were no male children. I can't remember."

"Or your father did something to make sure they weren't around. Maybe he could justify giving those children away or killing them," Rowan said thoughtfully. "Obviously more questions need to be asked." He walked to the door. "Okay, let me keep digging." He stopped at the doorway and looked at her. "Once you get your personal belongings, you can contact me on your phone."

"I thought I left my phone in either your car or Haro's truck."

"Let me check with the front desk," he said and disappeared again.

She relaxed against the bed, her mind humming. She had heard nothing but silence regarding the cult for all these years, literally nothing. The original investigating cops had checked in on her once or twice afterward, but, realizing she was doing okay, had gone their merry way, content with having given her a chance at a better life.

Whereas now somebody had shot her, and the geologist died. Was that a random shooting, or was she targeted? She had to think it was intentional, yet there was no reason for such a thing—except to stop her from tossing that letter into the lava.

And the only one who knew what they would do at the Burning Fires that night was his grandmother. And that was something else in and of itself.

When Rowan returned, he had her cell phone in his hand. "Your purse is at the front desk and locked away. We can bring it here if you want, but I figured your cell phone is what you needed."

She reached out a hand and accepted her phone. "What about your grandmother?" she asked softly.

"What about her?" he asked as he walked back to the door.

"Would she have told anybody what we were doing?"

He stiffened and slowly turned to look at her.

"I'm not accusing her," she said quickly. "But she is the only one who knew what I was doing."

He stared over her head for a long moment, as if working out something. And then he smiled and said, "I guess I'll go ask her then, won't I?" And, with that, he disappeared.

ROWAN HEADED BACK to his office to work through several different threads for this investigation. Because now it was another murder on his home turf, and what the hell was he supposed to do about the poor geologist? There wasn't even a body, but he had seen it with his own eyes as the arm and head had disappeared into the lava. So basically he could confirm there was a deceased male. Thankfully he had several photos. As poor as they were, they were something. And he could call it what he wanted, but he didn't know how to prove if it was murder, suicide or an accident.

Back in his office, he slammed the door hard behind him, just an outlet for his frustration and rage. Frustration that Haro had been killed. Rage that somebody had tried to shoot Phoenix. Angry that he wasn't getting to the bottom of this nightmare. And none it answered Theo Hogarth's death.

Were they connected? The crime scenes were nothing alike, … yet the two men were neighbors.

He needed to talk to his grandmother. And he needed to get more history on Phoenix's background. How many children were in that cult? Were they all deceased? Where were the males? Had there been any males? He knew some families could have ten or twelve females in a row, but eventually the odds went to having a male child.

He feared the cult didn't keep good birth records. And, even if they did, surely Phoenix's father had burned up any evidence before that fateful day when he was sure to die by police gunfire.

Rowan wrote furiously, dumping everything from his mind. The anger, the frustration, the pain at seeing Phoenix's X-rays was something he had never even thought a child could survive. He hadn't seen any of her scars firsthand, except for the one along her face. But, if her body was as bad as the doctor said, and they'd certainly seen a lot of her, it was amazing she was alive. And Rowan kept coming back to that. How was that possible? Was her psychological state something he could trust?

Or was this all a mask for some incredibly traumatized child on the inside? And that was just sick but maybe, in her case, understandable. Yet he couldn't see anything evil in her energy. He picked up the phone and called his grandmother first. "Hi, Grandma. Did you tell anyone about our visit?"

"No," she said, her voice low and dark. "I didn't. Since you were here, I've locked myself in my apartment and haven't gone anywhere."

"Why?"

"Because something here is dangerous."

"Did you think it would visit you?"

"It's here, in town," she said. "It might always have been. I don't know. But what was locked is now open, and what was dead is now alive." On that note, she hung up on him.

He swore and wrote down what she'd said and stared at the words. *Maybe it was always here, and what was dead is now alive.* He didn't know where to go with that one either. He would have to stop by and talk to her. He knew of nobody else in town with the sight like she had, except himself, and, at that, he gave a short bark of laughter.

A knock came at his door. "I don't want to be disturbed."

"Pelchi is here to see you," Anna said from the other side of the door. She turned the knob and pushed it open and looked at him. "Not sure what's going on here," she said, "but he looks distraught."

Irene's husband. He had plenty to make him distraught. "Bring him in," Rowan said. "To bring you up to speed, there was a shooting and also a death." He filled her in, ending with, "And that's on top of Hogarth's father being murdered."

She gasped. "Oh my. I didn't know."

"I know. We have a team out searching the woods right now, hoping to find some evidence. I haven't heard from anybody. Outside of the fact that, so far, they haven't found anything."

"Let me go get Pelchi," she said. A few moments later she showed him into Rowan's office.

Rowan stood and shook the young man's hand. He motioned at a chair. "I'm sorry for your losses, Pelchi. I know this is a very difficult time for you."

"There's something you need to know."

Rowan watched him and waited.

"She killed him, you know?"

"She killed who?"

"Our son. Everybody said it was an accident, but it wasn't. Everybody said it was stress from her birth, but I know the truth." Pelchi took a deep breath and continued, "I came in one day, when she was screaming at the baby, beating on him. I tried to stop her, and she dropped him. With a whole lot more force than necessary." His face was hard, and his voice was hoarse. "If I'd gotten in just a few minutes earlier, I might have stopped her. But she killed our son. She killed *my* son."

Rowan sat down hard. "I did hear a suggestion during the investigation of why she committed suicide. Everybody said it was the loss of her son, but somebody suggested she might have been guilty of planning a murder-suicide." He didn't add in that the same rumor had said Pelchi himself might have been involved in that plan too.

Pelchi nodded. "She was very guilty," he said. "I don't think I could have lived with her any longer. We no longer shared a bed. I couldn't even look at her without seeing my dead son, and the look on her face was revulsion."

"Postpartum blues can act like that sometimes," Rowan said. "I wouldn't judge her too harshly, given that the baby was still so young, and she was too."

"I keep telling myself that," he said. "Honestly, I do. I tried not to judge her for it, but I keep seeing my son."

"Understandable," Rowan replied. "I'm sorry, and I'm sorry for your double loss. Because, without the one, it probably wouldn't have led to the other one."

Pelchi ran his arms up and down across his chest. "It's just so hard. I don't know who I should tell."

"You've told me now," Rowan said quietly. "Who do

you feel you need to tell?"

Pelchi stared out the window, his bottom lip trembling, then it firmed up, and he said, "I don't know. I know the news will devastate her parents. And her brother. And now that she's gone, I guess the question really is, is it necessary to spoil their view of who she was?"

"I'm not sure either," Rowan said. "I suggest what you should do is think about what you need to do to heal yourself, because that is what's most important now."

"We can't help her anymore," Pelchi said somberly. "Maybe we all failed her. She didn't get any help after the birth, and maybe she needed that."

Rowan nodded his head solemnly. "I do remember seeing her before she gave birth, and she looked absolutely delighted with the baby coming."

"She was," Pelchi said. "That's why I was so shocked when I saw the look on her face afterward. As if she was possessed."

Rowan's whole body became alert. "This look on her face. Did it still look like her features, or was it just dark and angry?"

"Dark, angry and twisted. I don't know," he said. "I was so worried about my poor son. I just shoved her away and brought him to the hospital, but it was already too late."

"Right," Rowan said. "I remember that. An accidental fall, wasn't it?"

"That's what they said," Pelchi said. "I think they just covered it up too."

"It's possible," Rowan declared, staring off in the distance. "And maybe it was just inconclusive."

Pelchi got up slowly and said, "Let me think about what to tell her parents. It's difficult."

"If you need help dealing with this," Rowan said, "please get it."

Pelchi shoved his hands in his pockets, hunched his shoulders and said, "I know it sounds terrible, but, now that she's gone, in a way, I feel like I'm free."

"I suppose in a way you are," Rowan said. "Take careful steps now. You need time to come to terms with the changes in your life."

He nodded. "It's like she was a dark cloud over my life for these last four months. I haven't slept. I've hardly even eaten. I mean, what do you do when everything you love suddenly takes a wrong turn?"

"I'm sorry," Rowan said. "It is always hard to deal with one death, much less two. But, when it's family and a child and brought on by somebody close to you, well ..."

Pelchi nodded and walked to the door. He turned toward Rowan and said, "Thanks."

Rowan stood, walked around the desk and escorted the young man back out to the waiting room. "You're welcome, although I didn't do anything," he said. "I just want to make sure you heal from this."

"I think I can now," he said and gave a wan smile. "It helped to tell someone." He walked out of the waiting room to the front doors.

Rowan turned and sucked all that confused, depressed, negative energy out of his office and out the door with the young man. Not to attach back to where it had come from but to separate to join the wind and to blow where it needed to go. Something he had to do often but had forgotten about recently.

Until Pelchi walked in, and Rowan got slammed with nasty, negative energy. So much anger and pain and guilt had been in that young man. But now, with Rowan having pulled most of that darkness from Pelchi's soul, Pelchi should be better.

Finally, with that done, he turned to see Anna watching him. He shrugged and said, "You know what I had to do."

"I do," she said with a half smile. "I just haven't seen you do it lately." She glanced at Pelchi's retreating back. "Is he okay?"

"He will be," Rowan said. "He's had a rough few months."

She nodded sympathetically and returned to her work. He headed back to his desk, picked up the phone and made calls about Phoenix's father. He had a lot of questions now. If only he could get some answers.

Interesting that Pelchi looked so much better now than when he went into the police station. Was Rowan doing energy work to help out the village? He was talented. He was powerful, but his power was wasted on the wrong things. Sitting here this past hour, drinking his coffee, the Supplier slowly watched the world go by, wondering what his next step was. Everything he'd seen so far showed him how Phoenix as the sacrifice had been the perfect choice.

But, at the same time, he didn't understand why Rowan was hanging around Phoenix. The Supplier didn't like unexpected surprises, and he hadn't liked to see them over there at Theo's when he'd barely had a chance to finish his work. Theo had deserved to suffer longer. And then later that evening at the Burning Fires? … That was a sacred place. To see her there was disturbing. And forced a change in his schedule. Something else he hated. He'd gotten greedy and had taken two for himself. That would never do.

The Elders came first.

The sacrifices were for the Elders. The victims were to keep the Supplier's own soul moving forward so he could keep up his work for the Elders.

He'd been one of the Chosen Ones, and something about Phoenix let him know she was as well. But had somebody else chosen her before him? The supplier could see some of the energy around her. It was how he determined which were his best victims and his best sacrifices. He could see the confusion and the pain, but he also saw the goodness and the light.

Striving to overcome and succeeding was pure gold.

The Supplier could appreciate that. The Elders would appreciate that. To have chosen somebody who had been beaten and had struggled and had risen over all their conflicts and strife was a much better sacrifice than an eighteen-year-old who had never faced a challenge in his life.

No, this woman was definitely his chosen sacrifice, but there was something else about her. Something he just couldn't put his finger on. The Supplier watched as the young man kept on walking away from the police station. Something was wrong about his walk too. As if a huge weight had been taken off his shoulders, he walked with a little more pep to his step.

The Supplier turned his gaze to the police station and frowned. He easily saw the negative energy flying out of the building, like somebody inside that station had helped this young man. Everybody was out to help people here. The Supplier was getting sick of it. How did he get people to stop being so nice and kind? What the hell was with that? The world was built on pain. How was it that nobody else could figure that out?

The Supplier had to study, understand his sacrifices to make sure they were worthy. Something he had yet to do with this young woman. She'd kept him at bay and he didn't like that. She was either very powerful with strong instincts … or maybe someone was helping her.

He needed to know more. Maybe he'd run a quick check at the police station and see who was inside.

CHAPTER 17

W HEN PHOENIX WOKE again, she felt much better. The
doctor and a nurse came in, and, after a complete
exam, Phoenix was helped to her feet. She walked around
slowly and nodded and smiled. The medical team spoke in a
mix of English with their native tongue, but most of it was in
English.

"So may I go to the washroom now?"

The nurse helped her to the small room, and Phoenix
went inside, closed the door, proceeded to use the facilities,
then washed her hands. She sucked in her breath and winced
when she tried to lift her sore arm.

When she opened the door, the doctor assessed her once
more and nodded. "You're looking just fine," he said matter-
of-factly. "Healing very well."

She beamed up at him. "I've always been a fast healer,"
she said in a glib tone.

He nodded but didn't say anything.

She was grateful he hadn't brought up the X-rays. The
last thing she wanted to do was discuss her childhood. That
she'd survived a nightmare was obvious. As she made her
way back to the bed, she sat down with a groan and said, "I
might be feeling better, but my shoulder is still sore."

"We'll put it in a sling," he said. "And we're keeping you
here a bit longer, but there is a good chance you can leave

later this afternoon. It will depend on how the rest of the afternoon goes."

She stared at him in surprise. "Really? That would be awesome."

"Maybe," he said. "I'm not promising it yet. We'll check on you in a few hours."

She smiled, sank back against the pillows and said, "Thank you. That would be great."

"As long as you aren't staying alone," he said. "I can't have you reinjuring your arm."

"Right," she said. "I was supposed to leave this morning on the bus. So I'm not sure where I'll stay."

"Let me talk to Rowan," the doctor said. "You rest now and keep healing."

A nurse came over and put her shoulder in a sling. The pain eased. Soon after the medical team left, Phoenix was served a hot lunch. She smiled in delight when she saw the food. "I *am* hungry," she said.

"We have orders to give you two dinners," the woman said with a frown.

As a quick explanation, Phoenix said, "I have somebody coming today."

The woman's face cleared. "Okay, good." She left a small tray with an extra serving.

Phoenix wasted no time. She had soup, a hot sandwich and steamed veggies. She worked her way through the first plate, set the dessert off to the side, poured milk in her tea and drank it. Then she switched out the empty plate for the second one. It was almost identical, and she had no problem polishing that off. With both plates empty now, and the desserts sitting waiting, she sank back on the bed with her tea and relaxed.

The extreme appetite was part of her healing process. She remembered in the past she always used to recycle everything in her mind to help her too—reframing, they called it. She called it trying to make lemonade from lemons. She could further heal herself by doing visualizations; she could heal others as well, by pouring energy out of various parts of her body. But to heal herself or others required energy. A lot of energy. Food was a weak source of energy but was less invasive than others, like taking energy from the people around her. It was the only way she'd survived the tortures of her childhood.

At one point, she had thought about killing herself. Well, if truth be told, she thought about it a lot. The memories were faint, just drifted in and out of her mind as she lay here.

Being only eleven years old had left her with just enough memory to get everything wrong. She hadn't been mature enough to understand that she'd always been so tormented and so in pain that everything was colored by these earliest of experiences for her.

She wanted to think the shooting was accidental, but she had no real way to justify that. She felt a presence and looked up to see Rowan in the doorway, holding her laptop. She gave him a bright smile. "I ate your lunch," she said, pointing at the tray with the two empty plates.

He laughed when he saw that. "Good," he said. "I told one of the nurses that I'd be here at lunchtime and to give you double. I knew you would be really hungry after being hurt."

"That was nice of you," she said, not sure what to make of his final remark.

"The food here is good," he said. He looked at her critically. "You're looking much better."

"There's a chance I can leave later today," she said. "I'm up. I'm mobile. Obviously I have to stay in town longer in order to heal, so no going home yet."

"And you're not allowed to be alone, I'm sure," he said shrewdly.

"No, the doctor made a point of saying that," she said honestly. "But, outside of the hotel, I have no other place to go."

"Unless I bring you home with me," he said. He put his hands on his hips and studied her. "But I don't know how much trouble you'll be."

"And why would I be trouble?" she challenged.

"Because you have been so far," he said with a laugh.

She wanted to shrug but knew it would hurt. She looked at him and her laptop and smiled. "Good," she said. "I wanted to research my family. Something I've avoided doing all my life."

"That might help," he said, placing the laptop on her thighs. "I requested more information on the cult files. They're being faxed over to me. As far as the original investigators are concerned, there were seven women, all dead, and your father died as well."

"Okay, well, that would put that to rest," she said. "What about all the kids?"

"Twelve children were found dead. You were the only one alive."

She stared at him. "Seriously?"

"You expected some to be alive, didn't you?" he asked curiously and sat down in the visitor chair. "According to the report, four of the twelve found dead were male."

"I don't remember those four," she said bluntly. "But I

do remember there being about a dozen of us."

"Would you have known though, if they were dressed like girls with long hair?"

"I don't know," she said. "Maybe not? I don't know. But it is sad if all of them are dead. That means my entire family is gone, which I'd assumed, but it seems more real now."

"Yes, and maybe that's okay too," he said. "This gives you a chance to start fresh."

"True," she said, but it worried away at her. "The day I was found, I could hear children crying."

"Are you sure?" he asked, leaning forward. "You have to consider all the nightmares and the times you heard children crying mixed up and blended into that night you were released from the compound."

"Father was shouting out orders, and I know all the mothers were rushing to grab up everybody."

"Your mother took you into the closet, didn't she?"

At that, Phoenix gave a bitter laugh. "She tried, but I saw the poison in her hand, and she told me it was time to leave. I knew what she was doing."

"Did she explicitly say she would kill you?"

"Of course not," she said. "But then my mother did nothing but follow my father's instructions."

"Right," Rowan said. "So chances are, all the women did die, and you have no way to get those answers."

"I don't know," she said slowly. "I don't have any reason or any proof, but it does seem to me somebody survived."

"Why is that?"

"Because I heard somebody calling out," she said, puzzled. "It's like I can hear them yelling at me."

"What are they yelling?"

"*You are not alone*," she said, a questioning tone in her

voice. Then she shook her head. "I really don't know. I'll have to think about it."

"That could have been anything," he said. "It could have been a cop telling you to fight whatever injuries you had. I don't know if you remember, but you were hospitalized. You were extremely malnourished. You had several broken bones, open wounds, welts all over your body …"

She stared at him, her eyes glazing over, going back in time. "I do remember some of it," she said. "I'd just had a major argument with my mother. Refusing to go into the closet. Fighting for my life. And she was telling me that I was almost dead anyway. I wouldn't last much longer, and this was the easiest way."

"I think she was correct in many ways," he said. "But the truth of the matter is, you are alive. You did survive. And whatever help you had since then, that helped you to deal with your trauma."

"I was dealing with the trauma while I was being trau-matized," she said gently. "I kept doing things, energy-wise, to stave off the pain, to stave off the physical damage. I don't know where or how I learned of it. But it seemed to help, so I kept doing it more and more."

"What do you mean?" he asked, straightening up. "You mean, like, using energy to heal?"

"Your own doctor just said I'm healing remarkably fast," she said with a crooked grin. "I could hear a voice in my head telling me what to do. As if I knew it instinctively but had forgotten and needed the nudge to remember."

"A voice in your head?"

"Sometimes a male angelic voice and other times a wom-an. Sometimes when I was screaming with agony, and other times when I was lying comatose. Often I'd call out to them, so I'd know I wasn't alone. Voices kept telling me it would be okay. Only it was never okay."

Rowan leaned forward. "I'm sorry. Your childhood must have been a living hell."

"It was." She gave him a wry look. "Like my father used to tell me. *Doesn't matter what we do to you, you'll always heal. You will always heal faster than normal.*"

"Maybe that was part of his fear and loathing of what he didn't understand about you."

"Yes, and yet he would call it love. His twisted version of love."

ROWAN DIDN'T KNOW how to tell her that a bunch of other inconsistencies were in the cult report that were bothersome. Not only had there been four male children found dressed up as females but also signs that another adult male had been around the compound. Just a few little things that the police couldn't reconcile. As in two shavers in two different bathrooms, both different styles with different shaving creams. No clothing was in one bedroom, whereas the bedroom where her father had slept with his massive king bed—big enough for however many sleeping partners he wanted to have—a lot of clothing had been found. Also a stockpile of arsenic and other poisonous liquids. All guaranteed to take out his entire clan. And yet, Rowan still couldn't get behind why there had been so much torture of this one child.

And then there was the fire, … something she didn't seem to remember.

It was one thing to have a case with no closure, but it was another to have a case with closure and a ton of unanswered questions. Had somebody else been involved in this? Had somebody else gotten off scot-free all these years? It was just a little too possible, and that bothered Rowan.

He glanced at Phoenix. She was now sitting up and looking around, getting a sense of time as she went vertical again. The doctor had released her, and Rowan would take her home to his place.

He smiled and said, "It's pretty warm outside. I've got your dirty clothes here. Do you want your sweater though?"

She looked at him, frowning at the bag he carried, and said, "It's likely covered in blood, isn't it?"

He nodded. "Yes, I imagine it is."

She carefully slipped to her feet and straightened up. When she managed to take a couple steps, she turned to give him a brilliant smile. "See? I'm as good as gold."

He shook his head. "Not quite," he said. "I have foot-wear for you, if you want to get them on."

She looked at her shoes, sitting on the floor and said, "Tying those things doesn't look like fun."

He dropped the bag beside him and bent down, rear-ranged the tongue, stretching out laces so they stayed tied but open. He lifted one up. "See if you can put your foot in that."

She slid her right foot in and then took a few experi-mental steps. "That's perfect," she said in surprise. "I've never worn them like this."

"As a kid I wouldn't wear them any other way," he said with a chuckle. "Anything to save me the work of tying them up." He fixed the left shoe accordingly and held it out for her so she could step right into it.

With both shoes on, she took several more steps and said, "I feel almost as good as new."

"Except for the bandage and the sling on your shoulder," he said in a dry tone. "Are you hungry?"

She brightened up. "Absolutely," she said. "Do you have food at home? Or can we pick up something and take it home?" And then she thought about it for a moment. "Depending on how far away you live, maybe we should eat in town."

He laughed. "I don't live far away at all," he said. "And I have food at home already."

"Good," she said and walked to the door. "Then let's get out of here."

He waved at one of the nurses in the hallway and escorted Phoenix out of the hospital. Outside, she took several long, deep cleansing breaths of fresh air.

Rowan smiled. "I guess you don't like hospitals much."

"Hardly been in any," she said cheerfully. "At least not that I remember."

"Right." He remembered the X-rays he'd taken photos of. "Rough childhood. You must have hated the other kids."

"Maybe," she said. "Hate is probably too strong a word. I was more concerned with healing and staying alive than expending the energy to focus on anything else."

"You did say you used energy to heal."

She nodded. "I know it was something I read. One of the books my father had. I snuck in there one day and found a book on energy healing. I figured if he had the book, it must be true," she said with a self-deprecating laugh. "What a fool."

"Not if it helped."

"Good point, and it did, as did my virtual friends," she said and turned to look at him. "What way? Which vehicle?"

He pointed to his cruiser hidden on the other side of

several vehicles. "We're going this way."

She walked along happily at his side, apparently just delighted to be out of the hospital. She hadn't fought being in there, but being free was a whole different story.

"What else did you learn from his books?"

"Way more than I wanted to about sex," she said with a snicker. "He had several books on positions and esoteric beliefs of sexual energy. I was pretty young for that, but, if I had stayed much longer, I'm not sure I would have been innocent for very long."

"Were you ever raped?" He hated to ask, but that question that had been deep in his thoughts ever since he realized the extent to which she had been tortured.

"No," she said. "I think he was waiting for my menstruation to start. Of course that didn't save me from being forced to take care of his needs in other ways."

"Bastard," he said under his breath.

"Well, he could have waited for a hell of a long time for that," she said. "I think all my injuries pushed my puberty way back. My cycle didn't start until I was almost seventeen."

"That is pretty late, isn't it?"

"It's on the late end of the spectrum," she said. "Which was probably a good thing for me."

"Were other girls raped?"

"I don't think they thought it was rape," she replied, joining him in his vehicle. "When you are programmed to believe this will happen and that it will be beautiful, fun and all the women before you do this on a regular basis, it just becomes one more stage of your growth. One they were quite eager to achieve because the other women were all much higher in the food chain. I wasn't having my menses, no matter how much my father really wanted me to. It was one more thing for them to hold over me."

Something odd was in her voice. He studied her for a long moment and turned on the engine, reversed out of his parking spot and took the next couple corners. "Did you do anything to stop your menses?"

An odd silence followed.

He looked over to see her looking at him under her hooded gaze. "Interesting that you would ask that," she said. "I wondered if it was a natural side effect of the torture or of the healing energy I used to try to stay alive. But I was only eleven so how would I know to do that? It's not like I read anything on that topic."

"While your body would require a certain amount of energy to get through puberty," he said, "maybe you needed all of that energy to heal?"

"Maybe," she said. "I know that mentally I was telling my body to not take that next step because I knew what was coming."

"You saw the other girls go through it and saw they were happy and had that same programming. Why is it you didn't think it would happen the same way for you?"

"Because nothing was ever the same for me," she said. "I figured it was another way for him to humiliate me, another way for him to hurt me."

"He would have," Rowan said, his voice low and deep. "He was already a sick bastard. That would have been just one more avenue for him."

"I don't know that it would have made any difference to me," she said. "I was terrified of getting pregnant though."

"So, you knew all about biology?"

"I'd helped several women have babies," she said. "I saw

the pain and torment they went through. Sometimes they were a little too free with their words because they were in such pain. I certainly understood it was a result of the sex act. I wouldn't do anything that would put myself in a position to have a child. That would give him yet another way to hurt me." She turned to stare out the window.

He watched her profile, wondering yet again how she had ever survived what she had been through, both physically and emotionally.

"You're trying to figure out if I'm normal, aren't you?" she asked suddenly.

He shook his head as he kept his gaze on the road, then turned to look into her eyes for a second.

"I doubt I am," she admitted. "I don't know what normal is."

"Your life since leaving the compound seems as close to normal as anything," he said, then added, "At least, I think. I can't imagine what your recovery was like."

"It was as normal as I could make it," she said. "I don't know …" Then her voice broke off.

"You don't know what?" He headed down the long street that would take them the last couple turns to his house. He lived at the end of a road and had four acres to himself, and it was all fenced in. He had several dogs he kept around as pets, but they were also great guard dogs and kept a lot of the wildlife away.

When she stayed quiet, he said, "I've been seeing energy since puberty. That's why I was curious about the puberty thing."

"Oh." She looked at him in surprise. "So, you started seeing auras and colors and energy around you then, not before?"

"Not that I know of. I don't remember seeing it, but then, around eleven or twelve, I started to see all kinds of things. Some of it was pretty confusing. Sometimes the world would just be Technicolor, and I wouldn't understand why, and then I could blink several times, and it would go back to normal. But then sometimes I turned my head, looked again, and it would be all bright."

"Interesting," she murmured. "For me, I was working at energy stuff since about eight, when I was into reading his books. I was already pretty broken by then though, so maybe that started earlier, just not as focused as I was after the books."

"At eight, it's amazing you understood."

"I don't think I did," she said. "There were lots of pictures. The text was about pulling energy from your feet down, from your hand, circulating it through your body, through the seven centers—asking for guidance, asking for help, asking for healing, asking for love and trying to offer life. My mother was big on love."

He once again turned to look at her. Her voice was so devoid of emotion he had to wonder what she meant. "Meaning, she had no love?"

"I think her version of love was very conflicted," she said. "Maybe confused. I was her daughter, and she professed to love me, but she was also very much in love with my father, who was abusing me. So I don't know how that makes sense to anybody."

"Hence the conflict in her," he said.

"Exactly."

"Did she ever give you anything to keep as a child?"

"Sure. The letter," she said. "When my father found out, he was very, very angry. It's the only time I ever saw him lash out at her."

"Well, that's one reason why she didn't fight him much," he said. "Fear is a great intimidator." Rowan pulled into his driveway and shut off the engine. But he didn't open the door and get out; instead he twisted in the seat and said, "I thought your father gave it to you."

"Yeah, well, he took it from me," she explained. "And gave it back to me years later."

"Do you know why?"

"Because he said I was the only one who could own it." She shrugged and laughed. "I figured there had to be some trick to it. It would burn me or something."

"Interesting." He opened the door and said, "Do you need help getting out?"

She shook her head and hopped out.

He was surprised at her agility. The nimbleness of her movements. If that had been him, he'd have been feeling like he'd been hit by a truck. Instead she was already walking toward his front door. "I saw one thing in the police file. A suspicion there might have been a second adult male on the place."

She froze at the bottom step, her hand on the railing, and turned to look at him. "What?"

He nodded. "The cops found two razors in two different bathrooms and two different shaving creams. Clothing in one bedroom and no clothing in the other."

She racked her brain. "I only remember seeing my father there." She stared at a point over his head. "I don't know if it's safe to trust my memories though."

He waited calmly, watching to see if anything would shake loose from her brain. A second male would be huge. "It's possible he had visitors or family. Maybe other people in the cult he looked up to?"

Her gaze shuttered.

And he realized she had remembered something else. He waited, hoping she'd share. And then she sighed and said, "There's a tendril of a memory, but I can't quite figure out what it is. It's just out of reach." She gazed at him in frustration. "But it has something to do with another male."

"I hope you can find it," he said. "The police worry somebody got away scot-free."

"Even if they find out, what difference will it make?" she asked curiously. "I'm sure there's a statute of limitations, and he's well past that point."

"I'm not sure about that. Not if he's the one who shot you just this week. But it would be nice to have closure on this issue. All those children, whose hand did they die by? Because an awful lot of dead bodies were there. If this second male had a hand in it, he could be tried—if not criminally, then in a civil suit—as part of the machine that drove those women to do whatever they did."

"I didn't remember anything about that until you said something now." She laughed. "My father was nothing but crazy."

"Exactly," he said.

"I used to think maybe I was crazy too," she said in that same conversational tone. She went up the last few steps to the large veranda across the front of his log house. She stopped, looked around and smiled. "This is such a perfect home."

"In what way?" he asked, unlocking the front door. The dogs wagged their tails, jumping about, then bolted around him, and when they caught sight of her, they stopped. Not a sound came out of them, and their butts hit the floor. They just stared up at her. Both were rescues, and neither one showed aggression, but neither were they friendly. Strange that they no longer jumped and barked for joy at having seen him, as if in shock at seeing her.

"What the hell?" he murmured. He turned to look at her and asked, "Do you always have this effect on animals?"

CHAPTER 18

S HE DROPPED HER gaze to the dogs and, in an even slower movement, dropped into a crouch beside them. She held out her hand, but neither dog moved—not a tail, not a nostril. When she brushed her hand closer toward them, they both leaned in, and then both gave heavy sighs, lay down on their backs and gave her their bellies.

She heard Rowan whisper, "What the …" above her.

She gently scratched one dog, then the other, wishing her other arm was back in operation so she could handle both at once. When they gave another round of deep, heavy sighs and seemed to relax even further, she scratched their ears, whispering the whole time about what beautiful animals they were.

She glanced up at Rowan and said, "I've never really had much to do with animals."

But his gaze went deep as he stared at her. She wasn't sure he believed her or not.

She shrugged. "Maybe it's my energy?"

He stepped over the dogs and went into the house. She realized she'd upset him but didn't know what she was supposed to do about it. She straightened back up and called the dogs in. They came in, reverting to the happy puppies they'd been when they first arrived.

She whispered to them, "Go say hi to Rowan." She shut

the door and turned to watch as the dogs bolted to Rowan, jumping up and around him to say hi again.

She leaned against the front door, wondering. She hadn't been around many dogs, but she did know birds often sat on her shoulder or beside her. She could hold out her hand, and a squirrel, in time, would crawl up. She never bothered taking any pictures of it because she didn't know what other people could do or not do. As far as she understood, this was normal. She talked to them as if they were the same as she was. She'd always communicated with animals that way.

Only Rowan's reaction showed her that, for his dogs, obviously part of his family, this wasn't normal behavior. Not a great start to staying at his house. She knew she would have to apologize, she just didn't know what for. And that made the apology seem awfully empty.

She glanced around at his beautiful home—a huge fireplace, a great big open living room, open dining room and an open kitchen.

She slipped out of her shoes and walked barefoot across the floor toward him. "I know I'm supposed to apologize," she said. "It's the thing to do. But I'm not sure why."

He gave a half snort and turned to look at her.

She nodded. "I know that means that the apology doesn't mean much but …" She looked down at the dogs and smiled. "I do sometimes see this reaction in other animals around me. I just haven't been around dogs much."

"What other animals?" he asked curiously.

"Well, sometimes, if I sit still long enough, a squirrel will run up my arm. Birds will sit on my shoulder. I've had deer walk up to me, and even a beaver lie down beside me," she said. "But some things you just don't know if it's normal or not. I worked at a university with tons of noise and kids, and, although I'd hear the birds, and I could see them land on the window when I was there, I didn't know others couldn't see them."

"Couldn't see the birds?" he asked, jumping on her for emphasis.

She groaned. "Couldn't hear. Couldn't see. I don't know," she said. "For all I know, the birds weren't real."

"We're just getting through layers and layers of stuff with you, aren't we?" he said. He turned his back on her and pulled the coffeemaker across the counter.

"I've never tried to hide anything," she said. "At least nothing important."

"I guess that's the problem, isn't it? We don't really know what's important until we bring it out in the open."

"I've never had a long-term boyfriend," she said. "Yet animals have always liked me. Sometimes I wondered if they were even real. Once I put my hand through one, and it just stayed there and stared at me."

He slowly turned to her. "A ghost bird?"

"I don't know. The next day, the same bird was back. When I went to do the same thing, it was real and hopped up on my fingers."

He spun back, ground the coffee and finished making a pot. Then he pivoted, leaned against the counter, his hands braced there, and she joined him. "A premonition?"

"Maybe," she said with a shake of her head. "I didn't understand it at the time but maybe."

"Have you seen any others?"

She took a deep breath and nodded. "Yes."

"When?"

"When I was a child. When I was still at the cult. I remember seeing the cops come into the house, and I went to my mother and told her that we had to leave. I told her what I'd seen. She looked terrified and disappeared. For the longest time after I was rescued, I figured I must have caused the death of everybody because, if I hadn't told her what I'd seen, she wouldn't have thought it would happen and wouldn't have made preparations for it. The next day the police did come. By then the cult was prepared, and everyone died," she said, tears slowly leaking from her eyes. "Do you know what it's like to hold that memory—that guilt—for all these years?"

He gently folded her into his arms. "It was not your fault," he said roughly. "Even if you did have a premonition of the cops coming, you were eleven."

"If I hadn't said anything …" she said, tilting her head back so she could look up at him. "If I hadn't said anything, they'd probably be alive today."

"I don't know about that," he said. "The police were on to him. Your father was shot several times. Chances are, without advanced notice, he would have used all the women and children as a defense and gotten them killed anyway. Several other instances of cults like that ended with multiple family members dying in mass suicide, whether by cop or by poison."

She wiped her eyes. "I keep telling myself that I can't go back and change anything. But it's all tied to throwing that damn letter into the lava."

"I saw you reach your arm back and throw it," he said cautiously. "Are you telling me that you didn't? I thought that was done with."

She looked at him in surprise. "Oh." She stared down at her hands. "I remember pulling my arm back, then the pain … Did I throw it?" She frowned. "Where's my clothing?"

He motioned to the front door, the bag he'd brought in. She grabbed it and brought the bag to the kitchen table and opened it. Her T-shirt, leggings, socks and sweater were all there. She straightened it all out as best as she could with one hand. She checked the pockets. But it wasn't there. She sighed with joy. "Maybe I did do it."

"Your purse is here," he said and pointed to it. "You want me to dump it?"

She nodded. "Let's find out for sure."

He upended the purse, using his arms to stop everything from rolling away.

As he removed the leather bag from the pile, she said, "I don't see it."

He separated the items a little more. Her passport was here. Her wallet was here. As was a pad of paper, various lipsticks, lip gloss. He wasn't even sure what half of this stuff was, it just looked like makeup.

He picked up the pad of paper, and she gave an odd cry, plucked it from his hand and flipped through the pages. As she did so, another sheet of paper fell to the pile in front of them. She snatched it up, looked at it and held it up to him. "I guess not," she whispered. "It's still here."

"We attached it to a rock," he said. "Where's the rock?"

She shook her head. "I have no idea. And did we do it, or did we just think we did it?"

"Like Irene. That would mean a shared premonition again," he said. "And that's not something I really like to think about."

"I don't believe it matters," she said with a broken laugh. "Because look at us. That damn letter is still here."

ROWAN STARED AT the letter with loathing. "That thing is enchanted."

She chuckled. "Well, if it is, it's enchanted with something I've never seen before."

"How much do you know about enchantment?"

She shrugged. "Only what I've read. And what started as a curiosity as a young girl has become a fascination ever since. I've read widely."

"Do you know people who work in this industry?"

"I know *of* them," she said quietly. "I've never contacted anybody. I've never associated with any of them or had private consultations with them."

"Why not?" That question seemed to surprise her.

"Why would I? Most of them would need some history or background. Information I don't share well. Most would see things I don't really want anyone else to see. Plus a lot of charlatans are out there. How would I find those who are truly gifted?"

"So you do believe in all that psychic stuff," he said.

"How can you even ask that after Irene," she cried out. "We saw her flung off the damn cliff and then reappear." She motioned at the coffee. "Do you mind if we get coffee now?"

He turned toward the machine. "Sorry. I was just wondering out loud if we could call anybody for help."

"Maybe," she said. "Didn't you contact somebody already?"

"Yes," he said. "He was supposed to send somebody who was nearby, but I haven't heard anything yet."

Just then came a knock at the door. He looked over at her, handed her a cup of black coffee. "We'll get the fixings in a minute."

She waved him off. "I like it black."

He opened the front door, aware she had come behind him and stood there too. In front of him stood a six-foot-plus male, with huge shoulders, arms crossed over his chest and almost silver hair.

Rowan spoke first. "Hello. May I help you?"

"Name's Grayse," he said.

Rowan's eyebrows shot up at the name.

The man nodded. "Right. Stefan sent me."

He brushed past Rowan and stopped in the living room. The dogs came running, but, instead of barking, they greeted him like a long-lost friend. He bent down and gently cuddled them for a few moments while he eyed Phoenix.

"So, you are her," he said.

"I'm who?" she asked, a touch of defiance to her voice.

"John Hopkins' only surviving daughter," he said, straightening up. He shoved his hands into the pockets of his jeans and rocked back on his heels. "I was there."

"You were where?"

"At the compound when the place was raided."

Rowan reached out to catch Phoenix as she faltered. Coffee splashed on the floor, and he glared at Grayse. "A little more finesse would help."

Grayse snatched the coffee cup from her hand. "Let's go sit down."

In the living room, Phoenix sat on a love seat, and Rowan sat beside her. He had yet to clean up the coffee spill on the floor, but Grayse seemed to have that in hand as he walked into the kitchen and grabbed a paper towel, came back and cleaned it up. "What kind of a name is *Grace* for a man?"

"Well, there's no *C* in it," he said cheerfully. "It's G-R-A-Y-S-E."

"It's still an odd name."

"It is, indeed," he replied. "However, that doesn't change the fact I was one of the psychics who directed the police to save Phoenix. Along with Stefan—in energetic form."

Rowan didn't dare touch the subject of Stefan in an energetic form. "Psychics and saving. Stefan didn't mention anything about this," Rowan said. "You better take us back to the beginning and explain."

"Glad to. I'm happy to see Phoenix is doing well. We weren't sure she would be cognizant of anything back then."

"What do you mean?" Rowan asked and glanced down at Phoenix.

"She was in shock. We didn't know if it was the shock from the raid, the amount of poison her mother had managed to get in her, or everything that had gone on just before then. Her body appeared to be severely burned over a good forty percent of it, and, considering that, for her to still be walking was a miracle. She was sent to the burn unit immediately."

Phoenix made a startled sound.

Grayse smiled at her gently. "But you didn't stay long, as you were healing beautifully. You had already started the healing process yourself. Good job, by the way. We don't get too many young psychics like you who can heal so beautifully. But, then again, we also don't get too many who have been through the kind of trauma that required that level of healing."

"What made you look for her?" Rowan asked.

"We knew a lot of energy was coming from one particular part of town. Stefan had been called psychically to help a young child heal from horrific injuries somewhere in that region several times, but Stefan never could find the location of the abusive home," Grayse said. "We had no real way to know what was going on. I would wake up sometimes with really strong premonitions of children dressed all in white, laughing and having fun, and yet such darkness came with the premonition.

"I could never figure out what it was. I drove the neighborhood for years, but I couldn't pinpoint where all this energy was coming from. As soon as I'd get a premonition, I would get into my vehicle and drive, trying to trace it. But the trouble with a premonition is, it's a forward vision. I would never have any energy to track it. I tried meditation. I contacted several other psychics to see if we could zero in on what was going on. But we never located this hot spot."

"Until?"

"Until Phoenix reached out to Stefan—and Maddy, an incredible healer who works closely with Stefan. This last time they managed to loop me in to help locate her," he said smoothly. "Obviously she doesn't remember doing so."

Phoenix shook her head. "I cried out for help to anybody who would listen, and I had two people who helped to heal me, but I didn't have names or faces, just a feeling when they were there helping," she said. Her voice was faint but growing with strength. "I often called out. I didn't expect anybody to respond."

"Sometimes it is like that. When you don't really believe anybody is out there. It depends how much power is in the energy you send out. And somebody also has to be listening. Think of it like a receiver. You can send out a signal, but somebody has to receive it. I saw premonitions, but they were ahead of time, so I was of little help until Stefan looped me in, and I could send out inquiries. Then a friend men-

DALE MAYER

tioned some weird disturbance came from his town and
wondered if I could help him narrow it down."

"But you were already trying, weren't you?"

"I was," he said. "But I went to the cops this time. One I
had worked with a couple times, and I told him that I
needed to find the person sending out energetic cries for
help, but I had no way to locate them. I wanted him to tell
me what areas of town I would find families being watched
by the cops or where foster care or social services were
looking. He told me there were just too many. And, in most
cases, they never found anything wrong." Grayse stopped for
a moment to collect his thoughts.

"In one of my premonitions I finally figured out I saw
schoolbooks. Not normal schoolbooks though. They looked
like religious schoolbooks, and I talked to my friend and
asked if he could tell me who was being homeschooled in the
area. He laughed and told me that he didn't know, as no
rules or regulations governed homeschooling. I thought that
was a terrible shame. But together we managed to get a little
more information as to some of the homeschool groups in
town. I walked to a couple locations just to wander around
the outside, so I could check out the energy, but I never saw
anything and realized we had somebody living completely
under the grid. Likely a religious group.

"When I talked to my friend about that added detail, he
told me of a place they had heard rumors about, and every
time they went to check on it, only a couple women were
there. Raising their families together. When I got the
address, I drove by and knew it was the place. But I had to
come up with proof. About six days later I saw the premonition of the poisonings and the mass suicide. But, even then,
the authorities couldn't just move in on the compound. I

214

had to have more than that. Not just a suspicion."

Phoenix looked at him. "Nobody ever came."

"No," he said. "Obviously food came in and out of that compound, so I kept track of deliveries. I parked myself in the shadows for days. Finally a group of women headed into town to do some shopping. They wore their white dresses and went into one of the grocery stores. They came out with quite a bit of food. They went to three stores but always very quietly. Didn't say much about what they needed and left. When they were gone, I asked the storekeepers about them and was told they came like clockwork, always paid, never spoke, and the owners had no problem with them. I asked if they had any children with them, and one said sometimes they had a couple but most of the time none."

"What did you do then?" Rowan asked. "Because a couple women shopping is hardly grounds for a police investigation."

"Exactly," he said. "Except, when I approached the group to speak to them, one of the women appeared terrified. I asked her if she needed help because she looked like she wanted to escape, but two women from their little group grabbed her by the arm and took her away."

Rowan heard a startled gasp from Phoenix and turned to look at her. "One of the women disappeared, didn't she?"

She nodded. "They told me that she died. That God had called her home."

Grayse's face turned dark. "I contacted the cops and said I thought we had a captive situation, maybe a kidnapping. But I didn't understand all the details. I told him what I saw. I had also taken a picture of the women's faces. The cops ran them through facial recognition and found that, years ago, all three women had dropped off the face of the Earth as far as their families were concerned. The cops then went to the property. I warned them about the poison. About a chance of a mass killing. They went in with a full SWAT team."

Rowan made a choking sound at the back of his throat. He knew what it took to get something like that going. But then to have three women missing for that long, and one obviously terrified and looking to escape, maybe that had been enough grounds. He probably could have gotten that done through his office too.

"You said you could feel the energy I was sending out," Phoenix said to Grayse. "How long was I sending it out?"

"A couple years, I think Stefan said," he said apologetically. "If we could have pinpointed what was going on earlier, I could have saved you a lot of pain."

She sagged on the couch. "Wow. I tried so hard to contact anybody out there, to believe somebody was listening to me, and … you were," she said in astonishment.

"Yes," he said. "By the time we were alerted to the growing strength in your voice, a few of us were caught up in what was going on. Again we had to play by the rules of the police though."

She nodded her head. "You said you were there the day of the raid?"

He nodded. "Yes."

"You know for sure my father is dead?"

He looked at her in surprise but gave a definitive nod. "Not only am I sure because of seeing him but I also checked for a pulse, and he was definitely gone. His chest was pretty much blown apart by bullets. He wasn't coming back. And, yes, I can see how, in your mind, that might be something he was capable of."

"Was a second man there?" Rowan asked.

"Not at the time," Grayse said. "There was always concern about that because we did see signs of a second male."

"Did you find all the women?"

"Twelve children, seven women, and one grave with one woman. That was the one I had seen in town."

Phoenix turned her gaze out the window as Rowan asked her, "Were you around when she was murdered?"

She nodded slowly. "I think I saw her afterward in a vision. She looked so peaceful. She was lying on a bed with her hands folded, and our father kept telling us that she had chosen to go home to God. She was surrounded by candles, and strange symbols were painted on her gown. Just like Hogarth's father ..." She twisted about and looked wordlessly at Rowan.

"Shit. Another connection to Iceland. So he probably poisoned her?" Rowan turned with a look back at Grayse and filled him in on Theo Hogarth's case. "On the surface the connections are slim but if, with this piece of information ..."

"I wonder how many other women are buried on that property?" Phoenix asked.

"Do you suspect more?" Grayse asked. "I know they did a search, but they didn't find any proof that other bodies were there."

Rowan studied her. "What's the matter?"

"I often worried I was killing some of the others. Because I was always injured, so I always needed energy, and I didn't have enough myself, so I pulled energy from people," she said, for want of a better explanation. "Wherever there was energy, I took it to try to heal. I know it's wrong of me, but I didn't know it at the time. After seeing the dead woman's vision, I wondered if I'd had a hand in her death."

Grayse, with a wave of his hand, brushed that aside. "You were in terrible pain, and you were being tortured," he said. "Anybody would have granted you that energy."

"Are you sure? I might have taken too much." She chewed her bottom lip in worry.

"You can put that to rest," he said gently. "She was poisoned."

CHAPTER 19

PHOENIX SAGGED IN relief. "I've carried that one with me for a long time. I knew what I was doing was necessary, but I also knew I wasn't supposed to take from other people," she murmured, looking from Rowan to Grayse. "I knew it was wrong, but I couldn't stop myself."

"It's only wrong if you take so much you kill them," Grayse said. "In this case, as a child taking energy from an adult, you didn't. And neither could you have because it generally takes permission for somebody to do that or an incredible amount of energy to override the other person's will."

"What do you mean by *permission?*" Rowan asked. "This is getting more confusing. I understand Phoenix was tortured. She healed extremely fast because she accessed other people's energies to help her and, in turn, created more torment for herself because then they kept pushing her limits to see how much she could take."

Grayse winced. "Right. Don't we just love the evil human mind-set," he said. "We did wonder if we'd find other graves, but we saw no sign of them. And I don't think the dogs ever found anything on the property."

"Maybe not," she said, "but I wonder if anybody checked the basement."

Grayse leaned forward slowly. "There was no basement,

Phoenix. None at all."

"Yes, there was," she said. "At least I remember a basement." She turned her gaze inward. "We had to go outside to get there though, so maybe not."

Grayse stood and frowned at her. "You mean, like a bomb shelter?"

She nodded. "I think so. Something was definitely down there. And it was pretty big inside."

"So, how about a trip back to that property, and let's take another look? It would be nice if we could tidy up some more loose ends. We have an awful lot of missing women in the US. If one happens to still be there, surely a trip to the property is worth it," Grayse said persuasively.

"Not to mention the fact you'd be safer there than here," Rowan said. "Although you're likely too injured to fly."

Grayse looked at her shoulder, frowned and said, "You were shot?"

She lifted her head, startled. "How do you know that?"

"I've seen bullet holes before."

She gasped. "But you haven't seen my shoulder, so how can you say that?"

"Maybe not," he said, chuckling, "but I can see through a bandage."

"Do you have X-ray eyes?" she demanded.

"Not quite," he said. "I have some medical-based intuitive skills. I can see wounds, and, when I say *see*, I mean see them in my mind. And that's definitely a bullet hole. Somebody shot you. Who?" He turned his gaze to Rowan.

"We don't know," Rowan replied. "A geologist was with us and died in the lava field at the same time, and we don't know if he was shot, pushed or jumped."

Phoenix got up, walked over to the kitchen table and

came back with her letter. "Ever seen anything like this?" She held it out for Grayse to look at.

Grayse took it in his hand and gasped at the shock. "My God," he said. "Where did you get this?"

"My mother gave it to me initially. My father took it away, and then he gave it back to me not too long before the raid," she said. "I came here specifically to throw it into the Burning Fires. My father named me Phoenix Rising, saying I was born to rise from the ashes. And, as a punishment, or a part of my training, he consistently burned me so I could become accustomed to the feeling, and so I would rise again."

"The purpose of throwing this into the lava is what?"

She took a deep breath. "It's for me to walk away. Because that's part of my childhood. It's part of whatever it was my father belonged to. My father was a psychic or at least could burn flames at the end of his fingers."

Her news seemed to have the effect of a bomb. Grayse sat back down again and stared at her and then ever-so-slowly he nodded. "That would explain why I couldn't always pick up your energy," he said. "Because somebody was shielding it. Somebody was shielding the compound. We had no way to know. It never occurred to us that somebody was actively doing that. We just figured whoever was calling out was too weak to get through to us."

"Which is quite true," she said. "I was, most of the time."

"Did your father know what you were doing?" Rowan asked. "Did he have any idea you were sending out messages and using other people's energies?"

"Who knows what my father knew or believed," she said. "He had diaries. Lots of them. He used to keep a running journal of everything that happened. He said it would be important one day."

"And where would he keep those?"

She turned to look at him. "In the basement. With Uncle." She clapped a hand over her mouth as she stared wide-eyed at the two men. "He was always there too. He was Father's brother."

"I THINK YOU should go find the bomb shelter," Rowan said after they'd spent an hour going over and over the details. "Things are bad here. And you're injured, but there is no reason you can't fly now or in a day or two. Go sort this out. So that you'll be a whole human at the end of the day."

She looked at him and said, "Only if you come."

He raised his eyebrows at that. "I have a job here," he said gently.

"Yes, you do," she said. "But you're not alone. And other people can take your job for a few days."

"A few days?"

She shrugged. "You know as well as I do that whatever is going on affects both of us. And I think it affected both of us from back when I was a child."

"I'm not part of your childhood," he said. "Grayse is."

"But I don't think it can be separated now." At least she didn't think it could.

"Why?" Rowan asked in confusion. "I don't have any of the abilities you do."

"That's not true," she said. "You're keeping your chief of police alive, aren't you?"

Those words were like a soft punch to his stomach. His breath whooshed out, and he sagged on the couch, staring at her. "No, I'm not," he denied. Then he groaned, adding, "Maybe a little." He turned to look at Grayse. "My boss shot himself in the head," he said. "He's been in a coma ever since."

Grayse nodded. "An awful lot of psychic energy is happening here," he said. "Some of it is pretty ugly."

"Suicide season," Rowan said, his voice harsh. "As soon as the lava starts flowing every spring, we end up with people coming to commit suicide."

"Maybe the energy is attracting people of that mind-set," she said, looking at Grayse. "Is there anything we can do to stop that?"

He raised an eyebrow as he repeated, "*We?*"

She shrugged. "I've been doing this stuff all my life. Rowan has too, to a certain extent. But let me explain what's happened since I arrived here."

She told Grayse everything that had gone on since her arrival. "None of this is normal," she admitted. "I just came to throw that letter into the lava. I wanted a new beginning. A new start. I wanted a chance to get rid of the only thing I was given by my father."

"There has to be other ways to destroy it than coming all the way here."

"My father was from here," she said quietly. "He said the paper itself was from here. And, if you think I haven't tried to destroy it, you're wrong. I've tried to burn it. I've put all kinds of things on it, like acid, vinegar. I've held it over open flames on a stove, and nothing ever, *ever* touches it. The only thing I could figure to do was to throw it in the lava and let the lava consume it. If, by chance, it was not destroyed, the lava would take it into the bowels of its fire, and nobody else would get a hold of it."

"So, was this just a symbolic gesture for you?" Grayse asked. "Or is there more to it?"

"It was important to my father," she admitted. "Another reason I want to destroy it. Like he tried to destroy me."

"Why did he give it back to you?"

"He said I was the only one strong enough to wield it. I figured that meant I was the only one strong enough to destroy it. And I thought we did, but ..." She explained what happened earlier, when they wrapped it around a rock, only to find it in her purse after she'd been shot.

"Interesting," Grayse said. "Are you against going back to the US for a few days? I know it's a long trip, but you only have to be there a day or two, three tops, and then come back here and take care of the letter."

"Or I take care of this first," she said with a nod at the letter now in her hand. "And then I go home via that property."

"Do you think you can?"

She frowned. "I'm not sure. Do you think I have to put everything in my childhood to rest first? I've deliberately avoided going back to New Mexico. Since moving to Seattle, that's been home. I can't say I want to travel to the place of my nightmares."

Grayse nodded. "If there's more to find on that property, then I think the answer to that question is yes. And then you can come back here to his hometown ... and finish this off." He looked over at Rowan. "Have you looked up her family tree?"

"Yes," Rowan replied. "I only found a grandfather and her father, both locals here. Her grandfather committed suicide in the lava way back when, and her father apparently went off his rocker. I didn't find any mention of a brother.

Her father disappeared from this area soon after his father's death. As he'd been difficult to be around, the locals were happy to see him gone."

"And her mother?"

"I haven't had a chance to do any research into her mother's side of the family yet."

"I hate unfinished business," Grayse said. "It has a way of coming back and biting you in the ass." He looked over at Phoenix. "Please do this in the right order. Let's go back to the compound. Do what we need to do to close it all up, put an end to it. Then, if you still feel that strongly, you can come back here and put that piece of strange material, your letter, whatever you want to call it, in the lava. Where it can stay forever."

She nodded. "Fine, but I don't want to be at the compound long. And I'm not going alone. I have enough nightmares. I'm either going with Rowan and you and anybody else who might need to come, or I'm not going at all."

Grayse nodded. "Done on my part. Rowan, what about you?"

He groaned. "If you insist, but we have to be back here in *five* days. That's all the time I can give to this."

"Done." Grayse stood. "We'll leave for the compound in the morning."

THE UNUSUAL ENERGY brought the Supplier here. He sat outside Rowan's house, just close enough to see the stranger arrive. Multiple energies circled the man's head, as if he was in contact with many others at the same time. Interesting character. The Supplier mentally wondered if this was someone to look at closer, then decided the dangerous aura around him would be too much trouble.

Rowan he knew well. But this new man was an unknown. Yet the two together spelled trouble. And the Supplier didn't need anyone interfering in his plans at this late stage. The Elders were rumbling. The Supplier needed to give them their offering soon. He already knew she was no longer at the hospital. He'd gone to her hotel only to find she'd been checked out.

That left Rowan's house. And the Supplier had found her there.

CHAPTER 20

O NCE UPSTAIRS ROWAN lowered Phoenix's suitcase, opened the door to the left and showed her the room. "Hopefully this will be okay."

She raised her eyebrows and said, "It'll be lovely. Thank you. Besides, it's not the hospital."

He gave her a wry smile. "True, it's not the hospital, but it might not be quite as comfortable as the hotel."

"Hotels aren't comfortable. They're temporary and completely miss out on being homey. This is a lovely home." Her gaze swept the room, picking up on the hardwood floors, the beautiful four-poster bed and the fluffy down comforter. Even though it was summertime, she knew she could snuggle under that and sleep beautifully. Also a bathroom was attached. "This is really beautiful."

"Good," he said. "I want you to feel at home."

"I'll be fine," she said. "Any chance of food?"

"Yes. I had a stir fry in mind for my dinner tonight, so I've got that started already." He walked across to the other door in the hallway and showed Grayse his room. She peered in. It was a more masculine version of her room.

Grayse nodded and smiled. "Perfect, thanks."

The three trooped back downstairs to the kitchen.

"Do you need me to run to the store?" Grayse asked.

"If you're okay with home-cooked food," Rowan said,

"we're good."

"I prefer that," Phoenix said quietly. Her arm, although in a sling, throbbed. She sat down quietly, holding her arm snug against her chest. "Is there anything I can do to help?"

Rowan looked at her arm and said, "I'll be fine."

"Even one-handed, I can probably do something to help," she protested.

"Then set the table." He pointed to the large dining room table. At his direction about where to find everything, she managed to pull out the cutlery, placemats and even plates. She carried everything over a little at a time, using her good arm, and listened in on the conversation between Rowan and Grayse, discussing the energy of this town and if it was attracting the suicides to this location.

As she came back to grab glasses and to fill them with water, she asked, "Is that what's happening here? With suicide season?"

"It's possible," Grayse said. "Negativity attracts negativity, so the issue, if left unchecked, grows."

"Right," she said. When she came back for the third glass, Rowan had put vegetables into a frying pan with some cooked meat and was slowly adding a sauce. As she watched, he added a dash of red wine. The dish looked and smelled absolutely marvelous.

At a beep behind her, he opened the rice cooker and pulled out a pan of something that smelled a little more aromatic than she expected.

In another five minutes, everything was ready.

During the meal the men kept up their conversation as she listened. She knew most of this, having studied it on her own. She'd never found anything about the healing arts at the level she operated at though. She kept hoping to learn more but figured she'd learn more by doing more.

She'd also spent her professional life studying and teaching mythology, which covered a lot of this work anyway. In her research was a lot of data about using fire to cleanse, the sacrifices to honor the Ancient Ones and the gods, and of course the ferryman, who ferried the newly deceased from this life to the next. She'd always felt a kernel of truth lay behind the myths.

While eating, she could feel fatigue setting in. The flavors were delicious, and the warm food was a comfort she hadn't expected. Just knowing she was out of the hospital, not alone handling this, soothed her own nerves like never before.

Only as she sat here, studying Rowan, did she realize how alone she'd been all her life. Nobody to help her as a child, and then, although her final foster parents had been marvelous, they'd also very much treated her like a foster child—almost like a project to take on and to improve, which, under their tutelage, she had done. There had been an affectionate air to it, but it hadn't been loving. She didn't really understand what a loving atmosphere even meant. She'd had several boyfriends, but she was just too odd for them to stick around long. She didn't think she was odd, but she knew her upbringing had made her something others couldn't really understand—except for maybe these two men at the table.

Grayse frowned and asked, "Are you okay?"

She nodded and forked up the last of her dinner. "That was excellent," she murmured quietly. "I hadn't realized how tired I'm getting, though."

"The drugs are wearing off," Rowan announced. "You'll need pain pills before you crash."

"Only if it's fast. I'll crash soon," she admitted.

"We can arrange that," Rowan said and looked to Grayse. "Do you want seconds?"

"I'm good," Grayse said, holding up his hands. "That was good though."

"It really was," Phoenix said. "I can cook a few basics, but I'm no chef."

"Don't have to be," Rowan said. "Good hearty food is preferred over fancy gourmet food in my house."

"Haven't had much of either," she said. "The professors ate simple meals. They did go out a lot later on, though."

"How did you handle that?"

"I stayed home mostly," she said. "When I first joined them, we had meals all the time together. But I couldn't eat much because of stress. I lost more weight while I adapted. When I calmed down and realized the whole compound was gone, and I wouldn't have to go back, I settled into a better routine. We had dinner every night. I think more to give me stability. A routine they didn't deter from until I was about fifteen, and then they started taking a few evenings away."

"Were you okay with that?"

"Yes," she said, "because, even though it was a good place for me, it wasn't *my place*. Still felt like I was visiting, like I was a student being tutored. We worked on my education every night," she admitted. "Always one or the other working on my studies with me."

"You're lucky," Grayse said. "Because, if you'd ended up in a different foster care family, you might have had someone who didn't put any stock in education."

"I know," she said with a smile. "But there was absolutely no misunderstanding that I was their adopted daughter. That separation remained between them and me. They were a pair, whereas I was a visitor. A project they were working on."

At that Rowan frowned at her.

She shook her head. "No," she said, "it was all good. Because I wasn't ready to be a part of anything. I was disassociating from my past, my family, and I didn't understand how my foster parents could be as nice and as kind as they were." She smiled a self-deprecating smile. "I expected to be abused and tortured, so I eyed them with distrust for a long time. And I think they understood that. They didn't know a lot of my history, but they knew enough that they moved slowly, didn't make any sudden movements, never tried to hug me or grab me up and play with me," she said with a half laugh. "I wasn't exactly a child you could pick up and throw in the air."

"I'm sorry," Grayse said. "I think those are milestones in every child's life. Playtime is important."

"It is," she said smoothly. "But I was thirsty for knowledge. I was thirsty for control and power that would allow me to never be in that victimized state again."

"I think you did well," Rowan said. "I can't imagine what you went through, but I can see who and what you've become through it all. You owe your foster parents a lot."

"I absolutely do," she said.

"Do you keep in touch with them?"

"An email on birthdays is about all." She chuckled at the look on their faces. "And I think that's the way they like it too."

"Interesting," Rowan said. "Any suggestion they had anything to do with the earlier part of your life?"

She shook her head. "No, I don't think they had anything to do with the cult. Maybe because they were as cool and detached as they could be," she said, "made it the perfect relationship for me at the time."

"And what about any relationships since then?" Grayse asked curiously.

"I tried to make friends," she said. "I really did. I did the whole boyfriend-girlfriend thing and the party thing, but I was always the duck out of water. I never really learned how to socialize easily. Not until I was older, and then people saw me less as odd and more as reserved. Of course seeing many sexual acts in my childhood … didn't make for a healthy upbringing."

Grayse nodded. "Cults are known for that, unfortunately."

"I think they're just an excuse for people to sexually abuse children," Rowan said, his voice harsh. "In your case it was even so much worse than that."

"It was in many ways. The good news," she added, "is I'm gone from there. And that stage of my life is well and truly over with."

"Thankfully," he muttered. He collected her plate and said, "Let's get you upstairs to bed."

"I think that would be a good idea," she said as she slowly rose. The room swayed around her.

"Whoa, whoa," Rowan said, grabbing her good arm.

She shuddered as pain racked through her at the jolt. "Ouch."

"Yep, that's the message I needed to hear," he said. "Come on upstairs to bed."

"Says you," she muttered.

"Yep, says me," he said, laughing. He led her upstairs, even offering to carry her.

"I can walk just fine," she said. "It's my shoulder, not my

legs."

"It's your shoulder," he said, "but it's also a major wound."

"And yet it's much better," she said. "I think I'm just tired."

"I hear you, but that's not enough for me. Take your medication and go to sleep." In her room he pointed to the bag and asked, "What do you need out of there?"

"My pajamas would be nice," she said.

He lifted the bag onto the bed, pulled out the items she needed, and then turned to look at her with a frown on his face. "Anything else I can do to help?"

She could sense the intensity of his perusal. She shook her head and smiled. "I'll brush my teeth, and that's about it."

"And sleep," he said.

"Yep." She chuckled. "I'll probably need to take those pain pills though, like you suggested."

"They're downstairs still," he said. "Get changed and I'll be back up in a minute."

"Will do," she said as he disappeared. She took the opportunity to get out of her pants, but her shirt was harder to maneuver. She managed to get it off but couldn't unhook her bra. She stepped into the pajama bottoms but was stuck standing here in a bra when she heard his footsteps. She called out, "I need a hand if you've got a moment."

"Sure," he said, coming in with a glass and the pill bottle. He stepped up behind her, and she swept up her hair so he could access the bra strap. With that unclipped, he said, "Are you okay from here on in?"

She nodded but kept her back toward him and slid the bra off her shoulders.

He stayed behind her and helped her get her injured arm through the sleeve, then tugged it over her head. "Might have been better to sleep without your pajama top."

"Maybe," she said with a half smile. "But I'm tired enough that I don't want anything else to feel odd while I'm sleeping. I usually sleep in both the top and bottom of my PJs, so …"

He handed her the glass of water and her pain meds.

She took them while he pulled back the comforter on her bed. She placed the glass on the night table, then crawled in. She whispered, "I really need a good night's sleep."

"You'll get it. It's still early, but, with any luck, you'll knock out for a good twelve hours."

"I hope so."

"Do you want the lamp left on?"

She shook her head. "No, darkness is my friend."

He clicked off the light and bent down, kissing her gently on the temple. "Now sleep," he whispered.

She was happy to oblige.

HE CHECKED ON her several times that evening. He and Grayse cleaned the kitchen, and, soon afterward, Grayse, after all his traveling, called it an early night too. Rowan went to his room, planning on a hot shower. As he walked back in his bedroom, a towel around his waist, he heard whimpers coming from Phoenix's room.

When she didn't stop, he pulled on his boxers and headed down the hallway to check on her. He opened the door slightly and peered around the edge. She was tossing in her sleep, and, as she rolled onto her injured shoulder, the pain made her cry out. He walked to her bed and sat down beside her, placing a gentle hand on her head and stroked her hair. "It's fine," he whispered. "You're safe now."

She calmed at his touch.

He stayed and gently stroked her hair, helping her ease into a deeper sleep. Finally he stood and slipped from the room, this time leaving her door open. Once he got into his bed and turned off his own lights, he heard her start up again. He walked back to her room to see her tossing and turning again. This time he closed the door, slipped into the bed beside her and just gently held her. Against her ear, he whispered, "It's okay. You're safe."

"Rowan?"

"Yes, sweetie, it's me. Just sleep."

With a heavy sigh she snuggled in close and drifted off again.

He held her, wondering how his life had come to such a surprising place. He'd known right from the beginning that something was between them by the way their energies had entwined so easily. More than that he knew it was almost impossible to separate their energies now. He could fight it all he wanted, but there was just something about her, about the situation, about who they were together, that he knew was meant to be.

He closed his eyes and drifted in and out, but he was always so careful to not hurt her that he didn't sleep deeply himself. He woke up several times to hear her whimpering. At one point he woke her up to give her more pain meds. She took them obediently and curled up again. He crawled back in bed with her, and, as soon as he was under the covers, she backed up until he was wrapped around her again. He smiled and whispered, "At least you know where you belong."

"I do," she whispered, "but do you?"

He lifted his head to see if she was awake, but her breathing was slow, steady, her face lax, as if sound asleep in a deep-breathing state. He tucked her up closer and whispered, "Absolutely."

When he woke the next morning, he found a heat he hadn't experienced in a hell of a long time coursing through his body. The warmth coming from Phoenix beside him made him smile. He only slept with people he really cared about. Something about always having to watch his back bothered him. When he opened his eyes, she whispered, "About time you woke up."

"Really?" he said, turning to look at her with a smile on his lips. "Glad to see you're looking so chipper."

She pushed the blankets back, sat up and stared down at him. "I feel much better," she said.

He gently stroked her cheek. "I'm glad to hear that," he murmured, "because you didn't have a terribly easy night."

She smiled. "But thanks to you, I did get some sleep." She looked around the room and said, "At first I wasn't sure if it was my room and you coming to my bed or if I had crawled into your bed."

"Either works."

She leaned down and kissed him gently on the cheek. "Thanks for being a white knight and helping me get through the night."

The last thing he wanted was to be a white knight. "You're welcome," he said. "I'm not sure you realize just how much our lives are already entwined. … How's the arm?"

"Better. Not quite 100 percent but much better."

He frowned. "You can't do too much," he warned. "It'll be easy to reinjure it."

"I wasn't thinking about doing too much," she said with a smile, her finger gently stroking his lips.

He kissed her finger as it went past and then kissed it again.

She smiled and said, "You're playing with fire, you know?"

"You're the one playing with fire," he said, "but then that's what you do, isn't it?"

"Maybe," she said, "but not this kind of fire."

"Have you ever had a serious relationship?"

"I told you that I have," she said. "If you're worried that I'm a virgin, the answer is, no, I'm not."

He nodded. "I didn't expect you to be at your age."

"Given my history, you mean?" she said. "But I was more detached during the whole process. I wasn't engaged emotionally, and I think that was a downfall of the whole occasion."

"Absolutely," he said, sliding his fingers through her hair. She leaned into his touch. "*Sex* is just that," he said, "an animal ritual. But, once you add in feeling, it becomes something very special."

She looked up at him, her gaze glowing with emotion, and murmured, "Show me."

This time his fingers stroked her lips. She kissed his finger before giving it a tiny nip and then taking it in her mouth and gently suckling on it. He could feel his body responding immediately. He frowned. She shook her head. "No frowns," she said. "I'm an adult, not a child. This is something I want very much."

His mind went to her history and then realized she needed good memories as much as he needed not to dwell on what she'd been through. His gaze caught sight of her bandage. "You're injured," he protested.

"In that case you'll have to be gentle, won't you?" she teased.

"With you? Always," he murmured, sitting up. And he caught her chin with his hand and kissed her lightly. It was hard to hold back the gates of passion once the energy flared between them. He could sense them in an inferno of hot energy, twisting tightly around both of them. He pulled back, gasping. "Was it ever like this before?"

"No," she groaned. "I don't know what this is. But I want more." She threw her good arm around him and kissed him passionately.

He could do nothing but respond, his body already taking over. It was all he could do to hold back some semblance of control so he didn't hurt her. It was still dim in her room with the curtains closed. Maybe that was a blessing too, so he didn't have to see her scars, but he could feel a few of them. They rose under his fingers as he stroked and caressed, gently exploring her lean muscular body with just enough spare flesh to soften the hard edges. The strongest aphrodisiac was her response—she was so natural, wanton even, as she went with the emotions inside her.

She glorified in the feelings of her body, the release in her soul, relaxing into the energy. He'd known lovemaking could be so much more than he'd experienced. He'd never been with somebody who was so completely at ease with energy work like he was.

It was an incredible feeling watching her energy warm and surge around her hand, leaving a trail where it touched. Her lips carried heat and an inner passion he'd never felt before. When he couldn't hold back anymore, she whispered, "Please, now."

His head tilted back toward the ceiling as he struggled to control everything inside himself that wanted to take her hard and fast. She lay down on the bed spread-eagled, her arms wide as she sent gentle waves of energy toward him, telling him how much he was welcomed and wanted.

It was intoxicating. It was enticing, and it was incredibly erotic. He lowered his head and kissed her as he positioned himself at the heart of her. And, when he stroked deep inside, she froze and then undulated beneath him as if getting more comfortable, which had the actual effect of sending him over the edge. His control shattered as he surged into her again and again. She reached up with her good arm and held him close, and he could feel the energy holding them tighter and tighter as everything twisted inside them, until finally she crested beneath him, crying out in joy, and he followed her in the wash of his own climax.

He sagged beside her, catching his breath. "Did I hurt you?"

"No," she murmured dreamily. "And, if you did, I'd say let's do it all over again because I've never felt so warm, so cared for, so loved and so fulfilled in my life."

He kissed her gently. "That's how it's supposed to feel."

"I don't think most people feel this," she said, motioning to the energy cocooning around them.

"I think they do, they just don't know about the energy," he said. "If they can't see the energy, they can feel it, but it would feel more like an emotion and love."

"Yes," she whispered, "*love*. So damn special." She snuggled close. "I know we have to get up and leave soon, but just to have this moment together," she murmured, "it's so beautiful."

"It is," he murmured. "And I would do that all over

again, but I don't want you to reinjure your shoulder."

"It's fine," she said. "Stop worrying."

"Well, it isn't," he said, leaning over to kiss the bandage. "If we do this again, you have to heal first."

She smiled up at him. "Just being here with you, that's already incredibly healing."

"And that deserves another kiss," he said and proceeded to kiss her long and hard.

She wrapped her good arm around him and said, "I think that deserves a little bit more than that." And she rolled over on top of him.

He couldn't believe he was already ready for her. When she slid down his shaft, he groaned and shuddered. But he let her do her thing as she slowly rode him into the early morning dawn. He thought his heart would shatter into a million pieces, but then, when he climaxed, she picked up all the pieces of his heart and held them close.

All the while making sure they were both right here, right together, both needing and receiving what they each had to offer, which was *love*.

Even if they hadn't figured it out in their minds, their bodies already knew. Their hearts already knew, and their energies had already made that decision.

He'd never experienced anything quite like it before, and he knew he never would again with anyone else. If one person in his life was meant to be his partner, it was Phoenix.

And he was just so damn grateful she'd survived what she had so she could be here with him right now and forever.

CHAPTER 21

P HOENIX SAT IN the front seat of the SUV which Grayse had rented at the Albuquerque airport. The trip had been quiet, uneventful. Which was a good thing as she still didn't want to be here. However, Rowan was at her side, and that made a huge difference. Even though she knew Rowan hadn't wanted to come to New Mexico, he had done so to support her. She appreciated it and knew she would go straight back to his Icelandic hometown as soon as this nightmare was over. Their connection was undeniable—their future uncertain.

With Grayse driving, they headed out to the cult compound she'd hoped to never see again.

The thirty-five minute trip to the property was made in silence, until finally Grayse drove onto the rough driveway, then stopped one hundred yards in.

Without saying a word, Phoenix jumped out of the parked SUV and slammed the door a little too hard behind her. Within seconds Rowan stood at her side, a hand on her shoulder, whispering, "Easy."

"I don't know what you mean by *easy*," she said, her voice strangled. "What happened to the house?"

Grayse, at her side, replied, "It burned down. Didn't you know?"

She turned to look at him and asked, "What do you

mean, *didn't I know?*"

He stared at her for a long moment. "What do you remember from that night?"

Her eyes widened as she tried to think back. "I remember the police coming. I remember the shrieks. The shouting. The panic. My mother trying to get me in the closet. My father. Gunfire." She shook her head. "What else was there to remember?" she asked. "Seems like everything happened so fast."

"It wasn't all that fast," he said. "Do you remember the police talking to you? The ambulances?"

"Sure," she said. "That was all at the same time though." She motioned toward the stark shell of burned timber in front of her. "Did somebody hate the compound so much that they burned it to the ground?"

"It burned down that same night," he stated bluntly. "You don't remember that? It was on fire when the cops arrived, and, by the time they did a full sweep, the blaze was out of control, and it couldn't be stopped."

"No," she said. "I don't remember that."

"Let's walk," he said.

As they headed toward the burned house, she stared at it, trying to remember. Bits and pieces remained of the veranda she remembered standing on. As she walked around, she couldn't help but feel that maybe it was a good thing it had burned down. At least nobody else could use it for the same purpose her father had. They walked all the way around it. Time and Mother Nature had brought even more decay upon the burned-out hull. It was full of water damage, and rainwater still collected in one of the corners of the foundation. She looked at the foundation. "It's much shallower than I remember." She shook her head. "Something here is wrong." She turned to look around. "Are you sure this is the property?"

Rowan looked at her in surprise. "Are your memories that confused?"

"I don't know," she cried out. "It was a pretty rough time in my life though—you might want to keep that in mind." She didn't mean her voice to come across as harsh, but no doubt it had. "I'm sorry," she said. "I don't know what I'm saying."

She stepped back and looked around, seeing parts of what she could remember, and yet other parts were so far away. Everything had become overgrown in her absence. She turned and walked toward where she thought the other building had been. As she stood, she turned back and looked from one to the other spot and then took several steps. She looked at the ground and spied three rocks piled high in a triangle.

Memories crept through her mind. Memories of other children. Memories from their games about how this spot was secret. She slowly dropped down to the three rocks, lifted the first one to see the other two in hollows in the ground underneath. She removed them and reached her hand in and pulled out a large key. She held it up for the men to see.

"Well, that answers one thing," Rowan said. "Obviously you remember something."

She nodded slowly. "This is the key to the other shelter, the basement."

"Show us," Rowan said in a harsh voice.

She straightened, instinctively put her heel right against one rock and took three large steps forward. There was more debris, part of it from the house sprawled in front of them.

She motioned at it, looked at the men and said, "We have to move this."

They removed the timber, roofing tiles, plywood and a bunch of plastic garbage bags. With that all cleared away, they could see a trapdoor.

She held up the key. "This opens it." Her voice had gone from harsh to faint, as she realized maybe underneath were things she didn't want to see.

Grayse took pictures with his cell, then put away his phone and grabbed the key. With Rowan's help, they brushed back enough of the dirt so they could find the keyhole. He slid the key in. A lock snapped open.

It wasn't a visible lock; it was more like an underpinning lock. Pulling up the flattened handle, they lifted the lid, opening it wide for them to see in. Stale air wafted up and out. Both men coughed several times.

She nodded. "It was always like that. Even when we went in daily."

"Why did you go in here daily?"

Her voice dropped. "I don't know," she said. "I can't remember. Apparently I don't remember anything in sequence or correctly. It's confusing. I would have thought my memories were better than this."

She now doubted everything she had remembered. If it weren't for the scars on her body, she wondered how much of her childhood she would have remembered. She looked over at Grayse. "Is my mind forgetting all this because it's easier than remembering?"

"I would think so," he said gently. "Don't make light of everything you went through. I saw you that night. And you were barely alive."

"What condition was I in?"

He gave a heavy sigh. "I guess that's why I wish you'd remember. Then I wouldn't have to tell you." He motioned down at the great big hole. "How do you get in and out?"

"There's a ladder on the inside, built into the rock."

He bent down and grabbed at the edge of the hole and slowly lowered himself. "She's right," he said. "You have to know it's here though."

And just like that he disappeared from view. When a flashlight shining up from below, he called out, "Are you two coming down?"

She groaned. "If I have to, yes."

"I think you should," he said. And his voice had an odd tone to it.

She wrapped her arms tightly around her chest and looked at Rowan. "I guess I should go next, huh?"

He gently hugged her close and whispered, "We're here with you. Remember that."

She gave a strangled laugh, nodded, then crouched, one leg dangling over the side. Going by memory alone, she reached out for the first rung and let herself slide down into the hole the way she always had as a child. It didn't look any different. The rungs were still there. The scratch marks on the wall going down were still there. She slowly made her way to the bottom, where the ground was still dirt—or maybe concrete. She didn't know.

She stood at the bottom, trembling, hating this window back into the darkness of her past. She looked over at Grayse, who studied her carefully. "You look at me like I should know something about this."

He nodded. "I would think you should."

Rowan landed beside her. He turned to face Grayse, his voice echoing oddly in the darkness. "We should have brought some flashlights."

"We have our phones," Grayse said. He turned his on again and shone it around where they stood. All she could see were just four walls and a dirty but concreted basement.

"Similar to a bomb shelter but I haven't seen any like this," Grayse said. "Although this one was a decent living space at one point."

Phoenix took two steps forward, catching sight of something behind them. "Are any books or shelves or journals here?"

"We can take a look," Grayse said. "Do you realize other things are down here?"

Rowan stepped forward. "What do you mean?"

Slowly Grayse turned his phone's flashlight away, shining in the direction behind him. On the ground, in front of them, were several corpses. Now long dead.

Phoenix cried out and ran forward, and Rowan caught her.

"Take it easy," he said. "Let's approach slowly." He held her close to his body, and they approached the bodies on the ground. More odd-looking symbols covered their clothing, and they lay spread-eagle on the ground.

She stared down at an adult and what appeared to be several children.

"It's probably Uncle. He stayed here …" Another memory clicked into place. "With the boys …" She turned to look around, search the darkness. "After a certain age, they came down here."

"These do appear to be male children," Rowan said. "At least from what I can see."

"How can you tell?" Grayse asked.

"It's not easy at this age," he said. "There's two, who

look like young teens. Their pelvises are a different shape. They're all so tall. I wonder if all the men from the cult were kept here."

"As prisoners?"

"Considering three of them have stakes through their chests," Grayse said, his voice harsh, "I'll suggest maybe they were sacrifices."

ROWAN COULDN'T UNDERSTAND what he was looking at. "I count seven bodies in all."

"Yes, of various ages. A couple small ones," Grayse said, crouching beside them. He used his phone's flashlight to check as much as he could, then took several steps past the corpses to look deeper into the shelter. "Quite a bit of space is back here too."

"Did they survive the police raid?" Rowan wondered out loud. "Or where they killed first?"

Phoenix stared at the bodies, an odd look on her face.

Rowan knew memories were flashing back. Although she had enough really horrible ones, maybe these were even worse. "Do you know anything about this?"

She gave a strangled sound in the back of her throat and turned away with wild eyes. "I don't know," she said. "How can I possibly know?"

"So they were already dead?" Rowan asked Grayse.

"Most likely drugged," Grayse said from farther in the darkness. "Maybe they knew about the raid and killed these people first. This would be an honorable death."

"Why these stabbed victims?" Rowan wondered out loud. "What does any of this have to do with that letter Phoenix has?"

"This might help," Grayse said. He walked back toward them, holding a stack of books. "These are old, like very old." He stacked them on the ground. "We need to check out more stuff back here."

Rowan held out a hand to Phoenix. She willingly placed her hand in his, and he tucked her up close. It seemed to be a habit lately. But this was an awakening that she had never expected to deal with. He whispered, "It'll be okay. You survived this. That's what you have to remember."

"But they didn't," she said as she walked by the corpses, casting a glance down. "They have been here all this time, in the darkness. Nobody knew. Nobody had any idea what happened to these people."

"Come on. Let's go see the rest of the bunker," Rowan said. "We'll have to phone the cops because these bodies need to be removed and identified."

She gave him the briefest of nods.

Clinging tightly to his hand, they navigated the uneven ground back to the area where Grayse stood. As they got there, he could feel a coldness he wasn't expecting. "Am I smelling water?"

"It looks like a well is here." Grayse turned his flashlight so they could see where they were walking, and sure enough there was a small well. He lifted a bucket and shone the flashlight down. They could see the glistening water below. He dipped a finger into the bucket and nodded. "It's sweet too. Depending on food, they could live down here quite a long time."

"Except for the darkness," Phoenix said, her voice dreamy as she slid back into a childhood memory. "They came out at night."

"Why?" Rowan asked, pushing her memories gently.

Her gaze turned inward. "Something was wrong with them," she said. "They preferred to come out at night. Their eyes hurt them in the daytime."

"If they stayed down here all the time," he said. "They would have to come out at nighttime because their eyes couldn't handle the sunlight."

"There was something else," she said. "They were being fed something. I can't remember who or what, but there was talk about them. I think that was my father again. He thought they were special for a different reason."

"Your father was obviously very special himself," Rowan said, barely holding back his anger. "He made a lot of people suffer for no reason."

"Isn't this interesting," Grayse called back to them from the darkness ahead. "I'm at the end of the space in here. There are bunks and what looks like sleeping chambers."

They hurried along to see that, although small, the chamber itself had a surprisingly coordinated and organized space for living. It was pretty scary to think somebody could live down here for so long. It wasn't the life Rowan himself would want. He loved fresh air, nature and freedom. This would get claustrophobic and confining in no time. But the books, these people living in such darkness needed those.

He held up a notepad, still sitting here, covered in dust. "A note is here. *Police are coming. It's time for the end. Phoenix will rise, and we will all live again.*"

He heard Phoenix gasp, and, too late, he turned to see she had crumpled to her knees, tears now running down her face.

He bent down, wrapped her up in his arms and held her close. "What is it, Phoenix? What does that mean?"

"Father killed them all," she cried. "I remember now. He

killed them all because he thought I would resurrect them. They burned the house to the ground with me in it, knowing I'd live and could start this all over again in a newer, better world. One just for them."

CHAPTER 22

PHOENIX SAT, HER knees pressed against her chest, as her father's words played through her mind. "It's hard to even explain," she said, "but something about it not being possible for me to die, like that letter. I would live forever." She gave a broken laugh. "As if he knew."

"But maybe, in his own crazy mind, he thought you were the answer. You were the future."

"He definitely thought that," she said, "because I could heal. And I think that's why he thought I'd never die. But he said this world was so corrupt that they needed to find a way to live without society. The people who lived down here in the bomb shelter lived here by choice. They were slowly adapting their eyes and would only go out at nighttime when people weren't around. They became more isolated every day."

She got up and shook out her arms and her legs. "I have been down here several times. My father brought me down to meet the others. He kept telling them how I was *the Chosen One*."

"And how did they treat you?"

She shrugged. "I don't remember very much. More a case of them just sitting there and staring at me in wonder."

"But why would he want to burn down the house and take everyone with him?"

"I don't know," she said. "I only remember the police coming."

"Yes," Grayse said. "I was with the police. I also watched you in the middle of the fire. We had just gotten several of the bodies out when somebody warned the place would blow. A series of minor explosions followed, and the place was fully engulfed in flames."

"I don't remember that," she said. "I do remember fire, but it's as if I'm a long way away, watching as something burned to the ground."

"You weren't that far away," he said, his voice harsh. He crouched in front of her. "You were right here in the middle of it. I watched you walk out of the fire."

Rowan stared at him. "Was she on fire?"

"She was surrounded by fire," he said. "As if she was a part of the flames herself. I know most of the cops were screaming to get her help, but she didn't need any help. She just kept walking, and, as she separated herself from the fire, the flames burned down around her. And, like a Phoenix, she rose from the ashes."

She gave a broken laugh. "It's all just crazy. You know that, right? I mean, I'm covered in scars, and I was heavily burned, so that must have been me getting caught up in whatever fire was burning at the time. And I don't remember that."

"Do you remember the state you were in when you were rescued?"

"What do you mean?" she asked, not sure she liked where he was going with this.

"The burn unit is for people badly burned," Grayse said. "The officials definitely discussed the fact you didn't need to be there. You were doing so well. Even though you were hurt, you weren't badly burned. Somehow you had come through the fire without needing intensive care."

"But I was in the hospital for a long time," she exclaimed. "Are you sure you aren't thinking of somebody else?"

"You were in the hospital," Grayse said, "but not for a long time. Just for a little bit. That was more because they needed to see how badly injured you had been over your lifetime. Then they kept you out of wonder. Don't kid yourself. You were never in any burn unit. Nobody understood. Nobody said anything, but they had all seen it, the same as I had. You walked right out of that fire completely unscathed."

"But my body is covered in burns," she cried out.

"True," Grayse agreed, "but they were most likely from before the big fire."

"From your father, weren't they?" Rowan interjected. "Inflicted on you in preparation, you said. Teaching you. Training you to become what he expected you were born to be."

She stood up to him. "So? What? His training worked? He burned down the house around me, and I'm still alive, so I'm supposed to be thankful?"

"No. Of course not," Rowan said. "That's not what I said at all. Obviously there's nothing to be thankful for, other than you survived. But you did come out of that fire relatively unscathed."

"According to Grayse, yes," she said. "That doesn't mean I have to necessarily believe him."

"Oh, absolutely not," Grayse said. "Did you see her file?" He looked over at Rowan.

Rowan nodded.

She turned her gaze on him. "Did it mention a fire?"

"It did," he said. "Lots of mentions about the fact the house was burning, and you didn't appear to be hurt from it."

"Does it say I walked through the fire and came outside?" She didn't know why she was being so persistent. "It just seems so far from what's possible," she said.

"Really? Given everything else you know about your father?"

She groaned. "Okay. Maybe. It's one thing to find a way to heal from everything my father did to me with flames from his fingertips burning me, but it's another thing entirely to believe I walked out of a burning house in my condition as you describe it."

"Maybe," Rowan said. "But there really is a bottom line to all this. You're alive, and they're not. That's definitely something to consider."

HOURS LATER ROWAN got them out of there, removing as many of the books as possible. They had her sitting in the front seat of the rented SUV, while he and Grayse read through the journals they had found.

She had been offered a journal to go through and laughed. "Why? I lived it. I don't need to read it."

Rowan understood that. Given that the reading was extremely brutal, he was grateful nothing inside her wanted to rehash that same torturous past.

The journals were daily records of everything these people did. The group of males, led by John's brother, Jenan, had decided, for whatever reason, they had the ability to live without sunlight and were becoming special visionaries of the future.

Maybe they'd had some internet or intercom system whereby one brother told the other when there was a problem. Rowan didn't understand the stakes at all. It was so long ago that nothing was left of facial expressions, since all the skin was gone, leaving just skulls. With time and age, they had turned mostly to dust.

"I wonder if they killed the children after they realized the fire above had died, and they would miss the journey."

"I'm thinking something like that," Grayse said. "I don't know why the stakes. And not everyone was staked."

"Stakes are often used to drive out evil," Rowan said. "Maybe that's a lot of it. And maybe the rest died by poison willingly."

"Maybe," Grayse said. "Pretty sad if it is. When you think about it, an awful lot of lives were taken here that didn't need to be."

They heard vehicles approaching. Grayse walked around to the end of his rental SUV and waited. Two cop cars pulled up. He spoke to the first man as if he knew him well and then brought them around. He introduced them as Bruce and Jason, two cops he had worked with on the case way back when. The other pair of cops hung back, listening. All the cops were looking at her sideways.

Then they traipsed back to the bomb shelter. Rowan stood at the top, along with one of the cops and with Phoenix.

She hadn't said a word yet. When the three cops and Grayse had gone down into the shelter and came back up, their faces were grim.

Bruce said, "How is it that we didn't know this was here back then?"

Grayse nodded toward Phoenix. "Her memories brought us back here."

Bruce walked over. He was an aging man with a touch of gray hair and a portly belly. He stood in front of her, his gaze hard but clear. "You're the child who escaped?"

She looked him directly in the eye, then nodded.

"Were you ever in this shelter?"

She nodded.

"Did you see these men killed?"

She shook her head. "No," she whispered. "I remember they were part of the same group but different."

Grayse stepped in and explained about the journals and what they had read so far.

Bruce snorted. "The whole lot of them were crazy-ass nutcases," he declared. "Nobody else survived, just the one child. Even then, as far as I understand, she was in the middle of the fire." He cast a sideways glance at Phoenix and whispered, "Are you sure this is her?"

Grayse nodded gently. "Oh, it's her," he said. "And she's had a pretty rough go of it so far."

"I imagine," he said. "And if she's normal in any way …"

Grayse chuckled. "She's pretty overwhelmed by the ugly memories now resurfacing, but she's definitely normal."

Phoenix sighed. "I'm normal, more or less. I went through hell growing up. I was tortured repeatedly because supposedly I was *the Chosen One*."

"Of everything that we've learned so far," Bruce said, "you were the one. You were the only one who survived."

"Can you confirm that?" Rowan asked suddenly. "Can you confirm all the bodies that came out of here were dead?"

Phoenix studied Bruce's face as he nodded. "Without

question and I don't think anybody else could have gotten off the property."

Rowan pointed to the bomb shelter. "Except for the group who lived down here. For all you know, there could have been another group who lived in the damn trees."

Bruce let out another snort and said, "Given this evidence, then, yeah, maybe somebody escaped. But let me say that we didn't take anybody alive out of here, except for her. Everybody else was dead."

"Good enough," Rowan said. He slid an arm around Phoenix's shoulders. "Better?"

"Sure," she replied. "I can see this place burned to the ground. And what's left still makes my stomach churn."

"That's because we didn't eat," Grayse said. "And now we can't until the police say they are done with us." He turned to look at the nearest cop and asked, "Did you ever look at who owns the property?"

"Phoenix owns it," the detective said. "It's registered in her name."

Phoenix shuddered.

"Has been registered to her since when?" Rowan asked.

"Since the house burned down," the cop said. "Yeah, I know, very curious timing."

"I don't want this place," Phoenix cried out in horror. "I have no wish to have anything to do with it. It's the place of my nightmares."

"Maybe you'll sell it then," the cop said. "I know a shopping mall development is looking to come out this direction. Needs a lot of acreage. They were doing a feasibility report."

"You could probably sell it to them," Rowan stated.

Phoenix shook her head. "I don't know. That sounds

terrible too."

"Maybe, but it's an answer." He turned to the detective again. "Do you know who did the transferring on the title?" Rowan asked, apparently stuck on the legalities of the issue.

"No. But a lawyer would have handled it most likely," he said. "I can email you the documents." He looked over at Phoenix. "Or rather I can email Phoenix the documents."

"Email to both of us, please." She motioned to Rowan and said, "He's a cop too."

The detective eased back slightly and made a phone call, talked to somebody, then said, "They're emailing them to you now. I don't have access to them from here." He looked at the group and asked, "Where are you staying, and how long are you planning on being here?"

"We're going back into town," Grayse said. "We're staying for the rest of the day and tonight. Tomorrow, we have no idea."

"Good enough," the detective said. "Obviously we need a team to go over this place. And we'll have questions."

"Good," Grayse said. He looked over at Phoenix. "Are you ready to go? Let's get you something to eat."

She wrapped her arms around Rowan and nodded. "Yes," she said. "It's well-past time to eat, no matter what time zone we are in."

They loaded back into the SUV, and Grayse backed out down the long driveway. She felt better, a little more alert. "Glad that's behind me," she said. "I could use some food and then return to Iceland and get rid of my lovely letter."

"If he gave it to you, and you had that letter with you when you walked out of the fire, why didn't you drop it and let it consume itself then?"

"Yeah, that's a good question," she said in a dry tone.

"Maybe I'd have an answer for you, except I don't even remember it happening. I don't imagine I was in a state to think that far ahead."

"You also said you tried to burn it with a match, and you couldn't."

"That's also true. I don't know why." She shrugged. "Just another mystery of my childhood."

Whatever he'd expected to find, bodies were not it. Rowan checked out the email as it came in from the local cops, and, sure enough, it was the land title transfer. Done by a lawyer. But it didn't take long to realize it was a dead end.

He glanced over at Grayse as he turned onto the highway and took them back to town to their hotel. "We've got a problem with the lawyers," he said.

"Seriously?" Grayse looked at him in surprise. "Why?"

"Because their offices burned down about ten years ago," he said.

"Gee, what a surprise," Grayse said. "I'll drive by it." Once they hit town, he took a couple turns and ended up in front of a flat lot where the ground had been cleared. It was empty, and nobody had built on top of it.

Phoenix made a strangled noise. "Oh!" she exclaimed and hopped out.

Walking to the lot, she stood in the center and opened her arms, slowly turning in a circle.

Rowan stared at her, wondering what the hell was going on.

She looked at him and smiled. "I was here a time or two."

"Do you remember how long ago?"

"I came with my mother," she said.

"That's a very good point," Grayse said. "What's your

surname?"

"Rising," she replied. "Phoenix Rising. But I don't know what my mother's surname was."

He stared at her, but she shrugged. "My father's idea of a joke, I presume. I'm not sure that's the name I was born with but it's my legal name and the only one I've known."

"We should get it confirmed from your birth certificate," Rowan said.

"Wait, I think my mother's name was Roden. Maria Angela Roden," she said. "She changed my name to Rising to go along with Phoenix. I did search but couldn't find any family."

Rowan and Grayse looked at her, but she was turned away, staring up at the hills around them.

"What do you want to bet her family knew about the cult and disowned her?" Grayse asked in a low voice.

"Let's find out," Rowan said.

Urging her back into the SUV, Grayse took them to a restaurant, where they sat down and ordered dinner.

When it arrived, Phoenix inhaled hers.

Grayse put down his fork and looked at her. "Are you using energy to heal?"

She looked at him in surprise. "Maybe. Why?"

"Consuming food at this rate isn't normal, unless you're doing something with energy."

"I was focused on healing my shoulder," she said. She reached up and patted her shoulder. "But it is doing better now."

"You know something? I wouldn't be at all surprised, if you took off that bandage, to find there's no wound," Grayse said. "I doubt there was yesterday either."

She reared back and stared at him. "Are you saying you

think I made it up?" She couldn't believe anybody would think that.

Grayse shook his head. "No. Not at all. Just that you would have healed right away. The fact that you're still eating so much food is definitely a concern though."

She looked at his food and asked, "Are you done?"

"I am," Rowan said instead and slid his plate over. He had only eaten half his dinner.

Too much was going on for him to feel comfortable and to eat a big meal. He could almost sense this instinctive need to get up and run, but that didn't make any sense. He glanced around, looking for energy out of sorts or out of sync. But he wasn't seeing anything unusual. And that bothered him too. He glanced over at Grayse. "Are you picking up anything?"

But Grayse was still studying Phoenix and her empty plate. "I think we need to do some more analysis when we get you back to the hotel," he said, his tone abrupt.

"Give me five," Phoenix said and proceeded to polish off the rest of the food on Rowan's plate. She sat back and smiled. "That'll hold me for a little while. But, if we see a grocery store, I should pick up some groceries."

They stood from the table, and Grayse paid the bill and led them to the SUV.

As they walked over, he said out of the corner of his mouth to Rowan, "Keep an eye out, will you? I didn't answer you in the restaurant because I wasn't sure, but I'm definitely getting a disruptive energy here."

"Me too," Rowan replied. "Let's hit a grocery store for her and then head back to the hotel and maybe stay in for the rest of the day and night."

Grayse took them to a nearby grocery store.

Phoenix bought a tub of peanut butter, a loaf of bread, a pound of cheese, some ham, tea bags and milk. They stared at her in surprise. She shrugged. "I might get hungry."

"Wow," Rowan said under his breath.

She shot him a hard look.

He just smiled and said, "You eat as much as you need to eat. There's a reason for it. We just don't know why yet."

Soon enough, they were back at the hotel room. They had a suite with two bedrooms, a small living room, and a kitchenette. Phoenix put the food down on the small table and made herself a peanut butter sandwich. As soon as she finished it, she made herself a second one.

Grayse put on the teakettle. "Do you want some tea?"

"That would be lovely, thanks," she replied with a mouthful of sandwich. "What's the chance a family member is involved in this?"

"That's what we'll find out," Grayse said. "The cops are on it too."

"Wouldn't they have searched for family for me back when?"

"They did," Grayse said. "And found no one."

"Why would you find something now?"

"Because we'll go a little deeper," Rowan said.

She nodded and picked up two more slices of bread. This time she cut the ham and cheese to make another sandwich. She turned to look at Rowan. "I ate half your food in the restaurant. Do you want one?"

"Sure," he said. He sat down at the small table. He ate slowly, watching as she shoveled in her third sandwich. He glanced over at Grayse and saw a frown in his eyes.

Grayse nodded. "I'll grab my laptop and set it up with the Wi-Fi." He went into one of the bedrooms that had two single beds, where he and Rowan were staying.

He came back out with a laptop and started clicking away. As soon as the teakettle boiled, Rowan made tea for everyone. He'd rather have coffee, but they only had instant, and that wasn't his choice.

As soon as he sat back down again, Phoenix reached over to grab more bread, and he put a hand on hers. "Stop, Phoenix."

She looked at him in surprise.

"Have your tea first. Sit back and relax. Let that food digest."

She nodded ever-so-slowly. "I am eating too much, aren't I?"

He was gratified to hear the worry in her voice. "Yes," he said. "You are. What we need to know is why."

She pulled the sleeve of her T-shirt down over her shoulder. "Take this off."

It was time to check it anyway. He obliged and helped her arm out of the shirt. She held the T-shirt against her chest as he carefully undid the bandage.

When he took it off, he gasped.

She stared down but couldn't see anything. "I'll take a look in the bathroom." She hopped up and headed to the bathroom. When she came back out, her T-shirt was on normally, but her face was pale.

Grayse looked at her and asked, "No trace of the wound, is there?"

She shook her head. "Shouldn't there be a scar?"

"Not now," Grayse said. "The thing is, I'm not sure why else you're still consuming food if that is healed."

"Because I'm still not healed maybe, or something else needs to heal?"

"That's possible," he said. "That's what I'm figuring out."

She sighed and sat back down at the table, tucked the tea closer to her, then looked at it with revulsion. "Something inside me absolutely detests this tea," she said.

Grayse slowly stood and asked, "Is it not the same tea you always drink?" His voice was hard, and his gaze was intense as he locked on her.

She looked up at him, bewildered. "It is," she said. "I'm not sure why right now it seems like absolute poison to me."

"If you pull it closer toward you, what happens?"

She looked at it, and her face twisted with revulsion. "I can't even force myself to do that."

Rowan snatched up the hot cup and pushed it closer to her.

She screamed and backed away.

"Very interesting," Grayse said. "Where's that letter you were given?"

She stared at him. "What's going on? What the hell is happening to me?"

"Where's the letter?" Grayse asked again, his voice ever-so-soft but intense.

She stuffed her fingers in her pocket and pulled it out. "This is it."

"Put it in the tea," he ordered.

She reached her hand over the cup but couldn't force her fingers to drop it in the tea.

Grayse gasped and blurted out, "Aha! Now I understand."

"I don't," Phoenix cried out. "What's going on?"

"That letter," he said. "It's got his blood on it, doesn't it?"

She looked down at the paper and said, "I don't know if that's his blood or mine. I thought it was mine."

"No. It's your father's blood," Grayse stated. "He followed a couple rituals to put his energy into that letter."

"I was throwing it in the lava to get rid of it and him," she said. "Remember? That's what I was doing right from the beginning. Finding a way to destroy my ugly history without destroying myself."

"Do you realize why your appetite is so large right now? You are feeding him. Something about returning to the cult property has woken *him* up ..."

All the color drained from Phoenix's face. "What?" she cried out. "Surely that's not possible."

Rowan walked behind her and rubbed her shoulders and neck. He could feel waves of energy coming from her. It was not good, but he persevered and kept his hands on her.

Rowan stared at Grayse from behind Phoenix. "Seriously?"

"It's the only explanation," Grayse said.

"But my father is dead," she whispered. "You heard me even ask the cops about that, right?"

"That's why you keep asking?" Rowan asked gently. "Because you know in your heart of hearts something is wrong."

"Every once in a while, yes. But I figured it was just fear. Fear I didn't understand something."

"We definitely don't know something yet," Grayse said. "I suspect somebody all along has helped him. Tell me about your foster parents."

She looked bewildered but obliged. "Both are professors at the same university. One taught science. One taught math. They wouldn't have anything to do with this."

"What are their names?"

She gave them to him.

He brought them up on the internet and started working.

Rowan stopped rubbing her shoulders, feeling the negative energy receding slightly, and sat down, studying her face, studying the letter. Figuring out how this all worked. There was obviously a psychic issue. "How did he know early on you were special?" he asked.

"I don't know," she said. "Oh …" She stopped. "My mother said something about me running into a fire as a toddler and didn't get burned. When she told my father, he tested me. Apparently I did the same thing and did not get burned again." She shrugged. "It was probably all lies. Why would I walk through fire in the first place and not get burned? And why then did his fire burn me?" she scoffed. "It's one thing to see energy. It's another thing to use energy from other people to heal. But that doesn't make me fireproof."

"No," he said. "Not at all. But it could be part of your healing abilities. You can wrap yourself up in something to protect yourself. What are the chances that, when you left that house, you wrapped yourself up in as many energies as you could to protect yourself from the burning fire around you?"

She stood abruptly and stared at him. "Were they dead or were they alive, and I killed them?"

He gave her the gentlest of smiles. "Maybe that's an answer you need to give us."

She sat back down on the chair, wondering how they'd gone from a normal peanut butter sandwich to an esoteric conversation that bordered on ghost haunting. "I have no idea. It's too horrible to think about," she said softly. "This is so far from normal."

"Just think about it. If you knew that the place was on fire, and if you knew everybody around you was dying, whose energy would you grab in order to protect yourself?"

"Anybody's and everybody's," she replied instantly. "I didn't discern whose energy I would take to heal. I went for the strongest and then to the weakest. But, if it was me against the world, then obviously I was taking everything."

"Who was there?" he asked gently. "You would know because you would be reaching out for that energy."

She closed her eyes and put herself mentally back into the building, hating the fear trembling through her. So long ago, yet strangely as if it were just yesterday. "I can see myself screaming through the house. Crying out because the cops were leaving without me. They hadn't found me. I had been locked up in a room, and they hadn't found me."

"And then?" Rowan urged her to continue through the memory.

"The place started to burn, and I was crying because it hurt. It was so hot. I kept reaching for energy to cool it down. I was taking energy from my mother, which was normal. Then from the other kids and the other women. They were dying. Some of them had no more energy left. Their bodies were already cooling. My father was there somewhere. I could feel him. I knew he was dead because I had seen his body, but his soul was there. His spirit kept telling me to use it, to use his energy to save myself.

"I grabbed it and wrapped it around me to protect myself from that fire. I used him to cool it down so I could walk through the flames. There were other people too. Other men, cops. I reached for their energy too. They didn't notice.

They were still in shock over what they had seen. None of them noticed. I took a little bit from all of them just to try to protect myself, and I ran through the house. It was so bad, so hot. I was burning up. I had to take it all. I took more and more and more and kept wrapping it around my feet, my head." Tears streamed down her cheeks and sweat coated her brow. She twisted her fingers together.

"Keep going, Phoenix. This can help you. You need to know," Rowan encouraged her.

She took a deep breath. "There was a surge of energy, like a blue fire all around me, but it was cooling against the red-hot fire of the house. I knew I had to get out because, even though I was protected from the flames, the house itself was coming down. When I ran through the house, I saw the kitchen and ran to the front door, blasting through it even as the timbers behind me fell. I was covered in blue, but, at the same time, in the edges of the blue were orange flames. I could see myself. I could see the blue and the orange as I kept on walking, pushing the orange farther and farther behind me. Then I was outside, crying, and I remember being covered by blankets and men and strange energy. The voices. It was terrible. I kept pushing them all away, pushing it all back. I was cocooning my senses from the onslaught that was so hard to deal with."

"Right," Grayse said. "As a Phoenix risen from the ashes, you did exactly as your father said you would."

She nodded slowly. "It's one of the things he did at the end. He lit the house on fire." She shook her head. "What's that got to do with my appetite? What's that got to do with everything going on now?"

"I think all those bits and pieces of energy from the cult fire are still with you," Grayse said, staring at her. "I think you grabbed as much of your father's energy as he offered, and that's what he wanted. He wanted you to take him forward into whatever millennium came after this. His body was dead, but his soul survived. And you've been keeping it safe all this time."

She stared at him in horror. "Are you saying that the man who made my life a living hell is still alive?"

"No, not at all," Grayse replied, shaking his head. "His body is not alive, but that energy, that soul is, and going to the compound today woke him up. Maybe because you were in shock, traumatized from revisiting your childhood. Yes, his soul energy is definitely still alive, and it is attached to that letter you always keep with you. He's getting stronger as you get stronger. No wonder you felt like you had to drop it into the lava because that's the only place you could really, *really* get rid of it, isn't it? And I mean, get rid of him …"

"I figured it was the only place I could go and be free from it, yes. He came from the town where Rowan lives. I thought maybe, if it went back there, it would feel like going home, and the letter would let me go. I've been a prisoner of that letter all my life. … I just wanted to be free."

"It's quite possible you will be …" Grayse said. "But freedom from what? It's possible that it's planning on taking you with it—wherever that may be—including the Burning Fires in Iceland. Possibly the ultimate test for a powerful Phoenix. There you'd die and would rise yet again. Or not."

THEY'D GONE. ALL three of them.

Rage ate away at him. How could that be? The Supplier had been watching until late last night, and, by the time he'd rousted this morning and had returned to check on the trio, they'd left. He could feel the energy shift, the absence of the presences he sought.

Back in town he checked his phone for any news, then picked a coffee shop to hear the latest gossip. It wasn't long before he understood that Rowan had taken several days' leave, and he'd left the village and gone to the US. Because of her, no doubt. Although the Supplier couldn't discount the dangerous energy of the other unknown man with them.

Frustrated, but realizing all this did was delay his plans and didn't cancel them, the Supplier settled back to wait.

If they'd gone to deal with Phoenix's issues, then she'd be stronger, happier, theoretically a much better offering to the Elders.

As long as they could wait that long.

It all had to do with energy. Feeding the source to keep them alive.

The Supplier frowned as he contemplated her soul, her energy and those energies that surrounded her. Maybe she was better off alive and feeding the Elders little bits at a time. They had a few like that. Ones who had more value alive than dead.

Something was familiar about her energy. It bothered him. He needed to figure it out. Mistakes at this point were costly.

Deadly even.

CHAPTER 23

THE NEXT MORNING, Phoenix woke up alone in the hotel, feeling as if something in her life had shifted, something major. She didn't quite understand it, but the revelations about her childhood, how she had lived, how the ones had died in the bomb shelter had been enlightening. She didn't even know how to start processing it all.

To add in the possibility that her father was still alive in energy and existing as part of her was just terrifying.

She got out of bed, suddenly needing to get on the move, needing to do something, anything. She walked into the bathroom and decided a shower would be a great place to start. It took two shampoos to get her hair feeling clean. Being in that bunker made her feel like she was completely encased in dirt.

She had few memories of that group of males and not ones she could count on. And none in relation to the mysterious letter she still carried. She remembered her father saying it had been handed down from his father and his grandfather. He often called them his Elders. That the paper was ancient, whatever that meant.

Out of the shower, she dressed, braided her hair, then stepped into the small living room area of their hotel suite to find both men up. Rowan stood and opened his arms. She walked in his embrace, loving the morning hug. They'd slept like the dead they'd seen yesterday, but just knowing he'd been there with her had been wonderful. He smiled down at her. "Did you have a good night?"

"Sure," she said. "If demons and fire and death and life after death and ghosts count as a good night." She walked over to the kitchen and saw they had made a small pot of coffee. She got a cup, which emptied the pot, so she put on another one. "These pots aren't meant to hold much, are they?"

"No, we figured we'd go out for breakfast soon."

"Good, and then what?"

"Then we need to see a lawyer about your property," Rowan said. "I'd like to know the history of who has owned it."

"That's probably a good idea. I wonder if my father's father had it before him," she said. "I also woke up remembering my father said that letter was ancient and that his grandfather and others had it before him."

Both men looked at her.

She shrugged. "I don't know why that would be important though."

"I have no idea if that makes a difference, but I contacted Stefan this morning," Grayse said. "He said, if artifacts are taken from their homeland, sometimes they're imbued with energy that is much less than friendly. When generations of energy are added, it can corrupt as negative builds on the negative. He suggested it's behind your need to go to the Burning Fires. Not necessarily to destroy it but so it can go home. Often, when returned to its resting place, it will calm down. And your need to destroy it in the Burning Fires is likely partially driven by its own need plus your own to move forward and to leave your father behind."

"That's all very nebulous and unclear," she said, turning to sip her coffee. "I gather I was correct in taking it to its origin and wanting to drop it in the lava pit."

"Potentially, yes," Grayse replied. "It certainly is something worth following up on."

"I was trying to," she said. "But you guys wouldn't let me."

Rowan dropped a heavy hand on her shoulder. "We are going back. We can do it then."

She nodded but didn't say anything about that. "The lawyer is no longer in business, correct?" she asked.

"Correct, but somebody took over all his clients. I'm trying to figure out who that is," Grayse said. "The cops are getting us some information too."

"Food would be good in the meantime," she said quietly. She looked at Rowan. "And going home would be nice."

He studied her quietly. "When you say *home*, what does that mean to you?"

She started. "Oh. Wow. I wasn't expecting that," she said. "But you're right. I was thinking of heading back to *your* hometown." She shook her head. What the hell was wrong with her? Iceland was hardly home. She doubted she could even stay very long without applying for a visa of some sort. She'd have to get a work visa at a minimum. She seemed to be completely disassociated with everything. The only place that seemed to feel like home was his place, and that was so odd.

He squeezed her shoulder gently and said, "Maybe your homing instincts are stronger than you think."

She looked up at him. "Just because it was my father's hometown ..."

"And *his* father's and his grandfather's. So you have a lot of lineage there. It would be normal to think you were going home. What about where your apartment is? And your foster parents?"

She looked at him, and confusion and distress must have shown on her face because he opened his arms again. She didn't even hesitate, she walked into his embrace and snuggled close.

She murmured against his chest, "You're very cuddly."

He chuckled. "I can't say I've been told that before."

"That was very short-sighted of them then," she said, "because you are obviously a big teddy bear." She hugged him close. "Do we really have to stay here?" she asked.

He tucked her closer and said, "We can go home as soon as you want to, after we've cleared up any paperwork. We're booked on a flight tomorrow afternoon. Remember?"

"I forgot," she admitted. "I just wish it could be today."

"I think we have enough things to sort out today," he said.

Grayse stood and said, "Let's go get breakfast. I need to touch base with Stefan after that."

Rowan said, "Seems like you're fairly knowledgeable in this stuff."

"Too knowledgeable," he replied.

As they walked out and locked up the hotel room, Phoenix asked Grayse, "How did you get started in this?"

"I was part of a *shoot-him-up-dust-him-up* kind of a family massacre," he said calmly. "I was just a child, but I watched the spirits of every one of my family members cluster around me to try and protect me from the maniac gunman, who happened to be my oldest brother. I never forgot seeing them and once I did, I saw every dead person imaginable." He gave Phoenix a crooked smile. "That was just the start of it. After that, there were all kinds of images and colors and energy that I saw. Took a long time to train myself and to improve my abilities."

"I can't imagine," she said faintly.

"You do it all the time yourself," he said. "Look at you. You use energy to wrap up and protect yourself. You use energy to heal."

"Sure," she said, "but I'm mostly stealing energy. It always made me feel bad."

"What do you do about it?"

She shrugged. "If I care, I send the energy back with that much more healing attached to it."

He gave a bark of laughter. "That's the best thing you could do. Always give better than you've received. That's a motto everybody should live by."

Instead of driving, they exited the hotel and stood in the street. Phoenix pointed across the way. "A coffee shop used to be on the other side of the street, maybe down a few blocks. But I don't know if it's still there."

"Let's find out," Rowan said. He reached out of hand, and she put hers in his. They held hands as they walked across the street. The coffee shop was no longer there, but, as they carried on, another one was down a block farther. They walked in and took a table at the window and waited for service.

Rowan looked at her. "How's the appetite?"

"I'm starved," she said. "But it's not crazy out of control."

"Good," Grayse said. "That means some things are settling."

"It was bad yesterday," she said. "Just the thought that I might be feeding him …"

He looked at her with understanding. "It's always a good thing to know what someone is doing and why," he said. "And to understand that you do have control over that."

"I was wondering about that," she said in a low tone. "Just how much control does he have?"

"Any he has is because you've given him permission to have it," he said calmly. "That's the thing about the other side. They can only do what you allow them to do. Theoretically, in real life, that happens too. When you lose that physical body, you can only do what another person allows you to do. So, if you don't want him there, it's up to you to detach him and to toss him."

She stared at Grayse. "Is it that easy?"

He shrugged. "In theory, yes. In practice, no. But it can be done."

She sagged against the chair, picked up her coffee cup and studied him over the rim. "What if I may have picked up some energies from a bunch of other people?" she asked delicately. "And didn't return them?"

He stared at her for a long moment. "How many other people?"

She dropped her gaze to the table. "Quite a few," she replied hesitantly.

Rowan turned to look at her. She stared back at him and then looked away. "I can't be sure," she said. "But I spent a lot of the night thinking about the energy I have collected over the years. And, if I didn't give it all away, is it all still here? It's almost like a souvenir, and that makes me feel creepy, like a serial killer. Surely I didn't hurt those people, did I?"

"If you didn't take so much as to hurt them physically, then, no," Grayse said. "If you did it as a child, it's not something you can be held responsible for either."

"I'm not sure I like the direction you are going with this."

"I'm not sure I like the direction I am going with this either," he said. "How many people?"

She pursed her lips, mentally counting. "I don't know for sure but at least a dozen," she said.

He relaxed. "Do you think it's all because of when you were injured?"

"A lot from that fire at the cult," she said. "I was panicked and looking for anybody to help, and some people were dying. I don't know …" She hesitated to even say it. "It is possible I took the last of their energy to try to protect myself?"

"Did you know they were dying? Did you snag that energy from them so you could live and they couldn't?"

"Of course not!" she replied. "At least not consciously."

Rowan stretched out his hand and gently rubbed the top of her fidgeting fingers.

She stopped fidgeting and let out a deep sigh. "But I was thinking only of myself," she admitted.

"Anybody in that situation would only be thinking of themselves," Rowan said firmly. "It doesn't really matter. You did what you had to do to survive."

"What about since then?" Grayse asked.

"After getting shot," she said. "In the hospital, I was taking little bits of energy from people but not very much. Just enough that I could heal."

"Have you told him?" Grayse asked.

She shook her head and turned to Rowan. "I'm sorry, but I took some of your energy too."

"I know," he said calmly. "Remember? I see energy."

She stared at him, her gaze fathomless. "And you didn't mind?"

"I gave you a lot of energy," he said. "I also wrapped you up, protecting you in energy. So it's not as if you took anything from me."

She smiled up at him. "Thank you."

He squeezed her hand. "You're welcome.

Just then a waitress arrived with large platters of food. Phoenix stared down at the bacon and sausage and ham and eggs and potatoes and said, "See? Now this looks like just about the right amount."

A big platter of toast arrived and was set in the center of the table. "Okay, so, maybe with that, it's the right amount."

The men laughed and said, "Eat up."

She smiled and picked up a fork and dug in.

ROWAN FOUND IT interesting that her appetite had calmed down from yesterday, as if her father had been driving some of that ferocious appetite. He looked over at Grayse. "So, if her father is still here, can he affect her actions?"

Phoenix froze as she looked up at Rowan, then at Grayse. Rowan could see the fear in her eyes.

Grayse nodded his head. "Affect, yes. He can't control anything. This goes back to having permission. You might be doing a few things you wouldn't normally do, but you have given him permission to do that. Stop giving him permission to do anything, and he can't do anything. The trouble is, he already has a lot of control over you from your childhood. That's often why torture and abuse happens. It's all about power. Once you're afraid, you've already handed your power away, giving them the ability to take advantage over and over again. He's done that all your life. Until you started to fight back."

"I never fought back," she said in surprise. "What gave you that idea?"

Grayse chuckled. "Yes, you definitely started to fight back. As soon as you collected energy to heal, you were fighting back. You could lie there and take his abuse. Scream and cry out in pain and torture but know he couldn't stop you from healing. He could do his worst, and you'd still bounce back. And I think, in some way, he knew that, and that's why he treated you as badly as he did. Because he was so angry."

"He could have killed me," she said quietly. "If that was his intent, he never managed to complete the job."

"No," he said. "Thankfully. Maybe he didn't want to have the proof he could kill you. Maybe he wanted to believe in something bigger and better than him. Most people do, you know. Most of the time, people need to have something to believe in."

She frowned.

Rowan listened carefully. "What does any of this have to do with suicide season?"

Grayse looked at her. "Maybe it doesn't?"

"It does," she said clearly. "I just don't know how."

Both men looked at her. Rowan said, "What do you know about it?"

"It's energy," she said. "There's a nastiness about it, a neediness. As if it's rebalancing. And it is attracting what it needs and draws it in."

"But they're coming from all over the world, and they're not exactly jumping into this lava pit," Rowan protested.

"Yes, but that lava is drawing energy from all around it,"

she said. "It's not just from around the pit. I don't know if people have any idea why they are committing suicide or whether it's just instinct bringing them there."

Grayse stared at Phoenix. "Who is it who just said that?" he asked.

She frowned at him, then turned to look at Rowan. Rowan studied Grayse and what he saw had him shifting his vision slightly so he could see clearer. "Is that your father speaking?" Rowan asked in a low voice.

She gasped in horror, then understanding, and determination glittered in her eyes.

As he watched, the energy wrapping around her was suddenly picked up and tossed across the room.

"Maybe," she said indignantly. "Is he really affecting me that much?"

"I don't know," Grayse said. "I just knew somebody else was influencing what you said."

"That's terrifying," she said. "He has no right. He has no right to the way I think or what I say or how I believe."

Rowan glanced around, but nobody else was close enough to hear her words or to hear the fury behind them. Which was a good thing. Because she was getting very riled up. He reached out a hand and gently calmed her down. "Remember. He can only do what you give him permission to do," he said.

She took several calming slow breaths. "I'll assume the energy in that entire town is affected by his family line," she said.

"Negative or positive?" Grayse asked, studying her carefully.

Rowan watched as she answered instinctively.

"It doesn't matter," she said. "Because those are both

judgments. If people come without judgment, then they would not be affected."

Grayse chuckled. "Now *that* is you talking," he said.

"What is all of that supposed to mean in terms of suicide season?" Rowan asked in confusion. "And how do I change that energy so nobody sees it as a suicide spot?"

"It can take time," Grayse said, "but it is possible to change that atmosphere. You now have a history of suicide. Everybody has that expectation of suicide, so they're putting out that energy. What you need to do is get through a year without any suicides, so the next year that new mind-set's stronger yet again."

"That sounds like a ton of work on a day-to-day basis and goes well beyond what I can do," Rowan said.

"Yes, and no," Grayse said. "You have a group of us. So you can cleanse the area. Once it's cleansed, basically set up alarms, so, when darkness tries to creep in, you just boot it back out again."

Rowan started to laugh. "If anybody else could hear us now," he said, shaking his head.

Grayse grinned at him. "The whole world would think we're crazy, wouldn't they?"

"The whole world already thinks we're crazy." Phoenix leaned against her chair. "When are we supposed to meet the lawyers?"

Grayse pulled out his phone and said, "In fifteen minutes."

Rowan watched as she tucked into her food a little bit faster. He finished his meal, pushed back his plate and waited for the waitress to come refill their coffee cups. He figured he had just enough time to get a fresh cup down before they had to leave.

"Is it easier to affect one's own family members' energy?" she asked.

Grayse nodded. "It's always easier to affect family. Just think about it. You already have buttons you push for those you know and love. When you have somebody you've spent a lifetime with, you know their weaknesses almost instinctively."

Rowan only had one thing to say to that. "It sucks."

Grayse chuckled. "It does, indeed." He looked at the empty plates on the table and said, "You guys ready to go?"

"Yes," Phoenix said. "We need to." She stood and walked from the restaurant.

Rowan dropped some money on the table to help cover their meals and stepped out behind her, waiting for Grayse to follow. Once outside, the three headed toward the lawyer's office.

Grayse's voice was low as he said, "Remember. Not everybody looks at us in a positive light."

"Is that a warning about the lawyers?" she asked.

"Not so much," he said. "I'm just remembering your family may or may not have had a good reception here over all these years. It's definitely something we have to consider."

"Not to mention fueling that energy all around us," Rowan said quietly. "We need to be careful."

She nodded. At the lawyer's office she looked at him, took a deep breath, grabbed the door and stepped inside.

CHAPTER 24

P HOENIX LOOKED AROUND the lawyer's office. It didn't
resemble the super high-end ones she'd seen in movies.
It looked like a normal office. A woman behind the reception desk stood and said with a big smile, "May I help you?"

"We're here to see Mr. Lancaster, please," Grayse said.

"Of course," she said. "Do you have an appointment?"

"Yes, we do."

The woman consulted with her appointment book for a
moment and then looked over the screen. "Is this for
Phoenix Rising?"

Phoenix, hands in her pockets, gave the barest of a nod.
The woman's eyes locked on Phoenix. "If you want to take a
seat, I'll let him know you're here."

But she didn't move. And neither did Phoenix. Grayse
stepped forward and deliberately placed himself between the
two of them. "Hopefully we don't have to wait long," he
said.

The woman gave a headshake and smiled up at him.
"No, I'll let him know right now." She turned and left the
small room. When she came back out, she said, "He'll see
you now."

Phoenix stepped between the two men and walked down
the hall with her. When she was out of earshot from the
receptionist, she said, "What was that all about?"

"You're an oddity. Remember that," Grayse said. "A lot of history is here. A lot of people may not be terribly impressed with that cult."

She snorted. "You think? What about me?"

They stepped through a doorway into a large office. A fiftyish graying man in a casual gray suit to match his hair stood behind a large desk. He looked at them, but no smile was on his face. "Phoenix Rising?" He held out a hand. She nodded, stepped forward and shook his hand. He motioned at the three chairs and said, "Please, take a seat."

With the three of them seated, he said, "This is a pretty unusual occasion."

"In what way?" She might have been the burned, tortured child when she left this place, but she was now an associate professor in her own right with a lot of years of academia and experience in dealing with people. She didn't know why it seemed like she'd forgotten everything in her life up until now, but something about this lawyer's mannerisms made her draw a mantle of authority around her shoulders. She gazed at him directly.

"Because that property has always been a contentious issue," he said smoothly.

"By whom and because of what?"

He sighed and settled back. "A lot of people here were related to the people found dead on the property."

"And?"

"They think they have a right to that property," he replied.

"That's nice," she said. "Are they all blood relatives?"

"Yes," he said. "But not of John himself."

"Of course. And he had the title before me?"

He nodded. "Yes, he did transfer it into your name the

week before he died."

"The week before they all died," she exclaimed. So not the day of but close enough for him to have had an inkling of what was to come.

Again the lawyer nodded.

"So what's the problem?" she asked.

He looked at her in surprise. "Only that there's a lot of ill will toward you because of it."

"Toward the child who was tortured and beaten for all her life?" she asked in a curiously neutral tone.

He shook his head and said, "You're right. I mean, obviously you're an innocent victim in all this too. I'm just letting you know how the town generally feels about this."

"Is there any chance of it being sold or rezoned into something useful?" she asked.

"Potentially," he said. "There is talk of a big center going up. But I don't know if it will work."

Grayse spoke up. "Did you handle her father's estate?"

"In conjunction with my father, who had the law firm that burned down," he said with a nod. "Yes."

"Do you hold me responsible for that too?" Phoenix interrupted. "I don't know why you would. I was a child who had just been rescued from a cult. It seems like people want to pick on an innocent victim in both of these cases."

"It was suspicious timing," the lawyer said apologetically. "Something was odd in the way you were rescued as well."

"Odd how?" Rowan interjected.

"Just what some of the rescuers said at the time," the lawyer said with the dismissive wave of his hand. "There was always an odd history to that place. So, your rescue was just another part of it. Added to the legend."

"And what legend was that?"

He smirked. "That it was just a place people avoided. When the women came to town, they came in groups. They never spoke to anybody. They bought what they needed then they left."

"Where did the money come from?" Rowan asked.

Phoenix appreciated the fact that the cop in him was digging for answers.

"Good question," he said. "Her father's trust."

"What trust is that?" Rowan asked. "If there is a trust, why was it not passed down to her?"

The lawyer looked at him in surprise. "Well, it did, of course."

Phoenix leaned forward. "Are you telling me that I was supposed to get money every year from this trust?"

He stared at her. "Didn't you?"

She shook her head. "No one ever mentioned a trust to me. I've never received any monies from my father's estate."

He tapped the papers in front of him. "It's been deposited into this account every month. I don't have access to the account to see if any has been taken out, but the money should be still there."

She held out her hand. "What account?"

"It's in your name," he said with a puzzled frown. He handed her the sheet.

She checked the amount that had been deposited, and her jaw dropped. "This much has been paid every year?"

"No, that's monthly," he said. "Your father's family was very wealthy too, you know."

"Where did that money come from?" she asked faintly. "Because hundreds of thousands of dollars are in that account." She shook her head. "I had no idea."

"You're a very wealthy woman," the lawyer said. "From

your father's side of the family. Your mother's side were small business owners in Maine. I don't have much information other than she was an only child and the parents passed away years before you left the compound."

She didn't know what to say about that so said nothing.

"His family was from my hometown," Rowan said. "But I didn't find any sign of great wealth."

She frowned and asked, "Can you find any names?"

"Of course. Give me a minute." The lawyer tapped away on his computer. Within a few moments, he started printing documents. He looked at Phoenix and hesitated. "I know you are who you say you are," he said, "but, by law, I do need to check for proof."

She took her identification out of her purse and handed over her driver's license and credit cards.

He looked at them, compared them to the information on his screen and nodded. "Fine," he said. "I can give you the information now. Thank you for that."

"Make a copy," she said. "Just so we don't have to do this again."

He smiled at her. "That's an even better idea." He walked to the printer, lifted the lid and scanned her identification. He picked up the paperwork he had printed off and gave everything back to her.

"That's the information I have on the trust. That's the information on the bank accounts and how it's been set up. Just your name is on the account. I assumed you knew," he said. "I'm sorry. Could have made the last ten years a lot easier."

"Maybe," she said. "And maybe I wouldn't have appreciated it as much."

"What did you do with your life?"

She raised her gaze to his and smiled. "I was way behind in my schooling when I was rescued. I ended up with foster parents who were both professors. They got my education up to snuff pretty fast, and then I went on to university myself. Until a few months ago, when I was laid off, I was working as an associate professor."

He smiled a fatherly beam at her that was full of approval. "I'm really glad to hear that," he said. "I know at the time some suggested you might not have been right in the head," he said almost apologetically. "Partly because of your appearance."

"You mean the scrawny beaten-up bleeding and burned body that came out of that house fire?" she asked with a smile. At his nod, she added, "And with good reason. I don't blame anybody for that. I'm very grateful for the rescue."

"I'm sure you were," he said. "I'm just sorry that nobody else was rescued with you."

"You haven't heard, I'm sure," she said, "but, until a few days ago, I hadn't realized nobody knew about the bomb shelter. We opened it yesterday and found ..." She stopped, took a deep breath. "We found another seven bodies."

The lawyer sucked in a breath and leaned forward. "A lot of people here are still missing family members. I believe several children and possibly a couple adults. I don't remember exactly."

"It's possible," she said. "You'll have to contact the police. They have been working on the property all yesterday and likely today."

"Good Lord," he said. "Why the bomb shelter?"

"Because they all believed they could live forever," she said tiredly. "And, down there, they believed they could keep a different lifestyle. Honestly they were crazy. And I don't know how to explain it any more than that. They got sucked into my father's beliefs, and that's just the facts of life." She looked down at the bank information and said, "Do we know if any of his followers gave him money?"

"It's possible," the lawyer said. "There was a hefty bank account at the time, but there were a lot of funerals to pay for. So I did utilize that money to cover his funeral and that of the others."

"You're thinking that was money from the families?"

"I have no idea," he said. "None of the research I was given showed that the women had any money to give in the later years. I believe they did originally, but, after that, there wasn't much more to give. I think he collected around him some of the more vulnerable women of society."

He offered her a nod of understanding. "Well, you're certainly all set now. This trust isn't from the families you lived with. In fact, this is the money that kept those women and children in food. Regular withdrawals were taken to help support that cult up until his death. We transferred everything into the trust for you at that point."

She nodded and looked over at him. "What happens to the property now?"

He shrugged. "It's yours free and clear. The tax money has been taken out of his bank account on a regular basis. Several other accounts were used to pay the bills. You have about four more years of money left to pay those bills, and then I'm afraid you'll have to make some decisions."

"Thank you," she said, feeling incredibly freer than she had when she first walked in. "Much appreciated."

"One note is here from my father," the lawyer said, studying his screen. "Something your father left with us. Something about a box you were supposed to be given." He walked to a safe, unlocked it and brought out a box. He stared at it for a long time and then turned to them.

"I have been hanging on to this since your father gave it to mine." He handed it to me. "It's definitely for you. It even says *For Phoenix* on top."

She stood and hesitantly reached for it, turning it over in her hands. It was the size of a small cigar box, about six by eight inches. Her name was scratched on the top. She nodded. "Thank you. Did he leave this for me?"

The lawyer nodded. "There is a note on the account. It was the last thing to be dispersed from his estate. I can close that now."

"Were there other things to be handed out?" Rowan asked.

"A couple small bequests to the stores that they had worked with on a regular basis," he said. "Nothing that amounted to much. We never opened the box, so I don't know what's in there."

"You didn't, or you couldn't open the box?"

"Honestly I tried but couldn't open it. You hate to keep something if you don't know what's inside, but, the truth of the matter is, it doesn't open. Hopefully you know how."

She glanced at the lawyer and said, "Not a clue. Thank you for everything." She walked to the door.

Rowan followed her. "You don't want to open it?"

She hugged the box close to her chest. "I don't want to open it while he's watching," she said in a low tone.

Rowan understood and nodded.

The three walked back toward the hotel, with Phoenix clutching at the box and the legal documents in her hand.

"Do you want me to hold those for you?"

She nodded and let Rowan take the papers from her

hand.

He tucked them under his arm. It took them about five minutes to get back to the hotel room.

She walked over to the small table and sat down.

"Interesting that you're after the box and not the business accounts," Grayse said quietly. "A lot of money is detailed there."

She glanced at him. "I guess that's why I feel like I probably appreciated my education more. I had to work for it," she said smoothly. "Money is in there, maybe not enough for me to retire per se but enough for me to be comfortable. That makes a huge difference between poverty and not eating and having a roof over my head. I have an education. I can work when I need to, so I'll never be on the streets again. This is a piece of my history that I both loathe and find I can't let go of."

"That makes it very dangerous," Grayse said and sat down across from her, and Rowan took the spot beside her.

"It could be empty, you know?" Rowan suggested.

She chuckled. "We're hoping it is, aren't we? Because otherwise, what is in here could be something I really don't want to see."

"Then don't open it," Grayse said. "Nobody says you have to."

"Maybe," she said. "But it's definitely something I feel I *need* to open." She took a deep breath and then tried to pop the lid up. But it didn't move. She frowned and applied more pressure, as if it were stuck. She lifted it up, using her other hand, forcing it apart. She shook her head and said, "It should open easier than this."

She inspected it, rotated it, flipped it around, looking for springs or a latch to open it and then shrugged. She handed it to Rowan. "You try."

Rowan struggled as he looked at it, but there was no secret latch that he could see. He didn't have the strength to force it open but knew he could get a screwdriver and possibly pop the hinge on the back. He glanced at Grayse. "Do you want to try?"

Grayse already had his hand out. "You're not looking at it from the right direction," he said. "You're looking at it as a concrete or wooden block. You should be looking at it from an energy point of view."

As soon as he said that, Rowan stopped struggling. He could see where the energy was zipped around in a circle. "It's not possible to bind something closed with energy, is it?"

"Oh, yes, it is," Grayse replied. He tapped the top of it and slid it back across to her. "This has got energy in a band all the way around it. Not this way across the top but along the middle and around the sides."

She studied it for a long moment, reached out and pressed her finger to one spot.

Rowan could see the energy fall away. He looked at her. "How did you know to do that?"

"Because a weakness was there," she said softly. "I could feel it with my fingers." She slowly reached for the lid and popped it open.

Rowan wasn't sure what he was seeing, but it looked like paperwork.

She pulled out several pieces of paper and opened them up. She gasped. "It's made of the same material as that letter I'm trying to burn."

"Which could be why you couldn't get rid of it," Grayse said. "It's part of this piece, and this is completely wrapped in energy. If you can't feel that, then I don't know what to say."

"I can feel it," she said. "It's buzzing through my fingertips."

Rowan could see the papers were covered and surrounded in color, but it wasn't blue, and it wasn't gold. "There's a weird energy too," he said. "What is that?"

"It's ancient energy," Grayse said. "I don't know what the paperwork says, but the actual material and the papers themselves are very old, according to the energy on it. If you don't want to keep it, I do suggest we find a nice safe place for it and perhaps the letter you've been carrying around. Like in a couple museums and private collections, where some of these types of pieces are held."

"Held to keep them safe or held to keep the rest of the world safe?" Phoenix asked, raising her gaze from the paperwork.

"What's on the paperwork?"

"One is a letter to me from my father, one is a letter to him from his father, and one appears to be some sort of maybe recipe."

Rowan couldn't read any of the wording from where he was. When she folded the first and put it back in the box, he realized with disappointment she wouldn't share. But then, why should she? It was her life, her history, her childhood. She read the second one, her breath catching in the back of her throat. She folded it and put it back in the box, then looked at the third one.

"It's supposed to be a method of surviving walking through fire," she said. "At least as far as I can tell."

"And the letters?" Grayse asked bluntly. "What do they say?

"The one from my grandfather to my father says it was his gift to pass down, as it had been passed down to him and the Elders who had gone before, and he's supposed to pass it down to the firstborn in his family. And basically my father's is a repeat." She pulled them out again, opened them up and held them up for both of the men to see.

Rowan realized it really was just that. "No explanation. Nothing?"

"No, that would be way too easy," she said with a half laugh.

"No," Rowan said. "He died, I think, or at least he's been gone for quite a while. Maybe he's not dead though."

"There is a note in here about special energy," she said. "The recipe tells about special family energy. As if our energy is different."

"Meaning, you have abilities," Grayse said. "They're often hereditary."

"So, did my father love me because I was like him, hate me because I was like him, or hate me because I was better than him?" she asked. She glanced from one man to the other. "Or does it even matter anymore?"

"It only matters if it matters to you," Rowan said. "It's what you do with your life from now on. Your father is dead."

She shook her head. "No, he's not. I can feel him, but now I also understand what that other energy I feel is. It's my grandfather and possibly those who had gone before him," she said.

Both men stiffened.

She nodded. "His energy is here. The same as my father's. I'm wondering if that isn't part of what this recipe is, to walk through fire and to live forever. Walk through fire with a family member, die in the process, but latch onto the Chosen One and live through them."

"That doesn't sound very nice," Grayse said. "Is there a way to release them from our plane?"

She shrugged. "More writing is on the back, but it's harder to read." She read it quietly and then nodded. "Basically it's how to live in spirit form. And that's what they're doing. I'm the Chosen One because I'm like them, so their energies aligned easier to mine so they can live through me."

"Yet he tortured you."

"I think, in here, it talks about that," she said, pulling out her father's letter that she carried with her, tapping the bottom part of the letter. "Making sure the person is prepared for what's to come. I think my father took that and loosely applied his own idea of what being *prepared* meant." She took a look at the box, lifting it up, putting her letter inside with the other letters, shutting it and then shaking it. "I don't think anything else is in it."

Then she stopped and looked closer at the bottom. "An inscription is on the bottom here and a year—1612." She looked up at Rowan. "That's a lot older than my great grandfather's grandfather would have been," she said.

"It was over four hundred years ago, so, yes," he said. "Chances are this has been in the family since then, if not longer."

"Maybe," she said. "For that alone, it's nice to have the box, but all this other stuff? Maybe not so much." She turned to Grayse. "Is there any way to find out what abilities my father would have had?"

"Not that I know of," he said. "Wouldn't it be nice if we had a repository of that information? A database of everyone's ability. But I'm sure you can understand that would be a very bad idea."

Rowan added, "Think about the world at large and how many people would be afraid of them. I can't think of anything worse. We'd all be persecuted."

Grayse nodded. "So true. Anybody who doesn't understand us would fear us. And fear causes retaliation," he said. "Speaking of which, I highly suggest we leave this hotel, just in case."

Rowan looked at him in surprise. "From the lawyer's office?"

"The receptionist," Phoenix said suddenly. "Something was in her gaze."

"Exactly," Grayse said. "If we check out now, we can always go to a different town or another hotel."

"It's probably too late already," she said, checking her watch. "It is checkout time, but I don't know that we can hide our exit from here."

"Or we can just head straight home," Rowan said.

She looked over at him and smiled. "That sounds perfect." She turned to Grayse. "Are you coming back to Iceland?"

He gave a half a snort and stood. "I wouldn't miss it for the world."

"Let's get packed then," Rowan said.

Phoenix got up, headed to her room and packed the rest of her stuff. She could hear a commotion outside the hotel.

Rowan called out to her. "Come on. Let's go. They found us. We have to go now."

She grabbed the box, her purse, putting it all together in her single bag, and found him standing at a fire escape.

"We're going out this way," he stated.

She raised an eyebrow, and he shook his head. "We have to go, and we have to go *now*."

"Are they that angry?"

"I don't know about angry as much as wanting to destroy something they saw as evil back then," he said. "Mob mentality doesn't allow for rational thinking. We don't want to be here when they realize you are in this room."

Phoenix climbed down the fire exit with Rowan behind her and Grayse bringing up the rear.

As she went to dash left, Rowan said, "Stay here. We'll get the vehicle and come back for you."

She shook her head. "No, I can't be separated from you." She grabbed Rowan's arm. He motioned to Grayse. He disappeared around to the front.

She looked up. "Do you think he'll be okay?" she asked worriedly.

"You tell me."

Just then, Grayse was thrown to the ground in front of them, his clothes on fire, screaming in terror.

They both ran to him, patting him down with their coats and jackets to stop the flames. And, when they could, they yelled for help.

Phoenix grabbed Rowan's hand and said, "Stop."

He looked over at her. "What?"

"This is a precog."

He stared at her in shock. She motioned to the ground, and he saw no sign of Grayse. "We have to go help him now," she said. She raced out to the front, Rowan with her.

The roar of the crowd built as they got closer to the street. The crowd had surrounded Grayse and were chanting something she couldn't understand. He was shouting, explaining he hadn't been involved, but no one was listening.

No one cared.

They'd caught the scent of blood and, like a pack of animals, had him surrounded as he spun, reasoning with the unreasonable.

Then someone lit a torch on fire …

Rowan stepped in the middle of the circle and grabbed Grayse, plunging through the line to the other side, almost tossing him into the vehicle. Phoenix jumped in herself, hating the roar of anger from the crowd as they realized they were losing their prey. The smell of rage and fear and anguish. … That was what was really underneath it all. Had the crowd recognized Grayse from so long ago? Or was it just because he was here with *her*?

Neither made her feel better.

Rowan hopped in, turned on the engine and tried to back out. But they were surrounded by the angry mob.

"What just happened?" Grayse asked. "Talk about killer mobs."

"We'll explain in a minute. But we have to get out of here now. Rowan, drive," Phoenix ordered.

He was trying to, but the crowd wasn't going away. They were smashing rocks on the vehicle to get to them. He said, "If you guys have any way to stop this …"

"I do," Phoenix spat. She opened her window, stuck out her hand, and shot fire all along the vehicle, sending the crowd screaming backward. "Now, drive. Drive. Drive," she said, pulling back in through the window.

There was a space, and he hit the gas, and the SUV lunged forward.

She sagged against the seat and groaned. "I guess I don't get to come back to this town again."

"No," Grayse said. "I presume you guys have a reason

for what you did?"

She turned to him, seeing his gaze on her finger. She still held the fire in her hand. She quickly put it out and clenched her fist. She glanced at Rowan to see how he would react, but he was driving.

After taking a calming breath, she explained the vision they'd seen. "The last time we had seen one, it was about Irene. She had been there and fine, then running and jumping off the cliff and committing suicide. We didn't even get a chance to think. So, this time, we raced out and grabbed you, so they couldn't do whatever they would do to you."

He stared at her. "That was a very twisted precog you two shared."

"We've never had it happen before until Irene," she said. "I don't know why it's happening between us now."

"Because your abilities have blended to a certain extent," Grayse said. "They've helped each other develop—stronger, better. And you have created a new ability between you." He rubbed his hand across his forehead. He held out his arms and said, "I'm not burned, and I promise I'm not suicidal. I'm grateful for whatever intervention you did."

"Just make sure you stay close," she said. "I don't know how long something like this can have an effect because, last time, the energy snatched Irene up and dragged her away from the cliff edge, but, as soon as she was cognizant again, she got up and took off on us on her own. It happened so quickly we barely had time to react."

"So, what? I'm your prisoner for the next half hour?" he asked with a tilt of his lips.

She stared at him steadily and said, "It happened fast with her, but I can't count on it, so I would think for much longer than that."

ROWAN COULD SEE the shock and disbelief on Grayse's face. But Rowan was driving like a crazy man, without putting them in danger. His mind was consumed with the crowd and Phoenix's fire. ... She'd created and controlled it like a weapon. When he could speak, he said, "It's because we've seen it before. We just want to make sure you don't end up doing something completely freaky too."

"I don't like the sound of that," Grayse said. "I'm not without some of my own instincts and gifts here, and I could recognize major danger when we were there, so your rescue was definitely timely, thank you."

"Not a problem," Rowan said. "There's something about Phoenix and me now. Like you said, we're stronger together."

"That's not unusual," Grayse said. "We have several people with psychic abilities who partnered up, and it seems that, the longer they are together, the more their own abilities develop and grow, and, in a way, a third ability develops between them. Probably as a combination of their energies."

"That's a disconcerting thought," Phoenix said with a laugh. "I never really knew much about what abilities were because I was raised with creating fire being a normal thing."

"But only your father could do it, correct?"

"Correct," she said. "As far as I knew, none of the other kids could. If they were all his offspring, it would explain why I was the Chosen One."

"I wonder whether they were all his?"

"Some things you should just leave alone," she said.

"Nobody else survived that cult fire but me and potentially some of the energy of my father, which is … unnerving."

"You can't dwell on that now," Rowan said firmly. "We are heading to the airport, and we'll be back in Iceland soon."

"It's still a long set of flights," she said. "Hardly an easy trip."

"It will pass quickly. Just like all the rest of our trip passed." He watched as she nodded and sank back into the corner, her head dropping against the side panel of the vehicle and closed her eyes.

In the review mirror, he raised an eyebrow at Grayse. He nodded and said, "Sleep's the best thing for all of us. After an energy outlay like that, the adrenaline hits you, and then, all of a sudden, it stops and drops. Make sure you're okay to keep driving."

"I'm fine," Rowan said. "At least, until I get home again." He thought about it and said, "Is there any other paperwork we have to do, do you think?"

"We should hit the bank here, so she can access the accounts."

"Maybe stop at one closer to the airport then," Rowan said.

"Yes. It's one of the national banks. So it shouldn't be a problem. She has to get access to that account."

Rowan nodded and brought up the banks on his route. There were two. "She'll also need more food."

"She does burn through a nice amount, doesn't she?"

"And she's burned out right now. That's why she crashed. We're twenty minutes away from a bank. I don't know how quickly we can get our flights changed. I know another flight goes out today because I had to decide whether we would leave today or tomorrow."

"Today would be better for all our sakes, but let's hit the bank first. Deal with that, then maybe the airport and grab food there."

That was what they did. They pulled into the parking lot of the bank. Rowan gently shook Phoenix awake.

She startled slightly and looked at him and blinked. She smiled when she realized it was him. "Are we at the airport?"

"No. We're at the bank," he said. "We need to make sure you can get access to your account."

She nodded and said, "Good plan. I wonder if that'll be a problem."

"I don't think so. We got a lot of documentation from the lawyer."

They jumped out of the SUV. Everyone stretched, and then they walked into the bank and inquired about speaking to a manager. They managed to get cards for her and to set up online banking, so she could access the money as she needed to.

With that done, Rowan shepherded them from the bank and back into the vehicle. He noticed Grayse was ready to collapse. "Now we'll go to the airport," he said. "I've already got a couple calls in about our flights, and they were checking. If we can get confirmation that we are cleared to fly out today, then we'll take the rental back and go have a meal at the airport."

As he was about to turn on the engine, his phone rang. Their flights were confirmed for today. With that in mind, he backed out of the parking lot, drove to the rental drop-off at the airport. Seeing that both of his travel mates were getting even droopier, he pushed them through baggage check. They headed to a restaurant and ordered coffee immediately and food.

Phoenix sat with her eyes half-closed and head resting in her hands, elbows on the table.

Grayse crossed his elbows and just dropped his head on top of the table and said, "I'm out." By the time the coffee and food arrived, he was capable of lifting his head and looking around blurry-eyed. "Wow. That was like a ton of bricks hit me."

"Energy's like that," Rowan said.

Grayse looked at him suspiciously. "But nothing affected you?"

"I'll make it to the first flight," he said. "Then I'll be out." He gently squeezed Phoenix's fingers. "Phoenix, honey, wake up."

She slowly opened her eyes and looked at him. "I'm not really asleep."

He grinned and said, "Glad to hear that. There's coffee and food. Let's eat. We'll be boarding in about two hours."

She nodded. "It'll seem like a very long two hours."

"Maybe," he said. "But just think about it. Your life has changed completely. You have money. You know more about your heritage. As for your own property, you can take some time to think about it. Although that crowd was disruptive, and we're away from them now, I highly doubt they'll start anything at the airport."

A look of concern crossed her face. "I hope not," she said. "I didn't even consider that." She glanced around, and he watched as she shivered gently. She rubbed her arms, warming up.

He placed the coffee in front of her. "Get some of this down," he said. "It's not that you're cold because of the temperature outside. It's all the events that happened which make you chilly."

She nodded and reached out to hug the cup of coffee. She glanced over at Grayse, who was doing the same thing. Her gaze went from Grayse to Rowan. With a look of suspicion, she asked, "How come you haven't crashed like we have?"

"I will soon," he promised. "But, right now, it's important that one of us at least be cognizant enough to keep going."

"Can't argue with that," she said. "It's definitely weird."

"I don't think so," he said. "It is what it is. And, by the time we get into the air, I'll be more than happy to be the one who crashes."

"When do we land?"

"Midmorning tomorrow."

"That means nothing, with the time change, to me."

He laughed. "Exactly. So don't worry about it."

They ate slowly. The other two struggled to put the food in their mouths, but Rowan kept pushing to make sure they got a good meal. When they were done, he took them to their gate, and both nodded off again while he sat and watched. He was on his phone, checking in at home, and then doing more research on the crowd at the hotel. No mention of a mob was in the news anywhere. He sent the lawyer a message, telling him what had happened. But when he didn't get an answer, he wondered if the lawyer had been part of it.

Phoenix's bank account was now set up for her. The property taxes would be paid for the next few years, and then she'd have to figure out what she wanted to do with the cult site. As far as he was concerned, it should be left as a memorial, razed to the ground or sold off to somebody who wanted to do something for the good of all with it. Because otherwise the cult property would just be a piece of her past she didn't want to keep.

Almost as an afterthought he sent an email to the two cops he'd met at the property. The three of them would have to give updated statements to those cops, but, when Grayse woke, he could explain their mad flight from the area. Those cops were his friends, after all.

She had that box and the messages in it. That it came from his hometown was yet another one of those spooky moments that he didn't want to think about. But he had time right now, so he brought out his laptop and started researching the family a little more intently. He knew about her father, but he hadn't looked at her grandfather or great-grandfather. As he kept working through the research, he checked through his own database back home and realized he would have to go to storage to look at some of the older files.

But there were stats that would give him historical data back a good one or two hundred years, and he should find her grandparents and several older generations listed there, but that didn't mean he would find anything about what kind of lifestyle they lived. What he needed to do was find a way to stop his town from its suicide season and to stop Phoenix from wanting to throw her letter into the Burning Fires. He didn't mind her getting rid of the letter, but he didn't want anything to hurt her. He'd hoped she'd change her mind but doubted she'd be so willing to turn away from her lifelong obsession so easily.

Maybe, as Grayse had said, the box of papers would be better off in a private museum or some secret holding place where they would be secure. Something about that energy around the box really bothered Rowan. That her father's energy was still hanging around her was one thing. If Rowan could get that energy into that little box, he'd prefer to seal it up with his energy and not have anybody ever open it again.

He could feel almost ghostlike tentacles crossing his neck at the thought. He straightened and glared around, seeing an icy-blue energy beside him. Too many people were nearby for him to say anything out loud, so he reached through his mind and, with a finger, flicked it away. And it did disappear, but it seemed to latch onto the side of her that was farthest away from him.

She shuffled in her seat just then, turned sideways and dropped her head on his shoulder.

He watched as her physical contact with him threw the icy-blue energy into the ethers. He smiled and shifted so she would be more comfortable. She really was a sweetheart, and she'd been to hell and back. How could he get her to stay with him? Because he wanted to see where this relationship would go. He hadn't met very many people like her and none as interesting and attractive or who affected him as much as she had.

He'd had plenty of girlfriends, but no one had ever intrigued him enough to take the next step.

Now he couldn't imagine his future without her.

Finally it was boarding time. He helped his traveling companions get up and maneuvered them to their seats. They had three across, and he took the middle seat. As soon as they were settled on the plane and in the air, he closed his eyes, and that was it. He was out.

THEY'D BE BACK soon. The Supplier could feel it. He closed

his eyes and drew on his visions. He could see them traveling back home again.

Just in time. He couldn't wait much longer.

He frowned, sensing something had changed. Danger had amplified. Even the Elders were agitated. Did they know her? Did they realize she was supposed to come to them?

In his head he could hear one of them. *She's special. But she's dangerous.*

The Supplier knew that. Her energy had shifted. She was both freer, and yet burdened. She was too far away to see clearly, but his soul shivered with the recognition of her new energized aura and the ones she carried with her.

Was it possible?

Did she carry the very energy of the Elders he served?

CHAPTER 25

PHOENIX WOKE UP in the middle of the flight, noticing the plane was still flying level. When the stewardess came around the next time, she asked how much longer until they arrived. The woman smiled and said, "We're almost there. We'll start our descent in about ten minutes."

Surprised, and yet delighted because the long flight was almost over, Phoenix settled to stare out the window. Rowan still slept soundly. He almost looked like he was unconscious, he was in such a deep sleep.

But then she'd probably been no better earlier. Whatever the hell had happened back in the States had taken the stuffing out of her. Now Rowan had reaped the effects of having pushed past his normal reserves too. Grayse, on the other hand, was on his phone sending messages.

She leaned forward and asked, "Are you okay now?"

He beamed her a smile. "I'm fine. Really got sent for a loop back there though."

"Me too," she said. "I hope Rowan wakes up soon, or it'll be almost impossible to move him off the plane."

Grayse chuckled. "That's very true. He's too big for us to carry."

Just then Rowan muttered, "I'm here. I'm not very cognizant or mobile yet, but I'm here."

Content, she sat back, sliding her fingers under his and

holding his hand gently. He was such a protector. He'd been there to help look after Grayse and her when the two of them crashed; he'd been there for her every step of the way.

Hell. He'd been there for her right from the first time they'd met. She liked that in a guy. Still, it was hard to not keep looking around the plane and seeing if anybody involved in her cult history was with them on this plane. She wondered how long she'd be looking over her shoulder.

She was grateful when the plane safely landed, and they disembarked and walked out of the airport.

The three of them stood side by side, Rowan now standing tall, taking deep breaths of fresh air.

She studied his face and said, "It feels good to come home, doesn't it?"

He gave her a brilliant smile. "Yes. For you too?"

Their sense of togetherness was hard to beat.

Rowan glanced at Grayse. "Do you need your own wheels here?"

"No," Grayse said. "I'll catch a ride with you though, if you don't mind."

"Sure," Rowan said. "Let's go." He was parked in the short-term parking, as they'd only been gone for a couple days. As soon as they were in his vehicle, with the engine started, he patted the dash and said, "Now this is more like it." He pulled out of the parking lot, paid the bill and drove to the highway. Within minutes they were heading to his place.

Phoenix sighed, settled back and said, "Wouldn't it be nice to relax and not have any other weird stuff happen?"

Grayse chuckled. "Now that you are part of this world, that's not going to happen."

"Sure. But I don't have to hunt down crazy cult leaders

and other dead bodies and energy all the time, do I?"

"No," he said. "But, between the two of you, you could keep that town clear of negative energy too so suicide season doesn't happen."

She twisted in her seat. "How much effort would that take?"

"Not much," he said. "Energy attracts like energy. Once you get the suicide energy cleaned out, and since you can both see energy, you'll recognize when something's going on in town, and you can just walk by and mentally clear it away."

"*Mentally*?" she asked. "Is it that easy?"

"You'd be surprised," he said. "If nobody in town is deliberately or maliciously causing problems, then there's nothing to it. You can go ten to twenty years before something happens."

"That sounds perfect," she said. "I'm not at all sure how or what I would do in town if I were to stay."

"Maybe you could invite your foster parents for a visit?" Grayse said.

"That would be an interesting visit," Rowan said. "You haven't seen them in how many years? And look at how different you are now."

"Am I though?" She twisted once again to look at Grayse and then at Rowan. "I haven't even been here all that long."

"You've been here long enough to cause all kinds of chaos," Rowan said, half chuckling.

She snorted. "We'll blame you for that. All I did was hear a woman crying in the woods. It all went to hell from there."

"You came with a whole lot of energy of your own," he said. "Don't forget that."

"Right. So do you have to go back to work tomorrow?" she asked him.

"I should," he said. "I might even stop in this afternoon."

"Okay. Am I going to your house or am I going to the hotel?" she challenged.

He looked at her. "Well, you have the money to stay at a hotel, if that's what you want. But you are welcome to be a guest at my house, and you too, Grayse. I've got the room."

"I think I'll take you up on that offer," Grayse replied calmly. "I do want to check out Phoenix's background here. See just how much of her ancestral energy is here. Maybe we can clean up the village once and for all."

"That's possible," she said. "I don't know too much about my family line here, but obviously it is here. If we can find out where they lived, maybe that would give us an idea of what ancient energy is around. I do have the box with me, but I'm not sure what I want to do with it yet."

"No decisions have to be made right away," Rowan said. He looked through the rearview mirror at Grayse. "Right, Grayse?"

"No. As long as the box is left in a neutral spot, where the energy contained within can't do any damage."

Phoenix tossed that idea around, realizing just how new, and yet how old this energy was.

"So ... a safe place where nobody else can touch it and where it can't be opened and where it can't cause any distress by the wrong person who might know it's there?"

"Exactly," Grayse said. "In other words. A safe. Just like where the lawyer had it."

"Yes. That would make sense," she said. "I'll have to think about it."

They pulled up in front of the police station, and she laughed. "I didn't even realize we were so close."

"We are," Rowan said. "I'll go in and check things out for a few minutes. I'll be right back." He hopped out, shut the door and walked into the police station.

She turned to look at Grayse. An odd look came on his face. "What's the matter?"

Grayse smiled. "Nothing. Rowan just has an interesting trick of shielding his energy as he walks into the station."

"I think his job is probably a lot of bad news," she said, "but nowhere near as bad as if he were a police officer in a major city."

"Quite true. And all police stations have a certain amount of negative energy. This is what he was born to do though. I couldn't imagine, from his energy alone, any job that would be better for him."

"I just don't know what I'm supposed to do now," she said quietly. "I used to teach, but I'm not sure that's what I want to do now."

"I'm not sure either," he said, studying her face.

She glanced at him. "Can you see anything I should be doing from my energy?"

"Healing," he said. "You heal. What you could do quite easily is heal others."

"I don't think there's much chance of a job like that here," she said with a smile. "I already caused chaos here. Besides I don't know much about healing. I'd have a lot to learn."

"You don't need a job per se," he said. "You could do it anonymously, if you think about it. You could heal mentally, with your thoughts. You could walk through the hospital and help anybody who's struggling, even if you just focused on children. You could collect your energy and give them the healing energy yourself. And sure, you could learn a lot more specialized healing, but some great healers are out there you could contact and maybe learn from."

"Is that even possible? Who would do something like that?"

"Maybe Dr. Maddy would," Grayse said. "She works with Stefan and was part of the team who searched for you. They knew you were in acute distress and helped as much as they could. But they couldn't find you—something they would normally do. Now, realizing your father was psychic and keeping you all behind a curtain, that makes sense."

She stared at him in surprise. "I remember them. I thought they were like fictional characters, like a child's invisible friends, reaching out to help me. I didn't have names for them, but I could feel them. Then, in the hospital, after I got shot here, they came again. This time I got their names, and it was, indeed, Stefan and Maddy. I forgot about them," she cried out softly. "How could I have? They were my saving grace."

"They could feel you crying out," Grayse admitted. "And I know Maddy would love to connect with you on a physical level after all these years. As to whether she'd help with your training, I can't say for sure, but, given the power of your own healing that she saw firsthand back then, I wouldn't be at all surprised to hear she'd love to teach you some things."

"I'd really like that," Phoenix whispered, smiling. She sent out a message to Dr. Maddy as she had when she was sick and hurting, asking if such a thing would be possible. To Grayse, she said, "To help others with energy, … that would be almost a dream job."

"There are definite downsides to it," he warned. "It's not always light and sunshine. Some cases you can't help. You'll feel sadness and grief, frustration and anger. But …"

"There will be joy and love and a sense of accomplishment—a sense of rightness. To help to heal, after my father caused so much pain, to spend the rest of my life taking pain away …" She sank against the seat when a whisper slipped into her mind.

I'd be pleased to help. You're already incredibly talented. With a little direction, you could do so much more. We'll talk later. Over a phone perhaps?

And the laughing voice faded from her mind … but left a smile on her face. "I think I just asked and got a yes response from Dr. Maddy."

Grayse sat up and twisted to study her face. Then he nodded and said, "That's normal."

"Normal?" She stared at him. Then she snorted. "Listen to us. That was like dream-talking or a telepathic communication. Whatever it was, no one else will believe this is possible. Any more than they will believe I can heal. The hospital wouldn't likely let me in to see the sick or the injured, would they?" she asked. "That'll be weird for everybody to consider."

"Maybe," he said. "But it's also a really cool thing because you already know you can do it. You know how effective you are. You know that, once you learn a few tricks, you don't have to be right beside the patient, right?"

She twisted around in the front seat and nodded slowly. "Fascinating," she said. "I'd really like to learn more, do more …"

He chuckled. "It would be a real job in terms of energy workers. You're in an unusual position, or, maybe I should say, a lucky position of having money from the trust. You don't need to work. Although others might look at you and wonder how you support yourself. Yet the work you would be doing, with energy, would be incredible. You could heal everybody—well, maybe not everybody—but you could certainly help a lot of people. You could raise the energy of the town, and that will spread outward. Instead of having this be a suicide season, you could end up with people coming here because they feel so good. Because the energy is so strong, and it is feel-good energy."

"Ha," she said. "That would take forever!"

"What else have you got to do?" he said. "Really, it wouldn't take that long. Okay. It would take a little bit of time, yes, because the energy here has to shift and you're not used to doing it on a larger scale, but it's not as if it would be hard to do."

She studied him for a long moment. "Maybe," she said. But doubt still remained in her voice, and she knew it.

"Wait and see," he said. "If you and Rowan end up *together* together, that in itself will be a job."

"What? Being a wife is a job now?" she asked with a laugh.

He grinned at her. "Because of your energy, you'll see things well ahead of what's happening. So you'll constantly be reacting. It will be both rewarding and sometimes painful. You'll see the world around you differently, and you'll react differently. People will see you differently."

"But nobody'll know, will they?"

"No," he said. "And that's the joy of it. If you want them to know, you could tell a few, and honestly it's possible that, over time, as you build a reputation, you could do your work in the shadows. Wouldn't it be lovely to do all this and not have to worry about people knowing? To do it because it's the right thing to do and because you want to do it and to know that you can put a smile on a crying child's face or make an old woman feel not quite so lonely just because you're there? Because you have the way of touching somebody with energy that they don't understand."

"It sounds almost too Nirvana," she muttered.

"Each step you take," and he spoke deliberately now, each word having more emphasis than the last, "will help heal a piece of yourself. … If, through the act of healing others, you heal yourself, that's just good karma to me. You spent a lifetime in trauma. Why not spend the rest of your life experiencing joy?"

Rowan walked out of the station and hopped into the truck. He looked at the two of them and said, "The energy in this truck's heavy. What have you two been talking about?"

"The fact that you're doing what you're meant to do," Phoenix said blithely. "I don't appear to have any purpose in life, but Grayse has given me a few suggestions."

"I suggested she heal. It's something she knows she can do because she did it for herself, and she could do it for the people of your town."

"Remember how I told you about the energies who helped me back then?" At Rowan's nod, she continued, "It was Stefan and his friend Dr. Maddy. Grayse even suggested that Dr. Maddy might help me learn to do more specialized energy-healing work. Of course I'd have to talk to her about that. Maybe I'm no good at healing others, … just myself."

"That's a great idea," Rowan said. "I'd like to visit the chief in the hospital. Maybe you can do something to help him heal, as he's still in a coma."

"I'd like to see him too," Grayse said. "Didn't you say he tried to commit suicide?"

"Yes. He was the first one at the beginning of this year's suicide season."

"It would be nice if we could find out if any other energy is involved in that," Grayse added.

Rowan shot him a hard look and then said, "Sure. Let's stop by. I've been gone, so am due to visit him. I'd like to have a follow-up on his condition."

The hospital wasn't far. They were inside within ten minutes.

Phoenix walked at his side, studying the energy around them.

Grayse asked, "Can you feel it? The fear? The pain? The studied neutrality the medical professionals use to protect themselves from so much agony? They're all wrapped up in it to keep functioning. But you don't have to be like that, Phoenix. You're not hurting. You can reach out. You can touch some of these people who are hurting."

They walked past the emergency waiting room, and she could see a child whose knee was badly scraped up, all bloody skin and tissue, screaming at the top of his lungs. She sucked in her breath as she studied the wound.

Beside her, Grayse said, "You don't necessarily have to fix that. But does the child have to suffer so much?" She gave Grayse a look, and he shrugged. "What if you just gave him a little bit of energy or gave his energy level a chance to smooth it out?"

She reached out and, with a brush of her energy, dried the tears on his face and stroked his heart chakra to take some of the trauma back a bit.

He was still in shock, and his body was still injured, but

he wasn't screaming at the top of his lungs; instead he took deep, gulping breaths and cuddled into his mother.

She turned and walked on. Even from behind her, she could hear Grayse's whisper, "See? Told you so."

Rowan looked down at her and raised an eyebrow. She shrugged and nodded. He smiled, squeezed her fingers gently, and they walked down the hallway to a room.

Rowan pushed open the door already ajar, and they stepped inside. He walked over to the bed against the window where a huge man lay motionless. But his features were unmistakable.

She sucked in a breath. "My God," she said. "You didn't tell me that he was your father!"

He looked at her, his gaze steady and nodded. "I know. I didn't. The situation was hard enough without telling you both about the relationship."

Grayse walked up to the bedside, reached a hand down and touched Rowan's father.

She looked at Grayse and asked, "What's with the blue?"

Grayse smiled. "That's what I mean. You can see it and know it shouldn't be there. Do you want to lift it off him, please?"

She grabbed it with her hand, picked it up and flicked it out the window. She could feel something wrench from her own back as she did so. She stretched her hand up and rubbed her shoulders, frowning.

Grayse nodded. "See? You are connected in ways you don't realize."

She motioned at the chief lying in the bed. "The bullet doesn't look like it did that much damage. How is that possible?"

"The bullet went through the soft tissue and right

through the hollow where the jaw meets the skull," Rowan said. "He's not physically damaged, or at least not enough to warrant the coma he's currently in. Nobody knows why he won't wake up."

"Oh," she said, "I get it." She put a hand over his heart chakra, coming down almost like a slap.

A sudden moan came from his father. A moan that seemed to rattle all the way up through the inside of his chest before coming out his mouth. And then he shifted a little bit at first and then more as he tried to change his position.

Rowan stared at her. "What did you just do?"

"I removed the ice-blue energy on top, though I don't understand yet what that is. Then I reached out and gave him a smack, like a paddle from a defibrillator to wake him up—on many levels. He's lying here, locked in guilt and hatred for what he's done. So he won't fight back for life because he doesn't feel he deserves it."

"But why did he do it in the first place?" Rowan asked.

She noticed his hands clenched on the railing of the bed. "He didn't do it," she said. "That's the thing to realize here. It wasn't his hand that pulled that trigger."

Rowan's mouth dropped open all the way. He lowered his voice and leaned toward her. "Are you saying somebody tried to murder him?"

Grayse leaned closer too, his head right between the two of them. "No. It was an energy. Just like her father's energy. That's what's hanging around this town, and that's what's causing the suicides. It has nothing to do with your father pulling the trigger."

She looked down to see the chief staring back at them, shock in his gaze. She smiled at him and said, "Hi, my name is Phoenix. And I'm going to marry your son."

ROWAN FELT THE shock of her words initially but then the inner knowledge of the rightness in her statement.

He looked at her and whispered, "Are you sure?"

She beamed up at him. "I don't think I have a choice," she confessed. "It seems like we're two halves of the same whole."

He glanced over at Grayse to see him grinning like a fool. "Did you put her up to that?"

Grayse shook his head. "Nope. Not at all. But she's seen what I'm seeing. And you already saw."

Rowan did glance down to see his hand and her hand joined, as they had been so much in the last few days. Their energy also blended into something that wasn't his or hers but something uniquely theirs.

He squeezed her hand tight and looked down at his father, who was looking up at him.

"What happened?" his father asked when he could. He winced. "My mouth."

Rowan looked to Grayse and said, "Can you tell the nurse he's awake, please." He helped his father to sit up and held up a glass of warm water with a bendy straw.

His father took a small, slow sip and then another and afterward lay back down. "What the devil happened?" he whispered.

"Up until now we *thought* you tried to ... commit suicide," Rowan replied carefully.

His father's face took on a ruddy color; whether it was rage or shame, he didn't know.

But almost immediately the color was gone. He glanced at Phoenix, who was brushing the energy up his father's body and across his face. Rowan frowned at her. She smiled and looked down at his father and asked, "How are you feeling now?"

The chief lifted one hand first, then the other, moved his feet and said, "Honestly? I don't feel too bad." His gaze went back to Rowan. "Suicide?"

"You were shot through the mouth," he said. "The gun was found in your hand. It had been recently fired, and you had GSR all over your hand and the shirt you were found in."

His father's eyes clouded over. "I know I was depressed for a few days there," he said. "I just kept thinking about your mother and how lonely life was, but I never would have committed suicide. Not when it's been such a problem for our village."

"That's what I had thought," Rowan said. "I'm the one who found you, and I didn't know what else to think."

"I'm sorry. I wouldn't have wanted that for you," his father whispered. "I don't remember. I don't understand the sequence of events that led up to it. Last thing I remember was being at work in my office."

"Right," Rowan said. "That's where I found you."

His father stared at him, which was interrupted by the sound of running footsteps, and the door bursting open with a nurse and a doctor barreling in, practically out of breath. They stared at the chief in surprise. He looked at the new arrivals and smiled. "I guess I'm awake, huh?"

"And talking," the doctor said, coming in for a closer look. "How's the jaw?"

"Sore," the chief answered. "A shot of whiskey would help though."

"You're not getting that for a while," the nurse said, chuckling. She looked at him with a special smile and said,

"Very happy to have you back in the land of the living." She gently stroked his cheek, and the others could see a real affection in her actions.

He smiled and whispered, "I guess I am too."

"You won't get away scot-free on this," the doctor announced. "I don't know what happened, and I'm pretty damn glad you are awake, but, before you are cleared for work, you have to get some help."

"I didn't try to commit suicide," the chief said bluntly. "I just heard that theory from my son, but it's not my way. You know that. I've been against the suicide season here for a long time."

"Makes one wonder if something isn't in the air," Phoenix said lightly. "Or the water."

The doctor turned and frowned at her.

She just gave him a bright smile and stayed quiet.

Rowan knew she was suggesting other things, and he had to wonder. He hadn't even looked or seen anything different about his father at the time. Now he wished he had. He still had the crime-scene photos from the full investigation, but Rowan had found no sign of anyone else there. At least no one physically. ... But Rowan needed to take another look now.

The doctor said, "You all step out so I can give the chief a full examination."

Rowan straightened. "Sure." He looked down at his father and said, "Don't you go back into a coma. You got that?"

"Not going there," his father said stoutly. Although his voice was weak and his words a little slurred, his speech was becoming stronger. "Besides, we have a wedding to plan."

Rowan ushered Phoenix and Grayse out of his father's

hospital room.

In the hallway, Rowan stood there, almost shaking. He looked down at his trembling hands and said, "Hard to believe the old man's awake. And not only awake but appears to be completely cognizant."

"He probably is," Grayse said. "I suggest we do a search for energy. Can we go see his office? Do you have any photos? We do have a crime here that needs to be taken care of before that same energy can affect somebody else."

"What would make it affect one versus another?" Phoenix asked.

Rowan nodded. "Good question. Why would it go after my father, and how does it choose its victims?"

"It went after your father because he was doing something about the suicide season," Grayse said. "That's a huge problem for you guys. Or maybe this energy entity decided your father would make a perfect target to prove this guy could do what he wanted."

"We're giving it human qualities now, are we?" Phoenix asked in a half-raised voice, then looked around to see if anybody heard her.

Rowan gently tugged her closer and said, "I think it's just one way to refer to this energy."

"So it could be a human carrying this suicide-season energy?" Phoenix asked, her voice dropping and her body shaking. "Somebody bent on evil, like my father?"

"Maybe," Grayse said. "It's very common for this energy to attach itself to a much weaker person. Or for the energy to connect to a family member. Someone nobody would expect. It is fully capable of doing things you haven't thought of and possibly has been for a long time."

"What are you talking about?" Rowan asked. He glanced

around, but they were still alone, except for the team nearby, checking his father over.

"Somebody who is always there, somebody who is always friendly, who is always happy-go-lucky, maybe even simple," Grayse said. "Every village, every town, every city has multiples of them. The last person on Earth who you would think would have anything to do with this."

Phoenix gave a half a laugh. "Manru."

Rowan stared at her. "What?"

"She has the sight. She would know."

He shook his head. "For a moment there I thought you were blaming her."

"She is the kind to know everyone."

"Maybe. It's not like I can pick up the phone and ask her that."

"Why not?" Grayse asked. "I would."

Rowan pulled his phone out and said, "She'll think I'm crazy."

"She already does," Phoenix added.

He snorted at that and dialed his grandmother. When she answered, he said, "I have an odd question for you."

"I'm glad you're home, safe and sound," she said, her voice a calming effect in his ear. "What's your question?"

"Who would be the last person you would think of who would commit murder in this town?"

Silence came first. "What kind of a question is that?" she asked, puzzled.

"A serious one. Who is the absolute last person you would think would ever commit such a major crime? And that includes people who are simple-minded. People who are loving and caring and generous. People who are young. People who are old. Who?"

"Well, of course, I would think that about myself," she replied. "Because you know I would never do anything like that, but as for anybody else? *Hmm*. I guess everybody has their downside and their negative side and their dark side."

"Who else then?" he asked.

"Well, you," she said. "You are too honorable to be anything else."

He slowly lowered his phone. His heart was troubled though. "Did you guys hear that?"

They both nodded. Phoenix swallowed and said, "I can tell you that it's not you."

He hated the inner relief that washed through him. "Can we know that for sure?"

"Yes," she said. "I can see inside your soul. I can see your energy in the very heart of you, and it's not you."

CHAPTER 26

"**T**HIS SITUATION HAS taken a very strange turn," Phoenix said. "Makes me uncomfortable to think it's some person around us, who we've either known or interacted with. In my case, I don't know anybody here well, but, if it's somebody who's lived here or comes and goes on a regular basis, then it'll be somebody you know," she said to Rowan. "Does this person need a physical body to come for a victim?" she asked, turning to look at Grayse. "I know that sounds very esoteric, and I'm not sure that I should even be speaking like this," she said. "But I have to ask."

"Good thing you did ask," he said, "because, no, absolutely not. This person does not need a physical body. Chances are, it's easier for him if he does, or he's utilizing the physical body as a vehicle in order to facilitate some of what he's doing. But he could leave that physical body and potentially move to another. Although generally he'd have a close connection to that person."

"But why is he doing it?" Rowan asked, his voice harsh. "That doesn't make any sense. Why would any entity in this physical world or another make somebody like my father commit suicide? And how does it relate to Phoenix's situation?"

"It's not about committing suicide. It's about power," she said slowly. "It's about life and death. As with my father, when he used to light me on fire, when he put a bag over my head and tried to suffocate me."

Both men spun their heads around, their mouths dropped open.

She shrugged. "It was a long time ago. It was all about control. It was all about 'I have the power to make you live or die, so do what I want … or else.'"

"How does that apply to this?" Rowan demanded. "It doesn't make any sense."

"Maybe not," she said. "I suspect that, when we get down to it, there will be a reason. My father believed in the Elders or the Ancients—generations having gone long before him. My father believed in life after death. My father believed in all kinds of things. He believed in giving sacrifices. That's why the children were killed, as sacrifices to the Elders. He also thought that being a sacrifice would give them a better life."

"That's getting beyond freaky," Rowan said. "But then again, your father was loopy."

"He was. But what are the chances that somebody has lived here all their life and is just like him? Particularly when considering that my family line is here. What if Father has a cousin or brother or somebody, whether acknowledged or not acknowledged. Maybe my father was directing me to come back here so *Father* could return here. I know that was something he wanted but for some reason couldn't. I mean, the fact is, I am here now, which means he is here and his father …"

She nodded as she saw she had their full attention. "I have to ask. Does your grandmother know how to fire a weapon?"

Rowan stiffened.

She shrugged. "I don't think anybody's free and clear here. Your grandmother doesn't like me. She is in tune with this energy stuff. She's old enough to have learned a lot, and, like she just said, she would never expect you to kill anyone. Who we are looking for is not somebody who could do such a deed but could be affected by somebody else or forced or manipulated into doing that deed."

"By that definition a lot of people in town are possibles," he said, glaring at her.

"Exactly. We need a list of names, and we need to know who and why," Grayse suggested. "With a list we'd have to find a way to whittle it down to just a few."

"For example, Irene's husband? Was Irene chosen because of what she had done? Was your father chosen too? He was against the suicide season, so was it proof the suicide season was something he couldn't control? What about Theo and Haro?"

"Who knows?" Rowan said in frustration. "My head is spinning."

The door to the chief's hospital room opened, and the doctor stepped out into the hall. "Your father has gone to sleep for now. The checkup showed absolutely nothing wrong. When he wakes up again, I'll have one of my colleagues come take a look at him and assess his mental state. After that, you can probably pick him up and take him home."

"That sounds wonderful," Rowan said sincerely and reached out to shake the doctor's hand. "Thank you very much for the care you've given him."

"I've been looking after him," the doctor said, "but something else helped him to wake up. And that something, just maybe, was the two of you. Sometimes miracles happen." He smiled, and they watched him walk down the hall.

Phoenix muttered under her breath, "I have to admit, for a moment, I was afraid that was a joint premonition. And that your dad wasn't really awake."

Rowan chuckled. "I did too. That's why I was holding on to him tight while we were in there."

Grayse laughed. "You'll learn the signs of what's real, what's not real, what's a prelude, and what's not. You learned to act very fast with me."

"We did," Phoenix said. "Even then, we weren't sure. Now it feels like there'll be some confrontation with whoever is doing this, and it'll take all three of us to figure out the energy behind it all."

"You brought Rowan's father back, so that's a start," Grayse said. "Like you said, there could be some of your family here." He turned to look at Rowan. "Can you check that out?"

"I already had one of the deputies working on it before we left for the US. I haven't heard any results yet though."

"You need to check out that deputy and make sure he's not part of the family line and going to bury it."

Rowan laughed. "No, he's not. He is related to Irene's husband, however. But that's a different story."

"That's the thing about a small town. Everybody is related to everybody, aren't they?"

Phoenix and Rowan nodded. They slowly walked out of the hospital, stood on the front steps and took several deep breaths.

Phoenix could feel her body easing back, feeling the energy buzz from having used it. She looked at Grayse. "I forgot that buzz when I used to pull energy and use it for a purpose, that little weird buzz afterward."

He tilted his head. "You're surrounded by energy right now. Maybe shut it down, so you're not attracting entities."

She closed in her mind, envisioning a vacuum sealer hooking onto her big toe and sucking on all the energy, so it was tight against her body. The look on Rowan's face was priceless.

Rowan laughed. "I don't know what you just did, but you brought in your aura to the nearest tiny little channel I've ever seen."

She explained her visual, and he started to laugh.

"That's not bad," Grayse said. "Now you need to create a visual so something slides along the edge of your body and off again so it doesn't stick to you. Then it'll be interesting to see what happens around town."

"What do you mean?" Rowan demanded. "Are you saying these energies attached to her will find somebody else to attach to?"

"Possibly. But it's her father and grandfather I see."

Just then a vehicle arrived in the parking lot, and Rowan watched his grandmother hop out of the car and come toward them.

"I heard your father is awake." She had a determined look on her face. "Is that true?"

He nodded. "Yes, he is. He's doing fine. He's talking. He can move. He's still in a bit of pain and a bit weak, but there's a good chance he can come home today or tomorrow."

She stared at him. "You didn't think to tell me that on the phone? You asked me all those strange questions, but you don't even let me know that your father is awake?"

He shrugged. "Sorry. I was overcome at the time. I wasn't thinking straight."

She glared at him. "What is wrong with you?"

"It's been a tough few days."

She nodded. "I'll see your father," she said and turned to walk away.

As she did, Grayse grabbed her hand gently. "No," he said. "You won't."

She glared at him, shook her hand free and said, "And just who are you to stop me?"

Following her instincts, Phoenix stepped in front of her and said, "Not until you shed that energy."

Manru straightened up and said, "You are dangerous."

Phoenix nodded slowly. "To you, I am, yes."

Rowan stepped forward. "Hey. What's going on here?"

"Look at her back," Phoenix said.

Rowan walked around his grandmother, looked at Phoenix and motioned at his grandmother.

"You have the sight. You have all kinds of abilities. Yet you don't recognize the energy your grandmother is carrying?" Grayse asked him curiously.

Manru just raised her chin in defiance as she glared at the three of them.

"Oh, you *do* know about the energy you're carrying?" Phoenix asked. "And you're quite happy to carry it? How does that work?"

"He's righting the wrongs of the world. Fixing the things that can't be fixed any other way." She glared at Phoenix. "You're an energy worker too. You know how wrong everything in life is. How much the cops …" She shot a disparaging look at Rowan. "How little they do."

Rowan stared at his grandmother as if he had been kicked in the gut. "You're behind this? You're behind the shooting of my father?"

"He's responsible for my daughter's death," she said in a monotone, her voice losing all its inflection.

Phoenix gasped softly as she studied the older woman in front of her and saw an older man superimposed over the top of her face. Was that the energy she carried?

"Why should I care about him?" Manru said. "He never cared about her."

"That's not true!" Rowan cried out. "She died of cancer. What was he supposed to do? He can't fight a war against a disease like that."

"But neither would he let her visit a healer I knew," she said, her tone flat. "We could have gone to the US. American healers could have helped her. He wouldn't let her. He stopped us. He wasn't just saying no, he was actively not allowing her to come. I tried to get her to leave him. I tried to get her to leave all of you so she could live, but she wouldn't do it. My only daughter, and she died because he was so blinded, so black-and-white he couldn't believe in anything better than himself."

"Dad might very well be a blockheaded fool, but he's very good at what he does," Rowan said defensively. He was still reeling from his grandmother's tirade. "And Mom never once told me that she wanted to go. I would have told her to go, or I'd have gone with her."

"She wouldn't because she didn't want to leave you. You could have helped her," his grandmother snapped. "But, no, you were too busy in your little oh-so-important position. Always following in your father's footsteps."

"And you've hated him all this time? Hated me?" Rowan asked faintly, his shock and pain evident. "What about the other people? What about Irene?"

His grandmother shook her head, her voice returning to

normal, yet sounding incredibly tired, as if that other energy had stepped back, and now she was free to speak. "You don't understand even now. I loved my daughter. But her death, well, it was too much for her father. He'd been gone a lot already at this point. We'd traveled together and apart, but he wasn't here when she died. Our son died a long time ago. Your grandfather had taken off then, wandering the world, doing anything he could to try to atone for not being at his son's side—to protect him. He offered sacrifices to the Elders that they'd keep him safe. But he was losing it. He couldn't be left alone. He wasn't safe to those around him. He had only one choice to keep doing his life's work …"

"He committed suicide, and you carried his spirit with you all this time, didn't you?" Grayse stared at her in fascination.

Manru nodded slowly. "That is correct. My husband—he and I, we—have continued the work but knew we couldn't go on for much longer. But we go on for as long as we can—sometimes offering sacrificial souls to the Elders to keep them alive, and others are victims to keep our own souls alive. We needed to set these wrongs back to rights. Like Irene. It was an abomination that she should live while our son and our daughter should die. We had to correct this."

Phoenix didn't know what to say, but she could clearly see the double energies in the physical space of Manru's body. How sad that their grief sent them on this path.

"I already knew about Irene killing her child," Manru continued. "All who died in the suicide season were worthless. They all had a guilty conscience about something. They were all criminals who shouldn't be allowed to walk this earth. If the goodness and light of my children couldn't exist, then neither should their darkness."

"What is it that needs to be done?" Phoenix asked.

"You're not too afraid," Manru said, turning to look at Phoenix. "You watched them all die around you in the cult fire. You were totally okay to walk away and use their energy as you needed to, weren't you?"

"You're okay to be their tool? To help commit these crimes?" Rowan asked.

"I didn't commit any crime." Manru sneered at her grandson. "I didn't shoot your father. In practice, he shot himself," she said with a laugh. "Not my fault he's so weak he can be easily manipulated. I didn't shoot you either," she said to Phoenix. "The geologist, Haro Rahaun, did. But he had killed an infant over twenty years ago. His own child! He abused him so badly that he died. So, using him to kill you was not a problem. But then, of course, it was pretty easy to have him realize what he'd done and then walk to the edge and throw himself into the lava pit. I didn't want him to shoot Rowan though. That would have brought too much attention to these acts. Still, the Elders weren't happy with me." Manru turned toward Phoenix. "I told them you were dangerous, tried to show them. … but they wanted you anyway."

"They want her?" Rowan stepped forward. "What are you talking about?"

Phoenix stared at Manru. "I'm the sacrifice, aren't I? This is my father's energy. It's his ancestral energy here," she said. She shifted her purse to the other side of her shoulder, the small box in it weighing heavy. "That's why I'm a living sacrifice. Because they know I have their energy, and the Elders figure they can take it and feed on it and become stronger and live through me. Have you considered the fact you are also aging, and they'll need someone younger to replace you?"

"They already have the younger one picked out," Manru replied. "Yet I'm not done. I can go until I'm one hundred years old with them. I don't age as fast. But you"—Manru glared at Phoenix—"didn't want it. You kept fighting them on it."

"Them? Why *them*?" Grayse asked. "How is it you carry more than one energy?"

Manru turned to look at him. "They're connected of course. It's Phoenix's father and her grandfather, but he's also my old lover," she said. "He took his own life, and Phoenix's father and uncle died in that compound. But one lay undiscovered for so long. Now his soul is free." She faced Phoenix. "But they weren't quite normal. They were special. They were my lover's sons. By another woman. That woman was the local witch way back when. I'm over eighty, so we're talking fifty-plus years ago. It was a different time, and she was a very strong seer. And both of those men were her sons. My lover died, and I vowed to keep him alive in the only way I could. Only I was young and didn't understand. His sons carried his soul for me. When your grandfather and I fell in love, I was determined to learn more, so I was ready for my lover's time in need. Now we both serve the same Elders. Thank you for bringing the last bits of them home. They are so much stronger together."

They all stood, transfixed on Manru.

"That's why I was under the influence of my father so strongly after revisiting the compound this week. Bits of his energy and his father's energy were stuck in that bomb shelter with his son. But, when we opened it, we released his soul and his energy, and, of course, I was there for him. For all three of them …"

"The witch gave birth late in life, and, through you, her talents live on. They feel you are perfect because, without your physical body, they can then move that energy from their ancestors on to the next host."

"Who's the host?" Rowan demanded.

"She's been chosen already. She just doesn't know it yet. She can't host yet. She's too young."

"How do we stop that choice?" Grayse asked.

Manru laughed. "You can't stop this. But I can fix it. I want them to choose someone else, and only one way will that happen."

Rowan gave his grandmother a shake. "Stop this. You need to step out of this fog you're in. Realize these energies are dangerous!" he snapped at her.

"Only to sinners," she whispered. She turned to look at Phoenix. "I told my lover that you weren't worthy. But no one believes me. But, if you're dead, they'll be forced to join with me until we can find someone better …" She pulled out a small handgun and pointed it directly against Phoenix's chest.

Phoenix stared at the possessed woman with a gun. Phoenix was already drawing layers of energy in tight, like an elastic band, an almost trampoline effect. "I'm sorry, but, if you pull that trigger, it'll kill you, not me." She layered herself tighter with energy deep underneath the physical plane where the gun was tied in the same elastic aura.

Manru laughed, almost hysterical. "No, you're the one who doesn't understand. You aren't the Chosen One. You can't be. You're not good enough. I've seen into your soul. Seen what you've done. What you plan to do. … You already brought Rowan's father back. I can't have you undoing all my work. Healing people," she spat out. "So many more need killing." And she pulled the trigger.

Manru's body crumpled to the ground in front of them, a bullet hole in her chest, blood spreading across her body.

Rowan crouched at her side, a hand at her neck, and turned to look up at Phoenix. "She's dead," he said, almost dazed.

She nodded. "I know," she whispered. "I'm sorry. But it was necessary." She pulled her energy in around herself, then reached out a hand and spread protective energy around Rowan. "Protect yourselves. The energies she carried are looking to survive. They need a host. A source to live yet again."

Rowan stood, his face thinning as he pulled his own energy in close and slammed the door to any spirit looking to take over.

She looked over at Grayse and asked, "Are you ready?"

"Yes," he replied.

Phoenix placed a hand on each man and stepped forward into the energy that swarmed angrily at her feet. Her father and his brother and the remnants of their father and all the other generations before latched on to the energy tighter and firmer, growing as a big mountain on her back. Manru's energy and that of her husband, both raw, less tamed, less used to this form, swirled in agitation. Instinctively she knew they'd learn quickly.

She turned to look at both men. "In my purse is that box. Please take it out. But don't let go of my hands."

Rowan reached inside her purse with his free hand and pulled out the box. He laid it at Phoenix's feet. Grayse used his energy to open it, with her help. She placed her feet on either side of the box, holding it steady. She whispered to her father and his father and even to her uncle—all those energies from her family line who were here now, surrounding them all. "I'm here. I understand what you want of me. The energy is here—right here. You need it. Reach for it …"

Creating a clear and defined vision, she mentally created a vacuum, pulling from the base of the box, sucking up all the energy circling her own aura. In her mind she could feel an inner strength, and, using it, she cried out to the energies of her ancestors, "You will heed my orders and reach for the energy. … Now!"

As she did so, she reached out mentally and pulled the familiar but foreign energies closer to the heavy suction, pulling them into the box.

"Now," she cried out.

Grayse used his energy to snap the lid closed and then to seal it shut.

"Did we do it?" She released her hold on Grayse and Rowan, took several trembling steps backward, rotating her neck, shaking out her arms, flicking away remnants of energy, looking at Grayse and Rowan. "How do I look? Is it all gone?"

Grayse walked around her, then looked at Rowan. "You look too."

Rowan shook his head. "I don't know what I just saw, but I don't see anything odd about you now. It all swirled around and went into the box …"

"What about the icy-blue energy?" she whispered. "Is it still attached to me?" She already knew it wasn't. She already knew it was in the box but needed confirmation. "I think it's all in there," she said. "It feels like it's all in there."

Grayse placed a hand on her shoulder, bowed his head and closed his eyes. A moment later, he lifted his hand and smiled at her. "You did it," he said. "You pulled the energy from your system, and it's all in the box."

She smiled. "The question is now, what do we do with the box?"

Rowan stared at it with loathing. "I highly suggest we throw it in the lava, like you intended."

She looked up at him. "What about that idea of keeping it in a safe forever?"

He shook his head. "Hell no," he said. "We dispose of it forever. The damage they've done …" He shook his head. "So, did we save that little girl too?"

"I'd say so, yes," Grayse muttered. He took a slow and deep breath. "I have a good idea who she was."

Both Rowan and Phoenix turned to stare at him.

"Your child," he said. "A daughter. I just saw her now when I checked Phoenix's energy."

Phoenix's gaze opened wide, and she spun to stare at Rowan.

He blinked, and a gentle smile lit up his face. "Are you sure?" he asked Grayse.

"Yeah," Grayse said with a grin. "Something good to come from this."

"I can sense her," Phoenix whispered. "Oh my …"

And just like that, she threw her arms around Rowan's neck and hugged him tight. He picked her up and twirled her around.

When Grayse cleared his throat, Rowan put her back on her feet.

"I get that we have something worth celebrating," Grayse said, "but it's a bit unseemly if anyone sees us now." He nodded to Manru's body, collapsed on the concrete at their feet.

"Oh, Rowan." Phoenix looked down at his grandmother. "You need to get the hospital staff out here."

He nodded and said, "That's also my father's gun."

"You might want to consider the fact this makes his case attempted murder, not a suicide," she said quietly.

He looked at her with understanding. "Right, and we have a few other cases we probably need to look at too."

"There's time for that. Can't you already feel a change in the energy, in the air? It's different now, more peaceful."

"It will be." Rowan looked at Grayse. "You want to come with us to toss the box in the lava?"

"I wouldn't miss it for the world. But let's deal with this first."

Rowan pulled out his phone and called inside the hospital. Within minutes, the place was swarming with medical personnel. Then he called for several of his fellow officers to come. His grandmother was pronounced dead, but they had to wait to be questioned, and finally, hours later, they were in his vehicle and heading to the same place where Haro had gone over the edge of the cliff into the Burning Fires.

They all exited the vehicle.

Rowan turned to Phoenix and said, "This isn't the same material anymore. It's whole now, the box containing all the pieces you had, including your father's letter, given to you in childhood. What do you think will be required to get all that in the lava?"

She looked at it, smiled, lifted her arm high in the air, and, without further ado, flung it long and wide at the center of the lava, using her psychic energy to carry it to the center of the molten stream. Slowly, as the lava bubbled, the box sank, until one final air bubble popped from the surface, and it disappeared completely from sight.

Rowan and Grayse gasped at her long throw as they

watched it sink from sight.

She turned to look at both men and smiled. "I was re-born from the fire once and am now reborn a second time as my history is burned in the fire. The past is now in the past. For the first time I can relate to my name. My future lies before me." She slid her hand across her belly. "A future I never thought to have. Talk about a new beginning."

"That's exactly what it is," Rowan said, wrapping his arms around her neck and tucking her in nice and close. "For both of us. You'll have to marry me now."

"Ha," she said with a big grin on her face. "Good thing we had already agreed on that point."

Grayse said, "Sounds like a whole new beginning for a lot of people, especially this town." He looked at the two of them. "You have your work cut out for you though."

Phoenix smiled and said, "You know something? That's okay. For the first time, I feel like maybe I can rise to the challenge."

And she laughed. Life had never felt better.

This concludes Book 16 of Psychic Visions: From the Ashes.
Read the first Chapter of Stroke of Death: Psychic Visions,
Book 17

Stroke of Death

Cayce's art is well-known and respected among her peers, and, as such, has spawned forgers, copycats ... and enemies. But when her favorite model and best friend is murdered—the masterpiece painted on her skin cut off her body—Cayce knows she's up against a collector of a very different sort.

Detective Richard Henderson doesn't know much about art, but he knows what he likes. Of all the art mixed up in this case, it is the artist, Cayce, who fascinates him the most. While he understands her work contains an element of something extraordinary, he just doesn't know what that is exactly or how she embodies it in her creative works of art.

But, when other models show up dead, with more souvenirs taken from their bodies, both the artist and the detective realize much more is involved in this than just Cayce's art ... It's all about Cayce's soul.

Sneak Peek from Stroke of Death: Psychic Visions (Book #17) Chapter 1

C AYCE DIDN'T WANT to rush her work today. She didn't want to rush any day but definitely not today. This was the fifth day that she had put into this commissioned art piece, and today was all about incorporating the live model into Cayce's static artwork. Cayce had finished the backdrop. Today was all about getting the presentation of the model just perfect, merging with Cayce's background art.

However, the perfect model that the set director wanted was the worst model for the job. And yet Cayce had no *logical* way to explain that. Cayce had only found out about the change in the model yesterday. She'd been putting the final touches on the backdrop, when the company brought in the new model to show her. Cayce's normal approach was not to let others dictate her models to her, not even the client who had commissioned Cayce's artwork. But the client's representatives had pulled a fast one on Cayce at the very last moment.

To top off that insult, Cayce had taken an instant dislike to the new model, Naomi. Something about the sly curl to her lips and that look in her eyes all said she knew exactly what the world wanted, and she was prepared to give it up—

for a price.

But Cayce was a professional. She did what she needed to do. Today was no exception. Besides, the sooner she was done, the sooner she could move on. She walked from her vehicle to the art installation, putting down her large cases and turning to study the work she'd completed the night before. Finally, after a few moments, she stepped back and nodded. "It looks good."

"Looks darn good."

At the sound of footsteps she turned to see her replacement model saunter in, dressed in a bikini and not much else. Cayce nodded in acknowledgment of Naomi's comment, then said, "Okay, so right back to the same position we set up last night," she said, motioning at the wall— Cayce's painting—where the model herself would disappear into the actual painting background.

"And a good morning to you too," Naomi said in a snide voice.

Cayce shrugged it off. She was short on time as it was. She couldn't afford to waste more time by slinging words with Naomi when Cayce needed to be slinging paint. It was hard to be creative if she had adverse feelings for the whole scenario. She wished she had her regular model because Elena would have been absolutely perfect for this job.

Cayce had worked with Elena just two days ago on another art show, highlighting different masterpieces, and it had worked out absolutely stunningly, but that had been for a fancy house party, where Elena had been the artsy centerpiece of the ballroom. She had done a phenomenal job, and, when Cayce had told her best model to go home and to rest, Elena had laughed at her and said, "Now that I'm off duty, I want to enjoy the party and to mingle with the guests." She had given Cayce a gentle hug and had turned and walked away.

Elena's happy energy was so very different than Naomi's critical scowl, as Cayce tried to sort out what she needed to do next, other than deflecting Naomi's negative energy.

"You can start anytime," Naomi said in a bored voice. "At this rate we'll be here all day."

"I won't be," Cayce said. She bent down, opened up her cases, brought out her palettes and her paints, mixing the first color she wanted. When she was ready, she pulled on the energies around her, looking for that creative light, that rainbow, which she wrapped around her, almost like a blanket of good luck, spreading out into all the different colors. She was a firm believer in the colors of sound and the colors of nature.

When she reached for a certain color, she always called out to Mother Nature to help Cayce make a true representation.

Finally she stood up with her palette and walked over to Naomi and got to work. Cayce started with Naomi's left shoulder and arm, working down her elbow, Cayce's strokes sure, fast and accurate.

Naomi watched her in surprise. "Wow, when you get going, you get going."

Cayce didn't say a word; what could she say? It was beyond her to talk at this point because all the possible colors of the spectrum surged through her heart, through her mind, wrapping around her body and soul. She needed the same energy to wrap around Naomi, to help her model attract and pull in and blend with the same colors, the same energy. Only there was no blending with Naomi. Her energy was impatient, irritated—edgy.

Yet Cayce's work entailed a magical element, and she firmly believed it was due to the Mother Nature energy that she utilized. When the magic happened naturally, it was great, easy, wonderful. Sometimes Cayce could also *make* it happen, and Cayce was a pro at that. Which would desperately be needed here with Naomi.

Cayce worked incessantly for two hours, before she finally took a step back. She had the preliminary painting on the top half of Naomi, the background blending beautifully into the foreground. Although Cayce still had the other layers to work on, Naomi's hair was pulled back into a tight braid down her back, and Cayce had to blend Naomi's face and that hairline yet. She walked closer to the model. "Do you need a bathroom break or water?"

Naomi nodded. "Yeah, that'd be good." She walked toward the hallway, disappearing around a corner.

Cayce took a deep breath, let it out, gently twisting and stretching her spine and her neck. When she heard hard footsteps behind her, she stiffened. She hated on-site visitors, approved or not, when she worked. She just wished they'd wait to see the finished piece at the opening event. Not to mention that the energy preceding her visitor had a dark, disruptive influence attached. She pulled in her aura, then turned to face down the coming threat.

When she saw a man in a suit walking toward her, her eyes opened wide. His chiseled face was his most striking feature—but a model in a suit seemed incongruous here. "May I help you?" She studied his aura, seeing it snugged tightly against his body. A barely visible white line of energy surrounded him. Except it resonated with anger, ... lots of anger. Yet controlled. She raised her eyebrows ever-so-slowly. "What's the matter?"

"Why would you think anything is wrong?" he asked in a tight, hard voice.

Although he might not be aware of what his aura was doing, nevertheless he didn't want her aware of it either. Because now his energy had thinned even more. "Just that you look angry," she said. She waved her hand at the installation. "I'm kind of busy."

"You are Cayce Cormont?" At her nod, he continued. "And you worked with Elena Campbell?"

"Yes, all the time. We did a piece together two nights ago," she said, her face softening at the reminder. "She's a really good friend of mine."

Just then Naomi returned, instantly shifting the energy in the room. She took her position against the backdrop wall as she eyed the new arrival with a pretty smile on her face. "Oh, perfect. Somebody to come and watch me." And she bounced her bare boobs a little bit.

It was all Cayce could do to hold back her sigh of frustration.

The man looked at her, then looked at Naomi. "So do you know Elena too?"

"Sure," Naomi said. "Models in this business usually know each other. She's pretty decent. I'm better." She waved her hand at her bikini-clad body. "That's why I'm here, and she's not," she said smugly. "I'm Naomi Hartlet."

The stranger's gaze narrowed.

On the side, biting back her caustic response, Cayce watched Naomi's energy. The deceptive fluffy lights flitting off in a million different directions hid something dark inside, but everybody had something dark inside. Because Cayce had taken an instant dislike to the woman, Cayce had put up barriers, so she wouldn't have to deal with Naomi's energy on a firsthand basis, but that also made the painting of Naomi go a bit slower.

While Naomi seemed to think that Cayce was fast and on target, today wasn't really going as smoothly or as timely or as well as Cayce would have liked.

She turned to the stranger. "You haven't identified yourself," she said in a cool tone. "What's going on?"

"I'm Detective Richard Henderson," he said, pulling out a badge.

She frowned, reading the name on the badge. "What do the police want here?"

"Doesn't matter what they want," Naomi said with a throaty laugh. "They can send all their hunky detectives my way."

Naomi's words gave Cayce everything she needed to know, without even turning toward Naomi to see the same darkness oozing from her pores. *Nerves. Fear. Uncertainty.* Cayce studied her model for a long moment, then faced the detective, noting no change in his energy. He was completely unfazed by Naomi. Neither was he attracted to the mostly naked woman. *Interesting …* "Detective, why are you here?"

"Because we found your *friend*," he said, with added emphasis on that last word.

"Which friend?" she asked, not understanding where he was coming from. "What do you mean, *found*?"

"Elena Campbell," he said. "Remember her?"

Frustrated now, she gave a quick nod. "I already told you that she's a good friend of mine."

"Her body was found in a dumpster bin yesterday morning." His gaze was hard. … And angry. "What do you know about that?"

Cayce took the blow almost viscerally. Her body bowed

against the pain. "Are you serious?" she gasped out. "Oh, my God." She sank to the floor.

Her mind was completely overwhelmed as shards of pain splintered through her. *Was that why the last two days had been so rough?* She'd fought headaches and nausea, and, when a darkness had enveloped her, she'd really wondered what was going on. When she found out Elena had been replaced in this installation, Cayce hadn't been happy—as in seriously not happy—and had figured the ugly energy was due to that. She liked to choose her own models. Not deal with ones sleeping their way to the top. Naomi hadn't fit the bill yesterday. She hadn't fit the bill today. Cayce's models had to have that extra *something*.

Naomi didn't have it.

The detective squatted in front of her. "Breathe."

She drew in a deep breath, her gaze wide and painful as she stared at him. "How? When?"

"She had already been dead for several hours," he said softly, as he studied her. "And her throat was cut."

The shocks just kept reverberating. Her body shook involuntarily. Then she added her own headshake. "Oh, my God, dear God, no." She continuously shook her head, her lips firmed into a straight line, her eyes filling with tears. "Dear God," she whispered again, turning to the detective. "Elena was special. Why would anybody want to hurt her?"

"You body painted her, correct?"

She nodded, her gaze locked on his, searching for anything to say, but her throat had closed, her heart shutting down at the terrible horrors filling her mind's eye.

"And what did you paint on her that night?"

She stared up at him, and sadly she whispered, "A masterpiece. I painted her into a masterpiece."

"Well, guess what?" he said, his voice hardening. "A collector found something else to collect. Her skin."

At his last words, her stomach revolted, and she vomited all over the floor.

In her heart of hearts she knew the murderer hadn't just collected a masterpiece of art. Something was so very special about Elena. Her energy was pure gold.

When her killer took her life, her painted skin, he'd also taken a part of Elena's soul.

Find Book 17 here!

To find out more visit Dale Mayer's website.

https://geni.us/DMSoDUniversal

Author's Note

Thank you for reading From the Ashes: Psychic Visions, Book 16! If you enjoyed the book, please take a moment and leave a short review.

Dear reader,

I love to hear from readers, and you can contact me at my website: www.dalemayer.com or at my Facebook author page. To be informed of new releases and special offers, sign up for my newsletter or follow me on BookBub. And if you are interested in joining Dale Mayer's Reader Group, here is the Facebook sign up page. http://geni.us/DaleMayerFBGroup

Cheers,
Dale Mayer

About the Author

Dale Mayer is a *USA Today* best-selling author, best known for her SEALs military romances, her Psychic Visions series, and her Lovely Lethal Garden cozy series. Her contemporary romances are raw and full of passion and emotion (Broken But … Mending, Hathaway House series). Her thrillers will keep you guessing (Kate Morgan, By Death series), and her romantic comedies will keep you giggling (*It's a Dog's Life*, a stand-alone novella; and the Broken Protocols series, starring Charming Marvin, the cat).

Dale honors the stories that come to her—and some of them are crazy, break all the rules and cross multiple genres!

To go with her fiction, she also writes nonfiction in many different fields, with books available on résumé writing, companion gardening, and the US mortgage system. All her books are available in print and ebook format.

Connect with Dale Mayer Online

Dale's Website – www.dalemayer.com
Twitter – @DaleMayer
Facebook Page – geni.us/DaleMayerFBFanPage
Facebook Group – geni.us/DaleMayerFBGroup
BookBub – geni.us/DaleMayerBookbub
Instagram – geni.us/DaleMayerInstagram
Goodreads – geni.us/DaleMayerGoodreads
Newsletter – geni.us/DaleNews

Also by Dale Mayer

Published Adult Books:

Hathaway House

Aaron, Book 1

Brock, Book 2

Cole, Book 3

Denton, Book 4

Elliot, Book 5

Finn, Book 6

Gregory, Book 7

Heath, Book 8

Iain, Book 9

The K9 Files

Ethan, Book 1

Pierce, Book 2

Zane, Book 3

Blaze, Book 4

Lucas, Book 5

Parker, Book 6

Carter, Book 7

Lovely Lethal Gardens

Arsenic in the Azaleas, Book 1

Bones in the Begonias, Book 2

Corpse in the Carnations, Book 3

Daggers in the Dahlias, Book 4

Evidence in the Echinacea, Book 5

Footprints in the Ferns, Book 6

Gun in the Gardenias, Book 7

Handcuffs in the Heather, Book 8

Psychic Vision Series

Tuesday's Child

Hide 'n Go Seek

Maddy's Floor

Garden of Sorrow

Knock Knock…

Rare Find

Eyes to the Soul

Now You See Her

Shattered

Into the Abyss

Seeds of Malice

Eye of the Falcon

Itsy-Bitsy Spider

Unmasked

Deep Beneath

From the Ashes

Stroke of Death

Psychic Visions Books 1–3

Psychic Visions Books 4–6

Psychic Visions Books 7–9

By Death Series
Touched by Death

Haunted by Death

Chilled by Death

By Death Books 1–3

Broken Protocols – Romantic Comedy Series
Cat's Meow

Cat's Pajamas

Cat's Cradle

Cat's Claus

Broken Protocols 1-4

Broken and... Mending
Skin

Scars

Scales (of Justice)

Broken but… Mending 1-3

Glory
Genesis

Tori

Celeste

Glory Trilogy

Biker Blues
Morgan: Biker Blues, Volume 1

Cash: Biker Blues, Volume 2

SEALs of Honor

Heroes for Hire, Books 10–12

Heroes for Hire, Books 13–15

SEALs of Steel

Badger: SEALs of Steel, Book 1

Erick: SEALs of Steel, Book 2

Cade: SEALs of Steel, Book 3

Talon: SEALs of Steel, Book 4

Laszlo: SEALs of Steel, Book 5

Geir: SEALs of Steel, Book 6

Jager: SEALs of Steel, Book 7

The Final Reveal: SEALs of Steel, Book 8

SEALs of Steel, Books 1–4

SEALs of Steel, Books 5–8

SEALs of Steel, Books 1–8

The Mavericks

Kerrick, Book 1

Griffin, Book 2

Jax, Book 3

Beau, Book 4

Asher, Book 5

Ryker, Book 6

Miles, Book 7

Nico, Book 8

Keane, Book 9

Lennox, Book 10

Gavin, Book 11

Shane, Book 12

Bullard's Battle Series

Ryland's Reach, Book 1

Cain's Cross, Book 2

Eton's Escape, Book 3

Garret's Gambit, Book 4

Kano's Keep, Book 5

Fallon's Flaw, Book 6

Quinn's Quest, Book 7

Bullard's Beauty, Book 8

Collections

Dare to Be You...

Dare to Love...

Dare to be Strong...

RomanceX3

Standalone Novellas

It's a Dog's Life

Riana's Revenge

Second Chances

Published Young Adult Books:

Family Blood Ties Series

Vampire in Denial

Vampire in Distress

Vampire in Design

Vampire in Deceit

Vampire in Defiance

Vampire in Conflict

Vampire in Chaos

Vampire in Crisis

Vampire in Control

Vampire in Charge

Family Blood Ties Set 1–3

Family Blood Ties Set 1–5

Family Blood Ties Set 4–6

Family Blood Ties Set 7–9

Sian's Solution, A Family Blood Ties Series Prequel
Novelette

Design series

Dangerous Designs

Deadly Designs

Darkest Designs

Design Series Trilogy

Standalone

In Cassie's Corner

Gem Stone (a Gemma Stone Mystery)

Time Thieves

Published Non-Fiction Books:

Career Essentials

Career Essentials: The Résumé

Career Essentials: The Cover Letter

Career Essentials: The Interview

Career Essentials: 3 in 1

Printed in Great Britain
by Amazon

37368064R00205